ADVANCE PRAISE FOR ANTICIPATION

"A sweeping, immersive saga of love and loss, *Anticipation* enthralls from start to finish. Winawer's skill as a writer also shines through in the quiet moments, like the shared joy between a mother and a child, or the meditations on loss of a grieving widow. Truly magical."

— Fiona Davis, *New York Times* bestselling author
of *The Lions of Fifth Avenue*

"A compelling novel that weaves fantasy, philosophy, science, medicine, romance, and madness into a tapestry of intrigue and mystery. And, fittingly for a physician, Winawer ultimately writes a story of healing and hope. I loved every word and did not want it to end."

—Robin Oliveira, bestselling author of
My Name Is Mary Sutter and *Winter Sisters*

"An ambitious and beautifully written saga of science, history, and romantic mysticism spanning eight centuries . . . Prepare to be transported."

—Kris Waldherr, author of
The Lost History of Dreams and *Doomed Queens*

"*Anticipation* is a rich tapestry, meticulously researched, and woven with the threads of a sweeping romance, a wild ride through history, and a fascinating medical mystery. Settle in for a luxurious read!"

—Crystal King, author of *The Chef's Secret*
and *Feast of Sorrow*

"On the one hand, this is a pacy thriller, a historical tale of pursuit and murder across the centuries. On another level, I found myself reconsidering my views on medical ethics, reincarnation, and military occupation. Highly recommend."

—Jean Gill, author of *The World Beyond the Walls* and *Song at Dawn*

Also by Melodie Winawer and Gallery Books

The Scribe of Siena

G

Gallery Books
An Imprint of Simon & Schuster, Inc.
1230 Avenue of the Americas
New York, NY 10020

First Gallery Books trade paperback edition November 2021

GALLERY BOOKS and colophon are registered trademarks of Simon & Schuster, Inc.

For information about special discounts for bulk purchases, please contact Simon & Schuster Special Sales at 1-866-506-1949 or business@simonandschuster.com.

The Simon & Schuster Speakers Bureau can bring authors to your live event. For more information or to book an event, contact the Simon & Schuster Speakers Bureau at 1-866-248-3049 or visit our website at www.simonspeakers.com.

Interior design by Davina Mock-Maniscalco

Manufactured in the United States of America

10 9 8 7 6 5 4 3 2 1

Library of Congress Cataloging-in-Publication Data

Names: Winawer, Melodie, author.
Title: Anticipation : a novel / Melodie Winawer.
Description: First edition. | New York : Gallery Books, 2021.
Identifiers: LCCN 2020042623 (print) | LCCN 2020042624 (ebook) |
   ISBN 9781982113711 (ebook) | ISBN 9781982113698 (trade paperback)
Classification: LCC PS3623.I5894 (ebook) | LCC PS3623.I5894 A58 2021
   (print) | DDC 813/.6—dc23
LC record available at https://lccn.loc.gov/2020042623
LC ebook record available at https://lccn.loc.gov/2020042624

ISBN 978-1-9821-1369-8
ISBN 978-1-9821-1371-1 (ebook)

Anticipation

A NOVEL

MELODIE WINAWER

2489 96812

GALLERY BOOKS

New York   London   Toronto   Sydney   New Delhi

*To Dr. Michael Daras, who told me where to go,
and to my family, who followed me there.*

prologue

ELIAS OROLOGAS
July 2015
Village of Mystras, Peloponnese, Greece

On the day of the referendum, Mystras was closed to tourists. Our Greek nation voted overwhelmingly "*ókhi*"—"no"—to the austerity measures from the Eurozone. We voted *No* to taxes that left us barely able to feed our families. Some say Greece, in the hands of the European Union, is an occupied nation; we have been occupied many times over, with brief, precious moments of freedom in between. The Greek motto comes from a place deep in our souls: *Elefthería í Thánatos*, Freedom or Death.

Now Europe wants to control us again.

When the voting was done, I returned to Mystras, where I found two American tourists speaking to Nano, the owner of the grocery store on the corner. Outside his shop, the main street curves and divides around an old tree, where water from a spring trickles clear and cold from a spout in the trunk. I stopped for a drink. Inside the shop, Nano was cutting a slice of cheese from a wheel and wrapping it in white waxed paper. Even from outside the door, I knew the visitors were American: the straight impatience of the woman's back, their flat-sounding English, the way their voices cut through the quiet. Americans are a people used to talking over noise.

I speak English passably, after years caring for the historical site of Mystras, escorting visitors through the ghost city's streets. The visitors had come hoping to see the ruined city but, disappointed by the locked entrance, they'd made their way back down the hill to town. I watched them from the store's entrance where a tray of *thessaloniki* rested, the rings of dough clustered thick with sesame seeds. Nano explained patiently that the visitors should come back tomorrow.

"We have a tour guide here who knows a great deal about the site's wonders. He has been here forever," Nano said. He saw me outside and waved the hand not holding the cheese knife. Forever is a long time.

"Tomorrow," I heard Nano say, "please come back tomorrow." The woman sighed loudly and turned with her son to walk out of the shop. As they passed, the boy looked toward me. I thought, watching him, that the divisions between nations, and even times, are blurred in the young.

"Is that a bagel?" The boy caught sight of the tray of *thessaloniki* outside the shop.

"Not exactly," his mother said, smiling for the first time. Her tired face lit like a sunrise. "Do you want to try one?" She sorted through her change for the right coin.

"It tastes kind of like a bagel," the boy said, chewing happily. "We will come back tomorrow. Right, Mama?"

His mother ruffled his brown hair. "Yes, tomorrow." She sounded more than tired. Those who have known loss recognize its sound in one another.

"Promise?" the boy said. "I want to see the fortress." He pointed to the top of the conical hill, where the fortification built by the Prince of Achaea almost eight hundred years before still stood, its broken walls crenelated, sharp against the cloudless sky.

"I promise," she said, and they headed out across the tiny plaza of Mystras village.

Ω

I am Elias—*Ilias* in my mother's tongue. My mother was Greek, my first father—Jéhan Borghes—was a Frankish soldier in the Peloponnese who could not return home to France to find a wife. The Franks called us half-breeds *gasmoules*. But I do not consider myself only half-Greek. The Greek in me runs deep and wide, a river overflowing its banks.

Though my mother loved my father, and he loved her, their love was born of the occupation. So was I.

"Elias was your mother's choice," my father had often told me, smiling, as if he'd indulged her whim. When I was seven, my mother told me I'd been named for Profitis Ilias, the Prophet Elijah, our patron saint of the mountains, who left the earth for heaven and returned again. Then, I did not know that at his lonely shrine, on the top of the hill we once called Myzithras, my mother made a promise that I would have to keep.

part one

FIRST LIFE

What if some day or night a demon were to steal after you into your loneliest loneliness and say to you: "This life as you now live it and have lived it, you will have to live once more and innumerable times more; and there will be nothing new in it, but every pain and every joy and every thought and sigh and everything unutterably small or great in your life will have to return to you. . . ."

—Nietzsche, *The Gay Science*, sec. 341, Walter Kaufmann, trans.

chapter one

CHRYSE BORGHES
1237
La Lacedemonie

The moment one shared life explodes into two, both lives hang in the balance. Chryse had already lost two children and despaired that a living being would ever enter the world from her perilous body. She feared every kick beneath her ribs would be the last, and that she would look again into the dull eyes of a life snuffed out before its time.

She awoke in the night with a gush that drenched her bed-clothes, then a searing pain that made her feel as if she might tear in two. She had no time to send for the midwife, but she was a midwife herself, and she knew this child was coming early. Her husband, Jéhan, had marched with his regiment the day before and was encamped far from home. Tonight she was alone, crouching on the dirt floor while a rainstorm raged and wind wailed through the gaps in the wooden shutters.

After a minute's pause, the pain began again. Had there been a messenger to send, she could have found help in one of the other houses surrounding the residence of the Frankish prince Villehardouin, who ruled the valley and the land beyond. But there was no messenger.

In the end, it was not her experience that guided her when the time came; the knowledge came from the labyrinth of childbirth. At dawn, the pains came hard and fast with no time to breathe between, and then he was there, first head, then body, all four limbs—*blessed Theotokos, mother of God*. A boy with the sea-gray eyes of a newborn. As she lifted the slippery child into her arms, he took his labored first breath. His lips were dusky blue; he fought the air like an enemy.

Not this one, too, please no.

Chryse cut the baby's cord with the scissors she had used for others' births. Did she imagine the resistance in that twist of vessels, the reluctance to sever the last physical connection between herself and this delicate life? Around her neck the mother's amulet of protection swung forward, etched with the she-demon Abyzou being stabbed by a holy rider's sword.

You will not have him, Abyzou. This one is mine.

She rubbed her son roughly with a cloth until he squirmed and wailed. She had not had time to draw water from the well or to warm it on the fire to mix with salt. Chryse swaddled her son and put him to her breast. He struggled between sucks, pulling away while his little chest heaved with effort. Chryse had seen tragedy come to lives that started just like this one. She closed her eyes.

Profitis Ilias, who looks upon new mothers and babes with compassion, hear this prayer. Breathe air into his lungs . . .

The wind gusted, clattering the bare branches of the olive tree outside.

Profitis Ilias, answer me, and I will promise you whatever you ask.

The wind stopped as suddenly as it had come, and into the silence a voice spoke in Chryse's head.

Bring him to me now.

Ω

Chryse wrapped her son in a wool blanket and bound him against her chest; his heart beat fast against her own. She pulled her cloak around them both and closed the door behind her. At first the road was flat, winding through the valley's bare-limbed orange trees, but soon it began to climb. Myzithras, it was called, this solitary peak rising starkly out of the valley, silhouetted against the snowcapped Taygetos mountains behind. It was just daylight, and goats' bells echoed in the morning air.

Mud made the way treacherous, and the boulders were slippery with moss. Once, Chryse lost her footing, and she wrapped her arms around the bundle on her chest, rather than putting her hands out to break her fall. With that instinct, she realized she had become a mother. Chryse's knee hit rock, and the pain made her eyes tear, but then she was up again, her robe muddy and her knee burning.

Farther up, the trees thinned and the wind blew fiercely with nothing to block it but scrub and scattered gray-brown rocks. As Chryse neared the peak, the sun cleared the ring of mountains surrounding the valley. Finally she reached the tiny shrine of Profitis Ilias, its white stone bright in the sun. Chryse ducked inside the low doorway.

It was quiet in the shrine, the wind blocked by the thick walls, but the silence was receptive, an ear into which prayers might be spoken and heard. She unwrapped her son from her chest. His eyes were closed, and for a moment her heart stopped. But there it was, a lift of his shoulders, his next breath. She straightened her arms to raise the baby above her head.

"I have brought him to you," Chryse said. She waited until

her arms ached. When the answer came, she could not tell whether the voice was in her head or in the air.

In the years that come, a city will grow upon this hill, where my shrine now stands. The city will flourish as the heart and soul of this land and its people. You shall name your son after me, and he shall be mine. He will serve the city that grows upon the hill for all its days, and in return I shall breathe air into his lungs. But heed me: for when I call him he must come, and his lives will be in my service.

"I heed you, Profitis Ilias, and my son heeds you also," Chryse said. A wind rose again: first a hum, then a rush, and finally a keening wail, and at the sound's peak her son took the first strong breath of his life. His face flushed and his eyes opened to fix upon her face.

As Chryse made her way down the steep path back to the house, she heard an echo: *For when I call him he must come, and his lives will be in my service.*

Chryse's son felt suddenly heavy with the weight of that word: *lives.*

HELEN ADLER
January 2015
New York

It's a weighty name, Helen. I'm not Greek, or Spartan for that matter, which would be more accurate. No one is really Spartan anymore, not since Menelaus had the bad luck of marrying the most beautiful woman in the world. My mother, who was a New York Jewish girl, was reading the *Iliad* when she was pregnant with me and got inspired. My face is fine, but no wars have resulted from it. I consider this a good thing.

Names are the least of what we load on our kids' little backs, inadvertently or otherwise. "Parenting is not for sissies," my mom used to say. I would like to tell her, now that I am a parent, too, how right she was.

I was reading Mary Renault's *Fire from Heaven* when I found out I was pregnant, which partially explains my son's ending up with the name Alexander. I say partially because I'd always loved the name, but having Alexander the Great on the brain when a baby was beginning life in my belly hammered the decision home. Alexander seems to be handling his name fine so far, but there is an opacity about kids. You never quite know what they're thinking, even when they tell you, which they usually don't.

Alexander is particularly opaque, especially about what's bothering him. Until he blows. But, fortunately, that doesn't happen very often. He reminds me of his dad, Oliver—the way he thinks before talking, as if he is gravely considering the consequences. Oliver almost never got mad either, and I don't like to remember the few times he did—especially now. I am always looking for things that remind me of the best of Oliver, now that memories are all that's left. Alexander is a natural place to find them. I try not to look too hard. My kid is himself, he's not a window into someone else.

Almost a year later, I wonder whether my memories of Oliver are accurate. Was he actually perfect or do I just remember him as perfect? I suppose there is an advantage to dying suddenly. No one has time to think of you as sick, or failing, or needy. No one gets tired of your whining, no one has to watch you fade in the months before the end. Butterflies, I read once, die by just drifting to the ground, beautiful to the last second. Poetic, but it doesn't help me much at the moment.

I am not at the point of appreciating anything positive about Oliver's death, though some well-meaning acquaintances say at least he didn't suffer long. I don't know how long it takes to drown, nor whether drowning for a minute is worse than dying slowly, like my dad from Parkinson's disease. So I can't console myself with that, either. It is not a coincidence that I have devoted my life to studying the science of neurodegenerative diseases, while I watch my father gradually slow down to a nearly motionless state, except on those terrible moments when he falls and can't stop himself from hitting the ground. He went from playing tennis to playing checkers, from living alone to living with help, and finally, reluctantly, from his apartment to a nursing home. Our paths were linked: nursing home for him, neurodegenerative disease lab for me.

My last few months with Oliver were ordinary. Oliver and I ignored one another healthily, the way normal parents do once the child eclipse hits. I was writing a proposal for a National Institutes of Health grant, while trying to imagine how we'd host Thanksgiving dinner for my extended family in our six-hundred-square-foot Manhattan apartment. Oliver was preparing for a foster child's adoption case that kept him talking long after we'd turned the lights out.

In the meantime, we were preoccupied with ordinary things: complaints from the downstairs neighbor about my walking barefoot to the bathroom in the night, and Alexander's troubles with writing in second grade. Oliver coaxed Alexander through *p*'s and *q*'s and *b*'s and *d*'s, more patient than I ever could be.

At night, we had moments together, if not necessarily at leisure. "How's my sweet cellular biologist?" he'd say. Oliver was the only person I've ever met who used the words *sweet* and *cellular biologist* in the same sentence. The week before he died, Oliver came home after Alexander's bedtime to find me staring at a screen filled with incorrectly formatted tables.

"Bad at Excel," I said grimly. He kissed the back of my neck. "How about some help?" he said. Oliver's competence with Excel was legendary. He sat down next to me. I watched, letting relief wash over me.

A few months later I was on my own—with Alexander and Excel.

Ω

The first Monday in February blossomed into an epic child-care fail. The afterschool program I'd relied on to amuse Alexander until I could exit work—as usual, running, leaving multiple unfinished tasks in piles on my desk—had been shut down by a stomach bug. This meant Alexander, now a restless fourth grader who would have already spent seven hours that day sitting as still as possible in an overheated public school classroom, had to join me for a critically important, endless afternoon meeting with potential donors, a meeting that my lab's survival hinged upon.

My research is, for want of a better word, basic. This means that I study things that nonscientific people would find incomprehensible or downright dull. Most of the time, I work with cells growing in a dish. The implications of what I do are big, but the cells are tiny, and my job is tough to explain.

"So, how does it help people exactly, this, er, science you are doing?" my aunt Delia asked while filling her mouth with a roast beef canapé at our wedding. That was neither the first time I'd heard that exact sentence, nor the last.

Despite all that, the actual experience of growing nerve

cells is mesmerizingly beautiful: the elegant pattern of their delicate projections silhouetted like tree branches in winter, the gray-white grainy electron microscope images of mito-chondria, the cells' powerhouses, with their curious internal folds, hinting at mystery.

On the way to Alexander's school, I plotted the best ap-proach to avoid a work/life disaster. I could give him a device with a screen and headphones, then put him in a corner. There was also bribery—the $49 Pokémon box he'd been begging for. I was still scheming when I picked him up at Door "C," the eloquently named exit to the asphalt play yard behind his public school.

Alexander looked poignantly alone, his head turning while he searched for me. His backpack seemed impossibly big on his hunched shoulders. In that moment he looked, fleetingly, like Oliver on our first deliberate date, a boat tour of the Hud-son River. I'd seen Oliver first that day too, searching the crowds for me. That was the moment I'd fallen in love, when his face was filled with anticipation, the first stirrings of what would become our future. I barely remember the boat ride, but I remember Oliver—his light hair rising in the wind as we pulled out, the way he kept his eyes on my face, his generous laughter every time I tried to be funny. And I remember the two muffins that he'd brought for our breakfast, along with one coffee and one tea, just in case. We'd shared the coffee.

My voice broke when I called Alexander's name, my throat tight with remembering. Then Alexander's eyes caught mine and he was rushing past his harried-looking teacher and into my arms. He smelled of tuna fish and Elmer's glue. I bought him a pretzel that was as big as his face. Not exactly bribery, but I hoped it might help, and while he bit through the salt-dusted dough, I started to explain.

"So, Alexander, I have a meeting today, and since day care is closed, you'll have to come with me." I forced myself to pause and listen—something Oliver had tried to teach me. He used to say that I'd give Alexander something to worry about when he hadn't been worried to begin with.

Alexander went back to the pretzel, which he'd pulled apart. He took a bite from the right half, then the left half, then the right again. "I like to keep it even."

"It's a long meeting. I won't be able to talk to you. There will be a lot of grown-ups you don't know. There will be a lot of grown-ups I don't know."

"Why are you having a meeting with a lot of grown-ups you don't know?"

"To tell them about my science and convince them that they should give me money for experiments."

We were close to the subway station now, standing in front of the store with the best Pokémon cards. I stopped, wondering whether to introduce a bribe.

"What science?" He'd asked me before, but there was something different about the way he asked now.

The words I'd been planning for the funding meeting popped up first. *I culture rodent neural stem cells for experimental striatal transplantation into a mouse model of Huntington's disease.* Mom brain and science brain faced off inside my head.

"Uh . . . I take immature brain cells, baby cells that haven't turned into brain cells yet."

"Where do you get the cells?"

"From mice."

"How do you get them out of the mice?"

We were heading into dangerous territory, but it was too late. "I take them from mouse brains."

"You cut their heads open?"

"After they are put to sleep."

"And what happens when they wake up?"

"Ah . . . they don't."

Alexander looked down at his sneakers. I looked down, too. The soles were shredding off, and he'd broken both shoe-laces. I moved my gaze to Alexander's sweatpants, which were three inches too short.

"You have to *kill* them?"

"I don't want to hurt the mice. They help me make sick people better."

Alexander brought the two pretzel halves together and tried to get the edges to match, which, of course, they no longer did.

"I'm not hungry anymore," he said, handing me the pieces, which were slightly damp where he'd bitten them. I wasn't hungry either.

Ω

After the mouse conversation, I thought we were done talking about my science. It turned out, after I'd stocked Alexander with three packs of Pokémon cards, several of which he declared "super-rare," that we weren't.

"What problem are you trying to fix with the baby mice?" Alexander asked as our train stopped at a signal in the subway tunnel.

"I told you I study Huntington's disease, right?"

Alexander nodded. "The rare brain sickness?"

"Right. It makes people lose their memory and have movements they can't control."

"Can I get it?" He looked worried.

"No, it gets passed on from one generation to the next, from parents to their children."

"In the blood?"

"Not exactly the blood. Huntington's comes from a problem with the genes, the DNA, the messages in cells that tell them how to grow. Almost all cells have DNA in them."

Alexander looked only slightly less worried. "So I could get it from you?"

"Sweetie, no! Not at all. I don't have it."

"And you can't get it?"

"No—you can only get it if you're born with the gene."

He puffed out his cheeks with relief. "The kid gets it just like the mom or dad?"

"About half of the time," I said, translating autosomal dominant inheritance. "Often it gets worse from one generation to the next."

"Why?"

"Because the gene has too many copies of three chemicals in a row, called 'triple repeats,' and when the new cells of the new person are made, the copies multiply. The more copies, the worse things get, and the earlier the problem starts. That doesn't always happen, but it can."

"That sounds scary."

"It is," I said, ruffling his hair. My little scientist. "The worsening from one generation to the next is called 'anticipation.' That's one of the things I'm studying, so that maybe we can stop it from happening."

"I thought anticipation meant getting excited."

"Right, usually. In this case, it means that Huntington's disease in some families comes earlier and earlier, from the grandparent, to the child, to the grandchild. It's a different kind of anticipation."

He sighed again, wrinkling his forehead. I wanted to smooth out the worry with my hand, but that wouldn't touch what was troubling him. "Are you still worried?"

"No."

"It's good to talk about this with you," I said, risking directness. "Even though it's kind of upsetting, I'm glad you're interested."

"Of course I'm interested." Alexander shuffled through the cards in his lap. "This one is Hoopa," he said, pointing to fine print I could barely read. At thirty-nine, I dreaded reading glasses. I'd promised myself never to wear them on a beaded chain around my neck. Alexander had no problem reading the card. "He can summon these rings, and if you go through them, you get transported to another dimension. Hey, can I have my pretzel?"

The Pokémon cards worked for a while, getting Alexander through the dullest part of my meeting. The visitors today were identical twins, sisters in their midthirties named Alicia and Alina, patient-advocates who volunteered to tell their stories about life with Huntington's. They wore matching outfits: green turtlenecks and black pants, black sneakers with bright white treads. One sister had long red hair, loose and fuzzy about her face, the other had the same startling shade of red, but cut short in tight curls. Entering the room in tandem, they mirrored one another—as if one sister's twisting head, the dance-like jerks of her arms, were an invisible force reflected by her twin. As one head tilted, the other did, too, and their paired movements had an eerie, rhythmic beauty. Although they were courageous and inspiring, speaking eloquently about their fight to maintain as normal lives as possible, they knew they would worsen, in awful simultaneity.

They'd seen their father losing first his balance to the involuntary movements of chorea, then his mind, then his life, several years before their own symptoms began. They tried to hold on to the knowledge that every individual with Huntington's disease has a different body, mind, and heart. They told stories of family members who tested negative and were consumed with survivor's guilt. They recounted their agonizing decisions about whether to get pregnant, and about their mother, who, in her darkest moments of despair, had regretted having had children at all.

After everyone left, Alexander gathered his cards and stuffed them in his backpack.

"You said the bad protein, the one that gets made by the bad gene—doesn't fold right?"

I smiled. "Yes, kind of like how you fold laundry. But with laundry, folding badly is better than not folding at all." I saw he'd been gripping the Hoopa card tightly in his hand, so tightly he'd bent it.

He sighed, opening his hand up and flattening the rectangle of flimsy cardboard.

"It's okay about the mice, Mama," he said finally. "You have to stop the chorea." He put his hand in mine and we stood up together. "And I'll work harder on folding the laundry."

We walked back to the station to catch our train home.

EUDOXIA

She awoke from a dream in the dark. Once, she would have opened her eyes to see her narrow bed, the thin coverlet of threadbare wool, the earthen floor of the cave tucked into the mountain. Now she was blind—she could stare at the brightest sun without flinching. But her inner eye had sharpened, slicing through visions.

The prophecies come from the dark.

The night was warm, too warm for a fire. Her thoughts flitted like a moth around a candle while darkness brooded around her.

I have a fortune to tell, for those who have the stomach to hear.

It is a dream of generations, a dream of movement and madness. The house of Lusignan shall flock to me, hungry for an answer, grasping for a cure. So it shall begin. I cannot see the end.

chapter two

PÈRE VILLENC LUSIGNAN
1249
La Lacedemonie

Père Villenc Lusignan visited the fortune-teller alone while the rest of the house slept. His parishioners would not welcome the knowledge that a man of the Latin Church sought the words of a seer. The steep path to the cave was cut into the side of the hill, the entrance hidden by a copse of hemlock trees. Crumbling earth and rocks rolled underfoot, and wild grasses grew thick underneath the trees' overhanging branches.

Nettles stung Père Lusignan's legs as he climbed. Every few steps, his feet made a movement he did not intend: a jerk and snap, as if he were withdrawing from a sharp rock. He walked cautiously, mumbling a command to each errant foot. He reached the mouth of the fortune-teller's cave without falling, and the dark doorway beckoned.

Inside, the air was thick with smoke and stiflingly hot; a fire smoldered in a rough stone hearth. A narrow bed covered with shabby woolen blankets was pushed against the wall, and a three-legged wooden stool balanced like a dog with a missing limb. A niche with an altar was cut into the wall, the faded image of a saint painted on the stone.

Père Lusignan had followed the directions he'd been given. *Go at moonrise on the twelfth day of the month and you will find her there. She will speak her dreams, and you shall find truth buried in them.* The rumpled blankets moved, revealing matted dark hair, a lined face, two clawed hands.

What have you brought?

Père Lusignan flinched. "I have brought my question."

Not enough. She turned her hunched back. He pleaded and threatened, but she did not move. Finally—

Bring me what you hold dear, and then I shall answer. She waved her arm, a dismissive gesture that seemed to have magical force, propelling him out of the cave.

The next day he returned with food for the old woman, left over from his evening meal. The seer ate it ravenously, sauce dripping down her chin, crumbs of bread catching in her tangled hair. But "Bring me what you hold dear," she said, and again he stumbled home.

The third night he searched his house for a trinket that would please her. He found a broken necklace bright enough to catch the eye, with a chain too damaged to be worn. But he knew that if he wished to learn the truth, he would have to do her bidding. He went to the chest at the foot of his bed and opened the lid, drawing out his dead wife's clothes, musty with disuse, and then, carefully wrapped in linen, a curl of her hair.

"Keep this piece of me with you when I am gone," she had whispered, cutting the strand herself. He carried this last remnant of his wife up the hill in the dark. The prophetess took it in her withered hand, running the strands through her fingers.

Finally, her voice rasped, the sound of dead branches breaking.

You have come to know the source of your affliction.

Though he knew she could not see his face with those milk-white eyes, he felt the harsh cold of her stare.

The scourge will follow you and your family through the generations, a beast at the heels of the Lusignan line. Some will twitch and shake and fall to madness, others will watch as those they love writhe into death.

Père Lusignan felt one of those twitches now in his wrist, and he hid his hand in his robe.

You cannot hide from the beast, Père.

"And the cure, what is the cure?" His own voice sounded strange to him, high and strained.

While your line dies, and dies, and dies again, another will live, and live, and live. He has the beast in his body, but his blood protects him. He will have lives upon lives.

"Does his blood hold the cure?"

She was silent, a pile of rags and snarled hair, two white circles where her eyes should have been. The sound of breathing, the sound of the fire. This terrible riddle could not be all.

"Tell me, please—a name, just a name." Panic filled his throat.

The fortune-teller breathed. The rags on the bed rose and fell. *These are the four names: Elias. Ilias. Mystras. Myzithras. The blood of Franks and Romaioi come together in this place, two streams into a river.*

"Four names? Two boys and two places? One place with two names? A man and a prophet? A man of mixed blood? The person, or the place? Explain yourself, madwoman!" The flat, close air of the cave swallowed his words.

You have your answer. Leave me.

There was nothing more to do but make his way out of

the terrible smoky cave, away from the seer who foretold his family's doom and the tangled opacity of the hope she had offered him, as blank and unfathomable as her eyes.

ELIAS BORGHES
1249
La Lacedemonie

At twelve I thought I was too old for a child's stories. But on the day after my birthday, my mother told us a new tale. It was spring, the middle of Lent. A green haze dusted the trees in the Vale of Sparta, where Prince Guillaume Villehardouin lived with his retinue, and which the prince's soldiers—my father among them—guarded with spears and swords.

We were sitting on benches at the wood trestle table in the front room of our house. Our wooden beds clustered together in one small chamber in the back, and a third smaller room served as storage. We'd nearly finished eating *deipnon*, the main meal of the day. I'd learned the French word from my father, but we did not use it often in the house, my mother's domain. I'd polished off slices from a loaf of the morning's bread, a thick bean soup, and the tangy white cheese made of milk from the sheep that grazed on the slopes above the prince's residence, La Crémonie. My father had gone out early to drill with the prince's guard, patting the top of my head with his broad hand.

Today our meal was later than usual—that morning my mother had been called to attend a birth. I was used to her frequent, unexpected comings and goings; birth does not adhere to a schedule. She often came home spattered with blood, but, she said, when at first I was frightened, "Women bleed when we bring life into the world, Elias. That is a small price to pay for the miracle of creation." Even late at night I'd creep out to be with her as she washed herself and recorded the birth dates and names of the babes in her logbook. It was just bound parchment and ink, but I thought of the book as the embodiment of new life.

Today, our meal was delayed by my mother's late return. My little brother, Giánnis, and I were finishing our sweet of stewed dates when he asked for a story. I was about to help my mother clear the plates, but she motioned me to sit.

"Stay, Elias," she said. "This is a story for boys who will soon be men." The fire crackled in the hearth under the iron soup pot hanging from chains above the heat.

"Forty-five years ago," my mother began, "in the year of our Lord 1204—"

Already Giánnis was interrupting. "Mitéra, were you born then?"

She touched his cheek. "I was not even a spark in my mother's belly. But your grandmother and your grandfather were alive. They bid me tell my children and tell my children to tell their children." I imagined that I might have a child one day who would hear my stories and whose hand would be smaller than mine.

My mother sat down at the table. I thought she was the most beautiful woman in the village. Her long dark hair was parted in the middle, and she wore it pinned at the sides with bone combs. When she went out of the house, she kept her hair covered with a *maphorion*, but at home, she did not wear the veil.

"In those great days, our emperor ruled in the great capital of Constantinople, and Hagia Sophia was filled with the incense from swinging brass censers. Our patriarch preached from the holiest of altars in the Christian world, and a relic of the true cross gave life to our prayers. When the emperor walked the streets, he walked on fresh linden leaves, and from the buildings that lined the Mese flew white and gold silk and samite to welcome his passing. There was no city as beautiful as Constantinople.

"On the seventh day of April, ships of the crusading Franks, led by the swiftest Venetian galleys, entered the straits of the Golden Horn outside the great walls of our emperor's city. These men called themselves 'pilgrims,' and their aim was to conquer the Infidel in Jerusalem. But these so-called pilgrims came with their warships, their armies decorated with the cross, as if they acted in the name of the same God we serve. They dropped anchor in our harbor."

Giánnis could not restrain himself. "Is this a battle story?" He leaped up from the table and waved his spoon like a tiny sword.

She nodded. "It is a battle story, *to paidí mou*."

Her little one—she used to call me that, too—made a few vicious thrusts with his spoon. "I love battles," he crowed. But I knew, seeing my mother's face, that this battle story would not end happily.

"When the sun rose the next morning, the Frankish and Venetian ships sailed so close to the great city's walls that those within could see the faces of the enemy. They had fitted their ships with machines of war and great ladders rising from the decks to the tops of the city's walls. When the Franks and Venetians launched their attack from the sea, we battled them back. They came so close that our soldiers fought lance to lance from our ramparts to their ship towers, beating back the assault."

Giánnis could not restrain his outburst. "Did we win?"

Our mother smiled, ruefully. "That day we won, and the enemy withdrew to nurse their wounds and bury their dead. But that, alas, was only the first day."

I struggled to form the words in my head. "The pilgrims were bound for Jerusalem, so why . . ."

My mother finished my sentence for me. "Why did they attack our Romaioi capital, the greatest city in Christendom? For all their purported intent to bring the light of Christ to the East, the crusaders saw what they could take from us. They took it then, they take it now, and they will always take it, Elias." I had never heard my mother like this, so bleak and dire, like a prophetess. Giánnis was undaunted.

"Mama, did the bad ships go away?"

"No, little one. Their army bound their ships, the *Pilgrim* and the *Paradise*, together to bring our doom." I wished that my mother would stop the story. I wanted to stay on this side of the divide between my childhood and what lay beyond.

"Mitéra, finish!" Giánnis tugged at our mother's sleeve.

"The *Pilgrim* and the *Paradise* came so near to the walls of Constantinople that their ladders flanked the great tower and knights could leap from their ships' masts onto the tower it-self. The great wall was breached. The Latin crusaders, in the guise of holy conquest, tore through the streets. They slaughtered our people until their battle horses slipped on the rivers of blood. They took our holy icons, looted our churches for their gold candelabras and chalices, defiled our relics. They put a lady of the night on the patriarchal throne in the Hagia Sophia. They captured the emperor and executed him like a lowly criminal, far from the kingdom that was his by right. They sacked the city and took its riches back to their own lands. Even now the great golden horses of the first emperor

Constantine—crowned eight hundred years ago—decorate the Basilica in Venice, and the conquerors divide up the spoils and our lands like spoons of quince sweet among greedy children."

Giánnis frowned. "What's a night lady? And can I have quince, Mitéra?"

"No quince today, Giánnis." She did not explain the night lady; I was old enough to understand. It was at that moment I realized that my father was one of them. Though he had been born years after the city's fall, he was a Frank, and the Franks had led the charge to storm the walls and bloody the streets of Constantinople.

My mother put her hand on my shoulder. "Elias, will you take your brother outside while I finish in the kitchen?"

I went out with Giánnis to play at swords. But I was slow, my mind on my mother's story, and my brother broke through my defense to bruise my shin. That evening my father returned brimming with exciting news. Soon I was to begin service in the court of the prince and take a position in the newly built *kastron* of Mystras.

Giánnis leaped into our father's waiting arms. "Pèreas, can I go with Elias?"

"When you are older. But now, you must serve only your mother, as I do."

"Ah, Jéhan, always my gentleman," my mother said, and he enclosed her too in his wide embrace.

That lovely spring day in 1249, my brother beat me in a game of swords, I saw my beloved father as a stranger from an enemy land, and I began my service to the place that would engrave its name upon my soul.

ELIAS BORGHES
January 1250
La Lacedemonie

Writing never came easily to me, despite the hours my mother spent guiding me through my letters. I read easily, but when I held a stylus to scratch letters on wax or in ink on parchment, the shapes resisted my control. My mother tried to be sympathetic, though I saw her frustration. I wished I had been promised to a monastery rather than the military, but I took up the sword because the pen eluded me so persistently. In fact, I was not much better with the heavy weapon than the lighter one.

The *kastron*—Mystras's fortress—was built at the top of the hill named Myzithras. Some said the name came from a maker of sheep's milk *myzithra* cheese or from the conical shape that cheese was molded into. I thought it was as if God had finished the Taygetos mountain range and then, as an afterthought, set the last bit at the mountains' feet.

Prince Villehardouin used the Greek name Mystras for his new castle. The builders took old stones from ruins found in the valley, some from ancient Sparta, where Helen took Paris's hand and left for Troy, bringing war in her wake.

I was eager to join my father, who trained with the garrison. "With the *kastron*, our good prince protects his subjects from the savage Milengoi Slavic tribes," my father said. We stood in the small garden outside our house where we grew fragrant amaranth—*vleeta*—herbs, and a single silver-leafed olive tree.

"Have you fought the Milengoi, Pèreas?"

"Many times. They are brutal, hardened by making their home in the Taygetos mountains. They come down from the peaks, savage with the intent to reclaim the land the prince has captured."

"Will I fight them?" The thought was horrifying.

My father put one arm around my shoulders. "Soon, they will no longer be a threat, thanks to our prince and his new fortress. The tribes have been driven back to the interior of the Taygetos, and their chieftans will soon accept his governance. The appearance of might can change an enemy's mind." *Appearance of might*, not might itself. I tucked those words away for further thought.

"Do you see, Elias, how the fortress was built? On two sides, sheer cliffs drop into chasms, defense assured by God's hand. And to the southeast is a tower so tall that a guard can see miles in all directions. The citadel of Mystras is truly unassailable. Tomorrow you will begin training to join the guards that protect the city. I have looked forward to this day since you took your first steps."

My father said Prince Villehardouin loved the land as we did, and we were glad that the prince kept us safe. We might have remained glad. But the ambition of princes is legendary.

Ω

"We have a newcomer among us." Pantaleon, the head of the squadron, motioned everyone to sit. He was barely taller than I (and I was not large for twelve), but every sinew of his body was full of purpose that made him seem larger. His eyebrows were thick and dark, and grew together in the middle.

All the other heads turned toward me. My face flushed. "I am Elias, son of Jéhan Borghes, a soldier in the court of the prince. My mother, Chryse, is a midwife in the village."

"Welcome, Elias," Pantaleon said. "We are now The Six."

The number, as he said it in Greek, became an incantation of shared intent.

I was one of the *gasmoules*—half Frank, half Greek— employed in the *kastron*. On the day I arrived, Pantaleon called a meeting of our group in the chapel. Outside, the soldiers went through their exercises, swinging their swords and making sure their bows pulled true. Inside, the chapel smelled of wax, the long tapers lit in prayers that rose to heaven.

I was the youngest. Pantaleon, at eighteen, was our leader. Nikos, so huge his arms were the size of my thighs, was sixteen and, like me, had a soldier father. A half-healed slash on his arm was carelessly wrapped in cloth. Theodore, thirteen, had wide light-blue eyes that made him look perpetually startled. He had joined just the week before. He whispered in my ear, "Nikos makes sure everyone sees his wound, as if he got it fighting. But he cut himself with a knife he was sharpening. Let Nikos think you're impressed and you'll be better off." I took the excellent advice. Fifth in the group was Demetrios, serious and quiet. His dark hair curled behind his ears and he had a slightly crooked nose that made me wonder whether he'd been injured in a fight. I was afraid to ask. Something about him made me want to stare, but I forced myself to turn away, afraid I'd offend him. He was old enough to bear arms in the *kastron*'s guard, and I imagined that should he kill a man, he would neither enjoy nor brag of it.

Marceau was last to introduce himself, and he took his time. I knew at once that he was dangerous. He was the son of Evrard Lusignan, the garrison commander, and his pale, angular face sported a superior smirk. Unlike the rest of us, he was of pure Frankish blood. During introductions, when his dismissive look swept over me, a chill raised the hair on the back of my neck.

"My father commands all of yours," he said with a curl at the corner of his mouth. He spoke Greek laced with French. Marceau took out a delicate silver tool to clean his nails. I did not need Theodore to tell me that Marceau lorded his origins over us, the half-breeds.

Nikos adjusted his substantial weight on the bench, making it creak. "Marceau, why isn't your father a priest like your grandfather?"

Marceau sneered. "You may actually be even less intelligent than you appear, which is hard to imagine."

Pantaleon interjected. "Men serve God in different ways: some within the church and others on the battlefield." He turned to me to explain. "Marceau's grandfather, Père Villenc Lusignan, is a man of God. We are fortunate to have his grandson in our midst."

I wondered why the son of a Frankish commander would be thrown in with a regiment of *gasmoules* to train. We were not well-loved or fully trusted by the Franks, though they were happy enough to use us as soldiers.

"How does he have a grandson if he's a priest?" The audacity of Nikos's question left me openmouthed.

Marceau put his hand on his dagger, but Pantaleon touched his arm in warning. Even Marceau heeded Pantaleon. "The holy man turned to God after he lost his wife."

"I'd rather be a fighter than a cleric, married or not," Nikos said. His lack of guile made me warm to him.

"Some of us are better suited to kill a man than to lead him to God," Marceau said.

Ω

In February, a month before my thirteenth birthday, I faced Marceau Lusignan in the practice yard. I had never been paired with Marceau; I suspected Pantaleon had protected me from him. Marceau rolled up the sleeves of his shirt beneath his tunic, while I shivered with the cold he seemed not to feel. His mouth twisted at one corner like a fighting dog's, and he came at me, sword arm raised. I dodged his first blow, then the second. The third slash of his sword could have taken my ear or eye, had I not moved in time. Instead the point slashed at the skin between the two, cutting a burning arc in my cheek.

Marceau stopped and looked down at his own arm, spattered with red. "So this is what mixed blood looks like," he said. "The same red as any man's, despite *gasmoule* pretensions about your *noble* Roman origins." Marceau took a square of cloth he used to wipe the sweat from his brow and carefully cleaned the streaks of blood. He kept the cloth, folding it into the scabbard at his hip. It chilled me to see a piece of myself in his hand. Though he was in name one of us, for him the name was as shallow as the Evrotas river in the height of summer.

PÈRE VILLENC LUSIGNAN
February 1250
La Lacedemonie

Père Villenc heard his grandson enter the house, announcing his arrival with the clatter of weapons on the marble tiled entry floor. Twice, tiles in the mosaic had needed to be replaced from Marceau's carelessness. Was it carelessness? Over time, watching his grandson, Père Villenc had begun to see a wanton, deliberate destructiveness. He recalled Marceau's face when the household dog tipped a brazier warming the upstairs triclinium, and the fire spread to engulf the dog, who howled in pain. At first, Père Villenc had thought the boy was shocked into immobility, but when he saw his grandson lean back calmly against the tapestried wall to watch, he felt a chill. It was hard to believe that Marceau, then only eight, could possess such innate cruelty.

That pleasure in destruction and in the suffering of others had grown as Marceau matured; he was as cold as the steel of the blade he'd learned to wield. At least the boy showed no sign of the scourge, not yet. No movements distorted his young limbs. Evrard, Marceau's father, had an odd clumsiness about him, though Villenc wondered whether his fears were creating evils where there were none to see. Evrard was as bland as Marceau was vicious; the Lusignan curse could not be blamed for Marceau's cruelty, which came, Père Lusignan feared, not from disease but from the devil. This thought came with an involuntary twitch, a flick of an arm he could not suppress, and he stumbled as he walked toward the door.

"I met the new boy," Marceau said, "and I don't think much of him."

"You do not think much of anyone," Père Villenc said reflexively, then realized what he'd heard. His mind drifted more these days, missing fragments he was not always able later to retrieve. "New boy?"

"He's called Elias. His father's a soldier in the garrison. Can't say he'll make much of a fighter, but his father must think he will."

"You are sure his name is Elias?"

"He says it the Greek way. He's a *gasmoule*, Greek mother and Frankish father."

Père Villenc's head buzzed: *These are the four names: Elias. Ilias. Mystras. Myzithras. The blood of Franks and Romaioi come together in this place, two streams into a river.*

Blood. He saw Marceau was holding a cloth, spattered red.

"You've been hurt?"

"Not I," Marceau said.

"You wounded a fellow soldier?"

"If you can call Elias that. I taught him a lesson; he'll have a scar to show for it. I'd have brought you his ear but I missed my mark."

"Don't kill him, just keep your eye on him," Père Villenc said. "Tell me what he says, and does, and where he goes."

"You want me to follow the runt of the litter? That promises to be a dull business."

"It is Lusignan business." Villenc held out his hand. "And I'll take the cloth." His own limb writhed away from its intended target, as if it could not bear the contact.

EUDOXIA

The old man had come again. She knew his acrid smell, and the rustling of the dried grasses on the stone floor marked the irregular shifting of his feet. Now there was the smell of blood, hot and alive. How long had it been since she'd had a sacrifice to feed her visions? He handed her a piece of cloth. The feel and smell of blood. The words flowed through her.

This is the blood of the servant sworn to the Prophet, the blood of the guardian of the gates. The blood of the boy who watches and waits. The blood of the babe promised on the mountain's top.

This blood shall give him life, life beyond the curse that writhes the limbs and withers the soul. But yours, Lusignan, yours shall give you death and give your son death and your son's daughters and sons. For death is in the blood of your line, and the twitching of the serpent in your limbs is death tightening its grip. While the Watcher lives and lives and lives, you shall die and die and die. Death is in your blood as life is in the blood of the Prophet's promise.

The old man cleared his throat.

"Can the blood of this boy save us? Can it?"

The blood of the boy is life, she rasped. Then she was done, the river of words leaving her gasping on the shore.

ELIAS BORGHES
Summer 1250
La Lacedemonie

Pantaleon took me aside after the others had left. We were in the *kastron*'s chapel, where the soldiers came to be blessed by the military chaplain.

"How are you finding your time with us, Elias?" Pantaleon smiled encouragingly. When he asked me to speak, I felt a familiar tightness in my chest.

One summer when I was small, a rabbit intended for my mother's pot escaped its cage, bounding out the doorway of our house. I'd pursued it, running. But when my breathing narrowed to a high-pitched wheeze I had to stop, straining to find the breath I'd lost. My mother came quickly, wrapping her arms about me, and praying in Greek until I could breathe again.

After that, Mitéra made me wear an amulet about my neck, an *enkolpion* etched with an image of the Profitis Ilias. "Your namesake," my mother said. When I touched it, saying the prayer my mother taught me, my breathing eased. That night, we had no rabbit stew.

Now, with Pantaleon waiting for my answer, I took the amulet in my hands and words came. "I am proud to be a part of your company," I said, "though I'm not the most capable student."

Pantaleon smiled wryly. "Few admit weakness." He motioned me to one of the wooden benches in the chapel and sat beside me. "Like most boys in our company, you come from the merging of East and West. But *gasmoule* is a word of the West, and words are shaped by the struggle for power. The Latins call us Greek, we call ourselves Romaioi. Our language is peppered with French, the way the fleur-de-lis decorates stonework of our cities. Do you understand?"

I thought of the story my mother had told me. "I understand."

"Despite this mixing of our blood, the love that made us who we are, we remain true to our Roman roots."

I reached out to touch the back of the pew, where a fleur-de-lis was carved next to an eight-petaled flower. "Do we not serve the prince of Achaea?"

"We serve him loyally. But do not forget that the prince's own kinsman Geoffrey was among the soldiers who took Constantinople and chronicled its taking. When the double-headed eagle flies again over Constantinople and Mystras, we will rejoice because the rulers we serve share our blood. Can you follow the prince now and still keep the secret flame burning in your heart?"

Was this treason or truth? "I can," I said, deciding in favor of the second.

Pantaleon put his hand over mine. "When the time comes, you will know." We left the chapel together.

ELIAS BORGHES
1252
Mystras

I woke in the night to the sound of my parents talking. My brother Giánnis was snoring in his seamless sleep. Giánnis looked like our father: light-haired, with round blue eyes in a sunny face, and he had a disposition to match. Though he was ten years to my fifteen, he was nearly my height and, had he wanted to, he could have crushed me in a test of the wooden swords we once played with under the olive tree. I had my mother's dark hair and eyes, as well as her delicate build. Although I liked it when others commented on our resemblance, I knew that it was not always a compliment to compare a grown son to his mother.

Tonight an edge to my parents' nighttime conversation brought me fully awake. I crept out of the bedroom and stood, listening.

"Jéhan, I worry about Elias," my mother was saying.

"All mothers worry, Chryse."

I could imagine the way my mother narrowed her eyes when she did not agree. "Elias is ill-suited to fight." I agreed with her. But a renewed threat from Slavic mountain tribes required a battalion to defend La Crémonie, and Pantaleon had told me I was ready. Prince Guillaume's new palace, rising on the plateau below the *kastron*, was expected to rival his current residence, La Crémonie, in comfort and opulence. Inside the fortified walls there was already plenty to attract raiders—livestock, weapons, stores of food, and gold.

"Chryse, you swore our firstborn son to Mystras's defense." My mother had not told me that.

"This may not be the manner in which Elias is best equipped to defend it."

"Every mother of a soldier fears for her son's survival. But it is late, my Chryse, and we must sleep to manage the day ahead." After that, they were quiet.

Back in bed, I lay awake a long time. If my mother doubted my competence, why had she kept me on the soldier's path? I shared her fear.

Ω

The next morning, I woke early while Giánnis snored on like a spring brook. My mother was already in the kitchen, pouring a pitcher of frothing sheep's milk into a pot over the fire. Three lemons sat on the table, and my mouth watered at the promise of fresh *myzithra* cheese. A bowl of honey waited, too, and a loaf of bread.

"*Kalimera*, Mitéra."

My mother turned, spoon in hand. "Did the promise of *myzithra* and honey wake you?" I shrugged. My mother raised one eyebrow. "Tell me."

"I heard you and Patéras talking last night."

"Ah, I see." She stirred for a few seconds. "And what did you make of it?"

"Why am I training to become a soldier?"

She hesitated. "Your father and I dedicated you to the protection of Mystras together, before we knew your talents."

"When I was born, Mystras was only a tree-covered hill."

"I did what the Profitis Ilias asked of me." My mother always walked the line between the physical world and that of the spirit, and I knew she listened to voices beyond the range of others' hearing. "The prophet whose name you share saved your life. At the top of the hill where the *kastron* stands was once a shrine, and the spirit still lives on the hilltop, though the walls of the shrine have come down, and the stones have been used to build fortifications. There, I dedicated you to Profitis Ilias, who brought the wind that filled your lungs. In return, I promised you to Mystras: to the city that would flourish on the hill. I swore you would serve, for all your . . . life."

I noticed her odd pause. "Does my joining the prince's guard fulfill that promise?" Her response was half nod, half shrug. I wished, sitting at the table while my mother stood at the fire, that we could go back to the time when I thought my mother had no doubts. "Mitéra, how did you come to love a Frankish soldier?"

My mother sighed. "I wondered when you would ask. You mean, how can I make a life with a man who took our land and sent our emperor into exile?" I stared at her. She looked like the mother I'd always known. "How can I love a soldier from a land whose soldiers burned our homes and stole our icons from the Hagia Sophia? Is that what you mean, Elias?" My mother stirred the milk fiercely, as if she might beat it into submission.

I stood up from the table, my legs shaking. "Yes, that is what I mean." All the questions I'd never asked rose to the surface. "How can you love my father when you resent his origins? And how can I?" My throat burned. I did love my father, and so did my mother. This is what it meant to be a *gasmoule*, this insoluble mix of love and anger.

My mother took the pan off the fire. She came and

wrapped her arms about me—it did not matter that I was no longer a child.

"Love is a bridge," my mother said.

"What if someday the bridge connects two lands at war?"

"It already does, Elias. It already does."

Ω

I came back from my first skirmish with my first real battle wound—a slash in my cheek, in the same spot where Marceau had sliced me open two years before. The sheer terror of being in battle marked me more fiercely than the Slav's spear. There is nothing like looking into the face of a man who wishes to kill you. My enemy tried to with his spear, but Pantaleon's battle-axe, catching the Milengoi warrior's spear arm, saved my life. Pantaleon finished the man off.

"You shall carry that scar for all your days," my mother said that night. She was holding back tears. At the table that evening, while Giánnis plied me for stories, my mother held her mouth in a thin line.

"He will be better equipped for the next battle," my father said, resting his hand on my shoulder. I should have felt proud, but I felt only fear.

The scar healed, but as my mother foretold, my face shaped itself around that new line—red and angry, then fading, but never gone. I fought more battles, and, when I wasn't fighting, stood watch at Mystras's gates. We all accumulated scars, some visible, some in our hearts. I got better at fighting, but I never grew to love it. Then, the scar served to remind me of my mortality. Eventually, it would come to mean something altogether different.

chapter three

HELEN ADLER
Winter 2015
New York

"Mama, do you wish you could live forever?" Alexander shifted from one foot to the other.

"I'm having enough trouble making it through this week," I said, trying not to swallow the pins in my mouth. I was adjusting the hem of a pair of new pants I'd finally bought for Alexander, and since he was wearing the pants, it took extra attention. They were three inches too long. What nine-year-old giants were the template for boys' clothing designers? At least he'd have room to grow.

Alexander put his hand on my shoulder to steady himself. "Dad used to laugh when you said things like that."

I looked up, trying not to poke either myself or Alexander with a pin in the process. "Things like what?"

He didn't answer me directly. "Dad laughed a lot."

My thoughts spiraled grimly. *Dad laughed a lot. I don't. I'm not fun.* I restrained myself. "Yes, he did." To take the pressure off, I went back to pinning.

Alexander sighed. "You remember that time when we were watching *Hotel Transylvania*? That was really fun."

I did remember—Oliver had laughed so hard at the movie (and had such a distinctive goofy laugh) that everyone around us started laughing because he was laughing, and we went out for ice cream with the bunch of laughing strangers afterward. Things like that always happened with Oliver; every outing turned into a party. Oliver hadn't grown up in New York City the way I had. He had a small-town sociability that I—trained to be suspicious of interest from strangers as a sign of either a con act or a come-on—did not. So I took a while to warm up to the post-movie event. The city is not as bad as I make it sound; there is a gritty friendliness about New Yorkers that I both appreciate and embody. We are nicer than we look. But at the post-movie spontaneous dessert, I was the only one not laughing, and was acutely aware of not being able to. Plus, one of the kids in the group asked me whether I was Alexander's grandmother because I had "so many wrinkles." His mother looked like a teenager.

I took the pins out of my mouth so I could talk without injuring my tongue and thought about Alexander's earlier question. "I don't know whether I would want to live forever," I said. "Would you?"

"Only if other people did, too," Alexander said. "Otherwise it could be lonely, living while everyone else dies. But if you could live forever with your family, that might be nice."

"Yes," I said slowly.

"But it's too late for Dad now."

I put down the pincushion and pulled Alexander into a hug. He buried his face in my chest and wrapped his arms as far as they could go around me.

"It would be okay if it was just the two of us, living forever," Alexander said, his voice muffled against my sweater.

Ω

A year into widowhood I was still no expert at helping Alexander grieve, particularly not while grieving myself. Sometimes everything was so hard—getting Alexander out the door in time for school, coaxing him through his painfully slow writing, figuring out how to change the broken light bulb in the antique ceiling fixture that Oliver's mother had given us—the light that I'd always hated and now hated even more.

Oliver would have known what to say when Alexander got in trouble for reading Greek mythology in science class. The call from the teacher meant I was supposed to come home after a crushing day at work to reprimand my son about distracting kids with the story of the Minotaur. While making instant mac and cheese and silently criticizing myself for it, I found out the rest of the story.

Alexander, having more experience and maybe aptitude for science, had finished everything he was assigned in five minutes. So, when Alexander had finished with the assignment (correctly), he'd found something to read, since science class was held in the library. The library that had been closed because the public school couldn't afford a librarian.

"We never get to check out books," Alexander told me, sadly, over the mac and cheese he loved, which made me feel both better and worse about making it.

I was not as gracious on the phone with the school administration as Oliver would have been, and at the end I started crying. The assistant principal, probably thinking that I was an unhinged widow, quickly ended the conversation.

Alexander grew even quieter and slower. He drifted in the mornings when he was supposed to get dressed for school, and I'd leave his breakfast bagel to burn in the toaster while I found him buried in an illustrated version of *The Odyssey*, or playing puppets with his socks and an invented language that sounded like Greek. It was only in the brief moments between tasks that his thoughts came out, usually when I had no time for them.

At his afterschool program, his peaceful exterior hid some surprises. One day he came home with a classmate's 1953 wheat penny, which he returned reluctantly, after I discovered the "I traded it" story was not accurate. I had to have grave and apologetic conversations with several school staff, and then had to spend two days lecturing Alexander about stealing while he fidgeted and failed to meet my gaze. He gave the penny back and didn't do it again, as far as I knew. But it didn't help our flickering connection. We needed a break, but I didn't know how to take one.

Once my fall grant proposals were done and submitted, I picked up Alexander a few minutes early and suggested a movie. We got an extra-large popcorn and a mammoth bag of gummy bears and settled in for his film choice, which I am fairly certain was about penguins surfing. Afterward, we walked out into the Friday evening bustle of Union Square. We passed a vendor selling gloves and Alexander pulled me over to look. He fingered the wool and fleece, as if his hands were helping him think.

"Mom, can we go on a vacation together? Not just me going somewhere while you stay home and work." *Don't just ship me off to camp, you mean*, I thought.

"Where do you want to go?" I dreaded him saying Disney World. Or maybe he'd want to go to the beach. No . . . not the beach. I stared at a pair of mittens while remembering Oliver's frayed Hawaiian print swim trunks and felt my vision blur. I wondered how either of us would ever manage a beach again, now that Oliver had gone happily into the water and hadn't come out. He'd never been afraid of the ocean, but maybe he should have been. Who knows how much fear is the right amount?

When Alexander finally answered, so much time had passed I'd almost forgotten I'd asked him anything.

"I want to see Sparta."

I didn't want to disappoint him. "Sweet boy, Sparta doesn't exist anymore."

Alexander shook his head. "I know *ancient* Sparta doesn't, but there is a place called Sparta now. They call it Spárti in Greek. Just like there's a real Mount Olympus."

"Let's look up the details when we get home, okay?" He nodded, but he knew he was right.

Alexander pulled me toward a food cart, where we bought a hot dog to share. As we made our way to the subway, Alexander resumed where he'd left off. "I want to go to Greece, where Helen came from. Grandma told me you're named after her. Don't you want to go there, too?"

Suddenly I did. I wanted to go to the place where my name came from, the place my son knew more about than I did. I wanted to go on vacation with my kid, who was interested in everything, held my hand even though I hadn't laughed at his favorite movie, and reenacted Greek myths with his socks.

Of course, wanting and doing are different, and the exciting idea looked dubious the following morning when I arrived at work to a pile of tasks I'd let slide while racing to meet grant deadlines. After an hour of answering emails, I made myself feel worse by reading a news article about the challenges of travel in Greece with the looming vote on austerity measures from the European Union.

Why had my son, lost in a haze of ancient history, chosen a country that would take two thousand dollars and fourteen hours to get to, where banks might shut down and strikes might immobilize transportation, and where if either of us had a health problem we might be better off catching a plane to nearby Turkey? After Alexander went to bed, I looked up the modern town of Spárti. As Alexander had assured me, it definitely did exist.

Ω

As a result of his accidental presence at my Huntington's disease funding meeting, when Alexander next encountered the topic of HD, he was prepared. I was struggling with my new widowhood hobby, knitting. It wasn't going at all well. I'd heard crafts were relaxing, but cursed at dropped stitches as the misshapen scarf emerged from my needles. Alexander was watching the news.

I heard his program in the background while I pulled out yet another failed row and started over on the scarf no one would ever wear. I was imagining myself as Penelope, Odysseus's wife. While he traveled the world in the adventures Homer immortalized in *The Odyssey*, she wove and put off suitors, who were promised she'd become available once the tapestry was done. She effectively avoided getting married to someone else by nightly unweaving her tapestry, then blithely starting again the next day. I did not miss the irony of the comparison with my widowhood knitting. I wasn't exactly fighting off suitors, but I knew I wasn't looking for a new husband either.

I glanced quickly at Alexander's screen to make sure there weren't any nightmare-inducing violent images, but it was just landscape rolling by, azure water and white cliffs, then a flash to a street protest with signs in Greek. I managed to spell them out slowly—my recognition of Greek letters came mostly from science. *Omega-Chi-Iota?* It looked like *OXI.* How was that pronounced? I heard a snip of audio, and I realized OXI was pronounced "ókhi." It meant "no."

Then it was gone, and the talking head was back. I forced my eyes down to the knitting. I'd dropped three stitches.

"Mama," Alexander said, "look."

I went to stand by Alexander. The program was about the austerity measures imposed upon Greece by the EU, draconian economic restrictions designed to bail Greece out of hopeless debt. The piece alternated between shots of angry demonstrators and a reporter interviewing a university professor. He was going on about how, in return for the unassailable benefits of belonging to the Magnificent European Union, the ungrateful Greek people, who should be Eternally Grateful, were instead complaining.

But Alexander wasn't paying attention to the content; he was pointing now, touching the screen. Below the talking head was a yellow banner: DR. PIERRE LUSIGNAN, CHAIRMAN, THE HELLENIC FOUNDATION TO END HUNTINGTON'S AND OTHER NEURODEGENERATIVE DISEASES. What did HD have to do with a political broadcast? The professor sneered as he disparaged the protestors for their resistance. "This is the price Greeks pay for evading taxes, since they're too lazy to work," Dr. Lusignan concluded.

The announcer signed off. "This has been Christos Mourtzinos, reporting from Sparta. Thanks to our local expert, Pierre Lusignan, professor of Hellenic studies from the University of Peloponnese, for today's thought-provoking comments."

Alexander remained entranced by the television, which he rarely got to watch. "They have Huntington's disease in Greece?"

"They have it everywhere."

"Professor Lusignan is not very nice," Alexander said.

I agreed; he wasn't. Meanwhile there were peculiar details about this particular not-nice expert on television that bothered me. First, Pierre Lusignan's accent sounded French, as did his name. Second, why would a scholar of Hellenic studies be on the board of a society for neurodegeneration? Third, why was the Peloponnese a hotbed of Huntington's research? I needed to know more. That night as I lay in the dark, I kept thinking about Huntington's disease in Sparta and the Greek Pierre. Maybe I needed to read some history before we went to Greece. Assuming we were going.

Ω

One night, while Alexander and I sat companionably at our keyboards sharing an order of General Tso's chicken, Alexander figured out how to surf the internet. Why did I leave my nine-year-old unsupervised on his own computer? One-word answer: *dysgraphia*. Anything that begins with *dys* is generally not good. A Greek prefix, these three tidy letters are crammed with meaning and indicate something "bad, difficult." While *graphia* means "writing."

My son is neither bad nor difficult. But his writing is bad and difficult. Or bad because it is difficult. I knew it, and so did he, proven by the pencils he'd snapped in his frustration, the erasers chewed down to stubs. I'm glad rubber isn't toxic. *Dysgraphia* was the formal Greek name for Alexander's *dis*-ability.

Parent-teacher conferences without Oliver were misery, and not only because if I didn't save the occupational therapist's email address, no one else would. Keyboarding, the school said, would be so helpful. The occupational therapist handed me a sheaf of papers. "Resources," they called them—a bunch of websites. Fortunately, Alexander loved keyboarding. There is grace, in fact, in the universe. Grace, though, comes at a price. Alexander now had not only a reason to spend thirty minutes a night on a computer, but also an entry point into a world I'd limited before.

I make it sound dire, as if his attempts to bypass dysgraphia ended in cyberbullying or pornography. It was nothing like that. When he typed in "plane tickets to Greece," he found a shockingly cheap fare to Athens.

I was opening my fortune cookie when he turned the screen to me. "Look, Mama. Does 'round trip' mean we go all around the world?"

"No, 'round trip' means going there and coming back." I smiled at his way of dancing with words. I looked at the fortune I was holding and started laughing.

"What's so funny?" I held out my fortune to him. He read out loud: "You will be offered an opportunity for unexpected travel. Take it."

HELEN ADLER
Late Spring 2015
New York

I had thirteen minutes between my research team's weekly meeting and my journal club to eat lunch and look up Huntington's disease in Sparta. While chewing on a granola bar that I found at the bottom of my bag, I searched for reports of Huntington's in Greece. I finished the granola bar in two minutes and had eleven left for single-minded research. Yes, HD was common in Western Europe, but Greece overall was not particularly known for it. My lab members were assembling when I found what I was looking for. Academia.edu had a copy of a student thesis from a graduate program at the University of the Peloponnese. The grad student had focused on the geographical distribution of triple repeat disorders in the Mediterranean region. The paper was in Greek, but with a clumsy Google translation, it was good enough.

An unusually high prevalence of HD was reported near the modern town of Sparta. Preliminary research (which I thought was pretty impressive for a student, and I jotted down her name to look up later) suggested that one or two families had given rise to a population of affected individuals and asymptomatic gene carriers, with origins that might date to the thirteenth century. "Founder effect," the paper stated with exaggerated thoroughness, "is reduced genetic diversity which results when a population is descended from a small number of ancestors."

One of the most interesting findings was that some people had a severe enough mutation that they should have gotten sick but didn't. The exact genes suspected to play a protective role had not been identified.

I leaned back in my chair as the journal club attendees filed in. Alexander's interest in Sparta suddenly seemed like an excellent idea.

Ω

My sister Jennifer, hosting Passover this year as she usually did, lived in a roomy suburban Dutch Colonial. She had permanent seating for fourteen, and overflow could be easily accommodated by the (matching) extra furniture stored in her (finished) basement. Compared to our crowded apartment storage, a usable basement was as foreign to me as the moon.

A few years before, in a moment of irrational hospitality, Oliver and I had offered to host the Seder in our apartment. We'd borrowed a folding table and chairs, but space constraints meant that my aunt Edith had to get out of her seat every time anyone needed to open the door to the bathroom. Edith, intolerant in the best of circumstances, did not take it well. Also, the extra leaf of the table gave way and dumped the Seder plate in Edith's lap. Then we tried a group call to my dad in the nursing home, but the connection was spotty and his hearing unreliable.

This year, I came early to Jennifer's house, ostensibly to help, though my clumsiness in the kitchen was a family legend. Jennifer handed me a colander of brussels sprouts to trim, ensuring I was holding the knife sharp-side down before letting me cut anything. Alexander was paying homage to a huge tub of LEGOs with Jennifer's kids; they had the $400 Ninjago City I couldn't stomach buying.

While I tried to not leave a part of my finger on the cutting board, Jennifer risked a probing question.

"How's it going with Alexander these days?"

"Oh, it's perfect," I said, my frustration with rolling sprouts making me irritable. Jennifer was somehow managing to baste a turkey, pipe chocolate onto a tray of coconut macaroons, and whip up a cauliflower kugel, all while probing into the most delicate aspects of my life.

"Helen."

"Still here." I sighed. "But I am really bad at sprouts." I stopped to wipe my sweaty palms.

"Let me take care of it," she said, and kissed my cheek. I started sobbing. Jennifer guided me to a kitchen stool and put her arm around my shoulders while I bawled.

"It's impossible," I managed to say. ". . . Not the brussels sprouts." I wiped my nose on a dish towel, which unfortunately turned out to be dusted with pepper. My crying turned into sneezing, or some inelegant combination of the two. Jennifer helped me wipe my face. It had been forever since any adult had touched me at all. Her gentleness unraveled me completely.

"Any chance of taking some time off with Alexander?" she said gently.

"Lately he's been talking about Greece. But I'm not sure that fascination will last until I can get a break. Assuming we can afford the trip. It's been a challenge to adjust to one income." I hated to admit it.

"What if I bought you guys tickets?"

"I'm that pitiful?"

"You are that important to me, and so is he. Besides, the prices are probably low. I think everyone is afraid the Greek economy will bottom out. Say yes, please, Helen?"

Alexander chose that exact moment to emerge from his LEGO fog into the kitchen. He had a piece of paper in one hand, and a pen in the other.

"Look, Mama," he said, brandishing the page. I could see there was writing on it—a big deal for this kid, for whom writing was anathema. The letters were Greek.

"Eliot has a Greek gods LEGO set," Alexander exclaimed, "and Athena comes with her owl, and this tablet with her name on it. See how I copied it?" I looked at the painstakingly penned Greek letters spelling out the goddess's name—$A\theta\eta\nu\alpha$. "Isn't that totally cool?"

"It is totally cool," I said to Alexander. Jennifer and I exchanged a glance. "Charity accepted."

chapter four

ELIAS BORGHES
Early Fall 1255
Mystras

One morning on the way to the *kastron*, I met Demetrios on the path that led up the hill to the north gate. Of The Six, I knew him least well but found him the most compelling. He remained as quiet and serious as on the first day I'd met him. I never recalled hearing him shout. Once, Nikos knocked him face-first into the dirt during a practice session. Demetrios slowly rose to his feet and wiped the earth from his face with his sleeve.

"That was a bit much, Nikos," he said, patting our giant companion gently on the shoulder. And that, amazingly enough, was all. I wondered whether he was full of emotions that he managed to restrain, or whether he was so calm inside that restraint was easy. His silence intrigued me.

This particular morning, as we walked side by side, I was glad to spend a few minutes alone with him. At the beginning of the walk the trees clustered around us, some with leaves beginning to yellow in the crisp fall air. But as we walked higher the trees thinned, as earth gave way to rock.

"How do you find being a soldier?" I had many other questions, but most seemed too personal.

"Difficult," Demetrios said.

I could not hide my surprise. "You are so good at it, though."

"Competence does not mean ease." He frowned slightly. "I am constantly afraid. This is the soldier's life."

"No one speaks of it."

"We are all afraid to."

"Fear is worse alone."

Now the silence between us was companionable. The air smelled of woodsmoke from fires in the castle enclosure, and in the blue arching sky, flocks of birds turned, heading away from winter. We walked together up the cobbled ramp to the gate, a high arched opening in the imposing outer wall. The wall was built of limestone and studded with broken pieces of tile.

Demetrios and I both felt it at the same moment, I know, because we looked at one another, at the inexplicable sensation of movement. It felt like being on the back of a horse that shudders off a fly. I nodded—*I felt it, too*—and then came a magnified version of that first quiver, then a rumbling beneath our feet, and the world tilted.

I threw myself over Demetrios while rubble rained down on my back. I was strangely unafraid. I knew, as improbable as it sounds, that the stones of the *kastron* spoke to me.

You come from the rock
When your time comes, we will welcome you back
Again and again.

When it was over, Demetrios embraced me with wordless gratitude before we began to shift the pile of stones that blocked the passage into the sunny outer court. We did not speak on the path home.

Afterward, Demetrios said I'd saved his life. Everyone had a new image of me—brave and calm in crisis, selfless in the protection of my comrade. But it was my secret understanding of that day that truly changed me. I began to believe that the strength of the stone that had once walled ancient Sparta, and fortified the *kastron*'s walls today, might actually reside in me.

GUILLAUME VILLEHARDOUIN
1258
Patras, Greece

Guillaume surveyed his new wife. Agnes was her French name, but in her father's land, she was Anna. He used her Greek name tonight, the night of their wedding, since she was the daughter of the Greek despot Michael of Epirus, *a powerful man with powerful ambitions*. The eloquence of his own words pleased him inordinately.

Anna raised one eyebrow with more skepticism than wifely adoration. "My father told me he'd promised me to a man of culture, not just a warmonger. Was he placating me?"

"Your father spoke the truth," Guillaume said, pleased. "I shall read verse with you and sing songs of love from my native land." Guillaume walked to the table where their gifts were piled and picked up a leather book stamped with gold. "A book of songs with illustrations so fine they rival those in our great churches. This extraordinary book was made for us, on the occasion of our marriage." The songs were French—the language of his ancestors. Of course, he spoke Greek, but the book was a sign of their new partnership.

He casually let the book fall open to an illustration of Charles of Anjou, the youngest brother of the king of France. "Even the royal family blesses our marriage." He and Anna had come to Patras to wed, a week's ride from his new palace at Mystras. He was proud of the long throne room at Mystras, with its high windows and vaulted roof and the eight fireplaces that burned hot through the winter months. The fortress on the summit was impregnable, backed by a chasm with the mountains looming behind it. His garrison was strong, the Greek barons loyal, and his new allies in the north—Anna's father among them—powerful. Nearly the whole of La Morée had fallen into his waiting hand. *And now, a wife to share it with.*

Guillaume smiled. "Your father promised me the allegiance of Epirus, the land he rules, and a beautiful bride. Of the second, I am certain." With this alliance secured by marriage, Nicaea, the exiled remnants of Constantinople's Greek empire, would be defeated soon. Constantinople was now under Latin rule and must stay that way.

Anna let down her dark hair. She was barely fourteen and he past forty, but she was not shy. "About the partnership between Epirus and Achaea"—she used the Greek word now, rather than La Morée, the French—"my father keeps his promises. On the matter of my beauty, it is not for me to say."

Anna was a worthy match, with wit to match her birthright. But she was inexperienced in the ways of love, and he could barely wait to begin her lessons. "Soon, with your father's strength behind me, we shall defeat the Nicaeans, and their hope to reclaim Constantinople will be crushed. You shall be at my side, princess, to enjoy the fruits of my labors on the battlefield. And in my bed to enjoy my labors at night." He did not mention what they both knew: her father Michael's ambitions might someday extend to Constantinople and the empire's throne. But for the moment, this alliance of Achaea and Epirus served them both.

The gold *kolti* suspended from chains framing Anna's face caught the light. Her father had spared no expense. "You are ambitious, prince." She met his gaze unflinchingly.

"Of course I am ambitious. Did you not marry me for that?"

"*I* married you because my father willed it. *You* married for military aid and a substantial dowry."

"I shall enjoy you all the more for those benefits, princess."

Anna raised one eyebrow. "Ambition may end in despair, if stretched too far."

Guillaume placed the songbook on the table. "I reach for what is mine," he said, and kissed his wife. Her lips tasted of wine. Ambition and military prowess had given Monemvasia, the almost-isle of rock, to Guillaume, and the fortress Maina, too. These three jewels: Maina, Monemvasia, Mystras. Two he'd captured, the third his own creation. The Nicaeans would be next.

Anna's body bent to his, just as the Greeks of La Morée did to his rule—*a wise ruler is received like a worthy husband.* She welcomed him with a passion surprising for a virgin, but crying out in Greek, not French.

ELIAS BORGHES
February 1259
Lacedaemon Valley

"*Mon fils!*" My father burst into the house unusually early. Since Prince Guillaume's wedding, an alliance against Nicaea seemed unavoidable. That meant war, and war meant our battalion would fight. It did not escape me that I would be in my father's army fighting against my mother's ancestors. Our job was to follow the prince, whose rule provided protection and safety. Still, safety is no substitute for freedom.

My mother had just set out an earthenware bowl of dried broad beans, and Giánnis and I were picking out stones, when the peace of our task was ruptured by my father's unexpected entry. When he embraced me, I felt a twitch in his arms.

"Good news from the palace," my father said. "The prince has called you to pay him audience. This is an honor for our family."

"He wishes to meet with *me*? Why?"

My father laughed. "Do not be so surprised. You are well-trained, loyal, and honest." He did not say strong, I noticed. "We are on the eve of war, and he trusts our family to join his effort. Perhaps now we shall have a house within the walls of Mystras." When my father turned to my mother in celebration, she smiled carefully but did not fully join in his joy.

GUILLAUME VILLEHARDOUIN
February 1259
Mystras

Elias was smaller than one might imagine for the eldest son of Jéhan Borghes. Perhaps he resembled his mother. However, the story had spread of the soldier in training who had kept calm in the quake. After the quake, the soldiers had given this Elias Borghes a new name—Tin Íremi: The Calm One. Intrigued,

Guillaume had Elias brought before him. It was hard to imagine this small fellow could be great, but . . . *a great ruler sees the potential for greatness.*

Some princes held themselves aloof, luxuriating in their palaces while courtiers did the work to keep vassals loyal, but this was not Guillaume's way. *The more you know of your men, the better you can rule them. Such is the path of a great prince.*

"How may I serve you, my prince?" Elias's voice was more impressive than his physical presence.

"They call you Tin Íremi. How did you come to merit that name?"

Prince Guillaume watched Elias's reaction. Guillaume's brother Geoffrey, in the last days of his short reign, had told Guillaume one secret of his success: "Ask questions you know the answer to, and you shall learn more than if you asked those with answers you cannot fathom."

Elias did not answer immediately. This young man was not afraid of silence; his new name was well-earned.

"When the quake shook the *kastron*'s walls, I was not afraid," Elias said levelly. "But since I knew there was no reason to fear, I am not sure my behavior warrants any particular title."

He is modest, too, even better. "And how could you know there was no reason to fear, Elias Borghes?"

"If there is anything to fear, I am generally the first to know."

Prince Guillaume could not help laughing at the boy's description of himself.

"Tin Íremi, I look forward to your presence in the court. Do you speak French? The French spoken at La Crémonie is as elegant as in Paris."

"I owe gratitude to my father, who taught me many things, French among them," Elias said, in fluent French.

"I have need of an emissary. Have you experience?"

"I have not. But I have the will to learn, and I could not wish for a better master," Elias responded.

"You will join me tomorrow, when I ride out to visit the villages. My subjects are my children, whose well-being I assure. I shall ride through the countryside, taking stock of the lands I rule and the people who have put their lives in my hands. I shall dismount, to be at the level of the very peasants themselves, and walk about them, smelling the earth they till." Guillaume looked back at Elias to make sure the young man was still attentive and happily found he was. "You do ride?"

"Yes, of course," Elias said. "But I do not have a horse."

"You shall have one tomorrow. All men in my service are well-satisfied. Remember those words."

"I shall, my prince," Elias said. Once dismissed, he left quietly. Guillaume had little doubt—and he was confident in his ability to judge character—that Elias would prove himself useful on the long trip north to fight against Nicaea.

EUDOXIA

The boy had come. He brought food—a fresh loaf still warm. But he was quiet and demanded nothing.

It is good he knows how to wait. For he will wait and wait.

His labored breathing was the only sound in the cave besides the endless beating of her own heart. He pressed something into her hand, an amulet, etched with an image she could not read with her hands.

This one knows to give before he takes. She turned it over, the oval of metal warm from the boy's skin.

Keep it, she said. Some gifts cannot be given. *Your allegiance is to the place, not the prince.* She knew, with the unerring vision of the sightless, that the words had hit their mark.

In the sight of God, a thousand years is but a single day. Her words sank into him, water into dry earth.

HELEN ADLER
July 2015
New York

Alexander slept most of the overnight flight to Athens, but I didn't, and neither did the third passenger in our row. We sat next to each other for a few hours in respectful silence. I wasn't sure she spoke English at first, but once the dinner trays were cleared and Alexander was curled under an airline blanket, I realized verbal interactions with my neighbor were possible.

She smiled at Alexander's sleeping form. She looked the part of a classic Greek grandmother, with wise blue eyes surrounded by a web of wrinkles, and she was dressed all in black, including a black kerchief over her head, a black wool dress, a black jacket, and, I'd seen when she got up to use the restroom, sturdy black shoes at the end of her thick, slightly bowed, black-stockinged legs. Monochromatic dressing certainly makes matching your clothes easy.

She scrutinized my dinner tray. "You need eat more," she said, nodding sagely. "Too thin." I ate another piece of my chicken, which really wasn't bad.

"I forget sometimes," I said.

"Mother life like this. Only one child?"

It was easy to understand each Greek-accented word she said, but her phrasing was poetic. "Yes."

"God bless you both." Her voice was low, with a honey-thick accent. "First time Greece?"

"Yes." I suddenly wanted to tell her everything, this woman I'd probably never see again, but I didn't know how to start. "Are you going home?"

She laughed, a surprising bell-like sound, different from her speaking voice.

"Yes, but mine more than one home. Where is your home?"

I felt the tears come, sudden and startling. Sometimes grief sneaks up on you and then *wham*, there you are, tears pouring down your face over a plastic tray of half-eaten air-plane chicken. "I have a sister. But my husband died two years ago. Alexander and I are alone." Now I was crying hard enough that I could barely talk.

"Yia Yia family."

I looked at her, not understanding.

"Yia Yia is grandmother. Call me Yia Yia."

"Yia Yia," I said slowly. She met my attempt with a firm pat on my arm. And once I'd said *Yia Yia* I couldn't stop talking, and my new Greek grandmother let me alternately babble and cry into her black-clad shoulder.

I told her some of the details—Oliver's walk to the empty beach, the decision I'd made to stay home with Alexander that day (the rain, the wind, too cold to swim), his not coming back for an hour, then two, then never. Oliver's towel on the beach afterward, dusted with sand. I'd told the story before. But what I eventually told Yia Yia was something I'd been afraid to even think.

Where our problem arose, paradoxically, was that Oliver

was too happy. His parents had been faithfully married for thirty years, were doubles tennis players, and a formidable team at bridge tournaments. I, on the other hand, had only my dad, and he had four tenuously controlled illnesses and lived in a nursing facility. Oliver had been a doted-upon only child, he'd done well in school, and he loved his job, which loved him back. He made everybody laugh, washed the dishes every night, didn't snore, and never picked his nose. He'd never faced devastating loss, disillusionment, or doubt, at least not that he'd confided to me. And he wasn't afraid of the water. His life was perfect, until it was over.

I was surprised every time I got a grant funded, or a paper published. I questioned every decision I made, often a mind-boggling number of times a day. Oliver patiently put up with, for example, the countless times I switched from buffet to table service and then back to buffet again when planning our wedding. He indulged me by counting the number of revisits I made for the thornier decisions, like which elementary school district we should live in, and then buying me that number of chocolate kisses to celebrate the decision. We never finally decided whether we should try to have a second child, so I never got the kisses for that decision. It would have been a five-pound bag.

Maybe because of my parents' early divorce, my mother's death, my father's illness, or because of who I am independent of all that, I grew up with the expectation that loss is inevitable. Oliver's family had reunions, lived into their nineties, and never argued, at least not in front of me. Oliver thought I was dire; I thought I was realistic. Fortunately, he found my outlook endearing.

Optimism is a lovely quality in a spouse, and I certainly benefited from Oliver's way of moving through the world. But there were times when secretly I felt like he couldn't join me where I was going. Because he didn't know grief and doubt like I did. And now that he was gone and I was left with the greatest grief I'd ever experienced, the knowledge that his perfection was an imperfection that had divided us was hard to bear.

I didn't give Yia Yia all that detail, but I told her enough. Enough that when the pilot announced we were flying over Spain, she said: "Sleep, Eléni." She said my name in Greek; it had a beautiful sound. "You have sadness, even before you lose your husband. So maybe he did not understand. Not every husband understand everything. Even with love."

The relief of her wisdom washed over me. "I die soon," she continued, "but until that, I pray for you every day—for you and your son."

She didn't look like she was about to die soon, but I couldn't imagine a better person to be praying for us.

Ω

Alexander had a plan. We landed in Athens at ten in the morning—him refreshed by seven hours of sleep, me bleary. Yia Yia appeared unscathed, and energetically kissed us on both cheeks before she was collected by ebullient family.

On the train to the city, Alexander reviewed his intentions. "First, I want to see the Acropolis and Zeus's temple in Athens. Then I want to go to Mystras. There's a palace and a fortress. I saw it on . . ." He hesitated, realizing that my reaction to his internet browsing might not be wholeheartedly positive. I was too tired to rouse any disapproval. "On You-Tube. But it is real." He'd fortunately learned that not everything on YouTube was real. "There are these *churches* with real old *paintings* too—and a *museum*." Clearly, those were his strategies to capture my interest, in case the fortress angle didn't work. I wasn't even sure I liked museums, but I always felt compelled to take Alexander. Oliver had loved museums.

I didn't realize I'd gone silent, musing about museums and parenting, until Alexander piped up again.

"Can we go to Mystras, please? The video said it was a place where you could go back in time." Our train wound through the suburbs between the airport and the city of Athens. The recorded voice announcing the stops was melodic over the loudspeakers, serenely beautiful. *Eponymi stasi . . .* next stop. I loved the rhythm of it. Or was I just jetlagged? *Mystras* had a beautiful sound, too, like *mystery*, but not quite. *A place where you could go back in time—Alexander wants to be able to do that*, I thought. *I don't blame him.*

"Sounds amazing." I figured out how to access our international data plan and spent the rest of the ride looking up Mystras, with Alexander peering excitedly over my shoulder. Then suddenly, "*Eponymi stasi, Metaxourgeio,*" the mellifluous voice sang again, announcing our station. We stumbled off the train and walked the few blocks to our hotel, pulling our rolling suitcases over cracked, uneven sidewalks in the hot July sun.

Ω

Mystras—the historic site, not the living town where we'd booked a room in a funny little inn for a few days—was closed the day we arrived. Everything shut down for the referendum, the day Greece was to vote *ναι* or *όχι* on the EU's bailout measures, which were supposed to solve Greece's national debt crisis in a way I could not fully grasp.

My understanding was further muddied by the paradoxical fact that *ναι*, which was pronounced "neh," sounded negative, but actually meant yes, and was accompanied by a side to side shake of the head. A shining example of how the Greek language is not, in fact, English. Meanwhile όχι sounded slightly like "okay," meant no, and came with a nod. It's as if the language were designed to make tourists give up. In any case, Greece was voting that day, the people declaring their agreement or disagreement with an external solution for their economic struggles.

We gave up on touring the ruined city and instead spent the afternoon hiking through well-marked wooded trails that wound up the hills at the foot of the ominous-looking snow-capped Taygetos mountain range. Neither of us was a particularly vigorous hiker, particularly in the heat, but we were both intrigued by a tiny half-ruined church perched along the path, with rough white plaster walls and an encaustic black-and-white floor whose tiles were loose and in places broken. Alexander found a stick and pretended to defend the church from invaders while I agreed to play a frightened princess. He didn't tell me I was doing it wrong, for which I was supremely grateful.

I made sure to get back to the tiny town of Mystras before sundown—one street, two miniature plazas, a knotty tree with an old woman sitting under it, a cat winding around her legs, all nestled at the base of the hill that led up to the ruins of Byzantine Mystras. By then the vote was done, and the village was buzzing with "όχι"—for the country had voted overwhelmingly: *no*. We stopped in the grocery at the corner of the little square, where Alexander found a ring of bread shaped like a bagel with a too-big hole, dusted heavily with sesame seeds.

"*Thessaloniki*," the broad-faced proprietor of the grocery said, smiling down at Alexander incongruously over the long, sharp knife he was wielding over a massive wheel of cheese. "You like?" And Alexander did like, despite the seeds. *Traveling*, I thought, *might be good for him. For both of us.*

The news was blaring from an ancient black-and-white television perched on the counter. I didn't understand the Greek, but the cheering crowds with signs held high were clear, and the fervor filled the room through the little screen.

"We'll go see Mystras tomorrow, right, Mom?" Alexander said.

"Yes, tomorrow." I suddenly felt extra tired.

"You promise?" Alexander said. "I want to see the fortress."

"I promise," I said. Alexander tore off a piece of the bread for me as I looked back at the cheese man. "It is open tomorrow, right?"

He smiled. "Yes, yes, open. We have a tour guide here who knows a great deal about the site's wonders. He has been here forever." He waved his free hand toward the door, but from the grocery it was hard to see into the bright plaza.

When Alexander and I left, we walked hand in hand across the square, where the same old woman in black was sitting in the shade of the huge oak tree.

EUDOXIA

Alpha and Omega, Christ in the cosmos, shining in the dark before the beginning and after the end of time.

Kyriake.

The week's first and eighth day, the beginning and the end and the beginning.

The Prophet's promise.

The guardian of the gates.

The mortar of the walled city, the veins of ore, the ancient hill, the lost shrine.

Ilias, Elias, Elijah, Eliahu, Mystras, Myzithra, Mistra.

Alpha and Omega.

Beginning and End with neither Beginning nor End.

chapter five

HELEN ADLER
July 2015
Site of Mystras

The next morning Alexander woke up before dawn and leaped onto my bed.

"Mama, breakfast starts at six. It's already six *thirty*."

I struggled out of bed slowly. In the bathroom I forgot, again, to throw the toilet paper into the garbage pail as instructed by the ever-present signs. Even when I rehearsed in my head until the key moment, I almost always forgot until I saw the paper heading down into the pipes it was doomed to clog. I wondered how forgiving the Greek plumbing system was of the occasional error.

We arrived at the Mystras entrance at 7:59. The gates didn't open until eight.

"Start early to avoid the heat," the grocer in the village had told us, but it was hot already. We stood in the sun on the steep path and met our guide.

"Elias O-ro-lo-gas . . ." I sounded out the syllables on his name tag.

"It means 'watchmaker.'"

"Your family's ancestral profession?"

He tilted his head. "No, but the name suits me."

Alexander, who was usually slow to warm up with strangers, chimed in. "I read that in Mystras you can go back in time. Is that why you're called watchmaker?" Our tour guide took an audible breath, and I hoped we hadn't offended him.

It seemed we hadn't; Mr. Orologas smiled. "I shall have to say that the next time I'm asked." As we headed up the steep hill from the entrance booth, I noticed he hadn't offered any other explanation.

"We should start with the palace," the guide said, "then the fortress. If you have the strength, we can continue to the lower town afterward." He glanced at us. I wondered whether he realized that I was the weak link.

"Can we come back if we don't see everything today?" Alexander asked as we started up the path. It led to a plateau where restoration was interspersed with the weathered stone of the original. A crane stood watch like a skeletal dinosaur. The guide stopped. He crouched so his face was on a level with Alexander's.

"You can come back as many times as you like. It would take many lifetimes to learn everything there is to know about this place."

"Great!" Alexander said, and to me, "Can we?"

"Uh . . . sure." Had I just agreed to spend a huge chunk of our first international vacation visiting the same remote ruins over and over again? It reminded me of reading to Alexander when he was three years old—one more time through *Go, Dog. Go!* and I thought I might lose my mind.

The grassy plaza outside the palace was the only piece of flat ground anywhere; the rest sloped dramatically. Alexander immediately found a half-ruined guard tower to climb via an internal staircase, emerging high up to wave. *If it weren't safe, there'd be a sign, right?* I took my cue from our guide, who didn't stop him, and waited while Alexander pretended to fire arrows from the top. Once he'd shot us both, he headed down again, erupting with questions.

"Whose palace was this?"

"When it was first built, it belonged to Guillaume Ville-hardouin, the Frankish prince of Achaea."

"What was he like?"

"We know . . . from what is written, that he was ambitious. You understand the word?"

Alexander nodded seriously. "You mean he wanted a lot? And thought he could get it?"

"Precisely. He was Frankish—now you'd call him French—but he was born in Greece, at a time when the Franks ruled this part of Greece. And his ambition was to rule more of it. Nearly every battle he fought, he won. Until one day . . . he didn't." Elias laughed quietly. "He loved to hear himself talk. And thought others loved it, too."

The comment struck me as the sort of thing you'd say about someone you'd met at a cocktail party rather than a historical monarch.

"Do the Franks still rule Mystras?" Alexander sounded disapproving.

Elias shook his head. "Mystras belongs to the Greeks now. But shortly after we managed to free ourselves from the French, the Turks came in their place, and they stayed four hundred years."

Alexander chewed his lip thoughtfully. "Are you Greek?"

Elias raised one eyebrow. "I am Greek. But I do have French blood. Hundreds of years ago, during the prince's time, Frankish soldiers came to live here in Mystras and married Greek women."

"Who built Mystras?" We were standing outside the walls of the palace, but because of the restoration work, we couldn't go in.

"Prince Guillaume built it for himself. But he could not keep it."

"Why not?"

"It is a long story," Elias said.

"I like long stories," Alexander answered. "Like *The Odyssey*, for example."

Elias raised his eyebrows. "That is a very long story."

Alexander shrugged. "I read it with my grandma. She liked Homer. That's why my mom is named Helen."

Elias glanced at me. "Your mother sounds formidable."

I thought of my mother, who had probably been formidable even as an infant. "She was. I feel more like a Penelope than a Helen these days, though."

Elias smiled. "Are you unraveling a tapestry to put off unwelcome suitors, then?" I choked on my mouthful of water. Fortunately, I didn't spray our guide.

"I'm such an idiot," I said, mopping my face with a tissue. But what I was thinking was how perfectly this stranger had read my mind. My tangled, sarcastic, grieving mind. He was still smiling, as if we'd shared a private joke, which we had. I couldn't help smiling back. He had an exceptionally nice smile.

Ω

By the time we'd finished seeing the palace it was ninety-six degrees in the shade, and my Alexander the Great was fading. Elias suggested we head down to the village for refreshment and air-conditioning and resume later. "Free of charge," he said, reading my expression.

The air-conditioning in the little café was only slightly

more effective than that in our hotel, but it was good enough
to stave off heatstroke, especially when the waiter brought two
tall glasses of local sour cherry soda called *vissinada*. Alexander
crowed with delight at the dark red beverage. I'm not much of
a soft drink fan, but the tangy flavor was a perfect antidote to
the dusty heat. The waiter offered me a glass of ouzo to mix in,
but I declined, wanting to maintain consciousness.

Without asking Alexander, I ordered tzatziki, a Greek
salad, and, just in case, french fries. The waiter spoke no English, but I managed to communicate our order.

Alexander took his first pause from the *vissinada*. "Elias is
very old, Mama," he said.

"He's not *that* old, Alexander. Probably not much older
than I am." Alexander, I realized, might consider me old.

"He's older than you," Alexander said with a slurping
sound that heralded the end of the cherry soda. He looked
into the glass sadly, but, knowing my usual reaction to soft
drinks, didn't ask.

"You want another?"

Alexander's look almost made me laugh. The waiter patted
Alexander's head affectionately.

"*Omorfo paidi*," the waiter said, smiling, and headed back to
the bar.

"What did he call me?"

I fumbled with the Greek/English dictionary that I'd in-
stalled on my phone. "It means 'beautiful child.'"

"Oh, that's funny." Alexander shook his head.

"But you are beautiful." He was, especially at that moment,
his dark hair curling across his forehead, little beads of sweat
on the tip of his nose.

"You're my mom."

"It's true, I am. But you're still beautiful."

"Whatever," Alexander said. "And you are definitely much younger than Elias. He is *super* old."

The food came, and we both realized we were starving. And through some Greek magic, Alexander turned out to love tzatziki, and scraped up the cucumber yogurt so eagerly with the fries (which he loved, too, even though they were sprinkled with oregano) that I grabbed only a few bites.

Alexander wandered out into the tiny triangular plaza, and I moved to an outdoor table. I noted with relief that he looked both ways before stepping off the low curb. It was hard to imagine that moment when I'd let go of his hand and watch him walk off alone. For now, I didn't have to let him out of my sight. He made his way to the spreading oak tree at the plaza's center, where an elderly woman sat in a folding chair in the tree's shade, nodding off to sleep. Her long-sleeved black dress and black shoes reminded me of Yia Yia from the plane. I imagined Yia Yia with her family, the people who had opened their arms to her at the airport, and had to wipe my eyes with a paper napkin. Unfortunately, it had tzatziki on it—but better that than ketchup.

A cat wound itself around the woman's ankles—a calico whose splotches of orange, black, and white flickered in the speckled shade of the oak tree. Alexander knelt down at the tree's roots. I thought he was playing with the cat, but then I saw he'd found a faucet protruding from the tree's trunk and was kneeling to drink from it. The spigot had a weathered stone basin below it, and thick moss grew along the bark below its continuous stream. I was going to get up to join Alexander but felt slowed to a near standstill in the syrupy heat. The old lady's eyes opened, and she looked at Alexander. Her lips moved, but I was too far away to hear her words. Alexander stopped drinking to look up at this Yia Yia—I couldn't help thinking of her by that name—listening intently. I waved slug-gishly for the waiter—my arm felt unnaturally heavy, and the air was thick and hot. I called to Alexander, but my voice sounded strange, like a record played at the wrong speed. Shaking off my strange lassitude, I paid the check and went to the tree. The woman's eyes were closed again. I whispered to Alexander to avoid disturbing her.

"What was she saying?"

He stood up and whispered back. "I didn't really under-stand. It was Greek. Mama, you should have some water." I knelt down to fill my bottle and took a drink. The water was cool and tasted like rock, as if it were coming straight from the ancient mountains.

MARCEAU LUSIGNAN
Late February 1259
La Lacedemonie

The next time Père Lusignan left the house late at night, Marceau followed him. His grandfather stumbled in the dark and almost fell, sending rocks skittering down the hill. Over the past months, Marceau had awakened several times in the night to the sound of his grandfather's steps on the marble-paved courtyard. Perhaps he was paying a woman. He would not be the first priest to have succumbed to a longing of the flesh.

Halfway up the hill, his grandfather disappeared. Marceau climbed until he could see an opening in the rock face, barely big enough for a man to enter. Marceau flattened himself against the stone, listening. He recognized his grandfather's tremulous voice. The second voice was unfamiliar and harsh, like heavy fabric tearing. Marceau felt a shiver of unease.

How old is the boy?

"He is twenty and two years, training to be a soldier like his father."

Marceau had just turned twenty-two. Were they speaking about him? The voice began again without the lilting intonation of ordinary conversation. Marceau wanted to run down the hill—away from that terrible voice, back to his warm bed.

The stones will speak and show Tin Íremi the path to new life.

Tin Íremi? That was the foolish name the soldiers had given Elias. So the voice wasn't talking about him after all.

"How are *we* to find this path to life?" His grandfather sounded desperate.

The path is closed to you and dark. Where Tin Íremi walks, you stumble. Where he sees, you are blind. When the stones speak to him, you feel the crushing weight of walls. He carries the curse but defies it. He lives, you die. And soon the next of your line will feel the curse's whip in his limbs.

"My son, or my grandson? Tell me, woman, tell me!"

Silence.

"If the blood of the boy is life," Père Lusignan said, "in that blood, might we find salvation?" A cold rain began outside; then, as the wind rose, the sky split with a jagged flash of light.

If it could be taken, it would cure . . . The last words echoed in Marceau's ears as thunder split the air. When Père Lusignan emerged from the cave, hood pulled far over his head, he did not notice his grandson, drenched and crouching against the rock.

ELIAS BORGHES
Late February 1259
Evrotas River Valley

When I rode out with the prince, Marceau came, too. He wasn't my choice.

The whole week had been unseasonably warm, and snowmelt swelled the Evrotas river until it overflowed its banks and ran brown with mud. Broken branches rushed with the current. The water had risen to the level of the bridge, and our horses balked when we tried to turn them onto the partially submerged planks. Some dismounted to lead their horses, and I followed their example. My mount was particularly skittish— an irritable gray mare aptly named Maigre—skinny. She had been restless for our whole journey, but now she bared her long yellow teeth and tossed her head, refusing to move. I murmured calming words to her and eventually I managed to pull her at a reluctant diagonal, her hooves skidding on the slippery moss.

I heard Marceau before I saw him. He had managed to push his barrel-chested bay to cross without dismounting, and as he approached, Maigre stumbled, her foot catching on a heavy branch. Later, I was not so sure that Marceau's proximity and Maigre's accident were coincidental. As she began to fall, I realized my hand was tangled in the reins, and I went down with her, sliding on rock slime, and then we were falling together over the edge of the bridge. I hit the roiling water and went under.

Most of the villagers grew up dipping in the waters of the Evrotas, laughing and bobbing in the gentle summer current. I had always stayed at the edge. Some of us are not meant to swim, but now I had no choice.

The water was viciously cold, dark, and moving fast. I could not tell which way led to air and I panicked, thrashing in the river weeds and tethered by my wrist to my horse's reins. At last, my chest burning, I managed to surface enough to take a gasping breath before being pulled under again. Maigre's hoof struck a burning arc against my thigh. Underwater, I grasped the loop of reins and managed to loosen it. I surfaced again for another breath. Now Maigre was moving downstream away from me, swimming powerfully, her head high.

I could barely keep my head above the surface. A branch swept by, catching the side of my head. Dizzy, I struggled sideways toward the river's edge. Marceau was still on horseback, following my wild ride downstream. I made my way toward the riverbank and he stopped to dismount. He grabbed a fallen tree branch and held it out for me to grasp; I swam as hard as I could toward it. Finally, my hands wrapped around the wood, and he began to pull me in toward dry land. I was close to the riverbank when a flicker of movement shifted above my head, and a blow landed on the back of my neck, knocking me under again. A terrible weight pressed down on my head, pushing me under. There was an evil deliberateness to the steady pressure, and the more I tried to escape it, the harder the downward force grew, until my mouth filled with the river. Fatigue spread through my limbs, with numbing cold. *It would be so much easier to stop* . . . Suddenly I felt a tug at the back of my neck and, violently, I was dragged out of the water and dropped gasping on the river's muddy bank.

One of Prince Guillaume's knights pounded my back while I coughed up water, curled in agony and relief on solid ground. When I caught my breath, I looked up to see Marceau, off to one side, a strange look on his face. In one hand, he held the branch he'd offered as salvation, but on the ground next to him was another branch, glistening with water, a branch that could have pressed me down into the swirling river.

HELEN ADLER
July 2015
Mystras

We were planning to go back to Mystras the next morning for Part Two of the tour, but I balked at the weather report. "Alexander, it's not even seven a.m. and it's already ninety-eight degrees. Maybe we should do something else?"

"It will be hot everywhere," he said. "And we can't just stay in the hotel all day." He had a point.

"We could find a place to go swimming."

Alexander's face went blank. "I'm not going swimming," he said. "I don't want to die."

"Oh, sweet boy." I took his hand; it stayed limp.

"Alexander, look at me." I stared at the top of his head.

"We're all going to die," Alexander said bleakly, not looking up.

"That doesn't mean we should never go swimming again." A long, grim silence. "Does it?" I hadn't wanted to swim since Oliver's death either.

"I had a bad dream," Alexander said, by way of an answer.

"Do you want to tell me about it?"

He took a deep breath. "I was standing by a river. It was moving really fast, and it was brown, how a river gets when it's been raining for a long time. I was looking into the river, and I saw a hand." He shuddered.

"A hand?"

"It was Daddy's hand. I could see his ring." I looked at my own hand, where the complement to that ring still circled my finger, white gold with a small blue stone, the metal etched with leaves.

Alexander was trembling. "I went into the water to get him—I grabbed his hand but I went underwater. I kept trying to pull him up but every time I got my head above the water I'd sink again. I couldn't breathe, and I couldn't get Daddy out."

"Sweetie, that's such a scary dream." It took everything I had to keep from crying.

Alexander turned around and buried his face in my chest. "He wasn't afraid of anything. But now I'm afraid of everything."

"I know. Me too," I said.

Alexander sighed into my shirt. "Do you think maybe he was sometimes afraid but never told us?"

"Everyone is. We're just super afraid right now because we lost him."

Alexander looked up at me. "You know, sometimes you are kind of smart."

I hugged him again. "I love you, Alexander. Even if you think I'm only sometimes smart."

"I love you, too. And actually, you're smart most of the time."

We stayed with our arms around one another for a while. Outside the window, faintly, I could hear someone singing in Greek.

"The water is not our friend," he said finally. "And it doesn't care about us at all. It doesn't even know we exist."

chapter six

ELIAS BORGHES
April 1259
Mystras

After my near drowning, my cautious respect for the water turned to outright fear. Even the sound of the river brought back memories of submersion, and I awoke from nightmares gasping for air.

Soon, though, I had new worries. Our battalion would be marching north to meet our allies in the war against Nicaea: troops under Michael the Despot of Epirus. On a balmy spring morning, I was again summoned to Prince Guillaume.

"I trust you have recovered from your brush with watery doom?" he said.

"Indeed, and your words are the perfect balm to hasten my recovery."

Guillaume's smile broadened. "I have a task for you. You are acquainted with the Milengoi tribes in the Taygetos?"

I nodded, remembering the bloodlust of the warrior who had nearly killed me.

"Excellent. You shall bring their chieftain a message, requesting that the Milengoi send a coalition to join our campaign in the North."

"You want me to talk with them, not fight them?"

Prince Guillaume laughed. "Is that relief or disappointment? Soon you shall fight. For now, I want your words."

Ω

I had been warned to avoid the paths up the Taygetos as soon as I'd learned to walk. But at dawn on the morning after I met with the prince, I began a trip to the Milengoi settlement. The *kastron* looked tiny silhouetted against the stark *pentadaktylos*— the five Taygetos peaks that we called "five-fingered," like the vast hand of God.

My role was to obtain the promise of a great *droungos*—a battalion of mountain-born Slavs who would, in exchange for fighting for our cause in Macedonia, be exempt from taxation.

I decided to ask Demetrios to join me. If he spoke it would be for the right reason, and if challenged, he could defend our lives. I also (though I did not tell Demetrios) wanted to spend more time with him; his quiet intrigued me and he made my frequent silences feel easy, rather than awkward. I was delighted when he agreed to come with me. Demetrios met me at the entry to the ill-marked trail at the base of the mountain. We wore short swords and carried hidden daggers, but no armor. My father had given me the blade he'd carried to his first battle; it was nicked and pitted with age. HERE, TOO, VIRTUE HAS ITS TRUE REWARD was etched on the circular pommel. My father often quoted Virgil; the *Aeneid* offered much to inspire a soldier and a father.

At the beginning, the trail wound through oaks, wild olive trees, and, where the trees did not crowd and shade the path, low, dense shrubs of white heather. Demetrios and I chatted companionably, not discussing the danger of our errand. Demetrios's younger sister was to be married and planned to move to her husband's house nearby. I talked about Giánnis, now seventeen and sprouting a tufted beard that made him look like a piebald hedgehog. Demetrios laughed—watching his little sister head toward marriage made him squirm, as if she still toddled about the house with a wooden rattle in one chubby fist. When we talked, Demetrios smiled in a way I'd never seen, and once I caught him gazing at me. I smiled more than usual with him, too. I wondered what he saw in me.

As we walked, the trees changed to fir and black pine, and the thick carpet of needles underfoot silenced our steps. By then the way was steep, so we stopped talking and focused on the climb into the mountains. As the trees gave way to meadows studded with bare rock, I worried we'd gotten lost. So did Demetrios.

"Weren't we supposed to find the settlement before the clearing, Elias?" Getting lost in the Taygetos mountains, particularly when trying to find a tribe of warriors known for their savagery, is unwise. Demetrios and I stopped to look at the rough map the castle steward had sketched.

Snapping branches alerted us, too late. When we looked up, eight men surrounded us. Worries I'd had about seeming overly threatening seemed ridiculous; we were as ominous as a pair of rabbits compared to the band of armed men. All were tall and burly, with dark hair loose to their shoulders. They wore leather armor over rough brown tunics, leggings, and conical helmets with nosepieces that turned their faces into blank masks, shadowing their eyes. One, apparently their leader, had a tunic embroidered with red thread that reminded me of blood. They held round shields emblazoned with red and white, and their spears were long enough to strike before we could reach them with our short swords. We'd never win with steel; words would have to do. Fortunately, many of the

Milengoi—I'd been told by my father—understood a bit of Greek.

"We come with peaceful intent," I said. The Milengoi did not lower their spears. "We bring a message from Prince Guillaume to your chief."

The man in red pointed to the weapons at our hips. "No swords," he said in Greek. Demetrios and I handed over our visible weapons. The guards roughly patted us down and took our daggers, too. They led us more roughly than necessary back down the wooded path. I stumbled and Demetrios held out a hand, but my guard struck his arm with the haft of his spear, grunting a warning.

"At least it wasn't the point," Demetrios whispered.

After a few minutes of tramping through the evergreen wood, we reached a clearing by a stream. Houses made of stacked logs with thatched roofs were built along the water. Through the open doorway of the largest dwelling, I could see the haze of smoke that came from clay ovens. The house was big enough to fit at least twenty people. Outside, sheep hides hung on a rack, curing in the dappled sun. The guards pushed us through the open door.

The floor was firmly packed earth, and two wood columns made from tree trunks supported the roof. The walls were horizontally laid logs finished with dried clay filling the gaps. Demetrios and I were pushed onto wooden stools, where we waited, flanked by the spear-holders. We sat until my back ached and the stove's smoke and heat made me dizzy. Finally, the bright rectangle of the doorway darkened, and the chief entered. The guards bowed, pushing us to stand.

"I am Berislav Dragovic and gather glory as my name befits me." The Milengoi leader spoke Greek fluently. The Franks spoke Greek, too, but they were our masters. Dragovic's people had fought to be able to call this mountainous land home. They came with swords, but as they stayed, they put down their weapons and began to speak the Greek that my mother had used to sing me to sleep. When I heard Dragovic speak the language of my people, I understood that this bearded chieftain of a mountaintop band of savage fighters was as much my kinsman as Demetrios. So when I answered, I was filled with the promise of partnership, rather than the poison of fear.

"Most honorable leader, I bring words of peace from Prince Villehardouin and extend a hand in friendship, knowing that the spirit that animates all our souls is truly one and the same."

Dragovic towered above even his substantial guards, and he looked like a hawk with his fierce hooked nose and heavy slanted brows. "Welcome, men of Achaea, tell me your purpose," Dragovic said. The guards pressed us back onto our stools. Dragovic lowered his bulk gracefully into a carved wooden chair.

"The prince respectfully requests a battalion of your strongest fighters to accompany him to battle. He would be honored to have your men in his company."

Chief Dragovic was not the sort of man to be seduced by compliments. "And in return for our aid?"

"The prince will provide the Milengoi with his protection and exempt you, as his subjects, from taxation. He trusts that the Milengoi will see the wisdom of his suggestion."

"Suggestion." Dragovic chuckled. "Your prince chooses his emissaries well. Before I answer, I have questions of my own."

"*Knyaz*, I shall do my best to answer." I could see the term for a Slavic prince flattered him.

"Tell me your names, emissary." I told him Demetrios's, then my own.

"Ilija," Dragovic said. He pronounced it "I-li-ya" with an inflection like birdsong. "Where is this battle, and when?"

These were the questions I'd prepared for. But the answer might not please him. "We leave in a week to join the Despot of Epirus, in Macedonia."

Dragovic grunted. "Macedonia is months away on foot. And whom are you fighting against with these allies? Perhaps your comrade will enlighten me?"

Demetrios was ready to answer. "We will battle the Nicaean forces under Emperor Michael Palaiologos the Eighth. Our prince hopes to fortify holdings in Thessaly."

"This plan teems with intrigues and dangers—like a hive of wasps. Is all of Achaea not sufficient, that your prince must head north for more? He married the daughter of a Romaioi leader who schemes for the throne of Latin-occupied Constantinople. Through this alliance, they intend to fight the Romaioi emperor, who wishes to reclaim the throne as well. In this way, your Latin prince and Michael of Epirus will be temporarily yoked against Nicaea for their own eventual gain. And now Prince Villehardouin asks for *our* assistance when we were so recently his enemies. What a tangled bunch you are." Even more tangled if you considered that Demetrios and I were the children of both the conquerors and the conquered.

I answered carefully. "We are simple soldiers, entrusted with the task of defending Achaea from enemies, whoever they may be. If you choose to join us, all that has been promised shall be granted to you." One breath, two, three. In the oppressive heat of the meetinghouse, drops of sweat fell from my face into my lap.

Finally, Dragovic answered. "You may be soldiers, but you are not as simple as you say." He paused long enough to make my anxiety rise again. "Proposal accepted. You may tell your prince. And tell him that his messengers made it possible. You said that the spirit that animates our souls is one and the same; it is not often that I see that sentiment from Franks. Go in peace, and we shall meet, soon, in war."

Re-armed and relieved, Demetrios and I made our way back down the mountain to deliver the good news. After our experience with the Milengoi we had a new closeness—*shared danger*, I thought. *Like any two soldiers.* But it felt like it might be more than that.

PÈRE VILLENC LUSIGNAN
Early April 1259
La Lacedemonie

Evrard managed to consume a remarkable amount of dinner in a short time, then stood from the table, belching with pleasure. "Within a week, we march north with the prince. These will be your last meals at a table for many months, Marceau." Evrard wiped honey from his lips with the back of his hand. "You'd best enjoy them." They'd feasted on gray mullet, early spring asparagus, and emmer groats boiled and flavored with spikenard, honey, and cinnamon.

He thumped Marceau on the back and stomped upstairs. At the top step, he stumbled, cursing. Marceau's mother followed him with a worried look.

Père Lusignan waited until he heard the footsteps above cease. "Marceau, I heard Jéhan Borghes's son almost drowned on an outing with the prince."

Marceau smiled a slow incongruous smile at his grand-father's words. "He's not a good swimmer."

That smirk. *This is my grandson. I should not fear him. But I do.* "Did you have something to do with it?"

"The boy fell off his horse, but I was there to fish him out of the river before he went under for good." Marceau took a large, slow bite of groats.

Père Lusignan had lost his appetite. "I need to make something clear, Marceau."

"Please do, Grandfather." Marceau smiled again.

"I may have incorrectly communicated to you a desire that ill should befall the boy. You are about to go to war with a fellow soldier. I wish him to live; he may be useful to us. But if he is wounded and does not survive his wounds . . ."

For the first time Marceau looked interested. "If he does not survive? What would you have me do?"

Père Lusignan dropped his voice to a whisper. "I want his body, Marceau."

"What on earth do you want with that boy's corpse, if he is stupid enough to get himself killed?"

"Bring it to me, in whatever shape you can. Even just a piece. Do you understand? Our lives may depend upon it."

"An amusing, if grisly, task. I'll do my best." Marceau remembered the night outside the prophetess's cave—the only time he'd ever felt truly afraid. His grandfather did not know he'd heard, but now the words came back to him like the hollow sound inside a shell.

He lives, you die. And soon the next of your line will feel the curse's whip in his limbs. The blood of the boy is life . . . If it could be taken, it would cure . . .

If it were true that his life depended upon taking Elias's

blood from him, then ensuring that Elias came home in his possession, dead or alive, would be the wisest plan of all.

CHRYSE BORGHES
Late April 1259
Mystras

A few weeks before the army left to march north, Chryse lay awake in bed. Jéhan's sleep had become disturbed in the past few months—he often was up for hours at night and slept in the day. Chryse asked La Crémonie's physician for a draught. When the doctor came, she knew what the physician saw but did not mention: the way Jéhan fumbled with his cup of wine and snapped at her questions. The doctor took her aside—*perhaps he needs more rest*, he said. The draught helped Jéhan sleep, but it did not change anything else. Chryse saw now he'd been ailing for at least a year, hiding the movements with gestures designed to mask his illness. She tried not to imagine what might happen to her, with Elias about to march into battle, Jéhan growing more dependent, and Giánnis still young enough to need her.

That night, Chryse had a waking dream. The prophet came to her, faceless, with a voice like the wind from the night Elias was born. She was in the old shrine, whose foundation echoed below the walls of Mystras's new *kastron*.

Do not forget your promise.

"I have not forgotten," Chryse answered. "His name is your name, and he owes you his life." She could not say *lives*.

He is yours, but he is mine as well.

"I know this."

When I call him, when the stones call him home, he must come.
"He will come."
He must return to Mystras.
"Will I see my son again?"
He may be changed when you see him next.

A nightingale began to sing outside the shuttered window. It sang without reservation, pouring its heart into each note, singing as if this were the last song of its sweet life.

ELIAS BORGHES
Early May 1259
La Lacedemonie

Training for battle, even with a full battalion, did not prepare me for seeing the vast forces that Prince Guillaume had assembled for the trip to Macedonia. The men poured into the Lacedaemon valley, foot soldiers pitching tents, cavalry filling La Crémonie's stables with their restless mounts. Higher officers and barons who had sworn fealty to the prince found lodging in La Crémonie and the garrison's quarters. I had never seen so many people in one place, churning up the wet spring earth under their feet, filling the valley with shouts and the clash of weapons as they practiced, the smoke from fires clouding the air. An enormous train carrying food, spare clothing, axes, swords, spears, and cooking utensils began to assemble. Medical units, each with a surgeon, stretcher-bearers, and orderlies, added to the crowd.

The prince gave Demetrios and me the task of recording the arrival of troops. We walked among the men, speaking with the commanders. One battalion had ridden from

Monemvasia—the prince's rocky outcrop fortress surrounded by the beating waves of the Aegean Sea except for a narrow land bridge connecting it to the mainland. Prince Guillaume often boasted of his siege ten years before, which drove the citizens to eat rats and cats. I approached one of the Monemvasiots repairing his kite-shaped shield where the leather had separated from its frame.

"Was your ride long?"

He looked up, brushing a thick lock of hair from his eyes. "Not as long as it's going to be." His voice was gruff but not unfriendly.

"It is an honor to have the men of Monemvasia join us," I said.

He grinned, lopsidedly. "I suppose you've heard we're die-hard resistors, pirates who make the seas a hazard to sail?"

"All I've heard made me wish to meet a Monemvasiot in person."

"Well here I am, a rat-eating pirate in the flesh. My name is Spyridon, in case you care to use it." I introduced myself. His grip was strong and warm. "And in case you were wondering, Elias of Mystras, rats taste fine when you are starving."

I looked around us to be sure no one was listening. "You are willing to fight under the prince, despite all that happened?" He probably thought I was gathering intelligence about the troops' loyalty, but I wished to know for my own reasons.

"I'm a soldier; I fight when and where I'm told."

"Even against Nicaea?" I did not include "the true inheritors of the Romaioi empire." But I sensed he knew what I meant.

"You are Romaioi, aren't you?" He tilted his head thoughtfully.

"In part."

"And you fight for your prince."

"My father is a Frankish soldier."

"Well, then we both know what it means to fight against today's enemy. If the enemy changes tomorrow, we'll see." He smiled and held up his shield, the long triangle of hide now taut against its frame. "My shield is the same, loyal, and knowing its master. I hold it, and it protects me. For the next few months, it will protect you, too."

Ω

I was putting together supplies I'd need for the trip: tools, a tinderbox, the hard biscuits provided to soldiers in the unit, dried meat and fruit to supplement what the countryside might provide. My mother found me in the storeroom packing dried figs and put her hand on my shoulder. I could not imagine being so far away for so long.

"Can I help you, Elias?"

"You always help me, Mitéra."

She laughed, squeezing my shoulder. "Then I have done my job properly." She moved to help me pack, starting on the store of dried mulberries.

"*Moúro*," she said thoughtfully, turning one of the berries over between her fingers. "This fruit is why the Franks called our land La Morée, shaped like a mulberry, ripe for picking."

I thought of the double layers of her meaning. "How will I manage without you?"

"You will manage." She paused. "You must come back to Mystras, Elias."

"Ideally with all my body parts attached," I said with more humor than I felt.

"And you must ask those soldiers with whom you depart tomorrow to help you fulfill your duty."

"I will ask those I entrust with my life." There was a pressure behind her demand that I did not understand.

"Have the stones of Mystras spoken to you, Elias?" I had not told her what I had heard the day of the earthquake. But I had long ceased wondering how my mother knew the things she knew.

"They have."

"Heed them."

She handed me the berry she'd been holding, and I put it in my mouth. All of La Morée's summer was held in that fruit, the hours of sun and shining blue sky.

"I will, Mitéra. I promise."

Ω

My father, who could no longer hold a sword, had been released from military service. I knew Marceau's soldier father, Evrard, would be in the military party, leading a senior battalion of heavy infantry; the comparison with my situation stung. I, inexperienced and reluctant, was leaving to fight, while my father would wither at home. He touched my arm, and I could feel the ripple of alien movement. "I hope you are spared this misery," he said grimly. "When I left Paris, my father was in the clutches of the beast that has me now. I hope your mother's blood will keep you safe." He sighed.

I had never considered that my father's condition might reside in me as well, waiting for the right moment to emerge. Would my mother's origin protect me, as her love did?

"I hope I carry the best of both of you," I said, putting my hand over my father's. That was the least I could give him—he had shown me his heart; I held his hand.

"As do I, Elias." My father was crying.

Ω

Pantaleon, flushed with excitement, strode through the open practice yard barking instructions in a mix of Greek and French as we practiced donning our armor. First came chain mail *chausses* that we pulled to our thighs and fastened to our belts with leather points, followed by padded cloth over the mail. My mail hauberk had short sleeves, but even so, it was heavy enough to make my shoulders ache. Over our body armor went a quilted soft surcoat emblazoned with the prince's yellow cross on red. We covered our metal with cloth—as if trying to hide the steel beneath deceptive softness.

Pantaleon came to adjust the strap of my helmet, tightening it under my chin.

"I feel like a tortoise wrapped in blankets," I said, trying not to sound as irritable as the armor made me feel.

"There is a reason the tortoise lives so long," Pantaleon said, smiling.

"I will need all the protection I can get." By now, I was competent with my father's old sword but still the weakest in our group.

Pantaleon finished with the helmet and leaned in close. "Marceau has declared that he trusts no one more than you. He wishes to fight at your side in Macedonia. Did he mention this to you?"

"He doesn't talk to me."

Pantaleon frowned. "Something has changed."

"If anything has changed recently, it's been for the worse," I said. It was not wise to accuse without evidence, so I restrained myself from telling the story of my near drowning.

"Such a pairing is not to be taken lightly. Both your lives

would depend upon it. Marceau told me that there is no soldier in our group he would rather be defended by."

"I cannot imagine why."

Pantaleon laughed. "You have come far since the first days of your terror-stricken slashings in the practice yard. And I, too, would fight at your side gladly."

"I am proud to merit your trust." I had been about to say that I hadn't earned it. But this was no longer true. I had changed—the stones had spoken their strength into me and had reminded me of my own. I had saved Demetrios's life, made an ally of the Milengoi leader, and won the trust of the prince. Perhaps I did not possess the sort of power a soldier is celebrated for, but I trusted my own quiet strength.

Pantaleon was watching me. "Tin Íremi. I need your decision."

I did not trust Marceau. But I felt as if I were in a boat on a river with a steady current, pulling me inexorably forward. "Yes," I said. "I accept."

ELIAS BORGHES
Mid-May 1259
Mystras

The nightingales sang louder than ever on the morning Prince Guillaume's army marched from Mystras. My regiment included Knyaz Dragovic's battalion and the Monemvasiot contingent. My new acquaintance Spyridon grinned at me as his section went by.

Our march would cover a distance of 430 Roman miles. That was two weeks' walk on a flat road in good weather—but our path held neither. We struggled through spring mud and stones, steep slopes with scrub and nettles scratching our legs, swollen streams, spring-fed rivers. The route ran through forests with branches that slashed our faces and holes hiding poisonous snakes. Much of our route wove through farmed landholdings, where we gathered supplies under the prince's banner. The landowners and peasants knew that when his army passed through, their plenty was his.

The army's home was a village in motion, arriving each night before sundown and pulling out by dawn. Each evening, the battalion leaders found a site away from dense trees or hills that might hide enemy forces. When we stopped, the packhorses, mules, and donkeys were guided into a circle to protect the camp, wagons arranged around them. Engineers dug ditches around the encampment and spears topped the piled earth, forming a barrier. Guards worked rotating shifts through the night. We Six stuck our spears in the ground and leaned our shields against them before we pulled off our boots and ducked inside our tent for the night.

I took longer to fall asleep than the others. One night as I lay awake, my eyes open in the blackness, a line of light appeared as the tent flap opened. Demetrios exited, and I pushed off my blankets to follow. He turned to me with a welcoming gesture.

"Sometimes I come out to think," he whispered.

The moon was nearly full, high and yellow-white, lighting the tents that stretched in every direction, too numerous to count. The banners on their high poles hung with no breeze to lift them. "I thought everyone slept but me," I said.

"The wakeful always think that." Demetrios smiled, his teeth flashing in the dark. "Tonight I am preoccupied with my left heel, which has no flesh left."

It was hard not to laugh. "Shall we compare injuries?" We sat down to inspect our feet.

"I've got bandages from the medical tent." He held a roll of linen and a pot of salve. "Give me your foot." I put my foot on his leg, and he inspected it carefully. "You'll need to clean that first." He dipped back into the tent and emerged with a skin of water. He rinsed my foot gently while I tried not to wince, then rubbed the salve into my foot with his long fingers until the pain eased. He finished with the bandage and put my foot down gently. "That should feel better tomorrow. Unless you walk from sunrise to sunset on it."

"Which I will." I was reluctant to go back inside. "Are you tired?"

"Not as tired as I ought to be. You?"

"I'd rather stay out a bit longer."

Demetrios took care of his own foot while I watched. We sat, each of us with one bandaged foot, looking at the moon. We passed several minutes in companionable silence. An owl hooted from the wood that bordered our camp. Demetrios took a breath, and for a moment I thought he was about to hoot, too. Instead he said: "Elias, have you a love you've left behind?"

"Don't you think you'd know if I had?"

"There is much about you I don't know."

"I would say the same of you."

"I will tell you my story if you tell me yours," Demetrios said, "but you first."

"That won't be very satisfying for you," I responded. "I've got no one."

"Not even an inkling? A longing?"

I was about to answer no, but I wondered whether it was entirely true. My mother had questioned me as I'd entered my third decade with no marriage prospects. My father had suggested at least three young women from the village but did not press the issue after he failed to provoke an enthusiastic response.

"Aha, so there is someone. I shall keep your secret, Elias." Still, I didn't answer. "What if I say a name, and you nod yes or no?"

"I said there was no one."

"Yes, I know you did. Is it Pantaleon?"

I was glad that in the dark he couldn't see the color of my face. "Doesn't everyone love him?" I said it lightly, I thought.

"I won't judge you ill for it. He is certainly deserving. I loved him, once."

My mouth fell open. "Loved . . . how?"

"With great, unrequited passion. Now, though, I've found someone better suited to me. Someone I have half a hope of finding love from in return."

"You promised to tell me your story," I said. I was amazed Demetrios had not only tolerated my adoration for Pantaleon, but echoed it.

"You," Demetrios said.

"Me what?"

"You. I love you."

My head swam as I remembered all the moments of intimacy we'd shared, the sentiments I'd suppressed in my own heart. It was a few seconds before I could respond. "I have been thinking . . ." I stopped, then started again. "I have been thinking that I might die in this battle we are heading toward, without ever knowing love."

I looked at Demetrios's face: his dark brows, the slight crookedness of his nose, the untamed whiskers that had grown during our long march. I wanted to touch his face more than anything I could ever remember wanting. My hand moved of its own accord to brush his cheek.

Demetrios shook his head, smiling incredulously, and put his hand over mine. "We are a long way from home, and love is the best sustenance on a long voyage." His palm and fingers were calloused from wielding a sword, but breathtakingly gentle. As he put his arms around me, the lone owl cried again from the nearby wood. This time, a second answered.

chapter seven

HELEN ADLER
July 2015
Site of Mystras

"Alexander, if you make me climb that hill again in the baking sun, I will evaporate, and you'll be left with nothing but crystalline residue of your former mother." My warning had no effect on Alexander, who was used to my dire language.

"I want to go back to the fortress."

We stared at each other in the dim light of our hotel room, a mother-son face-off. Alexander's jaw was set in a square line I knew well. I'd have to bring my best weapons to this battle. "If we are hospitalized from heatstroke today, we won't be able to come back tomorrow. What about the Mystras Archaeological Museum? It's air-conditioned."

"A museum is not a REAL city."

"An eight-hundred-year-old ruin isn't a REAL city either."

Alexander's eyes filled suddenly with tears. "It IS real! Just because it's falling down doesn't mean it's not REAL!"

"Okay, okay, it's real. But the museum has things that come from the real city, too—clothing, jewelry—"

"Who cares about stupid *clothing*." Alexander clenched his

fists, and I realized, too late, that he was about to hit his rarely reached danger point. His red face contorted with fury. "You don't understand ANYTHING. No one understands me, not anymore! Especially not *you*." I felt like I'd been punched hard in the chest. He grabbed a water glass from the bedside table and flung it hard—not at me, thankfully, but at the wall, where it hit and shattered, spraying fragments of glass. The silence after his outburst was terrible, broken only by the sound of his ragged breathing. I could not think of anything to say— certainly not the miserable things in my head. *You lost Dad, and I'm a lousy substitute.*

Finally, Alexander looked at me and his eyes went wide. "Mom, you're hurt." I followed his gaze toward my leg, where a trail of blood snaked down my shin. His anger broke and turned to horror. "I'm sorry, I'm sorry, Mom, I'm so sorry." He ran at me and threw himself into my arms so hard he almost knocked me over.

I put my arms around him. "I'm fine, sweetie, I'm fine," I said. The cut was nothing, just a shallow stinging line. But of course neither of us was fine.

We stayed hugging for a long time until finally he stepped back. "I try not to make you upset," he said, his face pale.

"It's okay if I'm sometimes upset," I said.

"You are already sad enough," he said. I wished I could protect him from thinking he had to protect me.

"So are you," I answered. "It's not your job to make sure I'm not upset, really."

Alexander sighed. "Well, do you want a Band-Aid?"

"I'm okay," I said, "unlike the glass. Do you think maybe you could be upset without breaking anything next time, please?"

Alexander almost smiled. "Okay. I'm sorry." He wiped his

eyes with the back of one hand. "What is the museum like?"

I shifted gears as fast as I could. "Um, right." I tried to remember what I'd been saying. "The museum. Well . . . there's hair from a Byzantine princess."

Alexander sniffed. "Real hair?"

"From a body found in a *grave*." A long silence ensued. "And a stone carving of Alexander the Great."

Alexander looked at my leg again. The bleeding had stopped. "Fine."

"Fine?"

"Museum. But if it's hot tomorrow, too, we go anyway."

"Deal." Disaster somehow averted, we cleaned up the glass together and headed to the café for breakfast.

Ω

Elias met us inside the blessedly cool two-story building that looked out onto the courtyard of the Cathedral of Saint Demetrios in Mystras's lower town.

Alexander took Elias's hand. That surprised me—Alexander was usually slow to show affection. I'd given him the nickname Pineapple—tough and spiny on the outside, sweet inside. It stuck, with variations including, during our fight over his writing troubles, Spiny Piney. Elias welcomed the overture easily, folding Alexander's small hand into his own. Elias's skin was brown—that southern Mediterranean olive-gold—but Alexander had Oliver's coloring, pale and easy to burn.

Elias looked at me, and for the first time I allowed myself to actually take in the details of his face. His dark eyes were fringed with thick eyelashes, and his abundant brown hair was cut short enough to follow the curve of his head, but not short enough to suppress its curls entirely. I realized, with surprise, that he was beautiful, but even that brief thought made me uneasy. I had the feeling Elias sensed that my mind had gone elsewhere—not the details, but the distance. He waited while I composed myself.

"It's wise to start with the museum today," he said quietly, as if he suspected that I was, at that moment, fragile.

"Sorry, drifting isn't my usual mode. Vacation unhinges me." I wasn't in the mood for a soul-baring recounting of our family's tragedy. "I'd rather be listening to you talk about Mystras."

"There is ample time to learn about Mystras. It has been here for centuries and will likely be here for centuries more."

Alexander tugged Elias's hand. "My mom says there's a statue of Alexander the Great. Can we see that first?" Elias led us to the exhibit.

The statue was a plaque with a relief carved in gray stone about the size of a doormat. A big-eyed Alexander the Great was seated in his chariot, pulled by two winged creatures. The explanatory sign read: ASCENSION OF ALEXANDER THE GREAT, RELIEF, 2ND HALF OF FOURTEENTH CENTURY. SLAB USED IN THE FLOOR PAVING OF THE CHURCH OF THE PERIBLEPTOS, MYSTRAS. We hadn't seen any of Mystras's many churches. The way things were going, I wondered whether we'd ever get any-where else on this trip.

"What are those birds about?" asked Alexander.

"They are mythical eagles, or griffins," Elias answered. "Alexander put bait at the ends of two sticks that he held out in front of the birds, and they pulled his chariot all the way to heaven."

Alexander blinked at the depiction of his namesake. "After he died, you mean?"

"He didn't have to die to go to heaven. During his life he was a king transformed into a god. Have you heard the word *apotheosis*?" Elias was not, I was happy to see, one of those people who think you have to talk down to kids, and it made me warm to him even more.

Alexander was still staring at the stone. "*Apotheosis*? Is that like *anticipation*?"

"No, other than the fact that they both begin with *a* and have five syllables."

Alexander, who ordinarily would have run screaming out of the room at the mention of letters and syllables, smiled. "You're funny. But what does *apotheosis* mean?"

"I'm glad you think so. I'm not often considered funny. Apotheosis is deification: the elevation of a human being, usually a king or emperor, to the divine, like a god."

Alexander frowned again. "*A-po-the-o-sis*. I don't think I'd want apotheosis to happen to me. I think it would be too hard to be a god, having so much responsibility for ordinary mortals, living forever and all that. What about you?"

Elias turned back to look at the plaque. Finally, he shook his head.

"No, I wouldn't like it either. It would be hard to live forever."

He sounded profoundly sad.

ELIAS OROLOGOS
July 2015
Site of Mystras

After I left Helen and Alexander in the museum, musing about apotheosis, I felt a shift in the current of the long-running river of my life. The wisdom of Alexander's innocence nearly made me weep. Eight hundred years is not forever, but it is unimaginably long.

Now, nearly everyone reminds me of someone I have known before. Nano, slicing cheese at the corner store, looks like young Theodore, my companion from The Six. My brother Giánnis's features echo in the face of the man protesting outside the referendum polls. The land is familiar, too; the gentle curve of the Evrotas valley and the glittering bend of the river coursing through it are always the same. It is still achingly beautiful, and it is still home. The past interlaces with the present: an old black-and-white television sputters at Nano's counter, where once the only electricity was lightning scything through the night sky. Where Nano rings up the price of newspapers and Nutella, there once stood a blacksmith's shop. The layers of new on old remind me of spanakopita, the spinach-and-cheese pastry that found its way into our kitchens after the Turks came.

Rarely, a place, person, or moment in time will feel unfamiliar. But for some reason I do not understand, Helen is new. Other Americans have come through Mystras, and they have not felt so new to me.

Helen Adler is her name—she told me after she carefully read mine from my name tag that first day. Now there has been a second day, and I can see from her son's longing for Mystras that there will be at least a third. He is still so young that he imagines I might have met a prince who died hundreds of years ago. He is right, of course.

Helen surprises me, keeps me thinking in the dark when I ought to sleep. The plain directness of her gaze, the lack of artifice. She has hair the color of eucalyptus honey, green-gray eyes edged with hazel. A spray of freckles on her nose, like a child. Long limbs, small hands. When we stand, her head comes just to my chin. "It has been a rough few years," she said, but stopped herself from saying more. She has lost something profound.

It has been a long time since someone emerged from the blur of years for me the way she does. I finally drift off to sleep, imagining what I will show Helen and Alexander next. And in those last few minutes awake, I think, though I do not always, that I am glad there will be another day.

HELEN ADLER
July 2015
Spárti

I convinced Alexander to let us leave Mystras, just for the day. "Remember you wanted to see Spárti?" I asked hopefully at breakfast. I had an ulterior motive—Spárti was where Huntington's prevalence was reported to be surprisingly high. I'd not managed to make much headway with research before I left the United States, but maybe now, I'd be able to track down information.

An hour later we were on the one-euro, ten-minute bumpy bus ride to the modern town next to the site of ancient Sparta.

"I want to see the Sanctuary of Artemis Orthia first," Alexander said authoritatively. "It's where Spartan boys were flogged until they bled."

"That sounds horrible. Were they being punished?"

"How else do you think the Spartans became the best soldiers in the world?"

We hired a local guide and were joined by two overheated American women from Ohio. After the sanctuary, our companions looked queasy.

"Wasn't it cool how the really brave ones actually passed out from the pain?" Alexander smiled up at one midwesterner, whose name was Mary Louise.

"Yes, lovey," she said, but sounded doubtful. We lost them to a roadside café and headed on to the ancient theater.

In town, our guide pointed out a statue before ending the tour. "King Leonidas," he said, "the great Spartan leader."

"Wow." Alexander's face flushed with a combination of excitement and heat.

The guide pointed out the plaque at the statue's feet: *ΜΟΛΩΝ ΛΑΒΕ*. I sounded out the syllables slowly. "Mo-lon la-be?"

Our guide smiled broadly. "Excellent! But you say it La-VE. When the Persians, led by King Xerxes, attacked three hundred Spartan soldiers at Thermopylae, the Persian commander said, 'Lay down your weapons.' King Leonidas responded, '*Molon lave*'—'Come and get them.'" Our tour ended on that impressive note.

Spárti, I read in the guidebook, was where the residents of Mystras went when they abandoned the ruined town in the 1830s. I pointed this out to Alexander as we walked past budget clothing shops. If I needed a pair of leopard-print leggings for five dollars, this was definitely the place. I took note when we passed the General Hospital of Laconia, in case it might be a source of information on neurodegenerative disease in the Peloponnese. Feeling guilty about working on vacation, I went back to the guidebook.

"King Otto moved everybody out after the Greek War of Independence."

"Who was the war against?"

"The Ottoman Turks," I read.

"Greece had a lot of people trying to control it. But I guess they won the war?" Alexander's rapid mastery of the history of Greek occupation startled me.

I glanced down at the book. "Yes, I guess they did."

Spárti, it turns out, also had a stationery store with the best Playmobil collection in the world. As Alexander disappeared into the rows of boxes, I sat down in a folding chair and settled in for the long haul. I read the guidebook until I was seeing double. I looked up when Alexander emerged, arms loaded with options, wearing his I-know-it's-not-going-to-work-but-I'm-going-to-try look.

"One," I said preemptively. He sighed. Would it be the Roman gladiators with catapult (my preference), the pirate hideout (treasure included), or the emergency medical helicopter? While Alexander was making a final decision, the front door opened, making the bell on the knob jingle. The customer who entered looked familiar. He began trying out roller ball pens.

Alexander chose the gladiators and walked to the front counter. On the way, he looked back over his shoulder.

"I saw you on the news," Alexander said to the customer who had just come in.

The man turned slowly. "Is that so? Where?"

"I was in America. You weren't, though." I recognized him now, the snarky Pierre Lusignan with funding from a society studying neurodegenerative diseases. Maybe I wouldn't need to visit the General Hospital of Laconia to find what I was looking for.

"Children watch news in America?" He pushed his round glasses up his nose.

I felt a flash of irritation.

"This one does." I added a smile, not too nice but nice enough. I considered asking him about Huntington's disease, but he made me uneasy. I bought the gladiators, and we left Lusignan to his pen choice. When I looked back, he was staring at us through the window.

"Time for lunch," I said, taking Alexander by the hand. Choosing a random direction, I walked as fast as I could until we could get out of range of that gaze.

CHRYSE BORGHES
Late May 1259
Mystras

Jéhan stumbled on short walks, and began to drop his spoon when he ate, splattering himself with food. At times Chryse found him standing blank-faced, halted in an action whose purpose he could not recall. She ached watching him take out his sword daily to polish it—they both knew he would never use it again.

"I should be fighting alongside Elias," Jéhan said, but only once. Chryse gave up on the physician's treatments; only the sleeping draughts helped. At least in sleep he could forget the path his body had taken. Chryse, lying awake, could not.

On one of those nights, Chryse realized she had seen those movements before. Père Lusignan, the cleric whose grandson had gone to Pelagonia along with his father, looked the same. The thought filled her with dread. She had watched the priest for years as his stride faltered and his limbs began to flick and twitch.

Jéhan's deterioration had accelerated once Elias left—he spoke in a strangled voice, and his words were jumbled. If they were afflicted with the same illness . . . She thought hard, Jéhan drugged and snoring next to her. Had Evrard begun to show signs? Was it passed from father to son? Her husband was Frankish, but the Borghes and Lusignan families weren't related.

Chryse got out of bed and began to pace. Struck by an idea, she knelt at the chest where Jéhan kept the mementos of his former life, before the Lacedaemon valley became his home. She felt through the contents in the dark: the clothing he'd worn when they first met, the wreath of flowers she'd made for him, now dry and crumbling. It made her smile— he'd kept it all. At the bottom of the pile was a book with a worn leather cover.

She took it into the kitchen and lit a candle to read. It was a list of names: generations of marriage, birth, and death records from Jéhan's family, written in neat, cramped French. She leafed through the pages, reading each name carefully. There were pages still blank at the end; she'd keep the book for her midwife's birth records in the future. Then, as if it had been waiting, she found what she had feared. Jéhan's great-grandfather had married a Lusignan.

chapter eight

ELIAS OROLOGOS
July 2015
Mystras

Panos Economides, the keeper of the Mystras Inn, brought me a cup of strong Greek coffee with a frown rather than his habitual smile. Once there was no coffee in Greece; we had the Turks to thank for it—there are some benefits to occupation.

"*Kalimera*," Panos said, but not cheerfully. He lowered his bulk into one of the spindly café chairs. He was one of those big men who are miraculously light on their feet. "Elias, there is a problem."

I was often the first to hear, but not today. "Tell me."

"Something is missing from the museum."

I felt a stab of alarm. "What?"

"They have a new docent, have you met her? She is *Anglica*, I think, from her accent." He was right, the docent had come recently from England. I only knew her by sight.

Sometimes Panos required redirection, which I provided, gently. "You said something has disappeared?"

"Yes, yes, a book. The docent told Stavros, and Stavros told Nano, who told me, just this morning. A record of families from the time of Mystras's founding."

The coffee tasted suddenly like ashes. "Anything else?"

"No."

A waitress brought the plate of tiny *tyropitas* I'd ordered, but the flaky cheese pies no longer interested me. I pushed them toward Panos, who ate two rapidly. "They have called the police." He tilted his head toward the museum down the road, where I saw the distinctive black-and-white car parked. "I hope they will find the book, and the thief, and put an end to this trouble." Panos made sure I ate one of the pies, then finished them.

"I hope so, too," I said. I did not say what I was thinking: *The trouble is just beginning.*

Ω

For decades, I'd lived in the town at the base of the hill, working as a tour guide. I'd wondered whether that was how I was destined to spin out my years, talking about a place rather than living in it, the ghost town silent under the July sun, its tumbled stones baking in the heat. I ought to have known a threat would emerge out of the blur of years. This time, though, no one guided me.

Eudoxia dozed under the spreading tree, mumbling incomprehensibly when she woke, waving her gnarled hands in the air. She had done her job for longer than I and deserved her rest. I wanted to rest, too, to step off the endless spinning circle of years and live a linear life, sharing loves that I would not inevitably outlive. But instead I waited, off to the side like a stranger at a gathering of friends.

After I'd finished the museum tour, I went to find the British docent, who eyed me suspiciously. She could tell me nothing about the stolen book and went back to filing. I stopped in at the director's office. He confirmed that the missing book

detailed Mystras's families from the time of the Frankish occupation. It was handwritten, perhaps a midwife's or healer's
journal, given the detailed records of births, he said. I stopped
listening as time turned inside out. I had known that book
twice—from the museum, and from *before*. I'd seen my mother
writing late at night by candlelight after she'd returned from a
birth. Had she written my name on the day I was born? Standing outside the museum in the baking heat, I wondered who
might be searching for my family's history, and why.

*Whatever is asked of you in the service of this place, do not
shrink from the task*, my mother had said, long ago.

Danger to myself I could ignore, but danger to Mystras I
was sworn not to.

"Of course, Mitéra," I whispered to the empty courtyard.
"Of course."

ELIAS BORGHES
June 1259
Pelagonia

After crossing the Evrotas, we traveled north to the barony of
Nikli. There, Prince Guillaume tested my abilities as an emissary again, this time to persuade Nikli's lord Hugh Morlay to
join us. Lord Morlay could not have said no even if I'd come
without ten thousand troops behind me, but Prince Guillaume
took it as evidence of my diplomatic skill. "You've proven
yourself indispensable again," he said, nodding sagely. I let him
think so.

At the end of June, we crossed the Lepanto Gulf, leaving
the peninsula of the Morea behind. Then came the Pindus

mountains. We trudged through dry mountain riverbeds, dust caking our faces. We struggled in narrow gorges bordered by crumbling limestone cliffs where the path allowed only a single line of wagons. Pines clustered on the slopes, littering the ground with needles. Snowcapped peaks loomed in the distance.

In September, we joined our ally Michael of Epirus in Thalassinon. In my "indispensable" role, I joined the prince's retinue to meet Despot Michael at close range. Marceau insisted on accompanying me to Doukas's tent.

"Bastards," Marceau said under his breath, "both the despot and his son John. And John the Bastard married a Vlach wife; I suppose her beauty made her race bearable. Bastard sons of bastard despots do not have much to choose from." I ignored Marceau's nastiness, more interested in my first glimpse of a Romaioi ruler. Michael wore a red silk *tunica* with long, tight sleeves. Over that, his patterned silk dalmatic reached to the floor, wide-sleeved and decorated with embroidered flowers and studded with pearls. His sons, flanking him, were dressed only slightly less magnificently.

"I hope their sword work is as pretty as their dress," Marceau whispered. I agreed with his meaning, though not his manner.

John the Bastard (I could not put Marceau's slur out of my mind) reported to the allies. "Mercenaries have swelled our enemy's ranks. Two thousand Cuman cavalry have joined Nicaea." I tried not to imagine what two thousand screaming mounted soldiers bent on our destruction might look like. "Not only that, the enemy coalition has been joined by fighters from five other kingdoms."

"Their total number?" The despot's voice was gruff.

"Twenty thousand."

"We have more," John said confidently, though a muscle above one eye twitched.

Prince Guillaume chimed in. "We have numbers *and skill* to overcome the would-be emperor's forces. You know my successes in the Morea." He paused. He did inspire his soldiers, even if his flowery language made me smile. He had won battles for a reason. "If we attack the fortresses at Neopatras and Lamia now, we shall have a significant advantage."

Despot Michael shook his head. "A waste of time."

John nodded his assent. "The castles are a distraction." The united father-son front felt as forbidding as the *kastron*'s battlements. I was glad these men were our allies. After a heated argument, the council agreed: we would march to meet the Palaiologos army.

As Marceau and I exited the tent, he turned to me with a smirk.

"The two bastards together are not worth our prince's little finger."

Hugh Morlay, Nikli's displaced baron, followed us out and shook his head disapprovingly. "Who are you to take the measure of these men? You've barely outgrown the fuzz on your chin." He laughed, nastily. "Though I wouldn't mind being John the Bastard for a night. Vlach women are so easy their husbands have to hide them, but I found his." Hugh smacked his lips.

Unfortunately, our interchange had an audience. Demetrios, outside our tent cleaning his boots, pointed back toward Despot Michael's tent. "You see that woman?" She was elegantly dressed in a black velvet tunic embroidered in maroon and gold, and she wore looped chains of gold coins around her neck. Her dark hair emerged from a high square headdress and wound into a long, thick plait that reached to the small of her back.

"That is John Doukas's wife," Demetrios said. "She may not be on the council, but she knows more and hears more than many who are. She's been standing outside the tent for the whole meeting." My heart sank. If she'd overheard Lord Morlay's rash words, it could cause serious trouble.

Ω

As we were setting up camp in the plain of Pelagonia, the scouts returned with news: our enemies were a day's march away. Pelagonia would be our battleground.

That night I learned John Doukas's wife had, as I'd feared, heard Hugh Morlay's comments. I was with Prince Guillaume when John Doukas strode in without introduction. "Your pig Morlay insulted my wife," he said, slamming his fist on the table where Prince Guillaume had unrolled his maps.

The prince looked up slowly. He had developed a new mannerism; he ran the fingers of one hand behind his ear, as if to replace an errant lock of hair. "I'm sure the baron meant only to flatter your lovely wife."

"She is not yours to call lovely," John Doukas growled, leaning in so close I could see the sweat on his brow. "I want an apology, Villehardouin."

"No apology is needed when a man compliments a beautiful woman," Prince Guillaume said with a smile that failed to calm.

"He had the gall to proposition her like a common whore. Call your foul-mouthed lordling to task," John Doukas hissed.

"I shall not take orders from the bastard son of my wife's father," Guillaume said coolly. "Come back when you are civil."

John Doukas's face reddened dangerously, and he clenched his hands at his sides. "You'll wish you'd come groveling for forgiveness," John said ominously. Prince Guillaume cleared his throat as he watched Doukas's retreating angry back. Doukas was not a man whose alliance Guillaume could afford to lose. He replaced another invisible strand of hair behind his ear.

Ω

By sunset, the allied forces were encamped at Pelagonia. Weapons were honed on armorer's stones, burnished shields shone, and standards bearing the insignia of each battalion hung expectantly from their poles. Grooms tended to the battle horses, and troops hummed with speculation, anxiety, and fear. One young soldier began to cry like a baby until his commander took him into a tent to calm him down. He emerged red-faced and silent.

As we prepared to retire for the night, I stayed outside with Demetrios. In the hills surrounding Pelagonia's plain, I saw a gleam of light, followed by a plume of smoke. One fire became two, then four, then ten, then there were thousands of fires above us. Spyridon came up silently beside me.

"You're a stealthy one," I said, startled.

"Pirates tend to be," he said. "You see those fires?" Thousands of them edged the line where mountains met sky. "Those are enemy camps. In the morning, all those Nicaeans will sweep down and run us through."

Everywhere I looked a fire burned. "The council said we were prepared to overcome them."

"We'll see about that," Spyridon said grimly, watching until the hills were topped with flame. Then the shouts of thousands of men began to echo from the hills, filling the valley with sound.

A man appeared out of the dark, threading his way

through the tents. Demetrios, one hand on his sword, reached out to stop him.

"Who are you?" Demetrios said in the quiet, ominous voice I knew well. One threatening move and the stranger would be dead.

"I come from General Palaiologos with a message for the Despot of Epirus," the intruder said.

"Honest messengers don't creep around enemy camps." Spyridon drew his weapon.

"I speak the truth," the messenger said, voice tremulous. In one outstretched hand, he held a scrolled piece of parchment, sealed with crimson wax and stamped with a double-headed eagle.

"I'll escort him." My voice sounded more commanding than I felt. Demetrios walked with me until we were at the despot's tent.

Michael Doukas was standing outside looking at the fires, too. He was flanked by two guards, and torches driven into the ground illuminated the entrance to his tent. He was almost frighteningly lean, the sharp angles of his face exaggerated by the torchlight. His hand, marked by a jagged scar, rested lightly on the pommel of his sheathed sword. I stopped and bowed, as I'd seen the Epirote courtiers do; the messenger followed suit.

"I've seen you before." The despot looked at me.

"Kyr Doukas," I said, "I am Elias Borghes, emissary and soldier of Prince Villehardouin's army. This man bears a message from General Palaiologos." The despot's guards drew their swords with a metallic hiss.

The messenger raised his hands to show he was not armed. His fingers curled tight around the parchment.

"Inside," Michael said, motioning toward the tent's entrance. "Borghes, you too." The guards escorted the messenger roughly, and I followed.

"Honorable Kyr Doukas," the boy began, "your kinsman in Nicaea greets you with affection."

"Kinsman, eh?" Michael laughed. "How much connection can he claim as his troops prepare to stain the ground with my soldiers' blood?"

"He has sent me to warn you, for your welfare and the welfare of your men is his greatest concern. Kyr Palaiologos is very sorry that you have penetrated so deep into the emperor's territory with so few men."

"The emperor must have difficulty with numbers," Michael said.

The messenger cleared his throat. "For every one of your men, the emperor has one hundred. He fears you will be brutally defeated."

"Why would he send you to tell me this?"

"My master wishes you to abandon Prince Guillaume and go back to Epirus as secretly and quickly as possible. If you stay, not a single one of you will escape."

I had just heard something I should not have heard. If the despot decided to take the messenger's advice, I'd either be a prisoner or dead, before morning. If he didn't and the messenger was right about the size of the opposing army, I might end up a prisoner or dead anyway.

"Chain the messenger and keep him under close watch. His aim is to fracture an alliance that threatens the emperor's dominion." The guards grabbed the boy and dragged him out.

Michael Doukas turned toward me. "I shall speak with Prince Guillaume. Do not share what you have heard, lest you undermine your fellow soldiers' courage. We shall defeat Nicaea. Do not doubt it."

I walked back to my tent in the dark, trying not to look up at the hills, where the emperor's troops waited for dawn. As I lay down in our tent, Demetrios touched my arm. I took his hand and put it to my lips. His fingers smelled of woodsmoke.

"What became of the messenger?" Demetrios whispered.

"He's a prisoner now." I wanted to tell Demetrios what I'd heard, but the despot's warning rang in my ears. I might destroy the confidence that would give Demetrios strength tomorrow, putting his life and the lives of all who depended on his skill at risk.

"I pity the man who brings bad news into an enemy camp," Demetrios said.

I turned to him in the dark. "Will you promise me something?"

"Anything, Elias."

"If ill should befall me, bring me back to Mystras."

"I will bring you home if you are too wounded to fight," Demetrios said.

"I must ask you for more than that. If I do not survive, bring my body home."

"God forbid I should have to fulfill this promise, Elias. That messenger must have brought ill news."

I touched his cheek. "Promise me. I believe Spyridon or Knyaz Dragovic will help you."

"I cannot refuse you anything."

I leaned in and kissed the tears from his cheeks. Demetrios wrapped his arms around me, pulling me in. Before I fell asleep, I heard the despot's last words in my head. "We shall defeat Nicaea. Do not doubt it."

But it was impossible not to doubt.

Ω

That night a fierce storm blew in from the sea, and the wind battered our tent so viciously I thought it would tear away from its stakes. Water poured through the gaps in the canvas and thunder crashed around us until the ground shook. An army could have marched through our camp unnoticed in the savage maelstrom of sound.

We emerged from our tents and girded ourselves for battle in the muddy dark, waiting for the trumpets. But as the sun rose, vast stretches of empty space appeared where tents had been pitched. The flattened grass and packed earth were littered with the debris of a hasty departure: half-eaten food, smoking fires, piles of horse droppings, and standard poles stripped of their banners, thin and naked against the lightening sky. A few dogs wandered in the detritus, scavenging for a morning meal. Michael Doukas's Epirote army and John the Bastard's Vlach forces were gone.

Prince Guillaume summoned the commanders who remained: Romaioi barons from throughout the Morea, Knyaz Dragovic, and the impulsive Hugh Morlay. Spyridon stood to my right, second in command to the Monemvasiot captain. Our numbers were dangerously small.

The prince addressed us, his cape rippling in the light wind. I tried to listen to the speech that was meant to inspire, but the events of the night before played in my head.

"Dear companions, we have been betrayed." The prince paused. I saw a grace I had not seen in him before. He did not place himself above our fear and despair. "There is nothing left to do but fight. We are far from our homeland and in the midst of our enemies. I pray that on this day we may conduct ourselves in such a manner that people will speak of us with honor forever."

Had he stopped there, I would have gone to fight fueled

with the power of our unity. But Prince Guillaume did not stop. "Even if the enemy are more numerous than we, they are a worthless, miserable bunch made up of many races. We are fine, elite men. If we conduct ourselves well and behave like noblemen, then our enemy should easily be defeated."

Made up of many races. Knyaz Dragovic caught my eye. Demetrios whispered in my ear, "Spyridon the Monemvasiot, Elias the *gasmoule*, and a bunch of savage Slavs. There is no miserable bunch I'd rather fight beside." I wanted to embrace him.

Ω

Prince Guillaume ordered Hugh Morlay to lead the first battalion.

"I am prepared to be cut to pieces in your company," Morlay barked, pledging his allegiance in unpleasantly graphic terms. The Six, not surprisingly, were not in the advance guard; we made our way to a hillock where we could watch the battle unfold while we waited for orders. I was glad not to be on the front line. As the sun cleared the horizon, Nicaean trumpets blared and a dark wave swept down from the hills like a swarm of hornets. John Palaiologos's mounted knights thundered down the slope, their lances glittering.

Morlay was at the head of Prince Guillaume's army, his red hair hidden by his helmet, but I recognized his colors. Lances dropped as the horses sped toward one another, and then came a sound I will never forget: the ear-splitting clash of lances striking shields, the shrill whinnies of horses and the shouts of men as the front lines of knights collided. Morlay's lance struck the shield of his opponent so hard that the Palaiologos knight's horse was thrown to the ground, his rider slamming down with him. The downed knight's neck angled unnaturally, and his limbs went still. Morlay hurled himself at another knight, knocking his opponent off his horse, and then unseated a third, but this time, Morlay's lance shattered at the impact. He drew his longsword and pushed his mount forward into the mass of churning men, slashing through one man's arm, another's leg, splattering himself with fresh blood. Around him, knights fought until the ground was littered with the wounded, and dead piled underfoot so that the horses had to wade through the river of carnage, their hooves and legs streaked with gore.

Prince Guillaume, his red-and-gold standard flying beside him, pushed forward exultantly, calling for a second battalion to join the fray. His glory was short-lived; mounted enemy archers galloped onto the battlefield, letting loose a swarm of arrows that turned the sky dark and filled the air with a terrible high-pitched keening. One of Morlay's knights pitched from his horse, neck and chest bristling with so many arrows that he looked like a gruesome hedgehog. Wounded horses let out high-pitched squeals and folded to the ground, feathered shafts protruding from their necks and flanks, spilling their riders as they fell.

The signal came for the foot soldiers to mobilize; our wait was over. Pantaleon led us down the hill. I caught Demetrios's eye. *"Your request is safe with me,"* he mouthed, and then we were pressed into the advancing lines of fighting men.

The battle was chaos. Men shouted as they swung swords, axes, and maces, biting into steel, leather, and flesh. The metallic smell of blood was everywhere; I began to taste it. Vultures flew low overhead, waiting. Thousands more enemy soldiers poured onto the field bearing the Palaiologos double-headed eagle. I killed a man, my first, within minutes, burying my father's sword in the dip at his throat. There was no time to dwell on what I had done.

Marceau took down a man whose swinging mace could have split his skull in two. To my right, the Monemvasiot contingent slashed through the enemy behind rows of kite-shaped shields. Spyridon drove his spear into the groin of an infantryman who'd let down his guard and paid for the mistake with his life.

Out of the jumble of men ahead of me, a Palaiologos soldier emerged, his sword aimed at my chest. Nikos, roaring in like the rhinoceros he resembled, met my enemy's sword, then clubbed the man on the head with his blade until he crumpled to the ground. It was so like Nikos to use a sword as a blunt instrument—I might have laughed had I not been so terrified.

Then a space cleared around me, a circle of stillness within the maelstrom. Horns blared behind us, where Prince Villehardouin's reserve should have been. But when I turned, I saw instead a new army at our backs. The flags flying sported a white shield topped by a red band, and John the Bastard rode triumphantly at their head. I shouted a warning, and the men around me turned to see. It was bad enough that Michael the Despot of Epirus had deserted the prince on the night before the battle. But his son John had done worse—he'd joined the other side.

Now we were not only outnumbered, but also surrounded by our enemies, half of whom had been allies the day before. While the rear guard pressed forward to attack us, the emperor's battalions gathered around Morlay's knights at the front, cutting them down like wheat. The Cuman cavalry captain, a massive man wearing a half-round helmet topped with feathers, drew his bow, and Morlay's horse stumbled, struck with such force in the temple by the arrow that he fell to the ground in a heap, taking Morlay with him. I lost sight of the prince in the crush of men. Prince Guillaume's barons were taken prisoner, beheaded, dismembered, or left for dead in the mud.

Pantaleon, a few feet away, turned toward me. Blood poured from his helmet, and I realized, in horror, that he was missing an ear. I pointed wordlessly.

"The man who took it from me looks worse," he yelled, and pushed back into the press, undaunted.

Nikos and Theodore fought side by side, paired as they had been for years of practice together. And then in one instant, their partnership was severed. A Vlach soldier, silent and brutal, swung his battle-axe, crushing Nikos's neck. Nikos folded and lay still. Theo's stricken face echoed my despair. I looked for Pantaleon again, but I could not find him.

After that every movement was fractured, reflected in a broken mirror. I must have kept swinging, because I felt the heat and ache in my arms, but the sword had a life beyond me. Theo threw himself at the Vlach whose ax had taken Nikos's life, making a sound that was not remotely human.

Where was Demetrios? For a few panicked seconds, I could not find him. Then I found his broad, calm shoulders, the dark curls at the back of his neck where his helmet ended and his pourpoint began.

Thank God it wasn't you.

A Palaiologos knight, mounted on a massive black destrier, galloped toward me, his spear aimed at my throat. Outside of time, I looked at the double-headed eagle on the knight's tunic as he prepared to hurl his spear. One head faced east, one west, like the Romaioi empire with Ottoman foes on one front and Latins on the other. I could as easily have been fighting under the Romaioi eagle as the prince's cross; only an accident of my birth placed me on this side of the battle and not the other.

Marceau, my unlikely defender, aimed his spear toward the Palaiologos's soldier's chest, but at the key moment it veered and missed its mark, grazing the man's armor harmlessly. Had an involuntary twitch in Marceau's arm sent his spear off target? Had fear made him waver? Or had he missed his mark on purpose? He was already fending off an attack from another.

I raised my shield. Little Theodore, holding the ax from the downed Vlach, leaped toward me, knocking my enemy's spear off course. But the point still struck my side, searing fire along my ribs, and as I went down, the knight finished Theodore with the spear that had wounded me. Done with us, he directed his efforts elsewhere. Theo sat with a look of profound surprise on his face and one hand cupping his belly, trying to stanch the flow of blood.

"I don't want to go," he said simply. A small request, as from a child who wishes to stay late at a party. Then he was gone.

Ω

Marceau saw the spear strike Elias's side and slice through his tunic. Elias stumbled and fell, then dragged himself along the ground. The wound welled with blood.

The blood of the boy is life, Marceau's head hummed.

Elias threw himself on Theodore's body, and Marceau took a step toward them.

If it could be taken, it would cure.

Elias did not look up from his tragic embrace while the fighting raged around him.

A few steps more.

A line of Vlach soldiers thundered into the space between

Marceau and his target, and he was swept into a wave of fighting. Marceau fought back toward the spot where Elias lay, butchering four opponents in his desperation. He wiped away at his stinging eyes. His own blood, or an enemy's? Marceau did not care.

If it could be taken, it would cure.

He emerged into the clearing where Theodore's body still lay in the trampled grass, just as it had fallen.

The blood of the boy is life.

But Elias had vanished, taking his blood with him.

DEMETRIOS ASANES
September 1259
Plain of Pelagonia

Demetrios saw Elias fall. He ran, leaping over bodies to the spot where Elias lay, still breathing, thank God, his hands buried in the cloth of Theodore's pourpoint.

Demetrios knelt and touched the curve of Elias's back. "We must go. Can you walk?"

Elias looked down at the gash in his side. "I don't know."

"Try." Demetrios slung his shield over his back and put his arm under Elias's own.

The battle's ferocious center had veered away like a wheel rolling free of a carriage's broken axle. Demetrios saw Spyridon, wrapping a bandage around his bleeding left thigh, and shouted the pirate's name; he came limping. The three of them struggled along until they came to a copse of oak trees, where they let Elias slide to the ground. He closed his eyes beneath the tree's arching branches.

Demetrios knew that Elias walked the line between this world and the next; Demetrios had traveled that line with him the day of the quake. Anyone who loved Elias would know something of life along that fragile edge.

Bring him home. The disembodied words echoed in Demetrios's ears. He did not question their source.

Ω

"It's desertion," Spyridon said with a scowl, finishing dressing Elias's wound. "And it's a damned long walk. We should compound our crimes by stealing a mount."

"I'm going back to the camp for supplies," Demetrios said. He stuffed their rucksacks with as much as he could carry, turning at a sound behind him.

"Had enough of the fighting?" Knyaz Dragovic towered over him.

"Elias is injured," Demetrios said defiantly.

"But you are not." The Slav's hand moved to the hilt of his sword.

"I made Elias a promise to bring him home, and I intend to keep it." Demetrios would tie himself to Elias and go home as two corpses rather than leave his friend behind.

"Do you have help?"

Surprise pulled the truth from Demetrios. "Not enough."

"I will give you provisions, a mule, and my silence," Dragovic said. Demetrios exhaled with relief. "Elias makes us all love him, doesn't he," Dragovic said. It was not a question.

With a hastily loaded pack mule, Demetrios went back to the stand of oaks where Elias lay, Spyridon standing guard.

"I hope no one saw you steal that mule," the pirate said, raising one eyebrow.

"Knyaz Dragovic, leader of the Milengoi, gave it to me."

"How did you make such a powerful friend?"

"I had nothing to do with it," Demetrios answered. "Elias did." Spyridon laughed, but didn't disagree.

ELIAS BORGHES
September 1259
En Route to Mystras

For the first week, I managed to ride on the mule's back, drifting in and out of sleep with my cheek on its neck. Soon I could no longer stay seated on the animal. In the dappled shade of a copse of pines, I watched my friends build me a litter from tree branches. After that I lay flat, but every bump felt like a new spear wound. I shut my eyes against the light, and my skin burned. At night, Demetrios lay next to me. The days passed in a blur, but I still knew the sweet smell of his breath and the murmur of his voice in my ear.

Demetrios wanted to find a physician. "Just bring me home," I said, and Demetrios started to cry. He seemed unimaginably far away. I looked past him into the starry sky. Alpha to Omega, the arc of time.

"You will think I have left you, Demetrios, but I will not," I said, and then something like sleep came, and the stars went dark.

chapter nine

GUILLAUME VILLEHARDOUIN
September 1259
Plain of Pelagonia

Prince Guillaume was extraordinarily uncomfortable under the bale of hay. One errant straw tickled his right nostril, and several others had gone down the back of his neck. When the battle turned sour, Guillaume had—of necessity—absented himself from the most dangerous fighting. His allies' desertion and defection posed unreasonable obstacles, and it was essential that he survive, for the sake of the Morea and the family he'd left behind. Guillaume had donned a dress he'd found hanging in a peasant's empty house; the woman who'd once worn it must have been generously proportioned. A scarf draped over his head completed the disguise, and he'd managed to walk to the barn without attracting undue suspicion.

The irritation of the hay provided only temporary distraction from the battle he'd escaped—the worst Guillaume had encountered in his years of fighting. Many of his men had been captured, and more died at the hand of the emperor's forces. Despot Michael's disappearance had been bad enough, but when that bastard John came sweeping into view at the head of an opposing battalion . . . Guillaume could not bear to think of it.

Outside the barn's window he heard voices and stamping feet. A search party? They spoke neither French nor Greek. Guillaume felt a cold settle in the pit of his belly as he heard them more clearly. If the emperor's handpicked Varangian Guard—Northmen known for their savagery—were coming for him, he had no hope of escape.

Could he slip out of the barn unseen? Perhaps the axe-bearing barbarians would mistake him for a peasant woman. But if they were not fooled, he'd hardly be able to run in that skirt. It was safest to stay put, under the hay. *Mon Dieu, take care of your servant, so that I may survive to make La Morée a land dedicated to your holy name for my descendants after me. Let me live to bring children into the world who will praise your name.*

Before his prayer was concluded, the hay was torn away, and above him stood three Varangian guardsmen with long hair loose like lions' manes. Dragons were sewn onto their shirts, and each had a ruby in his left ear. They carried broad, single-edged Dane axes, the largest Guillaume had ever seen.

"Seems the prince has found himself a nice *tunica* to wear, but it can't disguise that face, and those big teeth," one of the guardsmen said in heavily accented Greek.

All was lost.

GUILLAUME VILLEHARDOUIN
Late September 1259
Court of Emperor Michael VIII Palaiologos at Nicaea

Nicaea, Guillaume was forced to admit, impressed him. Thick stone walls surrounded the city, which the prisoners had entered through a series of wide arched gateways. The city was built between a lake and olive groves; the trees' gray-green leaves shifted in the early autumn light. "You are in the court of an empire built on centuries of Roman rule," one burly Varangian escort said with a serene smile that contrasted with his barbaric appearance. "Do not expect to be master here." He and his barons had been imprisoned for a week in Nicaea before being granted audience. The longer supplicants waited, the weaker their will became; Guillaume knew that trick well.

As he was escorted into the emperor's audience chamber, he tried to hide his disapproval of the golden throne, wide enough for two. These heretics actually believed that each Sunday Christ himself would join their emperor, sitting side by side as equals! Smooth-faced eunuchs prostrated themselves before the emperor in rhythmic rows. Perforated brass lamps swung from the high ceiling of the throne room, illuminating the emperor's gold diadem and gem-encrusted scapular. The garment was so stiff with embroidery and pearls that it could stand on its own.

"Behold the Emperor Michael Palaiologos the Eighth, son of the Megas Domestikos Andronikos Palaiologos, Oh Sublime and Wonderful Splendor, His Serenity, His Outstandingness." The chief minister prostrated himself and kissed the emperor's red-slippered feet. Guillaume had never kissed a man's feet and had no intention of doing so, but he bowed in his own fashion.

The emperor had a long angular nose, and his eyes were deep-set and sharp. A thick beard and mustache framed an unforgiving mouth. But his mellifluous voice surprised Guillaume. The emperor's power came from control, not the loss of it.

"Prince Villehardouin, my prisoner." The reminder was unnecessary. "I shall tell you what I want from you. Grant it or you will never leave this prison. You must give me the Morea peacefully, or I will take it by force. This would be easy, since you and your most trusted lords are not there to defend it." The emperor cleared his throat. "I am a reasonable man, and I will give you enough from my treasury to enable you to return to *your* country. France." The emperor nodded, giving the signal that his prisoner might respond. A scribe scribbled madly.

Guillaume spoke slowly. "Lord Holy Emperor, La Morée was conquered by my kinsmen. If I, to save my own liberty, were to disinherit the descendants of the Frenchmen who won the land through prowess in war, I would be committing a terrible wrong. I implore Your Holy Crown to speak no further of this matter. Release me and my companions for a ransom, as is customary."

A slow flush rose on Michael's face. Guillaume felt stirrings of alarm. Guillaume imagined himself blinded, disemboweled, and castrated, in that order. Michael rose, and four imperial guards stepped forward, weapons drawn.

Michael spat his words. "You are so clearly *French*. You believed you could escape through arrogance, but instead you have doomed yourself and your followers. You will never leave here." The emperor waved his hand to his chief minister. "Take this man back to his cell, along with his lords."

Prince Guillaume returned to prison with his barons, wordless for the first time in his life.

chapter ten

CHRYSE BORGHES
Late October 1259
Mystras

Even on a diet of only porridge, Jéhan spluttered, as if he had forgotten how to swallow. One day he began to cough, complaining of pain in his chest, and the next he grew flushed with fever, his breath coming short and fast. Chryse sent for the doctor, a skilled Romaioi *iatros*, who worked in the valley.

"Your husband inhales his food and spittle. It has lodged in his lungs, and he burns with the fever of it." Whether the doctor's interpretation was correct or not, within a week, Jéhan was gone. Even through the agony of loss, Chryse wondered whether it was a backhanded gift from God, for him to be spared more suffering.

So she was alone when two men arrived at the house in Mystras late at night, carrying Elias in a makeshift litter. Chryse knew Demetrios Asanes from La Lacedemonie; the Monemvasiot was a stranger. They'd left before the battle's end, Demetrios said, and did not know the outcome. They carefully lifted Elias into his bed. There was no hospital in Lacedaemon, so Chryse told Demetrios to fetch the doctor who had treated Jéhan before his death.

The doctor cleaned and dressed the wound, then felt Elias's pulse at each crucial point. When he was done, he shook his head, his face etched with sympathy at the condition of the soldier whose father he had just seen buried.

"I am sorry. I have treated your son's injury as best I can, and I shall give him a medicine for the derangement of his inner organs. But his condition is grave."

Chryse did not need to be told. "What more can be done?"

"Any further help must come from God," Kalopheros said, but then he saw Chryse's face. She was a healer in her own right and a parent. "And from his mother, of course."

The Monemvasiot fell asleep on the floor, but Demetrios stayed awake with Chryse. They sat together on stools at Elias's side, watching the rise and fall of his chest. Finally, Chryse put her hand on Demetrios's shoulder. "When was the last time you slept?"

Demetrios could not recall. Chryse made a bed of blankets on the floor beside Elias and led Demetrios to lie down.

"I brought him home," Demetrios said as he closed his eyes.

"Yes, you did," Chryse answered. And then, "You brought him more than that." But Demetrios was already asleep.

Ω

He may be changed when you see him next.

Is this what the prophet had promised? This weakened, silent shell of her son? Chryse prepared to leave the house with Elias in the dark, just as she had twenty-two years before. This time he could not be bundled against her chest, but he balanced on the same precipice, between this life and the life beyond. *Lives.*

She leaned forward to kiss his damp forehead, and he opened his eyes.

"Mitéra." His voice was rusty, like an unused hinge.

"I love you," Chryse said, knowing it might be her last chance to tell him.

"I love you. Where are we going?"

"Can you walk?"

"No," he said, but she took his hands to pull him up.

"We are going up the hill," Chryse said. She managed somehow to make it out the door with him, carrying most of his weight. It took more than an hour to climb the hill. The road was shorter than the one she had taken from the valley two decades before, but today her load was heavier. They struggled on the winding path to where the *kastron* loomed in the dark. There, though the shrine was gone, Chryse could still find the spot where the prophet had spoken.

Elias folded to the ground, and she sat, too, breathing hard, so he could rest his head in her lap. A light rain began to fall, the gentle sound of drops on the grass. She waited— minutes, hours. The damp seeped into her cloak and robe, and Elias's head grew heavy on her thigh. She was on the edge of sleep when she heard the prophet's voice in her head, quiet as a whisper.

You did not forget.

Elias went still, his breath tapering to silence.

DEMETRIOS ASANES
November 1259
Mystras

Demetrios barely spoke for days after Elias's death. His mother cooked with saffron, filling the house with its uplifting scent, but Demetrios did not eat. His father, Paulus, made unsuccessful efforts to cheer Demetrios, bringing the best cuts of meat from his butcher shop, and his sister, Ireni, insuppressible about her upcoming wedding, showered Demetrios with words he could not hear and ebullient embraces he returned mechanically. His family believed they understood—he was a soldier shocked by war—but they did not know the extent of his loss.

Over the next weeks, the remnants of the prince's army straggled back to Mystras telling tales of horror and despair. Their prince had been taken prisoner. Romaioi leaders were known to blind their own family members to win the throne; who knows what they might do to an avowed enemy.

Few survivors of Pelagonia escaped, and many were lost on the route home. Some succumbed to festering wounds and the demands of the steep Pindus mountain gorges, while others fell prey to bands of outlaws who took advantage of weakened men. Pantaleon had not returned. No one knew if he was rotting on the battlefield or shackled in a dark Nicaean prison. Demetrios heard that Marceau had made his way back to Mystras, alone on a stolen horse. Demetrios did not seek him out.

Demetrios listened to his comrades' stories as they returned, but he could not tell his own. Spyridon had left for Monemvasia—in name, like Mystras, still the property of the absent prince, though none knew whether he would ever return home to reclaim it. Knyaz Dragovic came back with a battered remnant of his forces and reclaimed his holdings in the Taygetos. Demetrios was alone with his grief.

One late November day he awoke at dawn, unable to go back to sleep. He dressed and left the house. A chill wind picked up leaves outside the door. Demetrios moved slowly, thinking of the night he'd held Elias's feet in his hands and crossed from longing to love.

He took the path up the hill to the *kastron*'s north gate, where he and Elias had walked years before. He remembered their conversation as if it were yesterday: Elias's ability to break through Demetrios's shell, their talk of hidden fears.

Demetrios could almost hear Elias's quiet voice, his words carefully selected and slow to emerge: *Fear is worse alone.*

Since the last time he had walked this route, someone had built a fountain at the path's edge. It was made of stuccoed stone with a pointed arched roof, carved with flowers and birds. Demetrios thought of the stoneworker who had poured his heart and soul into this structure, knowing it would give pleasure to the ordinary folk who came to drink. He stepped along the freshly laid flagstones to the fountain's enclosure. A pipe protruded from the wall from which fresh spring water flowed into a basin. The water rippled, and a single leaf floated upon its surface, turning slowly. Demetrios bent to take a drink and splash water on his face. It was bracingly cold and tasted faintly of rock.

Perhaps it was the way of all mourners, to imagine those they loved were close enough to touch: in the wind, the birds, the earth, even the stones of Mystras's *kastron*. The wind lifted, caressing Demetrios's cheek like an unseen hand. Later, his despair would turn to fury. But for now, the rock-cold water, the wind stirring the fallen leaves, the swell of memory, gave Demetrios an inkling of relief.

GUILLAUME VILLEHARDOUIN
Summer 1261
Nicaea

Guillaume had never imagined his life would include years in a Nicaean prison. At night he lay awake, limbs tense and head full of what he had lost. Some nights he sang to himself to keep demons at bay, songs from the book that had graced his wedding day. He learned that his wife had delivered their first child and named her Isabelle. To have his firstborn come into the world while he was a captive in another man's kingdom was like a knife in his chest.

It became increasingly clear that Michael Palaiologos would not accept Guillaume's offer of ransom. He wanted the land, not money, and no sum could change his imperial mind. Still, Guillaume held out hope—for the sake of his daughter, and her descendants. The final blow came one mid-August morning when Guillaume was sweating in the oppressive heat of his cell. The door swung open, and two guards entered, gripping spears. One of the men was so hairy that curls from his chest bristled over the neck of his tunic.

"You and your barons are going on an outing," the guard announced.

Guillaume hoped this news heralded a change of his captor's mind. "I expect a more thorough explanation. This is no way to treat a prince." Dignity was essential.

The guard spat on the ground, barely missing the toe of Guillaume's boot. "Here's your thorough explanation, *prince*. Constantinople is ours again. And you've been invited to watch our emperor—God grant the Megas Doux long life— accept the empire's crown and scepter. Front-row seats."

So Guillaume and his barons were allowed to leave prison,

only to watch at sword point while their enemy entered the Golden Gate, hailed by a cheering crowd. The trip from Nicaea to Constantinople was torture. Ragged and miserable, Guillaume and his companions followed the tail end of the great procession through the streets of Constantinople behind the new emperor Michael and an ancient icon of the Virgin Hodegetria, Orthodox protectress of the city. When Michael and his wife, Theodora, were crowned, Guillaume watched grimly as their two-year-old son and heir toddled about the apse of the Church of Saint Sophia.

That night, his dreams were full of detail, down to the earrings Anna had worn on their wedding night. She held a baby girl swaddled in hazy gold who smiled up at her father, a fuzz of pale hair on her head. But her eyes were gouged out, sockets hollow. When Guillaume woke sweating, he called the guards to request an audience with the emperor.

Guillaume's clothes fit loosely, and his face was dark with an unkempt beard. Emperor Michael Palaiologos had, in those years, not changed at all.

The emperor's voice was deceptively mild. "Prince Guillaume. I trust you enjoyed your visit to the capital. Soon we will be moving to the court of Constantinople. After all these years of incompetent Latin rule, the jails are not so pleasant as in Nicaea. You might do well to orchestrate your release before you learn it firsthand." He looked down his long nose to Guillaume's kneeling form.

Guillaume knew the emperor had been asleep when the city fell to his military commander, but he smiled blandly. "It is truly fortunate you have such accomplished generals in your employ," he said instead.

"God delivered the city to us," Michael said without a trace of emotion.

"God is great and deserving of praise," Guillaume said. On this, at least, the two could agree.

"Why have you come, Prince Guillaume, other than to congratulate me on my coronation?"

"To request my liberty, Basileus Palaiologos."

"The terms have not changed, Prince. You must give me land in return for your freedom. But as I am now in possession of an entire empire, it is easy to be generous." He ran one finger down the ridge of his nose. "I now ask for only three castles from you, Prince Guillaume. Does that not seem eminently reasonable?"

Guillaume felt his pulse accelerate; three castles was less to lose than the entire peninsula. "I am eager to hear more, Your Excellency."

"In return for your and your barons' freedom, I ask first for the *kastron* of Maina, in the Mani peninsula. Second, the rock fortress of Monemvasia."

"And the third?"

"The *kastron* at Mystras. Those three, and you shall walk free."

The Maina, Guillaume's first castle; Monemvasia, hard-won and nearly impossible to take back; and Mystras—his great triumph, his kingdom, and, with La Crémonie nestled in the beautiful valley below, his home.

"There is no point in bargaining, Prince Guillaume, for I shall not bend again." Michael rose to leave. Guillaume's head buzzed.

"Megas Doux," Guillaume said, finally, to the retreating emperor's back. "I accept your terms."

chapter eleven

MARCEAU LUSIGNAN
Early Fall 1261
Mystras

Two years after his return from Pelagonia, Marceau spilled soup into his lap. The memory of the day he ridiculed his grandfather for the same clumsiness flooded into his mind. Père Lusignan was gone now; he'd died writhing in his bed. His father, Evrard, now gripped the rail to climb the stairs of their house, and lately he'd begun to come back from practice skirmishes with inexplicable wounds. *What if the beast resides in me, too?* Marceau thought as he watched his father bandage his latest injury.

"Prince Villehardouin has sold not only his castle, but his loyal subjects, in return for freedom. Already the Greeks are building houses on the hill, as if they own the place," Marceau said bitterly at the evening meal with his father. Ordinarily Marceau loved *louanika*, the smoked sausage his mother made, laced with cumin and pepper. But today the meat stuck in his throat. If the news was true, Mystras would soon belong to the Greeks. The Franks, his family included, would be interlopers rather than leaders, as was their right. "I want to slice the smiles off those smug Greek faces."

Lately, his anger spun beyond his control, like a weapon let fly too soon. Was that, too, a sign of worse to come? "The *gasmoules* are so pleased with themselves now that Mystras is destined to change hands. They ought never to have been trusted. I knew those boys could not fight loyally."

Evrard grunted, mouth full. "The *gasmoules* in your little company fought bravely. In any case, all but Demetrios are dead, and he and his family have always been loyal to the prince. You'd best be, too. Our leader will be back soon, and your disrespect noticed."

There was clearly no point talking to his father about anything of import. Marceau turned his head away as Evrard jammed a too-large heel of bread into his mouth. Marceau scanned the room for anything else to look at—the wooden ladles hanging beside the hearth, the barrels of wine—anything other than his father's wet lips.

Elias's disappearance added insult to injury. It should have been easy to do his grandfather's bidding and carry out the prophetess's command. *The blood of the boy is life* . . . But at the crucial moment, Marceau had lost his quarry.

After the battle, as he'd made his way home with the few men left of Prince Guillaume's army, Marceau imagined that Elias must have died on the battlefield. When he heard that he'd died in Mystras, brought home by other deserters—Demetrios and the Monemvasiot pirate—Marceau had asked around the village where he might find Elias's grave, claiming grief. The family had not held a public funeral, though, and no one knew where the body lay. Marceau imagined digging up the corpse and bringing a severed limb to the prophetess in the night. But even that grisly possibility was denied him.

Evrard finished off the sausage and thumped up the stairs, tripping on the top step.

EUDOXIA

The sons of sons come with their questions, generation after generation.

She could hear the visitor's impatient steps on the stones of the path. He entered, bringing the rancid scent of fear.

"Tell me whether I carry the curse," he barked.

A jingling sound, a coin in her hand. She dropped it on the floor.

"Not enough for you?" Two coins this time.

Give me something you hold dear.

"I hold nothing dear, except myself."

The words had the ring of truth. *Then give me a piece of yourself.*

"Crazy old woman," the visitor said, but then a moment later a tuft of hair was in her palm, and she closed her hand around it. "Tell me whether I carry the curse."

You shall know when you know.

"And if I am cursed, then what? Tell me that, at least."

Why did they seek her out if it made them afraid?

Ilias sti Mystras.

"Elias in Mystras? Crazy woman. Elias is dead."

You will find him. Throwing her head back, she began to laugh.

CHRYSE BORGHES
Late Fall, 1261
Mystras

When Père Lusignan's grandson came looking for the grave, Chryse knew she had done wisely to bury Elias in secret. From their first training fight, when Elias came home with a burning arc cut into his face, Chryse suspected Marceau's intent. Then Elias's near drowning, and now, his deadly wound. She had no proof of Marceau's role, but when Demetrios brought news that Marceau wished to pay his respects, she trusted that Frank no more than she ever had.

"Tell him nothing," Chryse said. She did not know why Marceau wanted to visit the grave, but respect had little to do with it.

As she stirred the *myzithra* cheese Elias had loved so much, she recalled the cold, the moon shrouded by wind-shredded clouds, the slippery mud, the whipping wet branches. That night repeated itself in her mind endlessly. Spyridon and Demetrios had followed her with shovels to the place where Elias's body lay under the trees. They avoided the main road, taking a path up the wooded slope.

They were soaking wet and mud-spattered when they reached the spot Chryse had chosen: near the *kastron*'s outer wall but out of sight of the guards patrolling the gates and looking down from the circular towers. Once a shrine had stood here, where the prophet's voice rode on the wind.

They began to dig. The rain came down in sheets, running into their eyes and mouths so fast there was no use wiping the water away. They had no priest, no censer, no bloom of incense, no flickering candles or glittering icons. But as she dug, Chryse sang the Epitaphios into the dark.

They laid his body with his head toward the east, and Chryse set the customary words, inscribed on parchment, on Elias's lips: *Come all you that love me and bid me farewell, for I shall no longer walk with you nor talk with you.*

When Demetrios bent to return the first shovelful of earth, Chryse stopped him and reached down into the grave.

Elias still wore the *enkolpion* about his neck, engraved with the Profitis Ilias. She lifted the amulet off her son's neck.

"It must stay with the living," she said, "who need it more." She brushed the mud from the saint's face and placed the amulet over Spyridon's head. "Here in Mystras, it is easy to remember Elias, for he is in every stone on which he sat to rest, in every tree under which he took shade. Demetrios and I will have those markers to keep him in our hearts. But when you leave for your island of rock, wear this in his memory. Wear it for protection and for comfort, as a symbol of gratitude for the friendship you gave my son when he was far from home."

Spyridon held the amulet in his hand like a prayer for his lost friend. "Now," Chryse said, straightening, "we close the grave." They shoveled until the hole was filled again, and together they stamped down the earth and covered it with fallen leaves. Demetrios knelt on the ground and pressed his face and outstretched hands into the fresh earth and leaves in a silent farewell. Chryse saw the grief in the curve of his back, and his dark hair glistened with the tears of the rain.

"*Ta léme*, Elias," she whispered. *See you*: the Greek farewell reserved for those we will meet again.

part two

SICILY

chapter twelve

CHRYSE BORGHES
Late November 1259
Mystras

Giánnis did not argue when he was apprenticed to the local ironworker. Watching his mother grieve, he knew better than to press to train as a soldier like his lost brother and father. Chryse still cooked for four, and Giánnis ate as much as he could to compensate.

One night the cold snapped, edging the olive leaves in frost and sending uneasy drafts through the shuttered windows of the house. Chryse lay under her woolen blanket, listening to the imaginary sounds of her lost men breathing around her. When the knocking began, she hardly heard it. As it grew insistent, she sat up. A visitor so late, and on such a cold night, must be a message about a laboring mother. Wrapping the blanket around her, Chryse lit a lamp and went to the door. Demetrios stood outside with a bundle in his arms. Chryse beckoned him in. The bundle was moving; a tiny hand emerged from the cloth.

"I found him by the fountain along the path to the *kastron*; I didn't know what else to do." Demetrios put the baby in her arms. "He was naked. It was so cold; I was afraid he might be dead. I hope I was right to bring him to you."

"You were right." She wondered why Demetrios had been walking on a night like this. Moving the fabric aside, she saw the baby's gray eyes staring into her face, the colorless color that newborns share. She checked him for injury and saw none. Not quite a newborn; the cord had healed already. She looked again at those eyes and felt an unexpected shock of recognition. *I know you.*

Chryse whispered into the baby's tiny curved ear, forgetting Demetrios was there. The baby blinked, his eyes fixed on her face. She wrapped her arms tightly around his little back, feeling the heart beating fast against her own, like a bird's. He turned his head to search for her breast. Years since she'd borne her last child, she had nothing for him and would have to find a wet nurse. Then she saw, outlined in the light from the open window, the arc like a faint, healed scar across one cheek. *Lives.* She began to weep.

"I shall call him Elias."

She laughed through her tears, surprising herself and Demetrios with the sound. She laughed at the cycle of the cosmos, Alpha to Omega, knowing that a life had been created to follow on the heels of death.

GUILLAUME VILLEHARDOUIN
Autumn 1261
La Lacedemonie

Two years after he left for Pelagonia, Prince Guillaume returned to La Crémonie as the leaves were starting to turn. He tried to console himself with his old residence. His nobles accompanied him, shrunken versions of their former selves.

Anna welcomed Guillaume, holding their daughter; Isabelle's rose-gold hair was just as Guillaume had imagined it. His heart ached with the joy of return and the sorrow of what he had missed. Worst was the knowledge that the price of his freedom was his child's inheritance. The three fortresses—the castles where she could have learned to walk, steadying herself with a hand against the stone walls, the strongholds that should have become her base of power when she ruled in her own right—were lost. "My little princess, I shall win back Mystras for you," he promised.

La Lacedemonie was strangely deserted. In Guillaume's absence, the Greeks had moved up the hill to Mystras town. Where the streets had once buzzed with commerce, a few Frankish soldiers now wandered. Houses stood empty, stores were shuttered, and merchants had gone, taking their wares with them. The trees were losing their leaves, covering the ground with red and gold like an imperial carpet. Guillaume felt the transient beauty mocked him; soon the leaves would rot.

The sight of the Palaiologos double-headed eagle flying over the *kastron* dealt the final blow. Guillaume wept in Anna's strong arms. Anna had become a reigning princess, lawmaker, and mother, while he had withered from mighty prince to groveling prisoner. "I want my Mystras back, Anna. I made it, and it should be mine." Even to his own ears, he sounded like a petulant child.

Ω

Greek officials arrived in full force to take over Mystras castle just as Michael Palaiologos triumphantly reentered Constantinople. Guillaume, with almost delusional certainty, refused to accept defeat.

"They have taken Constantinople today," Guillaume said, fiddling with the lock of hair behind his ear, "but it will be ours tomorrow." Anna nodded to placate him. Her words on their wedding night seemed prophetic: *Ambition may end in despair*. The grim fact that her father had betrayed her husband shadowed their life together, though they never spoke of it.

Unwilling to give up his beloved castles even though he had vowed to do so, Guillaume visited Pope Urban, who obligingly declared Guillaume's promises unenforceable. Anna accompanied Guillaume to the papal audience; she knew where the pope's declaration would lead.

"An oath made by an imprisoned ruler to his jailer, when that jailer is a monarch bent on possessing the prisoner's own lands, is not binding in the eyes of God." Pope Urban folded his long-fingered hands before him, signet ring glittering, as he erased Guillaume's vows.

Back home, Guillaume donned his armor and paid an ostentatious visit to La Lacedemonie, his remaining loyal lords in tow, flaunting his lack of fear before Greek soldiers once loyal to Frankish rule.

"They will think you mean war," Anna whispered as their procession wound along the road below the *kastron*, where the double-headed eagle glared from the pennants.

"I am not afraid of war with the pope on my side," Guillaume said.

He ought to have been afraid. When Guillaume's army marched on Mystras, they met Greek forces expanded with new men. The Milengoi joined the Greek governor, and the *gasmoule* soldiers declared their allegiance to the Palaiologos regime. Guillaume returned from his failed attempt to retake

Mystras, riding away from the walls that stood as strong against their builder as they had against his enemies. Afterward, Guillaume lay staring at the ceiling of their bedchamber until the room grew dark. Once Isabelle was bundled into her crib, Anna gently undressed Guillaume and put him to bed as if he were another child.

A few months later, Guillaume could not bear to stay in the shadow of the palace that had once been his. Anna did not look back as they left La Lacedemonie for the final time.

ELIAS BORGHES, AGAIN
Pentecost Saturday, 1267
Mystras

I did not know who I was at first. I did not recognize my older brother Giánnis, who had once been younger than I. I did feel, growing up, that my mother had been there forever, but all children feel that way. Sometimes I would bring my hand to my chest, as if looking for something, but there was nothing there to find. Once my mother caught me in that instinctive motion, and her face went white. I asked her what was wrong. "All is well, little Elias," she said.

On an early spring morning of my seventh year, I woke to the nutty scent of boiling wheat and knew my mother was making *kollyva* to mark the Psychosabbaton, the Saturday of Souls. I found her in the kitchen, laying out the hot kernels on a cloth. On this day, I had to be careful; my mother's grief for those who were gone was close to the surface. My father had died before I was born of an illness my mother would not name, and an older brother, my namesake, of a battle wound that failed to heal. The less I spoke on those mornings before the *mnemosyno* memorial service, the better.

When I appeared at her side, she turned to me and kissed the top of my head. "Little Elias, up early again. Would you like to help?" I nodded, liking the rhythm in the kitchen, but also knowing that she'd give me at least a spoonful of honey.

As the soft wheat kernels cooled, we mixed them with honey, then walnuts and raisins. She showed me how to pile the kernels with my hands into a mound.

"It looks like a grave," I said, shivering.

"As it should." Her hands guided mine over the warm wheat.

"Why do we make a grave with wheat?"

My mother kept working as we talked. "What happens if you bury a seed in the ground?"

"It grows into a plant."

"And when we place the body of the departed in the ground?"

That one was harder. "We are not plants, Mitéra."

My mother laughed. "It's true, we are not." Her voice shifted into the rhythm of verse. "If a grain of wheat should fall into the ground and die, it abides alone; but if it dies, it brings forth much fruit."

"Dead people turn into fruit trees?"

"Of course not. But the *kollyva* helps us feel the connection between life and death and guides our prayers for those we have loved and lost."

"Why do we pray for dead people, Mitéra? Isn't it too late?"

"We pray because we love them, even though they are gone."

"So our love survives even though the people we love are dead?"

"Yes. Love transcends death."

I snuck a taste of honey while my mother wasn't looking. "Do we get to eat the *kollyva* after we pray?"

My mother laughed and leaned forward to kiss my forehead. "Yes, of course." She began to mound another *kollyva*. "Now help me finish these so we can bring them to the church."

Ω

We walked down the hill toward the church, gathering company as we went. Everyone talked to my mother. She was the best-known midwife in Mystras, and nearly every family had a baby she had helped into the world. Many of those babies were now parents themselves. Men also flocked to her side because they wanted to marry her. She had streaks of gray in her hair, but I thought she was the most beautiful woman in the world.

Paulus Asanes, an attentive widower whose son Demetrios had survived Pelagonia, walked so close to my mother that I thought he would step on her robe. From the way she held it up as he passed, it seemed she thought so, too.

"Chryse, you look especially beautiful today," Paulus said in greeting. My mother walked fast, and Paulus, as squat as my mother was long and slim, struggled to keep up.

"I look the way I always look," she said succinctly. But she did smile.

"I would be honored to join you in prayer for your departed," he said. "I grieve for my wife." He was trying for a more serious tone; it seemed to work.

"Your company is welcome." She nodded graciously, and

Paulus reddened with pleasure. We continued our brisk walk down the hill, Paulus managing to talk despite the pace.

"At last we can pray in our church, after so many years under the Franks. With a bishop of the true faith."

"At last indeed, *dóxa to Theó*," my mother said. *Thank God.* "At last we are speaking our language, worshipping as we were meant to, reading the names of our dead from the *diptychon*. We lived too long under the man who called himself Prince of Achaea."

Prince of Achaea. The royal title gave me an odd feeling, as if there was something I was supposed to remember. Governors from Constantinople lived in the palace on the hill, now that the prince with the strange French name was gone. My mother was still angry. Giánnis never mentioned the prince's name in my mother's presence. He had happier matters to talk about—his new wife, Angelina, who ruffled my hair and called me *mikrós adelfós* just as Giánnis did, like a real sister.

I looked down at the new church at the bottom of the hill. The red brick outlining the windows looked beautiful against the yellowish stone. The Metropolis of Agios Demetrios, dedicated to Demetrios, our saint of soldiers. I was proud that my father and brother had been soldiers, but I did not want a job that required me to kill. My mother did not want me to be a soldier either.

I'd sat for hours in the grass, watching the masons lay stone and the carpenters build the wood roof of the church, and shape the domes that would collect our rising prayers. They were still building it, but not on Psychosabbaton. Today the builders and masons, like us, would hear the names of their dead and pray for repose in death and resurrection. What if we prayed so hard that all the souls came back to life at once? An alarming thought. One must be careful with prayer, I decided.

Inside, the church was full of mourners holding lit candles, and smoke poured from swinging censers, filling the aisles. I loved the incense, though it made me dizzy. Frankincense, heady and sweet, balsam, like a carpet of needles in a forest, the musk of spikenard, the delicate bitterness of styrax.

"Elias, don't fall asleep. Marble is hard if you fall." Giánnis had arrived separately with Angelina. We placed our *kollyva* on the memorial table in front of the gleaming crucifix and candelabra, filigreed with gold.

"Each candle is a soul we hold in our hand," she whispered, and I lit and held mine as steadily as I could. My mother sang with her eyes closed, but I followed the paintings of the story of Saint Demetrios's life, bright against the white plaster of the apse in red, blue, and gold. Demetrios was one of my favorite saints: a soldier who rode a red horse. The paintings showed him locked in prison, still preaching the word of God to his disciples from his cell. I did not like the final image. Four spears pierced his body, their points emerging from his belly and chest. My side burned in sympathy. The bishop began to chant the *kontakion*.

My mother led me to the front of the church. I began to be afraid of the swirling smoke, the dizziness, the pain still sharp in my side. What if I died here, in this church on the cliff between our world and the next?

In the apse, the crowd pressed forward, making it hard for me to breathe. I gripped my mother's hand. The bishop began to recite the names of the dead, and I could sense them around us, drawn by our undying love. I heard my father's name, *Jéhan Borghes*, and Giánnis told me to blow out the candle. "As this candle is snuffed out, each of us will surrender our souls at the end of our lives," he whispered.

And then the bishop said the next name.

I knew my mother was crying. I could see the tears on her face, like shards of ice. My brother's face shrank until he looked like a baby, with golden curls and wide blue eyes. My hand went to my chest, groping for something to ease the rasp of my breathing.

"Elias Borghes," my mother said, echoing the bishop's words. Then the world broke apart. I remembered the moment of my first death, the sound of the stones of Mystras screaming my name, sliding against one another, cracking open to pull me back into the mountain's heart, to become part of Mystras's soul.

And so, in my seventh year, hearing my family mourn my first death, I knew that my mother had been my mother before. I knew that my brother, standing with his hand on my shoulder, had once been little to me. I did not remember everything, but I knew as much as my seven-year-old self could manage. And I knew that I had once loyally served the prince who had become our enemy. By the time I was eighteen, the prince was dead.

chapter thirteen

HELEN ADLER
July 2015
Mystras

Usually I wouldn't have checked my email at the dinner table, especially on vacation. But when we walked into the inn's restaurant, it was 11 a.m. in Bethesda, home of the National Institute of Neurological Disorders and Stroke, where the program officer for neurodegeneration was just leaving a meeting of scientists whose decision would dictate the next five years of my life. I was not the only grant-supported investigator with deep affection for a program officer, in my case Nolan L. Campbell. I'd never met the man, but our interactions, in which I poured my scientific dreams out to him and he told me (always) how exciting they sounded and (rarely but not never) told me that my proposals had been funded, were emotionally charged.

I was waiting to hear from Nolan when Alexander and I sat down to look at the Mystras Inn's tome of a menu. It was hard to imagine how they managed to keep such a huge selection of food available—there were only five other people in the restaurant, and one was Alexander. The two women who'd been on our tour of Spárti were ordering burgers. I suspected, having watched Alexander refuse to eat his Greek burger the day before, that it might not go well for them, as burgers here were flavored with cumin and cinnamon. Plus, they didn't come with a bun or ketchup. The fifth person was a man at a table in the other room of the restaurant, his crossed legs visible through the doorway.

I ordered too much food: two *mezedes* and two main dishes, in addition to tzatziki and fries. All the food came at once—eggplant stuffed with meat, phyllo spinach pastries, rabbit *stifado* (a stew with square nuggets of homemade pasta), and a shockingly large plate of pork chops covered with garlicky bread crumbs. I moved the fries and tzatziki to the far end of the table where Alexander couldn't reach them. He'd been reading a graphic novel from the local gift shop—*The Boy with the Cross on His Shield: A Story of the Crusades*—but looked up at me. "We ordered *this*?"

I nodded innocently. The book must have been pretty good, because he put a chop and a spoonful of stew on his own plate and went back to reading. I decided not to make him put the book down, in part because it allowed me to check my email without feeling guilty. "Oh my God." I read it again, hyperventilating.

Alexander looked up from his chop. "Are you okay?"

"I got a great score on my grant." Would I never stop being surprised by success?

"Wow, awesome." Alexander smiled. He had bread crumbs on his face. "Does that mean we can pay Aunt Jennifer back for the plane tickets?"

His question made me choke on my bite of chop—not long enough to make trouble, but long enough to make him forget he'd asked.

My project proposing to use reprogrammed neural stem

cells to treat a mouse model of Huntington's disease would likely be funded. I'd also proposed a plan to increase expression of modifier genes that might be protective against the development of Huntington's. The key was to make it radical enough to be exciting, but not radical enough to be shot down.

Alexander finished the last page of his book. I asked him how it was.

Alexander had managed, despite being absorbed with the story, to remove every piece of parsley from the stew. "It tries to make the bad guys look good."

"Bad guys?"

"The Crusaders. They called themselves pilgrims, but they took Constantinople from the Greeks," Alexander said, frowning. "Elias told me the story. How can you call it a holy mission when you are stealing and killing? What's so holy about that?"

"That's a great question."

Alexander pushed his plate away. "I don't want to talk about it anymore. What's your grant?"

"It's about those cells."

"You mean mouse cells?"

"Right. But in this experiment, we don't have to kill the mice to get their cells. We just take a few skin cells from their tails."

"Don't tell me how," Alexander said, knowing himself.

"Okay, but listen: we reprogram the skin cells using viruses so that they become pluripotent. You know what that means?"

"I know *potent* means powerful."

"And these are *pluri*-potent, so they have many powers. They can become any kind of cell in the human body. Even a nerve cell."

"Whoa, really?"

"Really. We grow pluripotent cells into nerve cells and put them into the brains of mice with a condition like Huntington's disease. We watch to see whether the cells will grow in the mouse brains and make up for the cells that don't do their job right."

"You can make one cell turn into another sort of cell? Could you take a drop of blood and get the cells out of it, and those new cells could fix people?"

"Maybe someday. We've made the cells, but we haven't put them into mouse brains yet. Now I'm going to get to do it." Exhilaration washed over me.

"Mama, you are amazing." Alexander grinned. "Can we have dessert?"

Ω

After dessert, we staggered into the next room. Alexander stopped at the counter where the inn's owner was arranging bottles of deep-green olive oil in rows. Alexander picked one up.

"We make," the proprietor said. He was tall and broad with a resonant voice and thick black hair. I imagined him as the lead baritone in a Verdi opera.

Alexander looked up from the bottle. "How do you make oil?"

"We pick olives, then press. You have seen the trees in the valley?"

"Yes, the short twisty trees with the silvery leaves."

"Exactly. I am Panos." The innkeeper smiled and held out one beefy hand for a handshake.

"Alexander."

"Would you like taste?" Panos opened one of the bottles and poured the oil into a white ceramic bowl. The surface swirled dark green on light. Panos handed us a basket of crusty white bread, still warm.

I was stuffed, and I assumed Alexander was, too, but we couldn't resist. The oil was slightly bitter, but full of fruit, as if the months of sun, the rocky soil, and the blue sky had been condensed into this magic liquid.

"Wow," I said. "I need more of that."

"Take," Panos said, his broad smile getting even wider.

Alexander dipped a second piece. "How do you make it taste like this?"

"We watch fruit to decide when to pick—olives stay longer on tree, taste changes. Color changes, too—when olives begin to turn color it is time. It depends also on type of olive, temperature, sun, rain."

"It sounds like science," Alexander said, taking a third taste. "My mom is a scientist."

"Ah yes? Excellent."

"She studies nerve cells," Alexander said, "and she's going to get a grant that will cure Huntington's disease."

"Brilliant family." Panos poured more oil.

"It tastes like Greece," Alexander said seriously, holding his oil-soaked slice up for emphasis. "I love Greece."

Panos reached out his hand to ruffle Alexander's hair.

"Greece loves you back, *to paidi mou*," he answered.

That's when I noticed someone standing behind us. It was the man from the Playmobil store, Lusignan. "Your mother is a scientist?" he asked.

I didn't like how he directed his question at Alexander.

Alexander stopped dipping his bread. "Yeah."

Lusignan turned to me. "I have a great interest in the sciences."

"I thought you were a professor of Hellenic studies."

He gave a mirthless smile. "Hellenic studies encompass great breadth."

"Breadth at the expense of depth, perhaps." I copied his smile.

He laughed as though I might be joking. "What is your area of scientific expertise?"

"Neuronal degeneration," I answered, trying to sound dull. It didn't work.

"Fascinating. There are funding opportunities for international collaborative projects here. If you give me your card, I can provide you with a list." I did not want to give Pierre Lusignan my card, but didn't know why. This man, however irritating he might be, was offering funding information. My name and work were already public. Maybe he knew something about the high prevalence of Huntington's here. I fished in my bag and found a business card.

"I shall certainly peruse your publications," he said, in that French-Greek accent. He handed me his. "I do hope you enjoyed your dinner. And such a delight to meet your son again." He pocketed my card and left.

Alexander put his unfinished piece of bread on the counter. "I'm done," he said.

"Thank you," I said to Panos, and elbowed Alexander to remind him to say the same.

Panos capped the olive oil bottle. "Come back in December and you will taste the fresh oil, just pressed."

Alexander turned to me. "I want to come back."

"We haven't even left yet." Alexander frowned. "I'll think about it." I bought three bottles, and Panos wrapped them carefully.

I'd had fabulous grant news, Alexander had mastered the

Crusades, and we'd shared an unusually successful multicourse meal, topped off with local olive oil. I had also found a potential source of information for my research. But I felt uneasy, the magic of the evening marred.

Ω

Alexander fell asleep quickly and assumed his usual position, taking up three-quarters of the bed. I squeezed onto the remaining quarter and tried to read a fluffy novel that I'd thought would be, if not scintillating, at least inoffensive. It turns out fluffiness can be offensive. I read four pages and gave up. Our run-in with Lusignan was nagging at me.

Using the hotel's spotty wireless, I looked up Pierre Lusignan, University of the Peloponnese, Department of Hellenic Studies. I saw a clip of the interview we'd watched live before we'd left New York, in which he'd disparaged the Greek rejection of the EU's austerity measures. It made me angrier now that I was here. The next hit was from the Socialist Union website. After a moment in which I imagined being blacklisted by our government and having trouble in customs on the way home, I clicked it.

> *Unpleasant sentiment has arisen in the wake of the capitulation of the Greek government to austerity measures imposed by the EU. Pierre Lusignan, the only French person on the faculty of the University of the Peloponnese, has taken an unsympathetic stand. His comments recall Nazi propaganda that justified Hitler's occupation of Greece under the Wermacht.*
>
> *"Today's Greeks are not Europeans," Lusignan said in an interview. "The purity of Hellenic blood is polluted in the*

*population of modern Greece. Europe has been forced to pay
for the spendthrift, drunken Greeks who dance with chairs
rather than pay their taxes. Greece is a third world country
and has no business in Europe using the euro."*

This was more interesting than the fluffy novel but vastly
more offensive. What did neurodegenerative disease have to
do with ethnic cleansing and the purity of Greek blood? The
combination made my skin crawl.

Ω

When I woke up the next morning, Alexander wasn't in bed. I
looked over at the window ledge, expecting to see him sitting
there, as he liked to do, watching the street. No. He wasn't in
the bathroom either.

Having a child is an exercise in the fear of loss. Even when
Alexander was still growing inside me, the realization that I
hadn't felt him move in an hour would turn me into a puddle.
After he was born, my fear got worse. The time his eyes rolled
back after he fell off a playground ladder at age two. And the
time our babysitter didn't answer her phone for three hours
and I thought for sure she and Alexander were lying under a
New York City taxicab.

Alexander kept not dying, and I managed to relax a bit.
But then, just when I'd learned not to worry, Oliver went
into the ocean and didn't come back. Now that I'd faced the
irrational cruelty of life, Alexander's absence threw me into
panic.

I raced out the door and around to the front of the building.
I scanned the plaza, the lobby, the restaurant. I barked a query at
the inn's openmouthed staff, then raced out again. No sign of
him at the corner grocery, or the tables where old men in white

shirts sat with their morning coffee and cigarettes. Then— *Oh thank God.* There he was, crouching at the base of the tree in the plaza's center. Totally fine and totally himself, curly brown hair, orange tank top and blue shorts, sweet face. I stood in my rumpled pajamas and thanked the universe for the reprieve.

Alexander, oblivious, was squatting in front of the old woman in black who'd staked out her spot on a chair in the early morning sun. I ran across the street barefoot and hugged him so hard he grunted.

"I didn't know where you were," I said, breathing hard.

"I didn't want to wake you."

"You can't go off without telling me."

Seeing my face, my sleep-tangled hair, my bare feet, Alexander looked chastened.

"I'm sorry." Alexander reached for my hand and pulled me down next to him. My anger at him melted into relief. "She's saying something. Can you understand her?"

The old woman's face was etched with lines, like fissured rock. Her clawed hands moved rhythmically, as if she were casting a spell. Her voice rasped three words in Greek.

"*Selídes pou leípoun.*"

"Seh-*lee*-days poo *lee*-poon?"

The old woman looked up abruptly, and one of her hands shot out and grabbed Alexander's wrist. "*Ne, ne.*" That much I understood—*Yes, yes.*

Alexander repeated the Greek phrase. The woman closed her eyes and let go of Alexander's hand, and her head dropped until her chin hit her chest. She seemed to be asleep.

"I'm going to ask Elias what it means," Alexander said, standing up and dusting off his shorts. "I saw him in the cheese store. Can I go?"

I'd just almost lost him, or thought I had, and now he expected me to say, *No problem, go somewhere by yourself.* But I wanted to celebrate Alexander's moment free of worry. Plus, he'd done just what I'd insisted he do—ask first.

Alexander put his hand on my arm, a strangely mature gesture, comforting me rather than the reverse. "Mama, don't worry. I've got this."

If he thought he had it, I should try to believe him. "Fine. But stay there until I meet you. I need to get dressed." Alexander, looking both ways, crossed the quiet street to the grocery store.

Ω

Alexander and Elias didn't see me at first, so I had the rare luxury of one-sided observation. They sat together at a small table against the wall, each on a wobbly folding chair. The table held an ancient napkin holder filled with the extremely tiny and delicate napkins ubiquitous in Greece. Alexander had a set of pens next to him; he held the blue one. In front of him lay a small notebook, open to a blank page. Elias was holding a pen, too.

I didn't want to interrupt the magic, so I stood at the counter behind an ancient humming beverage cooler, feigning interest in Greek periodicals. Alexander's shoulders hunched tensely, but the ink was going onto the page in lines that looked like letters. I turned to page two of an article I couldn't read. When I looked up, Alexander had written six lines.

"Beautiful," Elias said, his voice full of delight, the way mine would have been. The beauty was in the effort.

"I did it!" Alexander looked down at his own work with surprise. "*Selídes pou leípoun . . .*" he read.

Elias put one hand gently on Alexander's shoulder. "You

say the words beautifully—you sound Greek. I would never guess you were not from the Peloponnese yourself."

Alexander straightened proudly. "Thanks! What did you say it meant?"

"It means . . . the missing pages."

"Why would that old lady in the square say that?"

Elias frowned. "Has she spoken to you before?"

"Yeah. I don't remember the words that time, though."

I put down the incomprehensible periodical and came over to them. "Thanks for translating." Alexander's lines of writing were in Greek, the letters painstakingly neat. In several places, his pen had poked through the page from sheer effort.

"My pleasure," Elias said, rising from his chair. "Would you like to sit?"

I shook my head. "You know the elderly woman outside?"

"In a way," he said. "The way you know someone who has been in your life for a long time. By recurrence, rather than mutual understanding."

"I know what you mean," I said, thinking of a colleague who had recently died. I'd known her for ten years, had seen her every day, and one day she didn't come to work. Heart attack, I learned the next day, through an email from our department head. I felt like I didn't deserve to grieve her—we weren't exactly friends. But we'd talked a few times, and we'd exchanged a daily goodbye wave. Her death struck me hard because she'd always been there, then suddenly she wasn't.

"Recurrence counts for a lot," I said.

"Yes, it does." Elias capped his pen.

Alexander closed the notebook. "Why would she say 'the missing pages'?"

"I don't know. But if there are any pages missing in Mystras, the Mystras Archeological Museum—where you've already been—is the place to look for them."

"You mean the apotheosis museum? Can we go after breakfast?" Alexander leaped out of his chair. "And can you have breakfast with us?" Smiling, Elias looked at me, awaiting approval. I was impressed Alexander had remembered apotheosis, but not exactly surprised.

"Please do," I said, and although I'd agreed for Alexander, as we walked toward the Mystras Inn, I felt an unfamiliar wash of anticipatory pleasure.

Ω

I had a Greek coffee, which was so strong it made my heart race. (At least I think it was the coffee.) Elias ordered us break-fast—a vast platter of pastries. Alexander, predictably, chose the cake. I ate four flaky savory pies while the grandmotherly woman who'd made them circled our table, nodding with pleasure. Afterward, stuffed and happy, we strolled to the museum.

The Mystras Museum was deliciously cool at opening time, the air-conditioning undiminished by heat-radiating tourists. Elias, despite his proclaimed ignorance about the answer to Alexander's question, seemed to know what he was looking for.

"I recall something that might be useful to you," he said thoughtfully, as if the memory were rising to the surface. I liked his slow deliberateness, certainly not a characteristic I shared.

We stopped at an old manuscript behind glass, opened to a page of interest.

"They generally turn the pages weekly," Elias said. "But we can ask for help so we'll have an answer before next year."

Alexander stared hard at the letters. "Can you help me read it?"

"This is To Chronikon tou Moreos—The Chronicle of the Morea," Elias said. "There are four versions, all written in the fourteenth century, in Greek, French, Aragonese, and Italian."

"Could you read it out loud?" I said.

Elias turned to me in surprise. "You understand Greek?"

"No, but I like the sound."

His smile was slow and complete. "How lovely."

"It's beautiful," I said, "especially the way you speak it." He looked surprised; I'd surprised myself.

When he began reading, I closed my eyes to listen. Every few seconds I caught a word I understood, but finally I stopped straining for meaning. Elias's voice was low and melodic, like a stream over stones. He stopped, and I opened my eyes again.

Alexander put his hand on Elias's arm. "Is it about that French prince?"

"Yes. Much of this book is." Elias's forehead creased in concentration as he read. "This part is about Monemvasia. Do you know Monemvasia?" We shook our heads. "It is a remarkable place. Almost an island, off the coast of Laconia, linked to the mainland by a long, narrow causeway. Its name means 'one entrance.' The city is made from the rock; from the mainland, you can't see the town at all. It looks like a mountain in the sea. And when you are inside the walled town, it is as if you are on a massive ship. When it was built, a drawbridge could be pulled up when enemies drew near. It was impossible to take by force, especially because it was inhabited by some of the most ferocious and effective pirates in the world. But it was vulnerable to siege." Elias stopped.

"Read," Alexander said impatiently. Elias bent his head and translated as he read.

"When winter had passed and spring had come, the prince called upon his barons to besiege the castle of Monemvasia."

"Did the prince win?" Alexander said.

"Yes. But the book tells the story better than I could.

"The barons and the others from the principality prepared themselves, came most nobly, and went with the prince to attack the fortress of Monemvasia by land. The four Venetian galleys also came." Elias looked up.

"I've seen pictures of Venice," Alexander said.

The language was surprisingly gripping. Elias made the archaic turns of phrase sound natural. *"After the galleys had arrived, the prince ordered his siege by land and sea. But the people of Monemvasia, who knew how the prince was going to come and attack them, had already stocked up on everything they needed. When the prince laid siege, they were so well supplied that they didn't give a straw about him, or his siege, or his war. When the prince saw their great defiance, he was angry and swore by God that he would not lift the siege until he had taken Monemvasia . . . But the prince conducted the siege for so long—three years—that the people suffered from a great famine, all their food having run out."* Elias stopped.

"Why did you stop?" Alexander touched Elias's arm again.

"There's a note from a copyist in the margin. It says, *'Two pages are missing from the manuscript.'*"

We all simultaneously said, *"Selídes pou leípoun."*

Elias went to get the docent. She dryly told us that an English translation of the French chronicle that relied on commentary from a French archaeologist relying on the original Greek chronicle referred to lines missing in the Greek text, though it didn't provide the missing lines. And it was not clear why the note had been written on this page. I would have laughed at the convoluted references, but the docent—a dour elderly woman with tight ringlets of gray hair—seemed to have no sense of humor whatsoever.

"The missing pages," the docent said in a grave tone that seemed designed to put all but the most persistent scholar to sleep immediately, "are thought to explain how Prince Guillaume built Mystras. This castle is now a Unesco World Heritage Site. Copyists left these sorts of notes to direct future copyists, perhaps to leave room for those missing pages. Or to alert them of damage in the hopes it might be resolved. In this case, it seems the missing pages have never been filled in."

"I don't see anything missing." Alexander sounded impatient, and I didn't blame him.

The docent cleared her throat slowly. "We cannot see the exact spot where the pages are missing today because the book is not turned to that particular page." She looked over her glasses severely, as if she expected us to reach in with our filthy bare hands and start flipping pages. "As I mentioned, scholars posit that those missing pages relate to Mystras's founding." The docent paused, as if we were stupid.

"So no one has ever found the missing pages? And no one even knows what pages are missing?" Alexander cut to the heart of the matter.

"You could say that."

"So how Mystras was built is a mystery, and no one knows the answer, and we're looking for it. *Awesome*."

I heard the sound of a throat clearing behind us, and then, the French-Greek accent I'd come to recognize.

"How marvelous to be at the frontier of known history, just as your mother is, in science." We all turned around. I was unpleasantly surprised to see Pierre Lusignan again.

"Is your interest in this manuscript another example of the extraordinary breadth of Hellenic studies?" I didn't even try to sound cordial.

"I've looked up your articles; your area of expertise dovetails neatly with a specific interest of mine. I'd very much like to discuss it further with you."

My desire to find out about Huntington's in the Lacedaemon Valley warred with my personal discomfort. "It might be difficult to find time on vacation."

"Of course, so hard to schedule when traveling with children. You could bring your son along. I see you have a guide at your disposal." Lusignan turned toward Elias for the first time, glancing at his name tag. "Elias Orologas. Interesting name."

"Thank you," Elias said. "And whom do I have the pleasure of meeting?"

"This is Pierre Lusignan," Alexander said. Elias inhaled sharply.

"Pleased to make your acquaintance, Professor Lusignan," Elias said, sounding not the least bit pleased.

"Likewise." When Lusignan smiled, his thin lips nearly disappeared. "I am, by virtue of my role as a professor of Hellenic studies and ongoing projects specific to the Peloponnese, quite interested in local archives. I should very much like to talk to you further, Doctor Adler, to determine how our areas of expertise might intersect to mutual benefit."

I gave him a perfunctory nod that I hoped was not at all encouraging. When Lusignan had gone, I turned to Elias. "What did you say, just then?"

"I said *páli*."

"What does that mean?" Alexander still had hold of Elias's arm.

"Again," Elias said. "It means 'again.'"

Ω

I said a quick goodbye to Elias, which then turned into a longer goodbye, since I found it surprisingly difficult to stop talking, let alone leave his presence. "Thanks so much for helping Alexander, both of us, really. I mean, I know you were helping Alexander, but I got a lot out of it, too." I could feel myself blushing. "You're a really good guide. I mean really, above and beyond."

"I am deeply flattered," he said with a slow smile that made me feel slightly breathless. Or maybe I was just breathless from talking too much. "I certainly look forward tremendously to being your guide again." Maybe he said that to all the tourists. I left feeling pleasantly fizzy until I remembered the unpleasant encounter we'd just had with Lusignan.

I didn't realize I was pulling Alexander's hand in my eagerness to leave the museum.

"Mom, stop dragging me."

I stopped on the path. Waves of heat were already rippling over the flagstones. "Sweetie, I'm sorry." I kissed his hand. I hadn't done that in forever. He smelled like cake. "Listen, Alexander, I like it here as much as you do. And Elias is great. But it's time to go." I felt like the ruined village was closing in on us.

"You mean go back to the hotel?"

"I mean leave Mystras."

Alexander looked stricken. "Will we come back?"

"Maybe." Elias was a great guide, a *really* great guide, but I needed to get away from the Hellenic Studies stalker.

"How about we go to Monemvasia?" Alexander said, and then cleverly waited, counting on reason to do its work. I imagined packing our bags and leaving Lusignan behind. I imagined a vacation where we went somewhere other than Mystras. Monemvasia—an unassailable near-island of rock in the sea—sounded just right to me.

chapter fourteen

HELEN ADLER
Late July 2015
Monemvasia

When we arrived with our bags in the sun-baked central square of Monemvasia, Alexander immediately climbed the huge cannon in the plaza. He balanced on one foot on the end of the cannon's barrel.

"Be careful," I warned, pointlessly.

"I'm fine," he said.

I had to take his word for it. Alexander climbed three months before he could walk. At six, he shimmied up the pole of the schoolyard basketball net and intercepted layup shots, shocking everyone who watched. Everything had to be climbed.

Leaving him to it, I walked up to the whitewashed facade of the church in the plaza. Church of Christos Elkomenos—"Christ in Chains"—the sign read. A church had been on that site for more than twelve hundred years. I looked back over my shoulder at Alexander, who was pretending to load the cannon. I then fell deep into an informational sign about a life-size image of Christ that had been chopped into four pieces by thieves so it could fit through the door, then recovered and repaired.

Lost in thought, I took a few seconds to realize that a commotion was brewing in the plaza. The center of the commotion was, unfortunately, Alexander. I raced over to find him sitting on the ground with a big lump forming on his forehead, two skinned knees, and a sheepish look on his face. I made sure he was okay, and then thanked the elderly Greek first responder. She looked just like Yia Yia, our seat partner from the Emirates flight. Then I realized the woman actually was Yia Yia.

Ω

"But we've made hotel reservations." Yia Yia led us up a steep side street. Our suitcases bumped over the cobblestones.

"You cancel hotel," she said preemptively. "Stay with Yia Yia."

"I'll lose my deposit." I was short of breath from the walk; Yia Yia, tramping onward, wasn't.

"No pay, I call."

She turned up an even narrower street bordered by a low wall made of the same mix of stones as the rest of the buildings—mostly gray, some golden brown or rose.

The buildings in Monemvasia seemed to be part of the mountain rather than built on it. It was hard to tell where land ended and house began. Branches of gnarled fir trees with tight clusters of tiny needles arched over the path, casting welcome shade and filling the air with a resinous scent. Monemvasia felt made of a single substance; the tree was part of the house was part of the rock was part of the cliff was part of the island. And the island was bound inextricably to the sea. As we climbed, the glittering blue of the gulf appeared below, dotted with white surf.

Yia Yia stopped in front of a low doorway. On one side,

peach bougainvillea wound its way up the stone wall. "*To spíti mou*," she said gruffly, "my home." And after a second, she added, "*To spíti sou*."

Alexander looked up at her seriously. "What does *sou* mean?"

"Means 'your,'" she said, and opened the door.

Inside, it was blessedly dark and cool. Yelling into an ancient rotary phone, Yia Yia canceled our hotel reservation without penalty.

Yia Yia lived with her younger brother, Kostas, and his ebullient wife, Antonia. After introductions, simultaneously warm and awkward because of language limitations, we were shown our room: white-walled with a deep square window fitted with folding wood shutters, and a door to its own tiny stone balcony overlooking the sea.

Kostas and Antonia owned a taverna, and we were swept up into preparations for that night's celebration of the fiftieth anniversary of the restaurant. But first, Yia Yia led us to stools in the kitchen, where Antonia served an enormous lunch—she called it a "snack"—of chicken phyllo pies, Greek salad, and deep-fried local cheese. Afterward, we followed Yia Yia out to the steep hill behind the house to pick *horta* for the restaurant's dinner. *Horta* are mixed boiled greens, served with lemon juice and olive oil, a Greek culinary staple. Yia Yia told us the names of the plants in Greek: *moloha* (blue mallow), *radiki* (dandelion), *vleeta* (amaranth), and *glistrida* (purslane). We came back with heaping baskets and sunburned necks.

That night we chose our dinners from steaming pots on the stove, ate at tables packed with laughing Monemvasiots singing raucously in Greek while a traditional Rebetiko band played in the corner, danced with chairs and with each other until we were red-faced, laughing, and drenched with sweat, and finally threw plates across the room for good luck. Alexander, shocked at first by the deliberate breakage, hit his stride fast. As we downed honey-soaked pastry for dessert, Alexander leaned against my shoulder.

"Mama, do you think maybe now we can say we're a little bit Greek?"

"I'm sure Yia Yia would agree." I felt a little bit Greek, too.

Alexander fell asleep on a cushioned bench. When the night ended in a round of retsina-scented hugs and two-cheeked kisses, Kostas escorted me home, carrying Alexander in his arms, then tucked him gently into bed.

When I awoke at nearly noon, Alexander stood on the tiny patio overlooking the gulf. I followed his gaze to the straight hazy line where the sea met sky. The air smelled like wild thyme, mixed with buttery dough baking.

I sidled up next to him. "What are you looking at?"

"The water."

I knew what he wasn't saying.

A soft knock on our bedroom door heralded Yia Yia's arrival. The baking smell intensified—some of it came with her from the kitchen, buried in the folds of her black dress and cardigan, her unvarying outfit.

Alexander's mouth was as straight as the horizon's edge. Yia Yia produced a wordless sound, a grunt crossed with a sigh. "You tell Yia Yia?"

The air hummed with cicadas, and below us the waves broke against the rocks: the sound of Alexander not answering.

"You think of *patéras*." We didn't need a translation. She reached out to touch Alexander's cheek, and he softened into it, like a cat. "Come." We followed her obediently.

Downstairs was dark after the bright terrace. She led us into a room smaller than ours. It held a narrow bed covered with a multicolored embroidered quilt, a spindle-legged chair, and a battered wooden chest. She opened the lid and rummaged inside, drawing out a box small enough to hold in one hand. She motioned Alexander to sit beside her on the bed, and drew an oval metal pendant from the box. It looked bronze but dark with age, strung on a chain. She held it up in the light from the tiny window.

"This Profitis Ilias," she said. "Today, twenty July, his day." The icon depicted the prophet with a raven sent by God to bring him food. "He heals who honor him. Take." Yia Yia lowered the amulet over Alexander's head.

"Wow," Alexander said, looking down at his chest. "Thank you. It looks really old."

Yia Yia nodded sagely. "Seven hundred years."

"SEVEN HUNDRED YEARS?" I was horrified. "Shouldn't it be in a museum?"

Yia Yia chuckled. "No museum. Family."

I tried again. "This is such a lovely gift. But we can't possibly take it from you."

"You take." Yia Yia brushed her hands together in a gesture that seemed to settle it. "Now breakfast." There was no use arguing.

I ate too many *amygdalota*, a local sweet made from almonds and sesame and dusted with powdered sugar. Yia Yia took us on a path that wound up to the entrance to Monemvasia's mostly ruined upper town, where a domed octagonal church perched on the edge of a sheer cliff. She brought us to a graveyard with a few stones still standing, so old they were hardly legible. She knelt in front of one grave.

"Yia Yia *oikogéneia*—family," she said, then repeated the Greek for Alexander: "ee-ko-YE-nee-ah." We knelt beside her.

Alexander traced the letters on the headstone. "Spy-ri-don. Spyridon?"

"*Ne, ne!*" Yia Yia beamed at him. "You know Greek!"

"Better than my Greek," I said, impressed. Elias must have taught him a lot. I had a sudden surprising pang, remembering we'd left him behind. "This was your ancestor?"

"Yes, Spyridon. Pirate. This his *enkolpion*. Spyridon have son and then his son and then his son and then finally my grandfather get *enkolpion*. Kostas wear it when he was small, but now his wife give him something else to wear." She gave a Wearily Tolerant Greek Mother-in-Law look.

"En-*kol*-pi-on." Alexander slowly repeated the syllables, getting another enthusiastic "*ne*" from Yia Yia. "Don't you need the protection?" Alexander fingered the amulet at his chest.

"I die soon," Yia Yia responded. She didn't look any closer to death than she had the first time we'd met.

Alexander frowned, and I realized how her refrain might affect him. "You will *not* die," he said fiercely. She put her hand on his shoulder, and gave a paradoxical Greek nod I was finally getting used to.

We stayed for a while on the cliff. Alexander wandered around the stones, reading the names. Yia Yia gathered wild herbs, depositing them in a basket. I sat on a low, crumbling wall, staring out at the hills dotted with green scrub, the cloudless sky, and the rippling sea. I imagined the centuries of prayer that this church had witnessed, the pirate who had worn the amulet around my son's neck, and the many hands that had touched the prophet's image, finding comfort there.

Ω

The next morning, I found Alexander on the terrace again. At this hour, the terrace was in shade, but the water reflected sun. "Where do you want to go next?"

Alexander turned the *enkolpion* over in his hand. "I want to go back to Mystras. But we can go somewhere else first if you want."

"Wow, thanks for letting me make a decision."

His smile faded slightly. "Are you making fun of me?"

"No, no, sweetie. I'm just . . . being an annoying mom, as usual."

He shook his head. "You're not annoying." After a few beats, he added, "Not usually anyway."

After a round of fierce hugs and promises to visit again, Yia Yia, Kostas, and Antonia pronounced us *oikogéneia*. We pulled our suitcases along the narrow spit to the mainland to catch the public bus.

I'd chosen Nafplio as our next destination, a once-Venetian outpost on the eastern coast of the Peloponnese. Compared to the eerie quiet of Mystras, Monemvasia had been a rocking party, but Nafplio made Monemvasia feel like the quiet car on an Amtrak train. The houses in Nafplio were painted in a candy jar mix of pink, pale green, and yellow. Handcrafted jewelry glittered in store windows, and happy crowds spilled out of packed tavernas. When we passed by, lilting music followed us down the lamp-lit streets.

On our second day, Alexander dragged me into a self-serve candy shop, where he filled two huge bags with gummies designed to extract teeth, and I indulged my obsession with locally made chocolates. Clothing boutiques sold breezy dresses that promised to make the wearer's life immediately carefree. I succumbed to a starfish-patterned scarf but had few illusions about its power to change me.

That night, when Alexander had fallen asleep in a candy-induced stupor, I flipped open my laptop while guiltily finishing off the chocolates. Guilt faded as I googled. The University of the Peloponnese had a branch in Nafplio, and the grad student who'd written her thesis on Huntington's in Sparta was on the faculty there. She was in the Arts Department, which I found as odd as a professor of Hellenic studies running a foundation on neurodegenerative diseases. The next day after breakfast I set Alexander up with five downloaded movies, a tray of pastries, and a promise of check-ins from the grandmotherly guesthouse owner, Irini.

Ω

The newly minted assistant professor was named Elektra Agathangelos, which sounded portentous, especially after I found out that *agathangelos* means "bearer of good news." Remarkably, she was happy to meet with me immediately. I suspected she was so newly appointed that my arrival was maybe a relief.

She had round cheeks and blond braids and looked about twelve, especially when she was enthusiastic. And her last name turned out to be accurate—she'd studied Huntington's in the region and was happy to talk to me about it. She served me Greek coffee so strong I thought my spoon would stand up in it. She bounced into her desk chair, and I lowered myself with comparative creakiness into mine. Once we got talking, I forgot her apparent youth in the mutual pleasure of academic interest and her obvious expertise. She spoke English with a faint accent that reminded me of Elias. A surprising number of things reminded me of Elias.

"You read my thesis?" She grinned. "I thought no one other than my adviser and defense panel knew it existed."

"I know what you mean." My defense was on an obscure interaction in a single-cell organism with distant relevance to human biology.

"You're the first person to visit me in this office. Other than my mother. She comes to stock the refrigerator." She opened a minifridge next to her desk. It was jammed with food. "Snack?" She extracted a huge slab of cheese pastry and heated it in a tiny microwave that sparked alarmingly. She gave me two thirds of the pie.

"So how did you end up in the arts school? That seems distant from your thesis."

She blushed. I wished I looked that nice when I was embarrassed. "It was the only faculty position near home. They offered me a job in a new departmental track—Americans call it STEAM."

The *A* had recently been added to the acronym that used to include Science, Technology, Engineering, and Math. Now Art was thrown in. The combination stretched the imagination.

"You're bringing the STEM to their *A*?"

She laughed. "Exactly. Except I'm not even a capital-*S* Scientist—I'm a historian. I think I'm the best *S* they could get. The department is dedicating resources to integrative projects. I'm creating a multidisciplinary project on the history of chorea. You're one of very few people with an interest in Huntington's disease in the Peloponnese, and I probably know them all."

That sounded promising. "Maybe you'll introduce me to the others." She smiled. "I study models of neurodegeneration—Huntington's disease in particular. You probably know that the discovery of a large HD family in Venezuela, all descended from one affected ancestor, led to the discovery of linkage to Chromosome Four." I stopped to make sure I hadn't lost her. "So when I saw your article I got excited. That's why I'm here."

"You think our local story might lead to a medical breakthrough?"

"You never know where a breakthrough will come from."

Elektra leaned forward. "Here in Achaea we have two informative families. In one family, the disease carried through the generations undiluted, and in some cases got worse with each generation. In fact, there are still affected descendants alive today."

"Anticipation," I murmured, thinking of my conversation with Alexander.

"Right. But in the other family, the disease suddenly stopped transmitting in the thirteenth or fourteenth century. It was recorded generation to generation, and then poof, it was gone."

"Do you know why it disappeared?"

"There are a few possible explanations. Since the child of someone with HD has a fifty percent chance of having the disease, it could be a coincidence. Except that no one in that family showed any signs again. Or my records could be incomplete." She smiled shyly. "But I have a more exciting theory."

"Tell me."

"The original HD family was French. Their descendants ended up in thirteenth-century Mystras under Prince Villehardouin."

"My son is a Mystras fan." Elektra laughed, knowing what I meant. "We know about Villehardouin."

"You are probably the only Americans who do. Around that time, the family with HD was living and dying in Mystras. It's hard to track, since the disease wasn't named until the nineteenth century, so we have to rely on descriptions of the time. Chorea was called 'the dancing mania.' The word comes from the Greek, *chorea*, meaning 'dance.' "

"English speakers have a lot to thank Greece for."

Elektra smiled so broadly she gained three dimples. "That description, plus the hereditary nature of the disorder, which we were able to get from diaries, letters, and records of deaths and births, helped track generations of a family from France who came to the Peloponnese during the Frankish occupation. Their descendants suffered from abnormal movements and insanity, and they died terrible deaths. The family was prominent in both France and Greece, so those records were easy to trace. Recently I found out that a French soldier who came to Mystras to fight in Villehardouin's garrison developed HD, too. His wife was a healer, probably a midwife, and kept meticulous records. The soldier's grandfather died with chorea. The soldier had two sons, and neither one got it. In fact, it never showed up again in any descendants of that family, even though the gene doesn't usually go into hiding."

"I like your wording," I said. "It's like the arts version of HD."

She grinned. "That's why they want me here." We took bites of our cheese pie. "Here's the exciting part. It turns out, from documents recently identified, that the soldier was related, several generations before, to that original French family."

"So there was one founder."

"Right. But what was special about the soldier's line that made them beat the disease while the originating family wasn't so lucky? The French soldier married a Greek woman, the healer. And after that, no more HD in that family. Ever."

I had a shiver of excitement, a hair-standing-on-end feeling. I slowly let the thoughts turn into words. "So you think the Greek family was carrying a protective gene that prevented HD from appearing in subsequent generations?"

"Exactly. And it's important from a sociodemographic perspective. The mixed-blood Greek/French population, called *gasmoules* at the time, were discriminated against. But it looks like they were, like many 'mutts'—no offense meant—healthier than the 'pure' line. When you contrast that against ethnic superiority theories—Byzantine, Nazi, white supremacist—it's a triumph for biology." I thought she was going to levitate right out of her chair.

I was levitating with her. "The Greek modifier gene, if it exists, is a gold mine."

"Exactly!" Elektra crowed.

My heart was racing, either from the coffee or the thrill of discovery. "You mentioned the descendants of the original French family are still alive? Are you in contact with them, by any chance? Or with the *gasmoule*'s descendants?"

Elektra wiped her mouth with a napkin. The phyllo flakes had a tendency to go wide. "The answer to the first question is yes. As for contact, we are working on it."

There was that "we" again. She did say she knew everyone in the field. "What got you interested in this? You can't have come to it by accident."

Elektra frowned, thinking. "Have you ever sat in a lecture listening to the speaker and then suddenly something clicks and you think—'That's it. That's what I want to study'?"

"Actually, I have."

"I was at a lecture about French-Greek relations from 1200 to the War of Independence. The professor was so passionate, like it mattered to him personally. It made me hang on his every word. Afterward I went up to the lecturer and asked whether I could work with him. He said yes, and here I am."

"Do you still work with him?" I'd managed to finish my pie, but only because I was wearing elastic-waist pants.

"I do. He has been gracious enough to mentor me from advisee to colleague. That's not an easy transition, but I got lucky." I knew what she meant. I'd left where I'd trained for that reason. "His passion is both academic and personal. He's traced his ancestors to that original French family; he came to the topic through genealogy research. Because he has family with HD it makes him kind of ferocious, in a good way. He might be more helpful to you than I am. I could introduce you."

"That would be amazing." I started to clear the dishes.

She took them from me. "Don't bother. The only sink is in the bathroom, and it is hopelessly clogged by yesterday's lunch." She sighed. "I'll give you his contact information. I'm sure he'd like to meet you. I hope what I've learned can make a difference." She wrote on a piece of paper and handed it to me with a smile.

I looked at the name, not believing what I was reading.

Professor Pierre Lusignan.

Ω

Alexander had finished the videos, his gummy candy, and the pastries by the time I returned. He was ready for an outing, so we climbed up to the Palamidi fortress, Nafplio's landmark monument. The ascent required either 913 or 999 steps (depending on where you stopped counting) to a fort overlooking the sea.

At the top, Alexander took my hand, interlacing his fingers with mine. "Mom?"

"Yes?"

"You know how sometimes you miss someone because you are having a really hard time and you wish you could talk to that person about it?"

I swallowed. "Yes, I know how that is."

"So . . . well, you know also how sometimes you miss someone because you are having such a good time you wish they could be here to share it?"

"Yes, I definitely know that, too. Are you feeling one of those things?" I tried not to sound like a psychotherapist.

Alexander let go of my hand and picked up a stray pebble. "Both." He suddenly threw the stone over the low wall surrounding the summit. I snuck a look to make sure there was no path below on which unsuspecting tourists might be walking. There wasn't, fortunately.

"Me too," I said. He sighed and picked up another pebble. "Hey, Alexander, can you get me one of those rocks?"

He turned to me, surprised. "Really?"

He handed me a pebble, and I threw it as hard as I could. "Can you beat *that*?"

Alexander smiled broadly. "I can *totally* beat that." We flung rocks down the slope until our arms ached.

After dinner, Alexander curled up on his side of the bed in our hotel room and drifted off to sleep. I missed Oliver, both for the misery he was not there to help me with and for the pleasure he couldn't share. But for the first time in two years, I missed someone other than Oliver. As I drifted off to sleep, I wondered what Elias would have said if he'd been at the Palamidi fortress with us. And I wondered how far he would have thrown his rock.

By the next afternoon, we were on the bus to Mystras.

chapter fifteen

MARCEAU LUSIGNAN
September 1281
Mystras

Marceau watched his twins for signs. Would his son or his daughter succumb next? Marceau's wife had lived only long enough to give them their names, Fedryc and Osanne, before she bled herself white into the linen of the birthing bed.

Twenty-one years before, Marceau had not called Jéhan Borghes's widow to attend the birth. Even if Marceau had wanted filthy Greek hands on his wife, he could not think of Chryse without breaking into a sweat. The sweats came more often now, leaving his clothing dark and damp. He believed Chryse knew what he had done—attempted to do. She must have suspected his plot, as fruitless as it might seem, to squeeze life from the corpse of her eldest son. The only one who knew the truth—his grandfather—was long dead. Marceau's mother, always a faint shadow flickering in the corners, had died of a tumor in her belly. Evrard had died at Pelagonia. Now Marceau had only his two grown children for company, and they might also harbor the Lusignan curse.

The young midwife, bright-eyed with a halo of fuzzy hair peeking out from her cap, had babbled cheerfully as she'd washed her hands. "A happy day for Mystras," she had crowed, telling them that Chryse had a new son, too. A foundling, but welcome. "She's named him Elias, in memory of her departed son. Someday perhaps little Elias and your babe will play together." *Elias, again?* And then "*Des jumeaux!*" the girl had exclaimed with joy when she saw there was not one baby, but two. Then the bleeding began. After the disastrous birth, the midwife fled, spattered with gore.

Marceau stayed in Mystras after most Franks had left. When his wife was still alive, she'd begged to leave. "What is there for us here, with all these Greeks, and our prince gone to Kalamata? Could we not follow?" She whispered because she thought it would make him less likely to hit her, but she was wrong. The quieter she became, the more infuriating he found her. He wanted to beat in the faces of the Greeks who whispered about him when he passed. He knew they saw his emaciated body, his continuously flickering face—an eyebrow lifted, an uncontrollable bend of the head, his clownish protruding tongue. They saw the arching of his back like that of a fish caught on a line, flopping and gasping for breath. He'd been allowed to stay in the castellan's house because it came with his years of service as castle warden for the prince, but charity was not friendship.

He did not tell his wife why he stayed in the town of ghosts, down the hill from the growing beauty of Mystras. *You will find him here*, the prophetess had said, even after Marceau's hope should have died, along with his quarry, buried in secret in an unmarked grave. *You will find him here* kept Marceau tethered to this place in which he was at best unwelcome and at worst an enemy. He did not know what he was looking for, but he could not leave until he found it or died trying. If one or both of his twins might harbor the curse, Marceau must unearth the antidote. He was prepared to fight for that slim hope and to pass the prophecy on to his children, when he could no longer carry out the task himself.

ELIAS BORGHES
October 1281
Mystras

Fourteen years after my epiphany at the Psychosabbaton, I had still not told my mother what I knew about my origins. I went with her to Matins services to chant the doxology at dawn, in the same church where I realized I'd been born twice. I did not tell my mother that I prayed for resurrection while living the heresy of transmigration of the soul. I did not tell her that a sort of magic had shaped my recurrence, a magic not in keeping with doctrines of our faith. I struggled to reconcile my faith with my knowledge, and I struggled alone.

Every day, small things reminded me of my past life. I'd help my mother clear the table to find, under my plate, faint lines I'd scratched with a knife while my mother wasn't looking, in the days when Giánnis was my younger brother. One day, when I was walking in the valley, I saw our old home. The yard that had once been a vast battlefield for my games with Giánnis now looked tiny, its one olive tree casting a small ring of shade. I still loved to watch my mother record a new life in her logbook late at night after she returned from a birth. Now the book was worn and stained, and she'd almost reached the last page.

I also did not tell my mother that I was falling in love with a Frankish girl. My mother might have been sympathetic, given that she'd married my Frankish father. But in my second look at twenty-one, I was old enough to realize that children are perversely drawn to what will pain their parents the most.

I was working in the governor's palace, once the palace of the prince. Guillaume Villhardouin had died three years before, holding desperately to his few remaining territories. Part of me felt sorry for the prince exiled from his beloved Mystras. He had been kind to me. But my current self, the boy raised in Mystras free from Frankish dominion, had no reason to be either loyal or sorry.

My mother presented me for employment to the governor as soon as I came of age. "You will serve this city all your days, Elias," she'd said. I did not yet know why she had insisted with such gravity.

I first saw the Frankish girl on the great lawn outside the governor's palace. It was the only flat place in Mystras; villagers congregated there for meetings, celebrations, and nothing in particular. The Franks, in their last few years of dominance, had built an elegant house near the palace for the prince's castellan. Even after the prince left, the castellan stayed on like a ghost of the dead regime. He had apparently gone mad, becoming a twitching, staggering shell of a man, prone to outbursts of violence. People said he once cut the head off his own cat when she'd deposited a dead mouse on his doorstep. When I first heard his name—Marceau Lusignan—I knew there was something I should remember about him. Some memories blurred, and no amount of effort could bring them into focus. My mother, usually tolerant of illness, psychic or otherwise, warned me away from him and rapidly silenced my questions. Since the mention of his name clearly angered her, I stopped mentioning him.

The Frankish girl looked like no one I'd ever seen: she was strangely tall, and her skin was nearly translucent, with a faint spray of freckles dusting her nose and cheeks. *Like dust fallen from stars.* Poetry was the first warning that my heart had leaped ahead of the rest of me.

One windy November day, I stopped to look at this tall, pale girl with a halo of red hair. She left it down, unlike other girls, so it blew about her in the wind. I could not stop staring. Gathering wild greens for *horta*, she had a basket on one arm and a knife in her hand.

"I won't stab you with it, in case that's what you're worried about," she said. I was too stunned to answer. The girls I knew did not talk to boys that way. She had an accent I could not place. Her hand with the blade flicked once; she gripped it tighter. Perhaps she'd almost dropped it. Realizing I was still looking anxiously at her knife, she put it in her basket.

"Where are you from?"

Her answer was unexpected. "You think I don't sound Greek. I speak French at home. Now you probably will think I *was* trying to stab you. But this is where I live, and that's what I am, and I can't help that."

I shook my head, bewildered. "You talk extremely fast."

She laughed. "I can't help that either. I don't suppose you speak French?"

I shook my head, but then that feeling came over me, and I wondered whether I might.

"I could teach you. But now I've got to go." She turned and left, running, her hair flying out behind her. I'd forgotten to ask her name.

I started to learn French secretly, using an old Bible of my father's as a text. It came surprisingly quickly.

The next time I saw her, I was practicing in a quiet spot

in the west portico of the Agios Demetrios church. It was my favorite place to sit and think. A shadow fell over my page, and I looked up to see her standing over me.

"*Bonjour*," I blurted out.

"*Bonjour*," she answered easily. She crouched down to see what I was reading. "Whose Bible is that? It can't be yours."

"I might ask what you are doing in a Romaioi church!" I said, stung.

"I'm sorry," she said immediately. "I ought not to have said that."

Her disconsolate expression made my resentment fade. This conversation had quickly exceeded my rudimentary knowledge of French, so I switched to Greek. "My father was Frankish; this was his. But he died years ago."

She sat down next to me, her dark-green dress and cloak spreading out around her. She was so close I could smell the chicory and dill that she'd been picking, but also something musky and sweet. I thought it might be the scent of her skin.

"When I am afraid or sad, I come to this church to stare at the painting of the Virgin. She calms me," she said.

"Why are you afraid and sad?"

"I am more often alone than I would like." She turned away.

I could not keep from touching her shoulder. She *was* crying, and another impulse made me brush her tears away. "I don't know your name," I said. "I am Elias."

She was quiet for a long time. "If I tell you my name," she said finally, "you must promise not to disappear."

I frowned, wondering what she could say that would make me do such a thing. "I promise."

I could hear her breathing. Finally, she answered. "My name is Osanne Lusignan."

Not only did I find a Frankish girl to obsess over, but I found the one girl who—from my mother's perspective—was the worst possible choice. I did not know why, but my mother despised her father with an intensity that rivaled any other emotion I'd ever seen her exhibit. But I was falling in love with her.

chapter sixteen

ELIAS BORGHES
November 1281
Mystras

"Sicily is closer than you imagine," Mystras's ambassador to Emperor Palaiologos's court in Constantinople said grimly. "Frighteningly close." The council meeting was off to an alarming start. A fire sputtered in the council room hearth, giving off mostly smoke, barely enough heat to take the chill edge from the room while cold rain beat against the closed shutters. The weather matched the mood. I stared at the map spread out on the table. By then, I was working in the governor's palace as part of the diplomatic staff. My mother, who had delivered the ambassador's son years before, a breech baby who would have died in less experienced hands, had secured me the post. Because of my position, I heard bad news early.

Our enemy, Charles of Anjou, already crowned king in Paris, had killed the other claimants to the throne of Sicily and was now king there, too. Charles wanted Constantinople next. He was amassing a huge armada in Messina, the port of his Sicilian holdings. I imagined hundreds of tiny ink-drawn ships making their way to Constantinople, crossing the parchment sea.

The ambassador told the council the details. "King Charles has a hundred ships in Sicily, and three hundred more in Naples and Provence. Those ships will carry eight thousand cavalrymen, two thousand iron mattocks, sledges, axes, iron shovels, ropes, and kettles for boiling pitch. Charles has ordered four thousand iron stakes from Venice, and two thousand shields from Pisa, decorated with the royal lilies. Those stakes take aim at our hearts, the axes at our skulls. Do not imagine yourselves to be safe, just because we are here in Mystras. In the spring, those ships will sail from Messina toward the Golden Horn. If Constantinople falls again into Latin hands, Mystras will be next."

That month, Charles of Anjou's longtime friend, Martin IV, ascended to the papacy, then took deadly aim against our emperor, using the church as a weapon. I brought the news home to my mother from the governor's office.

"Pope Martin has dared to excommunicate the emperor?" my mother asked through gritted teeth. She was kneading bread so savagely I was afraid she would break her hand. "No Latin Catholic priest, no matter how high his throne, can denounce a ruler of our church." *Pound, pound.* "Tell me the language of the papal bull."

"Pope Martin denounced Emperor Michael Palaiologos as a perfidious heretic," I said, "and has given his blessing to Charles of Anjou to reclaim Constantinople. He proclaimed *'the Greeks can only be cured of their religious errors by force.'*"

My mother slammed the dough again, then looked up at me. "The new pope has declared the next 'holy' crusade. The man *must* be stopped. You, Elias, must stop him."

"Me? I am no one. I am lucky to be in the room with the ambassador at all."

"I know very well who you are, Elias. And I think you do, too."

"What do you mean?" I asked, carefully. She waited. I looked at her hands. Her knuckles were swollen with age, but her strength was undiminished.

"Tell me what you know, Elias."

"I have been here before."

"Yes, you have. And do you know why?"

I had never thought to ask that question, even of myself. "Why?"

"At your birth, I dedicated your life to Profitis Ilias. He gave you your name and assured your survival. That dedication came at a price." She looked as if she were traveling back into the years. "You are my son, but you belong to Mystras, the heart of Romaioi renewal. You must do everything in your power to protect it. Whatever is asked of you in the service of this place, do not shrink from the task."

We were two specks of dust in the cosmos, two brief occurrences in the endless cycle of Alpha to Omega and back again. I did not know then that my second life was only the beginning.

"I will do what is asked of me, though I cannot imagine how," I said.

"For now, you can help me with the bread," she said simply, so I did.

Ω

The opportunity to be of use arose sooner than I expected. A *gasmoule* soldier returned to Mystras from Pelagonia, decades after being presumed dead, and joined the ambassadorial council. He'd been taken prisoner but, after swearing his allegiance to the Palaiologos Empire, had served Emperor Michael. "His Greek blood saved him," my colleagues in the governor's office said. After twenty years of loyal service, he was sent to Mystras to help establish the new despotate-governorship of the Morea. Pantaleon was his name, and when I saw his dark brows that grew together in the middle, and the asymmetry of his missing ear, the past flooded over me. I remembered his teaching, and the seed of doubt he'd planted in my heart, which had now grown into maturity. Then I'd been a *gasmoule* who served the prince. Now my Romaioi side had fought for supremacy and won.

Pantaleon could not know that we had met before, but once we began to work together in the governor's palace, he again trusted me with a secret. I often stayed late after work, copying notes I'd made of the day's meetings. Because I was a painfully slow writer, at the end of each day I privately wrote the records out in full. One late November day as I struggled with the task, I looked up to find Pantaleon watching me.

I blushed. "I need to rewrite the meeting's records," I said miserably, "to be sure they are legible."

Pantaleon could have asked the obvious—why in God's name was a young man who could barely write acting as a scribe?—but instead he smiled gently.

"Attention to detail is the mark of a man who strives not to make mistakes."

I put down my pen. "That is a kind interpretation."

"Not just kind," Pantaleon said.

"I may not be brilliant, but I am thorough."

"You remind me of your older brother."

"Giánnis?"

"Ah, no, I meant Elias. I was sorry to hear of his death. I extend my deepest regrets to you and your family."

Unexpected, to see the face of someone who mourns your death. "I wish I'd met him," I said.

Pantaleon sighed. "I feel like it was only yesterday that I left him on the battlefield. May you merit his blessed name."

"I hope to," I stammered.

"I have a task for you, one you'll probably do better than writing."

His honesty made me smile. "I can't do anything worse than I do this."

Pantaleon leaned forward. "What I propose carries risk and may take you far from home. But if all goes as planned, it will keep Constantinople from Charles of Anjou's grasp and assure Mystras stays in our hands. Will you hear what I have to say?"

Whatever is asked of you in the service of this place, do not shrink from the task.

"I will," I answered. And Pantaleon told me the plan.

Ω

My reputation as a slow secretary became a perfect cover for my double life. My night work also became time I could dream of Osanne: her asymmetric smile, the way her hands moved in the air like birds when she spoke, and the smell of hillside herbs she collected, which caught in the fabric of her clothes and in her loose hair.

The evening after my meeting with Pantaleon, Osanne found me writing in the governor's palace. She was strangely independent and often alone. She roamed freely, often exiting the city's protective walls and wandering across the grassy slopes. Because her brother worked in the governor's palace, too, she could enter at will. This made meeting her inevitable.

"I thought you might be here."

"I can never finish in the time allotted." I sighed.

"Being slow prevents errors, I've heard. Not that I've ever tried that method." She twisted a lock of her hair around her fingers.

"I'm slow of necessity, unfortunately."

Osanne looked over my shoulder at my work. Her warmth radiated onto the back of my neck. "Need help?"

I turned to look at her. "You aren't going to say 'Was your mother so busy pulling out other people's babies that she had no time to teach you your letters?'"

"I meant, can I help *you*? There is no shame in needing help."

I looked at her wide green eyes and the firm set of her jaw. For all her delicate beauty, she was a force not to be underestimated.

"If you can write better than I can, then yes."

She slid onto the bench next to me and took the pen from my hand. In a few minutes, what would have been an hour's agony was over. "Now we have time for other things," she said.

"Other things?" She was so close that I could hardly keep her freckles in focus.

"I am sitting close to you because I want to be close to you," she said.

On the current of her outrageous words, I kissed her. Her lips were slightly parted, and she tasted like mint and honey.

"That is what I'd hoped you'd do," she said, not even whispering.

"That is what I hoped I'd do, too," I answered, not sure whether I was making sense. And then, not caring, I did it again.

Ω

Unfortunately, Osanne's twin brother, Fedryc, worked in the governor's palace as a clerk. Fedryc was tall like his sister, but in other ways her opposite. Where she moved fluidly, he was unnaturally still. He had heavy brows, and his beard grew in uneven tufts. The day after I kissed Osanne, I was walking down the hill from the governor's palace, thinking of what Pantaleon had told me—*Sicily is the key to our future*—when I realized that Fedryc was standing directly in front of me.

"Stay away from my sister," he barked. I stepped back, out of the range of his fists. "I've seen how you look at her, *gasmoule fil a putain.*"

Even with my limited French, I knew an insult when I heard it—but he was armed, so I responded cautiously.

"I would defend your sister from any threat to her honor."

"She's not yours to defend, half-breed." Fedryc scowled, and took a step toward me again. He did not blink as often as he should. He had strange eyes, pale blue with a dark rim of black around the iris.

"As you wish." I put my hands up in conciliatory surrender, but he was not placated.

"Out of my way," he snarled. I stepped quickly to the side as he passed too close, throwing me off-balance. He looked back over his shoulder. "I'll be watching you, Borghes. Keep your filthy paws to yourself, or I'll take them from you."

I waited until Fedryc was far away before I turned my back. Now would have been the time to give up my growing fascination with a woman who had not only the blood of the enemy running through her veins, but also an unhinged father and a murderous brother. But I could not.

Ω

At our next meeting, Pantaleon made my role clear.

"Why Sicily? Don't we have enough work to do to rebuild Mystras?" I asked, refraining from staring at the spot where his ear used to be.

"Whoever controls Sicily will have the Romaioi empire in his lap," Pantaleon said. "King Charles treats it like a pawn, not a powerful kingdom in its own right, governed by proud and independent people. He taxes the Sicilians into poverty, using their money for his political ambitions. The soldiers he left to govern the island steal from the men and use the women for their pleasure. Sicilians hate the French already. That hate can be turned to rebellion."

"And Charles of Anjou's fleet is amassing there." I was beginning to understand.

"Precisely." Pantaleon leaned forward for emphasis. "And we are not alone in this effort. A powerful network of conspirators is moving toward the same goal from distances greater than ours. The plan is already two years in the making. Sicily, Elias, is where those devoted to the cause will carry out Emperor Michael's final will and upset Charles of Anjou's plans to claim our empire."

"How can a struggling scribe in Mystras help overthrow Charles's regime?"

"You won't stay in Mystras," Pantaleon said.

"You mean go to Sicily?"

Pantaleon's smile was fierce. "That is exactly what I mean."

ELIAS BORGHES
December 1281
Mystras

My mother's suitor Paulus Asanes had been coming to call for months, always bringing a gift. At first the gifts were for the household—a small box of mountain salt mixed with herbs, a string of sausages (he was a butcher), or olives stored in brine. As time passed, his offerings took a more personal turn. One day he brought a pair of earrings with garnet stones. My mother thanked him graciously, but to his visible disappointment, she did not put them on in front of him.

As Nativity approached, the residents of Mystras began to prepare for the holiday. Pigs, lambs, and goats were readied for slaughter, and we hung shallow wooden bowls on our doors, filled with water in which we suspended a sprig of basil wrapped around a wooden cross. Once a day my mother dipped the cross and herb in holy water and sprinkled each room of the house.

I did not think how strange our custom might seem until, while my mother was out at a birthing, I showed Osanne our house from the outside. I did not dare the impropriety of inviting her in.

"What is the bowl for?" she asked, running her finger around the rim. I explained how it protected us from the *kallikantzaroi*, the hairy goblins with red eyes and goat's ears who run through the streets at night, tearing to ribbons those who cross their path.

"They swarm in through the door and the chimney, destroying the house, devouring the Nativity meal, and smearing the house with their waste."

"Perhaps I should put up a bowl, too," Osanne said, surprising me, as she often did.

"I can help you." I thought of her brother and stopped. I had not told her about my encounter with Fedryc.

She seemed to understand my hesitation. "You could make me one, and I'll put it up myself," she said. I brought her fingers to my lips. It was a risk, but no one was there to see.

Paulus visited us on the eve of the Nativity. He came early with a huge grin on his face and a slab of pork. Along with the meat, he handed my mother a jug of *konditon*, the flavored wine I loved, steeped with cinnamon, cloves, and black pepper. I wondered whether he was trying to please her through me.

My mother had begun to prepare the Christopsomo, the round loaf symbolizing eternity—life everlasting through Christ. It reminded me of the *kollyva*, though tomorrow we would celebrate divine birth, not mortal death. Once I would have understood the celebration only as a Christian, without conflict. Now everything I believed was limned with the magic of recurrent life. Somehow, I was able to hold both truths in my heart, perhaps because I had no alternative.

With the yeast and flour came precious sugar, the finest olive oil, juice from an unblemished orange, then mastic crystals—smelling like a pine forest—fennel, cinnamon, and coriander seeds that I crushed in a mortar. We chose the best eggs from our chickens—only the most perfect ingredients were to be used in celebration of our Lord's birth—and we picked walnuts from the tree in the front yard to press into the loaf's soft center before baking.

Paulus made a fire in the hearth and prepared the meat, and I acknowledged to myself, as we worked side by side, that it felt like family. In our shared tasks we had the rhythm of familiarity, happy to be quiet.

The loaves had risen and were ready to bake, and the meat had begun to drip fat and sputter in the fire, when Paulus's son arrived with his wife. I'd heard his name but never met him; he was the head of Mystras's garrison. It was said he had fought bravely at Pelagonia when Mystras still belonged to the Franks. He had returned uninjured—one of the few who returned at all. When I'd first heard about him, I'd had that odd sensation of familiarity, as if I were hearing a song from my childhood.

I had a loaf of Christopsomo on a board in one hand when Demetrios and his wife, Despina, arrived. I looked up to greet our guests and saw not the lined face of a fifty-year-old stranger but the familiar smile of a long-lost friend. I nearly dropped the loaf on the floor.

Demetrios did not recognize me, but he must have seen something familiar in my face as I greeted him. He raised his eyebrows in a way I remembered, and he gave me a smile warmer than one for a near-stranger.

"It is so lovely to meet you at last, Elias." He drew out the name slowly, as if he held years of emotion in check, bound in those three syllables. "I knew your brother, and I mourn him still."

You do not have to mourn; I am here! I said nothing, but my thoughts were so loud it was hard to imagine they could not be heard. I shook Demetrios's hand and bowed to his wife, stepping back to let them into the house and then closing the door.

The afternoon passed in a blur. Voices rose and fell around me, and every now and then a sentence lifted out of the hum of conversation. Giánnis arrived with his wife, Angelina, and the happy news that she was pregnant. My mother embraced them both. The loaves came out of the oven, filling the air with their heady spice and citrus scent.

When the meat was ready, Paulus carved the pork from the bone, telling butcher jokes. "One day a rich man served a pork dinner to his guests, and they enjoyed the food and company so much that he decided he must have the very same party the next night. He went back to the butcher. 'I'd like another head of the same pig,' the rich man said, 'since the first went over so well.'" Paulus looked around the room expectantly. Everyone laughed. I glanced at my mother, and she was smiling broadly, her cheeks flushed.

Sitting across from Demetrios, I could not stop staring. Once, he looked back quizzically. After dinner, I excused myself on the pretense of collecting fresh eggs. I walked to the rear of the house, where our chickens made throaty noises from their coop. The black-and-white hen had laid an egg, and the russet hen another. The eggs were still warm, and my fingers curved around the smooth shells.

I turned at a rustle behind me. Demetrios stood shadowed in the doorway of the coop. It made me think of our soldiers' tent. "Any luck with the hens?" His voice sounded the way I remembered, disembodied in the dark.

I held up the results. "Twice lucky. *Sphoungata* tomorrow." I joined him in the yard. The moon was high and full, the sky clear.

"It is a pleasure finally to meet you," I said, feeling almost duplicitous. "I have heard so much."

Demetrios laughed. "I can't imagine why anyone would bother to speak of me."

"They speak of your military prowess."

"Being lucky enough not to die shouldn't be counted as prowess."

"You got me home," I said without thinking.

"What did you say?" Demetrios's head was haloed by the moon. His hair was threaded with a few strands of gray.

I had a choice. I could revise what I had said, wrap my error in a veil of words. But instead I pulled a memory from decades ago, words Demetrios himself had said.

"We are a long way from home, and love is the best sustenance on a long voyage."

Demetrios gasped. "Where did you hear that?"

"I heard it from you," I answered.

"I said those words to someone else, long before you were born."

"I am that someone."

Demetrios took a step back. I was afraid that I'd made a terrible mistake. He might think I dabbled in sorcery or sought illicit love. I tried to remember to breathe.

"I am glad you are back," he said finally, and opened his arms to draw me in.

Of course, we were different now. He because of time, and me because, even though I was in some ways the same person, I was also transformed. I had come of age in a new generation of Mystras, one in which Romaioi rule was the norm. I was in love with Osanne, and he with his wife. He had grieved me and gone on to love again. But that embrace was powerfully sweet, and the joy of being in his presence was as bright as the full moon. I told him that I believed the stones of Mystras had called me home, how I had returned to become part of the place, my heart beating in the pulse of the earth itself. He listened patiently, as he always had, and together we recalled the day I protected him from the falling stones. When an owl cried nearby, joined by a second, we laughed, remembering the owls that had called to each other on the night we first shared love.

"We have to go back inside," Demetrios said, smiling, "or our families will worry that we've been pecked to death by hens."

"I haven't said thank you."

Demetrios looked genuinely surprised. "For what?"

"You listened. You did then, and you still do now. You loved me, and you brought me home. I could not thank you then, but I can now."

"I did the only thing possible," Demetrios said gently, with the sweet seriousness I had always loved, and still did. We returned to the house with our two eggs.

chapter seventeen

ELIAS BORGHES
January 1282
Mystras

I set aside my French studies to learn Sicilian. Pantaleon introduced me to Vicenzu, a Sicilian I'd thought was the ambassador's new servant. But he had two secret roles: as a conspirator in the plot against King Charles, and as my language teacher. He was my age but as small as a ten-year-old, and he played the role of an obedient bumbler convincingly. The first word I learned in Sicilian was his name, which translated as "conqueror." The second Sicilian word I had to learn was *ciciri*, which meant "chickpeas."

"Chi-chi-reh?" Vicenzu made me say it a hundred times, correcting me until I had it right. It was extraordinarily difficult to pronounce. It seemed more useful for a shopkeeper than a conspirator, but he insisted I practice it until I had a pounding headache.

"The less you know about why, the better," he answered. It took several months before I could communicate clumsily in Sicilian. As the cold abated and the days got longer, Vicenzu began to train me to be a different person.

One night, Fedryc walked in on us. He brought his

strangely immobile face close to mine and pressed a dagger against my ribs. "Get back to where you belong, half-breed. I've been assigned to the night watch, and I don't want to clean up the bloody mess if you don't clear out in time."

Vicenzu saved us with a story about retrieving transcriptions and quickly found a new location for our plotting: the crypt below the Agios Demetrios church. The walls were damp and the air thick with the smell of earth. Vicenzu didn't mind that we were meeting in a burial place, pressed under the ponderous weight of a church's worth of stone. "When you're in Sicily you'll be the son of John of Procida," he said succinctly, "and you need information to pull that off."

"I don't even know who John of Procida is." Still largely in the dark, I tried not to sound irritable. "I have to learn another language, be another person, and travel to another country. What's next, a disguise?" I'd been half-joking, but to my consternation Vicenzu nodded.

"Yes, exactly." He handed me the folded robes of a Franciscan friar.

Vicenzu was an entertaining teacher, making me play the role I'd be taking on, rather than recite facts from memory.

"What's your name?"

"Francis."

"Your father?"

"John of Procida."

"Where is Procida?"

I hesitated.

"Too slow, *Francis*. Where is Procida?"

"Off the coast of Naples."

Vicenzu nodded approvingly. "What does your father do?"

"He is a physician of great renown."

"And whom does he serve?"

I thought for a moment. King Charles, in name, but truly King Peter of Aragon, Charles's enemy. "It depends on who is asking," I said carefully.

Vicenzu grunted. "Not bad for an amateur." From Vicenzu, an extravagant compliment. He asked his next question in Sicilian with an intensity fueled by his hatred of the oppressive rule King Charles imposed on his home.

"You are not from Sicily. Your home is far away, and your life bears no similarity to ours, where we suffer oppression under the French. Why should Sicilians follow your lead in rebellion?"

This was a question about not only my false persona, but also my real one. Why should I, a clumsy scribe in Mystras, serve Sicily's desperate struggle for freedom? I answered as if I were the son of one of the wiliest conspirators alive, a man who spoke with kings and emperors and gained the pope's favor. I was pretending to be the son of a physician allied with Michael Palaiologos, the emperor in Constantinople, in a plot to overthrow King Charles's rule in Sicily. But I was also my small self, dedicated to Mystras's survival. "My father hates King Charles as much as you do. The king confiscated our estates and sent his so-called knight to do the job for him: a French pig who raped my sister and killed my brother. I have earned the right to hate the French."

Vicenzu raised one eyebrow. "You know the facts. But can you embrace our people, as well as our cause? Can you understand our pride and our pain? Will Sicilians believe you when you swear you understand?"

I had been born twice to a people oppressed by the Franks. We were not so different, Sicilians and Romaioi. I spoke from my heart. "Our homes may be leagues apart, but our hearts beat together against the French. And I will fight with every

fiber of my being against your oppressor, who is also our own."
Vicenzu, breaking into a rare smile, threw his arms around me
in a powerful embrace.

ELIAS BORGHES
Late February, 1282
Mystras

Our ship would leave for Sicily at the beginning of March. In
addition to my doubly disguised self (pretending to be Francis,
John of Procida's son, who was pretending to be a Franciscan
monk), the vessel would carry a hold full of weapons packed
into wine barrels to arm Sicilian rebels. I added smuggler to
my list of roles.

The money for the voyage had come from Mystras's governor, ostensibly to secure safe passage of wine, oil, and
Mystras silk to Messina, Sicily's largest port, where King
Charles's fleet gathered. Emperor Palaiologos, too, had secretly underwritten the weapons that packed the ship's hull.

I had to see Osanne before I left. Early in the morning, I
took the risk of visiting the castellan's house. Since I dreaded
two of the three inhabitants, I did not knock. The door to the
stables on the ground floor was unlocked. Two horses stirred
restlessly in their stalls; I patted their necks until they quieted.
Standing in the straw of an empty stall with a window that
showed the house's front door, I watched from the shadows.

Osanne's father left first, walking with his strange, lurch-
ing rhythm. He headed down the steep path. A few moments
later, Fedryc took the road to the governor's palace. I slipped
out of the stable, carefully closing the door behind me.

I knocked once, then again. My hand was shaking. I'd almost given up when the door opened. Osanne stood in the doorway, dressed only in a white linen *tunica*. The *tunica* draped down to her ankles, and the sleeves covered her wrists, but I'd never seen her in so little before. My face went hot. "You're here," I said stupidly.

"I *live* here, Elias." She put her hands on her hips. "It is more surprising that you are here, no?"

I thought I'd blushed to capacity, but it seemed I hadn't. "I haven't seen you. I was worried." She tilted her head expectantly. I took a deep breath. "I *needed* to see you."

"You'd better come in. If anyone catches sight of you here, it will be difficult to explain." Osanne took a cloak from a hook and draped it over her shoulders. I was both disappointed and relieved, but it made conversation easier.

"I'll get us something to eat." She headed up the broad stairs to the first-floor triclinium. I followed her into the kitchen, where she motioned me to sit.

The Lusignan house was much more elegant than ours, with two stories supported by arches and set into the hill, so the top floor was at ground level in back against the slope. The upper story had a balcony and a view of the valley. Tapestries covered the walls, and the floor was an intricate mosaic of multicolored marble, not the packed earth and rough-cut flagstones I was used to. Osanne came back with a loaf of bread on a wooden board.

"*Katharos artos!*" It was the finest white bread, not something I ate often. She looked at me quizzically. "We get it every day from the baker in the valley." She cut a few slices and disappeared again, returning with a tray and two cups of *thassorofron*. I loved the sweetened milk of almonds ground and pressed with water. Another luxury, given the price of sugar. She put out a bowl of olives cured in thyme and honey, then joined me, as if sharing a morning meal with an unexpected male visitor while wearing her underclothes were the most ordinary thing in the world. I stared fixedly at the milky beverage instead of her.

Silently, I picked up a slice of bread. Now that I was actually in her presence, I didn't know what to say.

"I've been a bit ill," she said and, seeing my alarm, put her hand on my arm. "Nothing serious. Just a cough, easily mended with honey. But my father and brother insisted I stay inside. They like to control me." She grimaced.

"They are concerned about your welfare," I said cautiously.

"They are concerned about limiting my freedom." She put an olive into her mouth and chewed angrily. "*You* wouldn't restrict my freedom, would you?"

"What? There would be no point trying."

Her anger softened. "You are a strange man."

"I will take that as a compliment, from you."

Osanne took a sip of *thassorofron*. I noticed intermittent flickers of her fingers, a delicate movement she disguised with a brush of her hand to her mouth. It reminded me alarmingly of her father. "So you came because you were worried about me?"

"I am leaving Mystras."

She stood up abruptly. "How long will you be gone? Will you return?"

"I plan to."

She began to pace. She reminded me of lightning—bright, quick, dangerous. "When?"

"Within a week."

"That's very soon." She stopped pacing. "My father hates you. My brother does, too."

"That does not surprise me."

"You are so cool about it."

"How should I be?"

"Furious, regretful, vengeful . . . anything. You never seem to feel *anything*."

I reached out one hand and held her wrist. I could feel her pulse beating, like a frightened bird. "Osanne." I stood up to face her. She was almost as tall as I am. Her hand flicked in mine; again, I felt a wisp of apprehension. I imagined linking my life to her long, slow decline. *She may have her father's blood, but she does not have his heart.* "I love you," I said. "Is that better?"

She blinked. "It's a good start."

I took her other wrist. She was strong and wild, and could, if she wished to, easily escape my grasp. I leaned forward and kissed her cheek. "I would ask your father for your hand. But he would kill me."

Osanne jutted out her lower jaw stubbornly like a charming bulldog. "Well then, ask me instead."

This time when I kissed her, her lips parted so I could taste her: almond milk, olives, and her own herbal sweetness. I tasted the hills, the trees, the arching sky. We came away breathless. "Will you be mine, Osanne Lusignan? Even though your father despises me, and your brother wants me dead? Even though I speak little and appear to feel less?"

"I won't be anyone's. Will you still love me?"

I almost laughed. "That is why I love you."

She held her hand out. It wavered, then her head followed, like a dance to inaudible music. "You love me despite this? Even though I will end up like my father?"

"You are not your father." I touched her hand and stilled it.

"Fedryc told me that for me to bear a child would be an abomination against God."

"Your child would be a blessing," I said.

Osanne inhaled deeply. "All right, then. I will love you. But there is one more thing." I waited. "I speak French, the language of your oppressors. That is a shaky foundation for love."

"I speak it, too," I said. I remembered my mother's words: *Love is a bridge*. And with private vows Osanne and I affirmed our impossible love, across boundaries of language, history, hatred, and fear. When I took her in my arms, the scent of thyme surrounded us, and when I lowered her to the floor she cried out in Greek, the language of my heart.

ELIAS BORGHES
Mid-March 1282
Mystras

A few days later, Pantaleon told me our ship would leave from Monemvasia. "It's the only port not overrun by the Franks. Nafplio is the playground of the French, and they'll likely sell it to the Venetians soon, who are no better. But Monemvasia is ours again, and the Monemvasiots are the most feared pirates on the water. There's no ally I'd rather have."

I wondered whether I'd known Monemvasia *before*. I'd come to recognize the spark of inexplicable emotion, the unreasonable familiarity. But as usual, I could not force the memory.

Pantaleon was still talking. "You'll need to meet the captain. Symeon is his name. You can tell him everything." He saw me hesitate. "What are you thinking?"

I tried not to stare at his missing ear. "I am young, unknown, and have lived in Mystras all my life. Why choose me for a role in an international conspiracy?"

"We need someone from Mystras, Elias. Someone who cares what happens to this place, though we seem so far away from King Charles's grasp. We need someone to represent what the Sicilians call *Griko*—their word for *Romaioi*. This conspiracy is made of many small voices—together we shall make a great chorus. What happens in Sicily will alter the course of history, setting forces in motion that will have effects not only across distance but also centuries."

"Effect at a distance," I said.

"You are old beyond your years," Pantaleon said, smiling. "You remind me of your older brother Elias. Perhaps that is why I trust you with this task." He was right.

"I will go to Sicily, then, with Mystras in my heart. But I need to tell my mother."

Pantaleon nodded. "Your mother has kept many secrets. She will keep this one, too." He touched my shoulder, and I remembered how he'd adjusted my helmet, decades before, with the same hands.

Ω

After Pantaleon left, I climbed the Agios Demetrios bell tower. Unlike the church itself, which was topped by multiple domes, the tower had a triangular roof, and four windows pierced its facade. Because of the way the windows were spaced, I could look through to the blue sky behind. The tower seemed cut from the cloth of the sky.

At the top, the red tiles of the church's multidomed roof curved below like the scales of a dragon. I imagined the church as a fire-breathing serpent, defender of our faith. I stared out over Mystras hill, where new houses and shops appeared like spring flowers, and down, into the valley where the Evrotas wound. I wondered whether I would ever see it again.

Your allegiance is to the place, not the prince . . .

If the words of the prophetess were true and my mother's promise held, I'd more likely lose the people I loved than this place that called me unerringly home.

Ω

At home, my mother had just come back from a birth and was washing her dirty gown in the deep stone sink. I'd never gotten used to the sight of blood on her garments, even though the stain announced new life. Usually. She turned to me, drying her hands.

"Did it go well, Mitéra?"

"In the end, yes." Despite her skill, she sometimes came home downcast with loss—of a baby, or the mother, or, on the grimmest days, both.

"First child," she said. "Now there is a chance for a second." She caught the look on my face. "Talk to me."

I sat on the kitchen bench where once I'd heard the story of Constantinople's fall. She sat, too. "I am leaving Mystras. I can't tell you why." Telling her was a relief, but I already felt the anticipatory loss. "I hate to leave you."

"That is your job, as a young man, to leave, just as it is mine as a mother to ensure that you can. That is every mother's goal: to raise a child who need not look back." She sighed.

"Is it very hard, being my mother?"

She laughed and touched my cheek. "It is what I know. And at least I have had the good fortune to love you twice."

I threw my arms around her and buried my face in her neck, just as I used to when I was a boy. *You might lose me twice,* I thought. But I did not say it.

Ω

The next day, I escaped the governor's office early. Too much time underground made me desperate for the sight of bright new leaves fuzzing the trees. The clouds drifted high overhead, and by the side of the road, tiny wild iris pushed up through the grass. I walked up the hill to the *kastron*'s north gate, the path I used when my job required a sword, not a pen.

I stopped at a fountain along the path's edge, suddenly thirsty. It was newly built, with a carved border of diamonds like a snake's skin. I cupped my hands under the water flowing from a spout in the rock and drank. It was startlingly cold—the water had not yet learned that spring was imminent. Behind me, I heard a step on the path.

"I used to come here often, after you were gone."

I turned to see Demetrios standing on the flagstones.

I wiped my face dry on my sleeve. "Why?"

"The first time, I don't know. After that, I came because I found you here."

It was a strange thing to say, but if anywhere in Mystras blurred time, it was here, where the water and the rock met.

"I am leaving again."

Demetrios sighed. "When?"

"Soon."

We stood silently. I did not know what to do with my hands. Demetrios closed the gap between us, and in two quick steps he embraced me. I held him tightly. It felt like a brother's gesture, not a lover's, but it was no less powerful and sweet.

Demetrios drew back, still holding my shoulder. "Did you know I helped your mother bury you after Pelagonia? With Spyridon. You remember him?" I did, and smiled the way he always had, with half my face. "We buried you in the grove outside the *kastron*'s walls, where the shrine of the Prophet once stood. I kept my promise. I did not think I'd ever be able to tell you that."

"I am sorry you had to, and I am grateful," I said. It was unimaginable. We both shook our heads at the absurdity.

Demetrios dropped his hand from my shoulder and looked at his palm, as if there were something to read in the lines. "Soon I shall have to find a way to keep busy other than fighting. Unlike you, I have aged beyond a soldier's best years."

"What will you do?"

Demetrios paused before answering. "I might chronicle the events leading up to Pelagonia, and those that transpired afterward. The story should be told, and not just by the Franks."

"I look forward to reading your account," I said without thinking, and then the meaning of my words sank in. I might read it once he was gone. I felt the strange, punctuated shape of my existence, so different from those whose time on this earth ended only once.

"I shall strive to do the story justice," Demetrios said quietly, "and as I write it, I'll think of you." We walked down the hill together, arm in arm.

MARCEAU LUSIGNAN
March 1282
Mystras

Fedryc was out again. Where had he gone? "Osanne!" There was no answer. Was she gone, too? Marceau lurched to the kitchen, where he grabbed a hunk of the morning's bread and bit into it. He followed the bread with a gulp of wine. Even as babies, his twins had headed off in opposite directions, making the nurse who looked after them frantic. Old memories were clearer than the new.

Fedryc was likely plowing through another woman. Nearly every day he came home bragging of his latest, smelling of sweat and perfume. At least two village girls had swelling bellies thanks to Fedryc's wanderings. *His descendants will multiply.* Something about the thought bothered Marceau, but he could not unravel the thread. Marceau was surprised to see the bread still in his hand. He took another bite, chewed.

Was I like him? No. I had one woman, and now she's dead. And I have two children. Where is Osanne? She was always going out. Marceau forgot he was holding the bread and dropped it.

Fedryc, thank God, did not have the movements that twisted Marceau's limbs, throwing him off course. He was the opposite, eerily stiff and still. Who knew, though; the monster could lurk, hidden. But Osanne . . . she'd dropped a bowl at breakfast, not for the first time. *My daughter has the scourge. As did my grandfather, and my father, though he did not live long enough to show the worst signs. And I am almost dead of it.*

I must tell Fedryc. Marceau's mind skipped, like a faltering heart. His heart, at least, still ran as it should. *What was I thinking? I must tell him about the beast.* An image came to him, a slavering demon dog at his heels, claiming victims in each generation. *It is too late for me, but he has time.*

chapter eighteen

ELIAS BORGHES
Mid-March 1282
Monemvasia

In mid-March, I rode with my Sicilian tutor and co-conspirator Vicenzu to Monemvasia. Vicenzu's Skyrian pony had a dense black forelock like Vicenzu himself, who was always pushing his hair away so he could see. I rode a bad-tempered roan who bucked irritably every time I got in the saddle. I was glad the ride would take no more than three days.

Our plan, as far as anyone in the governor's office knew, was to supervise a shipment of olive oil from Mystras to Sicily via Monemvasia, the Morea's shipping hub. In my first role, as arms smuggler, I'd handled the funds from the emperor, bought and assembled the weapons, and supervised the packing into their innocent-looking oil barrels. They were transported to Monemvasia in a train of horse-drawn carts accompanied by armed guards. Once we got to Sicily, my second task would begin: inciting rebellion of the Sicilians against French rule. Parts one and two were intended to be complementary—rebellion fares best when weapons are provided.

Vicenzu and I stopped our horses at the narrow causeway that crossed to a mountain rising from the water.

"*Mone-emvasia*," Vicenzu said in Greek, shaking his head in awe. "*Single entrance*. Now I see why they named it that."

From the mainland, there was no sign of a town at all, no port, not even the *kastron* that had held against the prince. A narrow strip of land led out to the almost-island with its steep cliffs of reddish stone.

"Doesn't look like a town." Vicenzu echoed my thoughts.

"Not from here." The causeway bristled with armed guards.

Vicenzu kept staring at the remarkable configuration of the land, but I couldn't stop looking at that expanse of water. I'd never seen the sea before. It was nothing like our Evrotas river, meandering through the valley, shallow at the edges. The sea was something else altogether: a velvety deep blue, opaque and endless.

Ω

At the end of the long land bridge, we arrived at Monemvasia's main gate, where documents from the governor allowed us passage. We led our horses through the arched entry, and on the other side of the high stone wall, the hidden city appeared as if by magic. Monemvasia's central avenue was lined with shops and teemed with merchants, sailors, and customers who shoved past us, shouting, bargaining, and hawking wares.

We met the captain in the main square, where a massive cannon pointed out to sea. At the plaza's edge, a bright white-washed church kept watch, and a soldier stood ready, a stack of cannonballs waiting at his feet. I would not have wanted to be an enemy in Monemvasia's sights.

Captain Symeon was a hatchet-faced sailor whose first reaction to me was suspicion, which I later learned he applied to everyone. He led me down the steep cobbled streets to the port, where our ship, a two-masted trade *nava*, waited. I reviewed our contract of transport, knowing it was lies. Vicenzu pretended to be my servant. I'd suggested he take care of the whole transaction, but he burst out laughing. "I have some uses," he said, "but Emperor Palaiologos's funding transport of smuggled weapons via sea is best conducted by Romaioi, with Romaioi."

As we prepared to leave, contracts duly inspected and signed, Symeon grabbed my arm and pulled me close. "Outside the *portelo*, after dark tonight," he said. "We can finish our business." He released my arm. I would have to find out what the *portelo* was.

Vicenzu and I secured our horses and entered the church on the square to pay our respects. A young priest directed us to a life-size painting of our savior. Vicenzu and I knelt together, Sicilian and Romaioi, two men who were once strangers, paired in conspiracy and now devotion. I felt carried along by the current of our shared faith, even though that faith ran contrary to my recurrent life.

The *portelo*, I learned, was the only break in the thick sea wall that surrounded Monemvasia, a gate that led out to a narrow walkway edging the dark, thrashing water. It took all my will to walk through it that night. Symeon's bark of greeting startled me. He'd been waiting, pressed against the wall to one side of the *portelo*. I joined him, keeping one hand on the stone. I did not wish to be on the outside edge of the walkway. Vicenzu had stayed behind in the inn, where he would appear to be drinking too much wine while gathering information from patrons.

Symeon grinned lopsidedly, and he suddenly looked familiar, though we'd never met. "Let's not waste time," he said.

"I'm not just the captain of a merchant ship, and you aren't just a plodding bureaucrat."

I nodded. "I'll be in disguise when you see me next, in the garments of a Franciscan brother. And I'll call myself Francis."

"Easy to remember. But don't expect me to pray with you." He laughed, but without humor. We both knew I'd be taking on the robes of a church few Greeks bowed to willingly.

"You know what you carry in those barrels, then?"

"I know as well as you that no one will be cooking with it. Unless they are cooking up a rebellion."

This time, I laughed with him. It was hard not to, even though we were conspirators against one of the most powerful monarchs in the world, even though we were talking about smuggling arms, even though I was standing on a narrow ledge next to a dark sea. The wind picked up, and the waves rose higher, crashing against the stones that edged the path and frothing over our feet. I pressed myself flat against the wall.

"When do we leave, and how long will the voyage be?" Vicenzu and I had brought only enough food with us for the three days' ride, so we'd need supplies.

"King Charles's fleet is scheduled to sail out of Messina in the first week in April. He's set his sights on Constantinople, forcing Sicilians into service on his warships. As if they did not hate him and the French already, he's given them more to fuel their rage. We'll leave for Sicily within two days. At this time of year, in a little over a week we should be dropping anchor at Messina. We've been building the conspiracy for over a year, and now the Sicilians are close to revolt. In Messina, my job ends and yours begins, and I shall get you there in time to do it."

Symeon leaned forward to shake my hand and cement our

deal, his dark hand moving into light. Something else caught my eye, a metallic gleam just below the hollow of his throat. He wore an *enkolpion* on a leather thong about his neck. Many did, for the protection that a saint's image provided. But as the moonlight played across the pendant, I froze. Etched there was the face of Profitis Ilias: his thick beard, long hair, his gaze toward a raven, flying with food in its beak.

I was not the only child to grow up entranced by the story of the ravens, called by God to feed his prophet when famine struck. But this was not a random amulet around a Monemvasiot captain's neck: this *enkolpion* had once been mine. The past rose around me—the day my mother put the pendant over my head, the day my breath failed. The times when I reached for the prophet's image and his strength flowed through me. And much later, when I reached for something at my chest and found nothing there.

"Where did you get the amulet you wear?"

Symeon did not look surprised at my change of topic. "My father, of blessed memory, gave it to me in the last moments of his life. He said it would protect me, as it had him, and as it had protected another before him. It belonged to a loyal friend, a soldier like himself who did not survive his last battle. He did not tell me the soldier's name."

I heard my heartbeat in my ears. "Who was your father?"

"He was called Spyridon. A pirate turned soldier. He fought for a cause that was not his, as the Sicilians are forced to do now. My father fought bravely. I buried him with my own hands in the graveyard outside our Hagia Sophia church."

Spyridon. I remembered the first day I'd seen him repairing his shield, and the last, his face above me in the dark of my mother's house. And I remembered Spyridon's smile, one side of his mouth rising comically higher than the other, just like his son's.

That was when the wave hit, crashing up onto the narrow ledge where we stood, ripping my legs out from under me and dragging me into the sea with it. The water was brutally cold and rough; I went under and could not find a way up. The water dragged at my clothes and the cold pressed against my chest like a vise. My limbs burned. *Cold feels so much like heat.* I closed my mouth against the weight. *If I don't breathe soon, I will die.* But there was no air, only water.

Something firm brushed one of my hands. The something became a grip on my wrist that tightened and pulled, and then I was dragged up into the air, my face scraping along the rough stones of the path. I coughed up seawater while Symeon pounded my life back into me.

HELEN ADLER
Mid-July 2015
Nafplio to Mystras via A7/E65 and A71

The bus broke down on the way back to Mystras, so a one-hour-and-forty-minute trip took more than three hours. Just the way the hotel wireless rarely works. The way the shower is inexplicably cold, or hot, or dribbles when it should spray. The way the bathroom floods because the shower curtain is so flimsy, or nonexistent. I'd learned this about Greece. But I'd also learned how generosity flows like a river that never runs dry. No matter how dire the economic misery, how austere the austerity measures, how brutal the taxes, how desperate the lack of jobs and low the salaries, everywhere we went, people opened their arms and gave us what they had. In Athens, the hotel manager took one look at our jet-lagged faces and gave us lunch made by his mother. In Nafplio, we stumbled upon a wedding and were invited to join the festivities. In Monemvasia, we'd become family. In Mystras . . . I wasn't quite ready to classify our Mystras experience yet.

We sweated profusely while the bus driver stood outside. He was soon joined by a cadre of middle-aged men, passengers, plus a few extras who'd stopped their cars in the dry grass along the road and rolled up their sleeves to help. The issue seemed to be the right front wheel. Soon they were joined by another passenger, an Orthodox priest in full regalia.

Alexander looked out the window. "I've never seen a priest change a tire before."

"I saw a priest help push a car out of a ditch in Greece once." The voice, which had a distinctively Italian accent, came from behind us. Alexander got on his knees to peer over the back of his seat. I joined him. A woman about my age sat in the next row, remarkably not sweating at all. Her curly black hair bloomed around her head like a fabulous halo. She smiled. "Perhaps it's a Greek thing. I've never seen that where I come from."

"Are priests weaker where you come from?"

The woman laughed. "Maybe our priests aren't so likely to lend their bodies to the struggle."

Alexander wasn't deflected by the humor. "Where *are* you from?"

"Alexander, it's not nice to pry," I said.

"That's fine. It's investigative journalism. I'm from Sicily." She directed a question back at Alexander. "I'm a writer. Are you?"

"No way." Alexander shuddered at the thought. "SI-SI-LY. Is that in Greece? I love Greece."

"I love Greece, too. But Sicily is part of Italy. It's an island." She took out a ballpoint pen and an old receipt from her bag and drew a quick map, with the boot of Italy and triangular Sicily near its toe. Then she drew a curve of land until she got to Greece.

Alexander frowned. "It looks like Italy is kicking a Sicily ball."

"Sometimes we Sicilians feel kicked around. We are the world's most conquered island." She held out her hand, which was small and very brown. "My name is Catena." She turned to me. "How lucky you are, to be traveling with your son."

"Yes, I am," I agreed. "I'm Helen."

"I'm Alexander, and I'm lucky, too," Alexander said. "My mom is awesome." He had no idea how his words affected me. "Are you going to Mystras?" The bus route had at least seventeen stops on it, mostly one-street towns.

"Yes. It's a special place. I'm writing an article about it."

"It is special." Alexander thought for a moment. "Are there Greeks in Sicily?"

"There have been Greeks in Sicily for centuries. We call them *Griko*." At a loud thump outside, we peered out the window. The wheel's hubcap had fallen off, and the priest and driver were wedging it back on. "Are you going to Mystras, too?"

I turned away from the repair scene. "If the bus ever moves, yes. We're actually going back. Can't seem to stay away."

"Mystras is that sort of place," Catena said. "You know, the Sicilians saved Mystras about seven hundred years ago."

"Really? How?" Alexander hung over the seat back eagerly.

"The French king Charles ruled Sicily, but he treated the Sicilians badly. He wanted power over the whole world, and he saw Sicily as a tool to get that power. He planned to sail a fleet of warships from Sicily to conquer Constantinople, which was the capital of the Byzantine Empire. From there, Charles would have kept going until he had Mystras, too." She paused to make sure Alexander was following.

"What happened?"

"A conspiracy formed of rulers and rebels over much of what is now Europe. After more than a year of planning, the rebellion started in Palermo. We Sicilians fought back, the French were conquered, and Charles's ships never sailed. Our little soccer ball island changed everything."

Alexander chewed on his lower lip thoughtfully. "Was it super violent?"

Catena laughed. "Yes, it was. Rebellions usually are. But it worked."

"Thanks for saving Mystras," Alexander said. "I know you weren't there, but the people who were there aren't alive now anyway. So I'm thanking you instead."

"You sound like a historian."

Alexander looked at the map. "Sicily is so far away from Greece."

"Places are not so far apart as the map makes them look."

"We're from America. That feels very far from here," Alexander said. It was true, I thought. The longer we were away, the farther it felt. Alexander frowned. "So you never know whether something you do in one place could change something in another place."

"Exactly. That's history—how places are linked, plus the added dimension of time." I liked the way Catena talked to Alexander: without condescension, trusting him to understand.

Alexander leaned forward so far, I thought he might fall in Catena's lap. "Like something that happened a long time ago could affect how we are right now, on this bus? Maybe it's even why our wheel fell off."

"Precisely."

Alexander was quiet for a long time. "So if someone dies, maybe they are still somewhere, in some time, even though they are gone in ours. And that time still exists. And so do they."

She seemed to sense we were heading somewhere serious. "I think that might be true," she said. "I don't have any way of proving it, but I feel the way you do. I think time doesn't go in a straight line, and all times exist right next to one another. If we knew how, maybe we could step right from one time to another, just the way we do in space. We could talk to people who lived hundreds of years ago. The past—all the pasts—and the present are not so separate as they seem."

"Then you are a historian, too," Alexander said definitively. "Like me."

With exquisite timing, the bus engine rumbled to a start, and we were on the road again, our wheel in place and the priest back in his seat. Meanwhile, as usual, half the cars ahead of us were driving on the dusty shoulder, making two lanes out of one. *I love Greece.*

Ω

I think of my brain as a house built by someone with no sense of direction. To get from the bedroom to the bathroom, you have to exit through the back of a closet, walk through the kitchen, then outdoors through a field, back in through a side door, until finally the bathroom appears unexpectedly to the left of stairs you don't remember seeing before. My ideas come from nowhere, and once they appear, they can be hard to find again. It helps lead me to new scientific ideas sometimes, but mostly it's a pain. Especially when I am supposed to remember something but can't.

As the bus pulled into Mystras's familiar triangular plaza, a door opened in my head, and what I'd learned in Nafplio collided with what I'd found in Mystras. The unpleasant and omnipresent Pierre Lusignan carried the French thread of Huntington's in the region. Lusignan was also likely to be the most knowledgeable person in the country about Laconian HD prevalence. If I were serious about pursuing the source of a potential scientific breakthrough, I'd have to talk to him. But there was also a family carrying the gene with no apparent clinical manifestations, originating from a Frankish soldier with a Greek wife.

What Elias had said on our first tour came back to me in a rush: *I am Greek. But I do have French blood. Hundreds of years ago, during the prince's time, Frankish soldiers came to live here in Mystras and married Greek women.*

So Elias was descended from a French soldier and a Greek woman who'd met in Mystras. Coincidence? So were a lot of Mystras residents, probably. Right?

chapter nineteen

ELIAS BORGHES
Late March 1282
The Ionian Sea

The wind blew favorably, and Symeon said that if it held, we'd arrive in Sicily with a week to stir up revolt before the Angevin fleet launched for Constantinople. I learned three things on that trip across the Ionian Sea. First, a favorable wind means high speed. Second, high speed equals profound seasickness. My eight days were spent mostly hanging over the *nava*'s side rail. The only advantage I could see to our rapid passage was that it would end soon. My third lesson was that a Franciscan friar's robes itch viciously. Consumed by nausea and the desire to scratch myself to pieces, I found relief in the distraction when passengers approached me for words of religious wisdom. I felt guilty advising seekers, but in my more contemplative moments, I thought perhaps Divine comfort is just that, no matter its origins.

Ω

We arrived in the port of Messina the last week of March. I wobbled onto land with intense relief. Vicenzu grabbed my arm and turned me to look back at the port where we'd just anchored. The harbor was enclosed by a graceful sickle-shaped curve of land that protected the port from the open sea, and an imposing stone fortress stood on the hills by the water's edge, its battlements bristling with soldiers. The port smelled of fish and tar, but a breeze carried the scent of oranges, and citrus trees grew on the hills behind the harbor. The quay bustled with sailors and passengers, merchants shouted orders as their crews unloaded barrels and crates, and fishermen hauled nets of thrashing silver fish from their boats.

Vicenzu gestured me to look at an armada of hulking warships clustered near the shore. They flew the Angevin colors—gold fleur-de-lis on a field of blue—and the golden crosses of the Kingdom of Jerusalem, Charles's most recent acquisition. Alongside flew flags with the papal crossed keys. The decks were packed with soldiers. The ships menaced, oars ready with heavy iron chains pulled taut, sails furled and waiting.

"King Charles's fleet," I whispered. "And he has the pope's backing."

"*Sì*," Vicenzu whispered back in Sicilian. "He plans a crusade with Constantinople as the target, and Sicilian men as the weapons. We have a week to stop the ships from sailing."

We, Vicenzu said in Sicilian—*nuautri*.

We would arm the island against the absent, oppressive king, with the weapons we'd smuggled here. We would help incite the brewing revolt to overthrow his rule. Though this was my first moment on Sicilian soil, he included me in that *we*.

"*Nuautri*," I said, and Vicenzu gripped my arm.

Ω

Vicenzu and I stood on the quay with our meager possessions, watching as the crew unloaded the barrels from our ship.

Symeon barked orders, the *enkolpion* visible at his throat. I no longer considered the amulet mine. If it protected this man who had saved me from drowning, the son of a soldier who had fought at my side and carried me home, I was happy to let it continue to do so.

We did not stay in Messina that night. "Swarming with Charles's men," Vicenzu informed me. "We will find a warmer welcome in Palermu." Vicenzu made sure I knew how to say the city's name properly in Sicilian, just as he had with *ciciri*.

"When the time comes, your knowledge will save you," he said darkly, but would not elaborate further.

Palermo was no longer the capital. Charles had moved the seat of government to Naples. "Our *king* hasn't set foot here for sixteen years," Vicenzu said, spitting angrily on the stones of the quay. "He thinks he can leave French minions to keep us in line, give Sicilians no opportunity to air grievances, and move his so-called governing to a capital on the mainland. Meanwhile he taxes us into poverty and leaves us with French clerics to bring us the word of God. We see how well that strategy serves." If Vicenzu was a typical Sicilian, King Charles was in trouble.

When Vicenzu showed me the map, I realized with despair that the shortest route from Messina to the former capital was along the coast. "Back on a boat?" I shuddered. "I barely survived our last trip. And it ended only an hour ago."

"You'd rather spend five days we don't have braving the mountain passes?" I stared at the map grimly as Vicenzu elaborated: "Snowcapped peaks, deadly drops off cliffs, paths treacherous with falling rocks."

"It seems I do not have a choice." My nausea rose in anticipation.

"I'll try to find a fast boat so it will be over soon. You,

Father Francis, can pray while I do that." He left me sweating in my itchy robes.

Ω

We arrived in Palermo at night, and torches mounted along the quayside lit the port with flickering light. I stumbled after Vicenzu on the uneven paving stones along the water's edge. Palermo was larger than Messina, with multistory buildings clustered along the harbor. Even this late, lights burned in windows, and crowds lined the walkways. Mountains in the distance were silhouetted by a slice of moon.

We met our contact, a turbaned Saracen with a long dark beard, in a quayside inn. I'd never seen an Arab before, except depicted in books. I thought they had all been expelled to the mainland years before. I tried not to stare at his ballooned sleeves and curved sword.

Afraid the man might think me rude, I bowed apologetically. "I did not know there were Saracens still here in Sicily."

"There are not," he said slowly. "I've made a special trip back to help my friend." His voice was rich like the syrup of dates. If he'd lived here before the followers of Mohammed left the island, he had to be well over fifty, but he had a smooth ageless face. He looked carefully at Vicenzu, exchanging a glance that asked how much I knew. "A Franciscan friar?"

I pushed back my hood. "I'm no more a friar than you are."

Vicenzu grunted. "A subterfuge for the trip. Friend Mohammed ibn Al-Furat of Apulia, meet friend Elias Borghes of Mystras."

Al-Furat nodded. "You have come a long way in the name of friendship," he said.

I met his gaze. "We share a cause worth traveling for."

Ω

Al-Furat led us to the back of the building, where three horses were tied. Vicenzu deposited a handful of coins in Al-Furat's palm—denari decorated with the French fleur-de-lis on one side and the Latin cross on the other.

"For the horses," Vicenzu said. "Soon, we will have the Angevin soldiers in hand just like these French lilies."

What stayed with me most vividly from that remarkable night was the food. Our destination was the house of a Palermitano burgher named Ciau Trabucco, a co-conspirator who welcomed us with surprising enthusiasm for a middle-of-the-night arrival. Trabucco talked at high speed, stopping occasionally to breathe. His friendliness equaled his volume of words, and I preferred listening to talking anyway.

We were led into a cavernous stone-flagged kitchen, where we sat on benches at a trestle table. Servants appeared with goblets and a pitcher of wine. Trabucco introduced us to his wife, Itria, whose brooding silence stood in stark juxtaposition to her husband's intense verbosity. While we sat to plan rebellion, Itria moved about the kitchen preparing a late-night meal. I tried to focus on Trabucco, but my attention wandered to the cooking behind him.

"King Charles has done much to anger the Sicilians. The people are ripe for rebellion. Bursting, yes, exploding with fury, like a pile of tinder ready to be engulfed in flame, an Arabian racehorse twitching to run. The list of insults he has heaped upon us is endless, the indignities we have suffered beyond counting." Vicenzu opened his mouth more than once during the tirade, but, finding no entry point, closed it while Trabucco continued. "Each abuse adds power to our efforts to turn thoughts to action. If we are to succeed, we must fan the flames of revolt, bolster the barricades of resistance, fuel the fury, inflame the indignation—"

Ibn Al-Furat, who had been waiting for his moment, interjected his six words succinctly. "To stop the ships from sailing."

Vicenzu gave a half smile. He'd clearly chosen his collaborators carefully and knew their peculiarities as well as their powers.

"Indeed. Well said. To stop the ships." He cleared his throat. "King Charles's many injustices will be his undoing. He has the gall to run our government from afar, an affront. And the *subventio generalis* is a source of great frustration, which will be transformed into revolt."

Vicenzu explained. "Sicilian subjects of the king are required to serve in the royal army without compensation—at least ninety days but, in reality, always more. The only escape is to pay exorbitantly high fees. There is no limit to how much the king can demand."

"Except," Al-Furat said with his signature brevity, "the fear of inciting violence."

We were all silent, even Trabucco, acknowledging the wisdom of his interjection. "Exactly, violence," Trabucco said. "Violence—though I assure you it is a trait far from my soul's leanings—is what we must create, for no other means will enable us to escape from this oppressive prison. And that, my friends, is the second point we must hammer home, with all the force that drives a nail to its target." Trabucco inhaled a lungful of air. "The French officials he has left to do his business, these foreigners who cannot even pronounce the words of our language—let alone understand them—are vicious, ruthless, and profoundly corrupt."

A smell wafted from Itria's vicinity, and I glanced over at her. She was chopping fiercely. A pile of peeled onions sat next to her on the sideboard. Beside those was a comparatively small quantity of meat, though more than enough to feed us all. Trabucco was saying something about taxation while the onions went into a pot with the chunks of meat, water, and salt. Itria hung the pot over the fire. A slosh of oil from a jug followed, then spices. I recognized the scent of cinnamon, but others eluded me. When Itria dropped in handfuls of tiny balls of ground meat, my mouth began to water.

Trabucco stood up from the table, waving his fleshy hands for emphasis. "And finally, perhaps worst of all, these Frenchmen have no respect for our culture and customs. Sicily is to the French a bowl of soup from which they can scoop at will, to feed their appetites for power. But we were not born Sicilian to fill the bellies of the French. We do not walk this earth to help King Charles conquer more land, find more subjects to subjugate, or amass more gold to fill his overflowing coffers. We will not be press-ganged onto ships sailing for Constantinople to fight against an honorable emperor. We shall not, not today and not *ever*, bend to his will!"

I almost clapped at the performance. Al-Furat nodded his agreement.

Vicenzu patted Trabucco's padded shoulder. "He's got his defects, our Trabucco, as do we all, but his assets surely outweigh them."

I had to agree. But I wondered even more, listening to these men who knew so much, what my presence added. "Vicenzu, I am honored to be part of this fight. But I am not Sicilian, and my knowledge of your troubles comes secondhand. Why would the Sicilians listen to me?"

Vicenzu put a hand on my shoulder. "You are the representative of the Romaioi empire, a loyal subject of the emperor who supports our cause, with finance and force. You brought weapons across the sea to arm the rebellion, and you bring the promise of allies to conquer our oppressive masters. This rebellion cannot be accomplished by Sicilians alone. If we know foreign aid is coming, we will fight harder. Tell all you incite to rebellion that your friendship assures support that transcends their own struggling kingdom, and which comes from all over the world." *Whatever is asked of you in the service of this place, do not shrink from the task.* I would serve Mystras, whether I thought myself equal to it or not.

The meal Itria had prepared tasted even better than it smelled. The raw onions melted into a sweet caramelized sauce around the meatballs scented with cinnamon, spikenard, and black pepper. A vegetable with shiny purple skin called *melanzana* came pickled with garlic, mint, and celery. Flat, thin semolina noodles were boiled and served with a yellowish-white sweet sauce. Itria, so surprised by my interest she actually smiled, listed its ingredients: almond milk, sugar, and saffron, picked from the throats of lilies. We devoured a fresh cheese, which was soft and cylindrical, with a seeded flat bread we tore with our hands. When I thought I was too full for another bite, sesame candy came to the table. Itria had cooked the seeds with honey until the mixture turned silky and pale gold, then worked the sweet on a marble slab until it began to harden. We broke the candy into squares and ate, sighing our appreciation.

After our meal, I was shown to a bedchamber where I collapsed into dreams. I was in my brother Giánnis's smithy. Giánnis hammered at a piece of iron that glowed under the hammer's force, and I pumped the bellows, fueling the flames until they burned high and blue. Soon, the hammering became more insistent, as if the hammer were driving my brother, rather than the reverse. I had to drop the bellows to cover my ears and escape the relentless sound.

When I awoke soaked in sweat, the sound continued; someone was pounding on the front door. I stumbled into my Franciscan robes, which I was grateful to see had been washed.

Itria opened the front door, her white coif askew. Outside in the bright daylight stood five men, and at their head an armed sergeant wearing the Angevin blue and gold. His arm was raised, and I thought he was about to run Itria through with his sword. Then I realized he had been hitting the door with the butt of his weapon.

"We don't like to wait, *puterelle*. Where's your husband?"

Itria did not respond to the crude insult. "He is out."

"You'll have to do." The sergeant smirked. His face was ruddy, with vessels spidering his cheeks and nose. Sweat-matted black hair edged out from the brim of his helmet; a matching thatch poked up over his tunic's neckline. Itria stood stiff as a fire iron. "The king requires grain, cattle, pigs, and horses for the armada's expedition. As you are a loyal subject of the king, you will provide these expediently."

The pause before Itria's answer was uncomfortably long. "I prefer you return when my husband is here. Who shall I say came calling?"

"I'm Sergeant Drouet, and I don't care what you prefer." The soldier stepped forward, too close to Itria, and in the way of her closing the door.

I stepped out of the shadows. "Signora Trabucco, may I assist you?"

Itria turned slowly, relief on her face. She'd thought she was alone. "Please, Brother Francis."

My disguise, and my basic competence at French, kept the king's officers civil. We walked to the storeroom, the animal pens, and finally the stables, where Drouet chose the best horse with deliberate slowness. Itria gripped my arm.

She and I stood outside the house, watching the soldiers leave with their newly acquired supplies and livestock. Drouet and his men did not pay for what they took, and we could not argue. When they were out of earshot, Itria turned to me. Her voice was savage.

"Your job is to incite anger against King Charles and his French pigs." She let go of my arm, which had gone numb under her hand. "You are charged to ensure that rage runs hot in the blood of the Palermitani, hot enough to burn this brutal kingdom to ashes. These men, stealing in the name of their king, have done your work for you."

ELIAS BORGHES
Holy Week 1282
Sicily

Trabucco's house lay on the outskirts of Palermo, near the Oreto river. From there we could see the city walls. "The city is closer than it looks—an easy walk," Vicenzu said, stepping his fingers along the kitchen table for illustration. "And there we'll soon do our business." A fly landed on the table, and Vicenzu, punctuating his words, flattened it with one hand.

Each day of that week leading up to Easter, we started at dawn with a prayer in the Church of the Holy Spirit. Consecrated on the day an eclipse plunged the world into darkness, the church was, to my eye, severe, but I was not accustomed to seeing beauty in the Latin image of the Divine. The church was all straight lines where ours had graceful arches, and the windowless length of stone along the church's side seemed blind and uncaring, as if to make us fear God rather than love

Him. Whether the architecture echoed my sense of holiness or not, Easter was imminent, a holiday that I would share with the Palermitani and, with it, the departure of Charles's fleet.

I stood outside the church's narrow door, listening to the river rush along, full with spring rain. The churchyard was packed with burghers, farmers, servants, and peasants who thronged the entry for mass. A Cistercian friar gave me a brotherly nod, a gesture I'd never experienced in lay clothes.

Al-Furat appeared beside me suddenly. "Do you worship as these Latins do, Elias of Mystras?"

It was a difficult question to answer. "Not exactly."

"Exactness exists only in mathematics," he said, but kindly.

"Similarities between our churches are not sufficient to prevent the Latins from sacking the greatest city in Christendom."

"By which I understand you to mean the events of seventy-eight years ago?"

I calculated in my head. "Exactly."

We both smiled. "You were not alive then," Al-Furat said.

"My mother would not let me forget."

"Mothers," Al-Furat answered, "are a powerful force." I suspected he was imagining his mother the way I was imagining mine. "Despite what you have been taught, you will join hands with these Latin worshippers in the service of their freedom?"

"Yes," I said. "As will you."

"My people have suffered as much as yours for our differences. But so have the Sicilians. Today we stand and pray with them, against our shared enemy, and for our mutual causes of justice and liberty."

Ω

Each day, Al-Furat, Trabucco, Vicenzu, and I walked into town just after services at dawn and returned at dusk. We had a week to foment as much unrest as possible so that at the moment the match of rebellion was lit, the fire would rage uncontrolled. We ate in taverns, visited landowners, and spoke to peasants surprised anyone wished to talk to them. We prayed in churches and befriended merchants. We walked through the bustling port where King Charles's soldiers picked out young Sicilian men to force onto the galleys. Trabucco and Vicenzu introduced me to their friends, colleagues, and acquaintances, who seethed with resentment. When we heard a grievance, we echoed it. When we saw anger, we fueled it. And when we met silence, we told stories of the ills we had witnessed at the hands of the king and his corrupt officials.

On my third day, I made an error that almost jeopardized our plans and nearly cost me my life. I came to a house on a street off Palermo's port. A woman stood on the doorstep with two children—a small girl clung to her leg while a baby cried in her arms. She looked frightened when I asked whether we might speak inside. But she let me in, with a respectful nod and a quiet "*Frati*" in Sicilian. As she juggled the two children's demands and served me a drink, I offered to help her, but she shook her head vehemently. I began to cautiously ask her questions. With each one, she became more and more anxious, her gaze darting frequently to the closed front door. When I asked how she fared under the French, she went white and gripped her infant to her chest.

"You had better go," she said, but too late. The door opened and I saw why she was so frightened. Her husband was dressed in the uniform of a Frankish soldier. He scowled and drew his sword. I saw myself from his perspective: a strange man threatening his terrified wife.

She put herself between us. "Julien, please! He is a man of faith. Let him leave unhurt." The baby in her arms began to scream outright, and the girl at her leg burst out into sympathetic sobs. Her husband reluctantly let me escape through the open front door.

I chose my targets more carefully after that. Later I thought of her, when I saw the danger that a Sicilian woman's marriage to a Frenchman could create. Her fear for her life and that of her children was justified.

We avoided the Frankish patrols, staying apart to avoid suspicion. One by one, we returned every night to Trabucco's house, where Itria presided over the cavernous kitchen, to review progress and make plans for the following day. And every night, as befitted Itria's culinary mastery, we ate. On Easter Sunday, we celebrated the holiday with the Palermitani as if nothing were amiss, but late that night, Vicenzu took me aside. "People trust you, Elias. You have spoken well and done justice to our cause. But I warn you—what comes next may require more body than mind." He handed me a dagger in a tooled leather sheath. "This is your next weapon. Are you prepared to use it?"

I looked down at the blade. "I am as prepared as I can be."

Vicenzu nodded. "That is as much as anyone can ask."

Ω

The next day, Easter Monday, fell early that year, on the twenty-ninth of March. Before Vespers, we gathered in the square outside the Church of the Holy Spirit for the festivities, along with what felt like the entire population of the island. The night was warm and smelled of orange blossoms. A band of musicians played as churchgoers spilled out into the square. A man with a weathered brown face held a goatskin bag and pipes that somehow produced many songs at once, a high melody over three deeper drones.

"Our *ciaramedda*," Vicenzu said with pride as he saw me staring. The other instruments were more familiar: a plucked lute and handheld drums. When the music began, everyone began to dance and sing. Trabucco took one of my hands and Vicenzu the other, and soon I was dancing, too, though it felt more like being pulled than anything graceful on my part. Itria's cheeks were rosy, and her straight brown hair escaped from the edge of the kerchief. Dressed for the festival, she wore a shawl of saffron yellow over her white coif, and her gown was deep blue with a silver brooch pinned at her throat. But it was her smile, so surprising on her serious face, that made her radiant.

The drums sped up, and the music grew frenetic. A figure draped in yellow ran into the plaza, his face hidden in a devil's mask. Two demon-faced dancers in red raced behind. Young children squealed with delight, pretending terror as the devils grabbed a man from the crowd.

"*Diavoli!*" the onlookers shouted, and I joined in the chant. From the door of the church, priests emerged with statues of Jesus and the Madonna, which swayed over our heads. Around them ran a herd of children dressed as angels, their feathered wings bouncing as they drove the devils away.

Suddenly, at the edge of the square, a group of soldiers in blue and gold appeared. The music faltered like a missed heartbeat. Sergeant Drouet was at the head of the band. They strode into the square as if they owned it. A wave of disapproval spread out from their passage, but Drouet paid no attention. He walked up to a man selling marzipan sweets from a tray and grabbed a handful. He stuffed two of the candies in his mouth and chewed, the almond paste gathering at the corners of his lips.

The dancing came to a halt. "They look drunk," Vicenzu whispered.

"We're here to enjoy the festivities," Drouet said with an almond-filled grin. "The fun that you Palermitani are famous for. Play on, in the name of your king." He waved a hand at the musicians.

Trabucco shouted his answer: "We play for God's honor on this day, not for *your* king." Several Sicilians clapped, and a murmur of assent spread through the crowd.

Drouet's face reddened, and he pushed his way through to Trabucco. "You will do as you are told or be arrested for treason." Itria broke from the line of dancers to join her husband, and Drouet's eyes shifted to her. "Ah, this is your little wife?" He took a step toward her, too close.

Trabucco put his hand on Itria's arm. "I'll thank you to keep your distance."

"Today is a holiday, meant for enjoyment," Drouet said, grabbing Itria's breast.

Trabucco did not look like a man built for speed. But in seconds, he'd drawn his dagger and driven it into the sergeant's chest. Drouet's mouth fell open, still full of marzipan. Trabucco drew out the blade, slick with blood, and stabbed Drouet repeatedly, until he folded to the ground, blood burbling from his wounds.

Vicenzu pulled out his hidden weapon and held it high in the air like a banner. "*Moranu li Franchiski!*" he shouted in Sicilian, years of anger ignited by this final outrage. *Death to the French.*

The remaining soldiers rushed at us, brandishing weapons, but they were too drunk and too few, outnumbered by the enraged Palermitani. The mob turned on King Charles's men, hacking at them until the paving stones of the churchyard were slick with blood. I fought next to Vicenzu. The worthy cause did not erase the horror. The bells of the Church of the Holy Spirit began to ring for Vespers: a song of Christ risen, now a song of revenge. One by one, churches throughout the city joined the chorus.

"*Moranu li Franchiski!*" The call spread through the crowd: to burghers, peasants, and priests, to the children dressed as angels. And the words became reality.

Enraged Palermitani ran toward the city gates, calling fellow Sicilians to join against the French. Church doors flew open and worshippers ran into the streets, shouting. Some carried swords and knives, others whatever weapon they could find—pokers, brooms, pitchforks, shovels, a broken goblet from which red liquid still dripped. As I ran past, I did not know if it was wine or blood.

We were carried on the rising tide of rage. The mob tore down the doors of inns, killing every Frank they found—not only uniformed officers, but also old men with canes, youths with the first fuzz of manhood on their cheeks, kerchiefed matrons, even Sicilian women who had made the deadly error of marrying Frankish men. All were slaughtered and left bleeding in the streets. I could not bring myself to kill without provocation. But when a French soldier threatened me or my comrades in rebellion, I used my weapon until it was stained with the Angevin blood of King Charles's men.

That night I found out the importance of Vicenzu's lessons. The swelling tide of rebels threw open the convents and monasteries, confronting each friar.

"*Ciciri,*" a Sicilian rioter snarled at one cowering brother, so young he'd likely just entered the monastery. "Say *ciciri.*" The French Dominican struggled with the unfamiliar syllables of a language it was said the French could never master. The Sicilian left the Dominican bleeding to death from a gash in his pale throat, unable to make a sound in any language. I, thanks to Vicenzu, passed that test. But my immediate reward was taking others' lives from them.

Just before dawn, the mob dragged a pregnant Sicilian woman into a public square where, accusing her of lying with a Frenchman, the rebels cut the mixed-blood babe from her belly, leaving mother and child to die. After that I ran without seeing, my heart breaking. At dawn, I found Trabucco at the gates of the old royal palace, his jolly face incongruously streaked with blood. When he smiled, his teeth were white against the gore.

"Good news, Elias: more than two thousand French are dead. Palermo is ours."

That was just the beginning. The first night of killing bled into days, then weeks. One night as we took shelter in the burned shell of the French justiciar's once-elegant home, Al-Furat found me huddled against the wall while the other two slept. "Even when justice is served," he whispered in the dark, "violence is still violence." I wept silently with my head on his shoulder.

Two weeks later, half of Sicily was under rebel control, but Messina still held out, loyal to the king. When Palermo flew the Messinese flag to show that all Sicilians were brothers, their allegiance to French rule finally broke. The Messinese and Palermitani joined forces and burned Charles's armada to ashes.

chapter twenty

ELIAS BORGHES
May 1282
Mystras

I returned to Mystras at the end of May. This time I traveled alone; Vicenzu stayed home. I brought the good news from Palermo, and for three days we feasted and danced in the plaza outside the governor's palace, celebrating Sicily's victory and Mystras's salvation. Though I celebrated, too, the memories haunted me. My mother embraced me fiercely, as though she had thought I might not return. But I felt, as I leaned down to rest my head on her shoulder, that I was receding on a boat pulling away from the shore, leaving everyone I loved behind.

Ω

Not surprisingly, Osanne did not appear at the festivities. Since the city celebrated the overthrow of a French king's rule, her perceived allegiance to the crown might endanger her life. She did not come to visit, for equally obvious reasons. Finally, on my fourth day home, I could not wait another moment to see her.

I left the house at dawn. It had rained in the night, and the air smelled of green growth and damp soil. I climbed the hill under cover of the trees that lined the path. The castellan's house appeared suddenly, shrouded in mist. It looked unreal and flat, like a cut-out house.

I crouched in the bushes. The shrubs reverberated with the songs of hidden nightingales, claiming the last hours of darkness. They woke and sang when other birds still held tight to their branches. I remembered my departure for Pelagonia a lifetime ago; then, too, the nightingales' songs had filled the air.

No one appeared at the door, and my legs began to tire. I lay down in the grass behind the hedge and drifted off to sleep. When I awoke, Osanne was standing over me.

"You have leaves in your hair," she said. I sat up slowly. She frowned. "For a while, I thought you might be dead. You might have sent a message."

"I couldn't."

She crouched down next to me. I could see the spray of freckles along the bridge of her nose. "I suppose you can't tell me where you were."

I closed my eyes and saw the pile of onions on Itria's counter, the belligerent sneer on Drouet's face, the hot blue Sicilian sky. I opened my eyes again. "You have more freckles than before." I touched her cheek. "I wish I could have taken some with me to remind me of you."

"These are *my* freckles," she said, but I could see a smile at the corner of her mouth. Her head moved subtly, and though she tried to suppress the movement, I'd seen it. I wanted to kiss her. She took my hand from her face and brought it to her belly, which swelled soft under her gown. "And this is our child," she whispered.

"Not with this Greek scum for a father," Fedryc growled, appearing from behind a high bush, a sword in his hand. He lunged at me, and I put up my hands, all I had to stop him. But Osanne, throwing herself between us, stopped him first.

DEMETRIOS ASANES
Winter 1310
Mystras

At first, silence was a choice. As the years passed, not speaking became a habit, then a necessity, and then a way of being. Elias has not come back this time. At least not to me.

The story is rising to the surface, now that there is no one left who could be hurt by it. My father is in the ground, buried beside Chryse, the love of his late life, the mother of the man who won my heart. My wife is gone, too, and my little sister, who should have outlived me.

I walked up the hill to the *kastron* on that misty spring morning, years ago. May is always full of hope and renewal, that May even more so, with the news of victory Elias had brought from Sicily. I remember the sound of the birds; on my way up the hill, a chorus of celebration; on the way down, an elegy.

Above the path that ran past the castellan's house, two vultures circled lazily overhead. The grass was trampled near the path that led to the door, and there was a metallic smell in the air. I made my way around the side of the house, where the bushes grew high and dense.

At first, I saw fragments of the scene: a hand outstretched, dark hair in which a leaf was caught, eyes staring blankly at the lightening spring sky. Elias lay beside the castellan's daughter under the bushes. So much blood. They were long gone, beyond help. The savage way they had been dispatched sent me to my knees in the damp grass.

The guards came and found Marceau Lusignan raving, wandering the path that leads from the Nafplio gate. They put him in a cell in the *kastron* where, I heard, he stopped eating and drinking and soon died. Fedryc had taken one of the horses and disappeared. There was no proof, but everyone suspected he'd killed his sister's suitor in his rage while she tried, and failed, to come between them.

I told Chryse what I had seen, and late that night, for the second time, we buried Elias, together. In the dark, with only the insomniac nightingales to bear witness, we put him in the earth beside his love.

After that, I kept silent for a long time. But now that I have started to speak, I cannot stop.

Ω

This is the book of the conquest of Constantinople by the Latins, of the empire of the Romaioi, and the land of Achaea. Throughout the world, some people are easily bored, and it annoys them to hear a long history, preferring instead to be told in a few words. Accordingly, I will tell my story as briefly as I can.

I shall tell the story of how Frankish prince Guillaume Ville-hardouin went to the Lacedaemon valley for the winter, and there chose the mountain called Myzithras on which to build a castle. I shall tell how on that hill the shrine of the Profitis Ilias once stood, and how the Romaioi still climb its slopes to pray even now that the shrine is gone.

I shall relate how the prince built himself a castle there, and called it his own, though the stones were taken from the ruins of ancient Sparta, and the land was governed by Romaioi lords. The prince realized that he would not be able to master the Romaioi because of the strong country where they dwelled. Even when he ruled them, and even when they appeared to do the prince's bidding, the Romaioi were not cowed.

For though the fortress and the palace were built in the Villehardouin name, still the kastron's walls sang out the name of the Profitis Ilias. And they welcomed his namesake, Elias, the servant of the stones, the guardian of the gates, whose bones would be the marble and whose veins the mortar of the walled city, whose blood would nourish the ground and whose soul would sing from one generation to the next like the nightingales before dawn, as constant as the recurrent sky.

As much as I found, as much I wrote of this Chronicle of the Morea.

part three

PHILOSOPHY

Man is composed of two elements, one mortal and one immortal.
Every time the body is destroyed, the two parts go their separate ways,
but the process is repeated throughout all eternity.

—From *The Book of Laws* (*Nomoi*), by Gemistos Plethon
(b. 1355–1360; d. 1452)

chapter twenty-one

HELEN ADLER
July 2015
Mystras

The bus from Nafplio arrived in Mystras only four hours behind schedule. Three elderly women were settled on folding chairs at the bus stop, drinking coffee and sharing a pile of pastries on a chipped ceramic plate.

"I love Greece," I said as we stepped into the late-afternoon heat. The women vacated their chairs, which were folded and carried away, along with the empty plate and cups, by the owner of the café where Alexander had first tried cherry soda.

"Not as much as I do," Alexander said.

We checked back in to the Mystras Inn. Panos, the proprietor who'd fed us Greek olive oil, was at the front desk, as if he'd never left.

"You are back," Panos said, beaming, and opened his arms in a welcoming hug.

Alexander hugged back. "Yes, *finally*."

I raised one eyebrow at Alexander's dig, clearly intended for me. He smiled slyly. "Is Elias here?"

Panos considered the question. "No, not today."

Alexander frowned. "He's always here."

Panos laughed. "Almost always. But not today."

I had not imagined a Mystras without Elias in it. "Is he okay?"

Panos turned to me. "A small cold." He looked at me a bit too keenly. "I tell him you came for him?"

I nodded, blushing hard enough to remind myself of spin the bottle in seventh grade, when Joe Gleason kissed me on the cheek.

Alexander was not as daunted by Elias's absence as I thought he'd be. "Panos, can I see the olive oil press?"

"Of course." Panos tilted his head. "But I have a better plan. It is not olive season. Come pick *vleeta* for dinner. Then you will be truly Greek."

Alexander perked up. "I know *vleeta*!" Alexander crowed, pronouncing the *f*-like Greek *v* perfectly. "I picked it with Yia Yia!"

"You have Yia Yia?" Panos smiled at me. "Already he has a Greek grandmother, this is very lucky. *Vleeta* is my favorite. We have picked and eaten *vleeta* since ancient times. You pick and eat *vleeta*, and you are part of our history. Also you will help feed our guests. Very *nostimo*."

I looked up the word in my downloaded Greek-English dictionary. "Delicious?"

"Just so. You pick with me?"

Alexander looked up eagerly. "Right now?"

"Of course! Put suitcases in room and we go . . . if Mitéra says yes . . ." Panos looked at me. "Okay I take your son? You come, too."

"*I* want to go with Panos," Alexander said firmly, "*Mom*." He clearly meant by himself.

"Take water," I said to his retreating back. He smiled over his shoulder; he'd already swiped a bottle from the cooler. I took a few waters for myself, then rolled the suitcases along the outdoor path to our room. I'd booked the same room as before; at least I knew its problems.

I put the key in the lock, which always stuck, and applied the exact combination of lift and pressure I'd perfected. A voice behind me made me jump.

"You are back."

I turned to see Elias, looking just as I remembered him, except a little puffier around the eyes. "Just got here," I said, realizing that I was smiling so broadly it made my jaw ache. "You're sick?"

"I'm not sick enough to prevent me from welcoming you back." He smiled almost as broadly as I had. "And now that you and Alexander have returned, I feel much better. Panos told me he was taking Alexander on an outing."

"News travels fast around here. Amaranth-picking . . . what do you call it again?"

"Ah, *vleeta*." Elias got an odd look in his eyes, as if he were seeing something I couldn't see. "We used to grow it in our garden."

"We never had a real garden, just window boxes. Then the building made us stop because they said the plantings brought rats. On a fourteenth-floor window ledge? What rat is interested in snapdragons anyway?" Elias laughed out loud, which I'd never heard him do. "Does harvesting *vleeta* require wielding a sharp implement? I shouldn't be so worried, but I'd like Alexander to keep his fingers."

"What greater treasure to protect could there be than a child?"

He was, despite his charmingly archaic phrasing, exactly right. "Do you have children?"

Elias paused. "No, I don't. But that does not lessen my appreciation for what they bring into the world." He picked up my bags before I could insist on carrying them myself. It was nice to get some help, even for just a few seconds.

"What are your plans, now that you are unexpectedly left to your own amusement?"

I laughed. "I haven't had time to consider the options."

"May I suggest an adult tour?"

"Is this a professional offer?" After I'd said it, I realized I sounded kind of irritable. Not that I expected him to ask me on a date, but this sounded more like a business referral. "Sorry, I don't mean to be grumpy. We had a rough bus ride here."

He smiled. "I suppose it broke down?"

"Spectacularly." It was hard to stay mad at him.

"I am sorry about the bus. I ought to have said, would you like to join me on a nonprofessional walk through the ruins of Mystras? I would welcome your company if you are interested."

"It wasn't only Alexander who wanted to come back." Elias pulled honest answers from me like a magnet.

"Then there is nothing to stop you from joining me."

"Unless you're too sick?"

As if on cue, Elias sneezed. "I would have to be very sick indeed to miss this opportunity."

I handed him a box of tissues from a side table.

"We should not waste another minute. Unless you need to recover from your harrowing bus trip." Elias took a tissue and replaced the box.

"I don't need anything. Except a tour." *And you.* The last two words sprang into my head unexpectedly. I locked the door behind us.

Ω

"Is there anything in particular you want to see?" Elias drove his car to the main gate of the lower town and parked in the lot.

"How about you take me to one of your favorite places?" The guard waved at us, saying something in Greek. Elias answered, equally incomprehensibly. As we walked through the gate, I asked Elias to translate.

"He said he thought I was taking the day off," Elias answered, leading me along the cobbled path.

"I hope I'm not getting you in trouble."

Elias didn't answer immediately. "I told him there were some visitors for whom a sick day could be ignored."

"I'm honored."

"As am I, by your presence," Elias said. I half expected him to bow. The sun brought out the faint scar on his cheek. "Here is one of my favorite places. The church of Agios Demetrios—Saint Demetrios in English."

He'd led me into a small courtyard bordered by a covered walkway with rounded arches. A big tree grew over the wall to the right. A dry fountain against the wall made me thirsty. I opened my water bottle for a drink. We were alone, except for a pair of sparrows hopping along the stones.

"Why do you like it here?"

Elias sighed. "It was *our* church. The first built after the Franks left. Before that, Greeks were subject to Latin rule. You know Greece is mostly Orthodox, distinct from Western Catholicism?"

"I'm Jewish. Can you give me a quick summary?"

"Possibly." He sounded doubtful.

"Now I'm pounding you for a comparative religion thesis. Sorry."

Elias laughed. "It's a good challenge. First, the Orthodox

church does not accept the infallible authority of the Roman Catholic pope. The pope is considered equal to other bishops."

"Okay, I follow."

Elias raised one eyebrow. "The next concept is a bit more difficult. It has to do with the origin of the Holy Spirit. The Orthodox church declared the Holy Spirit to come from God, the Father. The Catholic Church later added the words '*filioque*'—'and the Son.'"

"So the Holy Spirit arises from the Father *and the Son*? That's it? One little phrase?"

"The new wording was considered heretical by the Orthodox church. That has been a major force in the schism between the churches for almost a thousand years."

"I see what you mean by difficult. What were you saying about the Franks?"

"The *kastron* was built by the Frankish prince Villehardouin seven hundred sixty-six years ago, and it became Greek thirteen years later, I am happy to say. You likely realize I take history personally."

"It makes you an irresistibly fantastic guide." I am a sucker for people who know what they are talking about. Especially mysterious, restrained, chivalrous, intellectual, child-friendly, attractive people who know what they are talking about. Elias started coughing; I offered him my water.

"You have a mother's preparedness," he said, handing the bottle back to me.

"One of the benefits of being anxious. I tend to overprepare, just in case." We shared a smile. "Why else do you like this church?"

"Because of its beauty, and the saint to whom it is dedicated: Demetrios, the patron of soldiers."

He didn't seem the military type. "Were you in the army?"

"You could say that." I didn't want to press him for details.

Elias led me into the shade of the colonnade. "This is the west portico. I often come here to remember."

"Remember what?"

Elias changed the subject abruptly. "I thought you might be in mourning the first day I saw you in Mystras town."

"I thought I hid it better."

"Now I've offended you." He looked pained.

"I'm not offended. But what do you mean?"

"I mean that those of us who have known loss recognize it in one another. And I do in you."

"That is the kindest thing anyone has said to me in a long time." I could feel myself start to cry. And then, amazingly, we were in each other's arms.

Ω

I think too much; it's a bad habit. But at that moment, my mind was blissfully blank. I don't remember a second in my entire life when the chatter in my head went quiet like that. Instead, a flood of pure sensation: the sound of Elias's breathing, the pressure of his arms around my back, his sweet smell of thyme and sweat. I heard my pulse in my ears, or maybe it was his. My head fit under his chin, and I buried my face in his brown neck, dusted with sun-gold hairs. I felt like I was sinking into him, the way your head sinks into a down pillow on a perfect night of sleep.

I must have thought something—how could I not? I hadn't hugged anyone other than my sister and Alexander since Oliver's funeral. But it wasn't until later that the words to describe being in Elias's arms came to me: absolute safety and heart-pounding risk. He felt like home and at the same time like a terrifying leap off a cliff. I felt like I could finally rest, that the weight I'd been carrying for two years could be shared by someone else. My insides went liquid and warm, and I ached in a way I'd forgotten I could—with a dizzy, fierce longing that made my legs feel wobbly. And miraculously—especially given that it was my first widowed-mom romantic embrace—I didn't censor the feelings at all.

"Wow, that was a mind-bogglingly stupendous hug," I said, after the spinning subsided.

"I absolutely concur," Elias said into my ear, and then we had another, even better.

Ω

We got back to the Mystras Inn just as Panos was returning with a very sweaty Alexander. "Mom, look how much I picked!" He showed me a basket full of plants with ridged leaves and clusters of tiny green flowers.

"I can't wait to taste them," I said. "They smell amazing."

"Elias! I thought you were sick," he shouted.

"Well enough to give your mother a tour," Elias said.

"Did you have fun, Mom?"

"So much fun," I said, "but I missed you."

"I missed you, too." Alexander put his basket down and threw his sweaty self at me for a hug.

That night, Alexander and I shared three plates of *vleeta* at dinner, doused with Panos's olive oil. Plus two cherry sodas; I had one, too.

HELEN ADLER
July 2015
Historical Site of Mystras

Two days later, I came down with a cold, having proven the germ theory. For the record, Elias and I didn't kiss (though I'd desperately wanted to, the combination of my celibate mourning and his restraint kept things medievally slow), but we had shared my water. Though comparisons are odious, he was completely unlike Oliver. In many ways, this was a relief.

I wasn't sick enough to keep us from another tour. Alexander pulled out his own creased map when we got to the gate of the upper town. He pointed to number 17, a square structure halfway up the hill. "What is this?"

I looked at the map's key. "House of the Castellan."

Alexander checked my answer. "What's a castellan?"

Elias looked surprisingly uncomfortable. "A castellan is responsible for the upkeep of a castle. In the early days of Mystras's founding, the castellan had a great deal of responsibility, but later, after it transferred to Greek hands . . ." He trailed off.

"Elias?"

"I'm sorry. I was thinking. Later, once the governors came from Constantinople, the castellan's role lessened but he remained, out of respect for his years of service. He had two children." He went quiet again.

Alexander traced the little square on the map. "I hope I know as much as you do someday. Do you know the castellan's name?"

"Marceau Lusignan," Elias said after a pause.

I was overcome by an intense fit of coughing that made my eyes tear. Elias and Alexander ministered to me with water and tissues, then Alexander went back to the topic with the stubbornness of a pit bull. "Lusignan is the name of that man in the museum. But we'd seen him before that."

Elias touched his throat, as if there were something hanging there. "The name has been in this region for hundreds of years."

"Well, I don't like him. And I am usually right about people," Alexander said firmly. "So be careful."

"Thank you, I will." Elias took Alexander's warning with great seriousness.

As we headed up the hill to number 17, Alexander took Elias's hand and turned to me.

"Mom, you can hold Elias's other hand."

"If he doesn't mind." Elias and I exchanged glances.

"Of course I don't mind," Elias answered, and we walked up the hill together.

Ω

"There's hardly anything left." Alexander looked at the shell of the building.

"Did you expect something else?" Elias asked gently.

Alexander sighed. "Everything is ruins."

"What if I describe the way it used to be, and you imagine it?"

"Okay." Alexander closed his eyes. I closed my eyes, too.

Elias cleared his throat. "The house stands on one of the few level areas in the city. All around, steep streets lead up to the fortress atop the hill. The streets are narrow, crowded with people talking, laughing, walking their donkeys and horses, taking their wares to the market to sell—fruit and vegetables, sheep and goats. The house is big and elegant; two stories high with a fancy balcony. From the balcony, you can see the whole city stretching down the hill, and after that the valley, green and gray with the leaves of orange and olive trees, and then lower, the Evrotas river sparkling in the sun." I heard Alexander sigh. "The front of the house is decorated with arches, and there are smaller arched windows up above. Even the balcony has little arches below it."

"How do you know all this?"

"I've studied," Elias said.

"What about inside?"

"On the lower floor is a storeroom full of supplies: grain, olive oil, wine in barrels against the walls. After you enter the front door, you walk up a broad staircase. At the top of the stairs is a large, beautiful room. The walls are hung with thick tapestries of flowers and animals, people in long gowns."

"Women, you mean?" Alexander interrupted Elias's rhythm. I opened my eyes; he had, too.

"Men, too," Elias said. "We all wore robes then."

We, I thought. How funny.

"Weird." Alexander snorted.

"Not so weird if that's what you are used to," Elias said.

I let my mind wander. Maybe historians (and by extension tour guides) are so connected with the past they think of themselves as inseparable from people who lived hundreds of years ago. Or maybe Elias in particular, growing up at the foot of a ruin, felt fully a part of it. If we are wise, we acknowledge the past as our own.

Elias continued his virtual tour. "The floor is mosaic, tiny marble squares set in patterns of leaves and birds. Imagine a carved wooden table set with goblets of *thassorofron*, a foaming drink of almond milk sweetened with sugar, a bowl of olives gleaming with oil, and a white crusty bread so perfectly baked that you could eat nothing but that every day for the rest of your life and be perfectly content."

Alexander had started to squirm, bored by the food rhapsody. "So were there battles here or anything?"

Elias looked startled. "All houses have ghosts."

Alexander perked up. "Are bodies buried here?"

"Adults were not typically buried in houses, no more than they are today."

Alexander sensed a loophole in Elias's answer and wouldn't let the topic go. "Were *children* buried in houses?"

Elias's face flushed slightly. "Babies born before their time might be buried under the earthen floor . . . near the hearth. It is not a happy topic."

I expected Alexander to back off, but he didn't. "But that way the baby would always stay with its family. That's a good thing, right?"

"It is," Elias said. We all were quiet for a few seconds.

"So, people *did* die here?"

Elias sighed. "Yes."

"Like, who?"

"It was probably centuries ago," I said, trying to give Elias a break from the ruthless questioning.

"Who indeed?" The unexpected voice made me jump.

"Professor Lusignan," I said unenthusiastically, and dropped Elias's hand.

"What brings you to number seventeen on the Mystras map? Does the 'House of the Castellan' offer particular interest?" He showed his teeth like a bad drawing of a smile.

"Numerical order," I said.

"You've already seen one through sixteen. Your tour guide is quite industrious." Lusignan looked pointedly at Elias. "I hear from the museum staff that you have been here for quite some time. Extraordinary loyalty."

"It is a lovely place to work." Elias's voice was mild, but I sensed danger.

"I'm sure. Do you have family in the region? Or perhaps ancestors? Local genealogy is of particular interest to me."

It was almost a staring contest, Lusignan waiting for Elias to respond, Elias not responding.

Alexander broke the silence. "Elias, *do* you have ancestors from Mystras? That's almost as cool as being a demigod, like the son of Poseidon."

Alexander's version of the question worked better; Elias nodded. "Yes, my family does date back to the beginning of Mystras. We've never left, in fact."

Lusignan inhaled between his teeth, a sibilant sound. "Imagine that. Generation after generation, in the same remote little place."

"Mystras is amazing," Alexander said. "I could stay here *forever*."

Lusignan raised one eyebrow. "You are too young to understand what forever means."

"No one can imagine forever except God," Elias said. His answer gave me chills.

"Doctor Adler," Lusignan said, turning to me, "what on earth brings a scientist to a ruin of a nearly eight-hundred-year-old city? There can't be anything informative for your work here."

"Scientists do have other interests."

"Is there anything in particular that interests you about number seventeen?"

"It's all interesting," Alexander said. I realized Elias hadn't told us who had died. Maybe he didn't know.

Lusignan nodded. "So it is. I look forward to more. Dr. Adler, I should be delighted to discuss funding for your promising research. Did I give you my card?" He handed me another one, which I took, being careful not to touch him.

"*À bientôt*," he said with a wave, and headed down the hill. We watched his back.

"What does that mean?" Alexander asked, once Lusignan had disappeared.

"It means 'See you soon,'" Elias said.

I knew I probably should see him again soon, given what he knew. But I didn't want to.

ELIAS OROLOGAS
July 2015
Mystras

Into the uncomfortable silence after Lusignan left, I suggested we visit the Pantanassa. It was the only part of Mystras that still lived in the present, and I wanted Helen and Alexander to glimpse the way the city had once hummed with life.

"The nuns still work and pray in the monastery. It is perfectly restored, even though it is surrounded by ruins. You won't have to imagine how it might have looked." I showed Alexander the location on the map so he could lead the way. Helen let the back of her hand brush mine as we climbed the steep steps cut into the hill. Three days ago, I would have thought it an accident.

Sister Iosiphia met us at the arched entryway, a dripping hose in one hand.

"Will she squirt me?" Alexander said, his face red from the climb in the heat.

"No, unfortunately." Alexander rewarded my humor with a smile.

The long, narrow courtyard of the Pantanassa was lined with flowering plants. Tall, spindly bushes blazed with orange blossoms, honeysuckle vines climbed the crumbling stone walls, and potted magenta geraniums filled the air with their musky scent. I loved to sit here and watch the bees hovering while cats looped around my ankles. Sister Iosiphia turned off the tap and beckoned us to join her.

"I love geraniums," Helen said, with so much emotion I suspected there must be a story behind it.

"For more than five centuries, the Pantanassa has been the only continuously occupied building in Mystras. There are six nuns here, and Sister Iosiphia is the oldest," I translated.

"Older than you?" Alexander said. Sometimes an innocent question strikes at the heart of the unimaginable.

Helen gasped. "Alexander, that's not appropriate."

"Age is not an insult," I said.

Alexander apologized grudgingly. "I just meant you know so much, that's all."

Sister Iosiphia led us to the reception room of the monastery, where she displayed an array of hand-painted icons for sale. Helen chose one—the Profitis Ilias with his raven. *There are no coincidences.* Another sister brought us a plate of cookies, which Alexander ignored. Helen shook her head. "He hasn't developed a taste for Greek sweets." She took three.

Alexander went to play with the cats in the sun. His absence allowed me to say what I'd been thinking.

"You both seemed afraid of Pierre Lusignan," I said.

Helen frowned and tipped her head so she could see Alexander through the doorway. "He keeps turning up. He wants to know too much about me."

"It seems he respects your work."

"He still gives me the creeps. He's interested in the disease I study, and he's told me he has sources of funding, so I should be more receptive. I've heard of him. Professionally, that is." Helen twisted her hands together awkwardly. I didn't like the thought of them working together, but of course it was not up to me. "I don't like the way he talks to Alexander. Or to you."

"Are you anxious on my behalf now?"

Helen sighed loudly. "Oh, brilliant. I've taught you my worst feature."

I had difficulty seeing any bad features at that moment. Helen was wearing a pale green sundress that left her lightly freckled shoulders bare. Perhaps she had more freckles than she did when she arrived, or perhaps I was paying more attention.

She grinned, and I wanted to kiss her. "I feel lucky to be among those you find worth being anxious for," I said, not sure of the syntax. When she blushed, I knew I had made my point.

Ω

I have lived too many times to believe in coincidences. She studies the *chorea*, and Lusignan is following her. He is watching me, too. In fact, he is more than watching. The morning after I met him for the first time, the docent Ms. Brathwaite, whose gray curls gripped her head like a helmet, conveyed a message.

"The esteemed Professor Lusignan, renowned for his scholarship at the University of the Peloponnese, extends his most sincere invitation for an in-person meeting to discuss Important Matters of History to which your knowledge might be particularly complementary," she said, with an intensity that implied too-frequent capitalization, "which, if I were you, I would accept with Enthusiasm, and Gratitude."

She penned a carefully written note, which included, in addition to the professor's (unpleasantly familiar) name, his contact information as well. It was written in a flowery script that reminded me of overstuffed velvet couches and lavender sachets.

I thanked Ms. Brathwaite graciously, murmuring vague assent. But I had no intention of returning his call, and certainly not of seeing the professor in person again. Despite my avoidance, he'd already found me twice, the second time on the path to number 17.

After I left Helen and Alexander at the door of the Mystras Inn, the encounter with Pierre Lusignan replayed in my head. Lusignan was not a common name in Greece. And this particular Lusignan found me at the doorstep of the house where a family that shared his name twitched and stumbled into madness, and where my second life ended savagely. It could not be an accident.

I returned to the museum. For me, a museum is a strange place. It keeps the past at a distance, but I know the past lives and breathes. I do find comfort in seeing the artifacts of my earlier lives: a dress like my mother wore, a book from the philosopher Plethon's time at Mystras, full of wisdom that would challenge and change the world. Today, though, I came not for reminiscence, but for answers. I came back for the Chronicle.

It was near closing time, and the docent, not recognizing me at first, waved me away officiously. She was severely nearsighted, so I forgave her error. Once I greeted her, she blustered apologetically.

"I need to see the Chronicle, out of its stand," I said.

She frowned. "You'll have to ask the director."

I went to find the museum director, who knew my competence in handling historical documents. Soon, hands washed and carefully dried, I was ensconced in a private room with the Chronicle, out of its case and resting in a velvet book stand.

I wanted to put down the pointed white book snake and touch the fragile paper and worn leather binding. I wanted to touch something that had been there, then. But, of course, I did not. First, I read the page about the siege of Monemvasia that I'd seen with Helen and Alexander, and the copyist's marginal note. I turned the pages. There was, as the docent had said, no information about the building of Mystras in the text. I would have to read the entire book. The writing was faded, but the language easy to understand.

> This is the book of the conquest of Constantinople by the Latins, of the empire of the Romaioi, and the land of Achaea. Throughout the world, some people are easily bored, and it annoys them to hear a long history, preferring instead to be told in a few words. Accordingly, I will tell my story as briefly as I can.
>
> For though the fortress and the palace were built in the Villehardouin name, still the kastron's walls sang out the name of the Profitis Ilias. And they welcomed his namesake . . .

The text stopped midsentence. I could see the place where pages were missing, torn from the manuscript. The edges were dull with years of wear. Whatever had been taken away had disappeared a long time ago.

I went back and read again.

And they welcomed his namesake . . .

When I came again to that fragment of a sentence, I felt the hair rise on the back of my neck. I knew the words referred to me. And someone had made certain the next section would not be found.

I read until I finished the entire chronicle, looking for an answer. I read the story of the prince I had served, of the battle I had fought, and of the companions I had lost in my first life, centuries ago. Several times I heard the director open the door behind me, then close it softly again. Finally, I reached the last page.

As much as I found, as much I wrote of this Chronicle of the Morea.
    —Demetrios Asanes, Mystras, In this year of our Lord, 1310

And for a moment in that little room I felt, though I had only paper and ink to keep me company, that I was not alone after all.

chapter twenty-two

ELIAS SARANTOPOULOS
Spring 1436
Mystras

I had no inkling during my third childhood that there might be anything unusual about me, other than the way I'd been found. My mother, after struggling for years to bear a child, had, on a walk near the *kastron*'s high walls, heard the sound of a baby crying. She found me, naked and squalling in a glade of trees, where a shrine to the Profitis Ilias had once stood. "The prophet sent you to assuage our loneliness," my mother told me, once I was old enough. My father, who ran a silk manufacturing business and tended more toward the practical than spiritual, smiled indulgently. The version he told was more mundane: a family too poor to raise me had left me to be found and cared for. In any case, when my mother chose my name to be Elias after the prophet, my father did not disagree.

My old memories stayed hidden. Looking back, I believe it was because there was no one left to remind me. My third life began almost a century and a half after my last had ended; everyone I had ever loved was long gone. And we had a new enemy to worry about: the Turks. Even though I was a child, I understood enough of my parents' hushed conversations to know that outside Mystras, enemy Turkish forces were gathering. But I was also young enough to think that we, in our mountaintop walled city of Mystras, were perfectly safe.

When I turned six, the looming threat of the Turks abruptly became real. At our evening meal, my father held his knife poised over the *aphraton*, ready to cut a piece of his favorite dish of fluffy hearth-baked chicken and egg whites topped with honey. A bowl of boiled grape hyacinth bulbs sat on the table, cooked with olive oil and fish sauce, drizzled with vinegar. My mother and father were drinking pear wine. The evening air was soft and warm, blowing through the open shutters that led to our balcony overlooking the Evrotas valley. My linen tunic was new, and the wool embroidery around the neck made me itch.

When the heralds came with news of messengers arriving from the Imperial City, we climbed the hill to the despot's palace. That was when my perspective shifted to see the wide, alarming world.

Turkish forces—the messengers said—under Sultan Murad had surrounded Constantinople, now under siege. My mother squeezed my hand so hard my fingers went numb. "They will come for us next," she said under her breath.

She was right. The following year the Turks destroyed the Hexamillion, the great wall separating the Peloponnese from mainland Greece. Crowded into the plaza again, we listened to the news as the sultan's troops advanced south, destroying everything in their path. General Turakhan Bey, Murad's commander, was said to leave the blood of his enemies on the blade of his curved *kilij* sword and smear it on his bread at dinner. The Turks butchered half their enemies and made slaves of the rest. My boyhood nightmares alternated between the two fates.

The Turks came as far as Mystras's lower town, stopping just outside the walls. I looked out at the army spread across the Vale of Sparta, a dark stain against the green, smoke rising from their camps.

Thanks to God and the masons who made our walls strong, a few days later Bey gave up and retired with his troops. We were able to breathe again. But when my father took me out riding afterward, the devastation was evident. Towns and fields were burned, villages looted, hundreds of soldiers and civilians left dying or dead. We were an island in a sea of destruction. We celebrated when the Turks retreated from the Peloponnese, and the siege of Constantinople lifted, but it was a muted relief.

My mother told me that Constantinople had been saved by the love of the Theotokos, the Holy Mother of God. Witnesses reported that soldiers saw a woman walking the ramparts of the city, haloed in divine light. The grateful citizens of Constantinople shouted hymns to the Virgin. The following day, the besieging army departed. My mother gave me an amulet to wear: an image of the Virgin carved into amethyst. I hoped the Theotokos would protect us, too, in our time of need.

Despite the political upheaval, I was raised with the security that I, like my silk manufacturing father and his father before him, would follow the same prosperous path. I learned the trade in the factory where workers soaked the cocoons in water, untangled the delicate strands, and spun them into thread. Spending hours walking through the white mulberry groves that covered the hillside behind the factory, I watched the worms eat themselves into a blissful stupor. My father told me how the silkworms find all their sustenance from the leaves. Although they were blind white larvae destined to die for the thread they create, the undiluted focus of their lives moved me. I wondered what I might accomplish with such single-minded devotion.

Ω

In March of 1436, when I celebrated my twentieth birthday, I encountered someone from my past. Like all twenty-year-olds, I thought I knew a great deal already, and like most of them, I was wrong. I'd left a meeting with a Venetian merchant whose ships would bring Mystras damask across the Arabian Sea. The trader was a ponderous man with three chins and no neck. He spoke Greek competently, and called me *paidí*—youngster. I tolerated his condescension silently; a sale is a sale. I escaped the meeting flushed with irritation and desperate for a walk.

I had found a new place to wander: the new Church of the Pantanassa. Its graceful bell tower rose from the steep hillside where the multidomed church perched, and the quiet sunlit cloister and portico with its colonnade of arches was the perfect place to walk in silence. On this occasion, though, I did not find the solitude I was looking for.

As soon as I crossed the threshold of the monastery, I met a wizened woman with eyes set deep in wrinkles, the corneas milky white. She wore a dark habit that reached to her ankles, but not the headdress of a nun. Bent with age, she was watering the plants that lined the walkway; she held a bucket full of water that sloshed over the rim to pool at her feet.

She opened her mouth, but no sound came out. She had no teeth, and her tongue was stained dark from chewing cloves. The silence was alive, undulating between us. I moved to help with the bucket, but she grasped it tighter. The water spattered the ground.

When she spoke, her voice sounded like a door moving on a rusty hinge.

You are the one to whom the stones speak.

A tendril of memory began to uncurl in my head. Her words made no sense, but I had heard them before.

Elias, Ilias, Mystras, Myzithras. These are the four: the boy, the prophet, the city, the hill.

I felt cold, even in the sun.

Give me something you hold dear.

I removed the Theotokos amulet and put it in her bony outstretched hand. She fingered it and shook her head.

No use to me.

I took it back carefully, afraid to touch her. "I have nothing else."

I shall take your blissful ignorance, she whispered, and she reached out and touched my cheek where a faint scar curved from an injury I could not remember. Her hand gave me a jolt, like an errant spark from a fire on bare skin.

The souls of the dead are sent forth into the generation of living things.

I knew the teachings of Plato. This was not a doctrine that most would dare to repeat, certainly not in a church, where transmigration of souls was heresy. She did not wear a cross about her neck. But if not a nun, who was she?

"I have studied Plato," I said carefully.

She leaned forward. Her eyes were white-blind, and I was afraid.

You know nothing, though you bear the Prophet's name.

Seek out the teacher who calls himself Plethon.

Follow him, and keep his words safe.

His enemies will be yours.

You are the watcher in the shadows.

The keeper of the word.

The sun disappeared behind a drifting cloud. Everything

froze, birds in their arcs, insects in midflight. The old woman dropped the pail; it clattered against the stones. She turned away, leaving me soaked to the knees and shivering from more than cold.

Ω

Not yet ready to return to the hum of our factory's looms, I went up the three steps into the cool dark of the church. Inside, the walls were covered with frescoes, glowing pink, blue, green, and gold. The Virgin looked down on me, the holy infant on her lap. I wondered whether her gaze held a reprimand, knowing that I had been prepared to give up her icon.

The arch of the sanctuary depicted the ascension of the Virgin; at the center, the luminous archangel tilted his head, haloed with gold. I walked from one scene to the next: the Virgin and infant lying in a cave, the entry into Jerusalem—so real I felt I could walk straight into the city where streets wound through fissured rocks and towers of stone.

In the north arm of the church, I stopped to stare at the image painted on the wall. A man was bound in a linen shroud, but he stood upright in an open coffin: Lazarus, with Jesus commanding him to come forth from the dead. Resurrection— all will rise at the Last Judgment, as Jesus once did—was what I had been taught and what I had believed.

Today the crone in the Pantanassa courtyard had shown me another path: *The souls of the dead are sent forth into the generation of living things.* Reincarnation, not resurrection, the flight of the soul from one body to the next. Belief in the transmigration of souls was Platonic heresy. But for reasons I could not quite understand, today the heresy had the ring of truth.

I shall take your blissful ignorance, the crone had said, touching the scar whose origin I could not recall.

chapter twenty-three

ELIAS SARANTOPOULOS
Summer 1436
Mystras

Nearly everyone had heard of Gemistos Plethon. He'd been a senator in Mystras and was one of the most respected judges in the Despotate of the Morea. He'd resolved one dispute for my father—a trader whose goods were lost at sea demanded compensation for his loss; however, a silk manufacturer is responsible only for the quality of the weave, not for the weather. Plethon favored our cause, and so my father favored him. My mother, though, as usual, had a different perspective. I often wondered what had brought my parents together at all.

"Plethon was expelled from Constantinople as a heretic," my mother said. "I don't care if he supports our business interests."

"He was not expelled," my father said, patting my mother on the shoulder as one might a child.

"Plethon was a menace to the faith, that's why he ended up here," she said. "The emperor's own religious adviser, Scholarios, sent him out of Constantinople so he wouldn't make any trouble. And then he gets here and calls himself Plethon, after Plato himself? And thinks he can espouse reincarnation while being a senator?" My mother grunted with disgust. "Let him deprive himself of meat if he thinks he might come back as a rat in his next life. I'll eat my lamb and aspire to heaven instead."

My father liked to pretend that nothing was amiss. My mother, on the other hand, expressed all her emotions visibly, and many were negative.

My father smiled indulgently at my mother and stroked her hair. "I love your passion and faith, Theodora," he said.

"You love my hair," she replied, pushing his hand away.

Ω

I'd seen Plethon striding across the plaza outside the despot's palace with his students in tow. He had the white hair and beard of an old man, but I'd never seen an old man walk like that, and I'd never heard him speak. My father's business schedule and my mother's distaste had kept me away from the philosopher.

Seek out the teacher who calls himself Plethon.
Follow him, and keep his words safe.
I'd memorized the words.

The day after I'd met the crone in the Pantanassa, I headed up the hill toward the palace. It was warm, and by the time I reached the plaza I was desperate for a drink. I threaded through the crowds of people and livestock to the fountain. A grumpy donkey butted me when I got in his way, and the man holding the donkey's lead apologized profusely. He had a long, narrow head and large ears that made him look uncannily like his animal.

"Terribly sorry. I've already offended you and I haven't even met you. Are you thirsty? Please accept a drink." The man took the bucket he'd intended for his donkey and thrust it in my direction. Unfortunately, his sudden movement resulted in half of the water leaving the bucket and splashing me.

His cheeks flushed. "Now I've made it worse. You're all wet. Why does everything always go wrong?" He took the edge of his robe and began to blot me with it unsuccessfully.

"It's a warm day, don't concern yourself." The water was refreshing, though not what I'd intended. I helped myself to a drink from the fountain, avoiding the donkey's bucket.

"I've made an idiot of myself, and I don't even know your name."

"My name is Elias Sarantopoulos, and I don't consider you an idiot." I couldn't help smiling.

"I should have introduced myself: I am Hieronymous Chrystonimos Charitonymos. You must have come here for some reason other than to be nosed by a donkey and doused with water by a perfect stranger. I'm here quite often, what with the donkey and the fountain and all, though of course, I have other things to do. I'm a scholar, but the stableboy doesn't seem to get along with this beast. In fact, just last week this little fellow kicked the boy in the kneecap. It swelled the size of a melon, and he can't walk now." I stepped backward instinctively.

Charitonymos turned an even darker shade of red. "He won't hurt you. At least I think he won't."

"I'm sure your donkey is very well behaved, and his owner shows abundant kindness." Poor Charitonymos wanted so desperately to be liked that I couldn't keep myself from obliging. "In any case, I'm looking for Gemistos Plethon. I know he lectures here in the square."

Charitonymos began to wring his hands, twisting the donkey's halter into a tight helix. "You're looking for *Plethon*?" He took a long, ragged breath, and then burst into tears. "You could not find a better man." He wiped his eyes. "Plethon is prudent, courageous, just, and wise. He has extraordinary knowledge of all things human and divine, in counsel and in action, in military and civil affairs, in scientific and practical matters. He has unprecedented mastery of things known in speech, theoretically and in practice, things known by the mind alone, and things known in harmony and diagrams and numbers and the revolution of heavenly bodies. He is the most important figure ever to have appeared on Earth."

I had not expected a speech. "I am glad to hear that. But why are you crying?"

Charitonymos hung his head. "Plethon has rejected me. I've begged him to take me on as a student, but he always refuses. I have implored our Lord to help his servant Plethon see my earnest desire to study and serve. I would do anything to sit at Plethon's feet." The tears rolled down his long cheeks.

I was moved by Charitonymos's earnestness. "Perhaps someday your longing will be satisfied, and Plethon will recognize your devotion and reward it."

"May God hear your words," Charitonymos said, pointing across the plaza. "But in the meantime, there he is."

ELIAS SARANTOPOULOS
Late Summer 1436
Mystras

I continued to learn the silk manufacturing process, and the business of local sales and export. The labor involved in producing silk thread meant nothing could be wasted; we made first-rate silk from the continuous filaments, and *koukoulariko*, a coarser fabric, from the floss that had to be spun before it could be woven. I supervised the dyeing. We used indigo imported from the East, and red made from insects that bled bright when crushed. Yellow came from onion skins, or for special occasions, imported saffron. Shellfish purple was regulated and worn only by the imperial court in Constantinople.

At the same time, I secretly became one of the *phratría*, or brotherhood of Plethon's initiates. It took many rounds of questioning to prove that my intentions were pure and my aptitude sufficient to merit entry. I, like his other students, hung on his every word. I could not bear to tell Charitonymos that I had won the prize he so desperately wanted.

Gemistos Plethon was in his seventies when I met him for the first time, but he overflowed with energy. For public lectures, he paced in the plaza as devoted listeners scurried behind. He was tall and his head rose above the crowd. He was easy to spot, but his stride was hard to match. He had a thick gray beard in the Greek style (he said he wished to be recognized as Greek without having to speak), and a long mustache that flowed into it. He wore his beard proudly but cared for it haphazardly. His body was a vehicle for philosophy; he paid little attention to it. One day Plethon arrived so preoccupied by a philosophical quandary that he did not notice his beard had trapped bread and honey from his morning meal. He also failed to realize that a small yellow butterfly, attracted by the honey, had settled there, too. The *phratría* were all hopelessly distracted by the fluttering.

The *phratría* met in Plethon's house in Mystras and included a monk named Basilios Bessarion who did not fit my preconceived notion of an inward-turning man of God. He'd come from Trebizond along the Black Sea and worked in the diplomatic service of the Emperor of Constantinople, John

VIII Palaiologos. Bessarion would have been a formidable teacher in his own right; here he was my fellow student. I felt completely out of my depth. On my first day, we plunged into a philosophical ocean, and I struggled to stay afloat.

"Today," Plethon said, spreading his arms, "we will debate Aristotle's and Plato's views on the nature of God." I had never before known it possible to discuss even one view of God's nature.

"Let us start with Aristotle," Plethon said.

Bessarion whispered in my ear, "The master is starting with Aristotle because he disagrees with him—be careful."

I was glad of the warning. As soon as Plethon got an unsuspecting student to commit fully to agreement with Aristotle, he proceeded systematically to take the answer, and the student, apart.

"Everything that is in motion must be moved by something else. Elias, do you agree?" My heart stopped. After several seconds of silence, Plethon said. "The question will not devour you, Elias."

I thought of a ball rolling down a hill. I thought of rain falling from the sky. I did not know what moved the ball or the rain. "Even if we do not know what moves objects in motion, something must."

Plethon smiled at me. "A good start," he said. "There cannot be an infinite number of movers. There must be some root cause of motion that does not move itself."

"The unmoved mover," Bessarion said.

Plethon looked at him. "Precisely. And this mover must be pure energy, an eternal substance. The unmoved mover, Aristotle tells us, is God." Plethon seemed to grow larger as he turned from Aristotle's to Plato's views. "But listen, brothers: How can we limit God's role to movement and change? Aristotle never calls God the creator, demeaning the grandeur of the divine. Plato teaches us that God is the creator of our entire universe. Plato's God is thereby both the end and the cause of existence."

That night, I fell asleep at the dinner table. My mother, worried I was ill, made me a poultice and put me to bed early, but I was the most well I had ever been.

Following Plato's teachings was dangerous; many considered them outright heresy. The most dangerous of Plethon's detractors was Georgios Scholarios, monk, theologian, and personal adviser to the emperor. Had I listened harder to my mother's and father's argument about him, I would have been better prepared for what happened and better able to stop it.

Plethon lived in the upper town, where the houses were large and far apart, enough to allow for terraced gardens along the slope of the hill and balconies facing the valley. The *phratría* always left his house a few at a time, to make our gatherings less obvious. The night Scholarios arrived, Bessarion, who had taken me under his wing, kept his hand on my arm, and we walked out together. Bessarion led me down through the Monemvasia gate to the lower town, where houses crowded close together, then outside the walls to the market, which teemed with vendors, shoppers, and livestock. The early summer offerings made my mouth water—*vleeta*, strawberries, blushing apricots, and the early crop of pistachios in their creamy white shells. Bessarion squeezed between two stalls, and we emerged into an alley where vendors' tents backed onto one another. He let go of my arm.

"No one will hear us, here," Bessarion said quietly. A few pigs rooted in produce too bruised to sell, but otherwise we were alone. I wondered why he'd brought me here. "Georgios

Scholarios is coming to Mystras. He is a man of great learning, well versed in theology and philosophy."

I could not tell where the conversation was heading. "Such knowledge is to be admired."

Bessarion smiled slightly. He had a thick beard like Plethon's, but his was carefully groomed and parted down the middle. "Scholarios is a theological adviser to the emperor, may God give him long life."

I wondered if Bessarion was trying to decide whether to confide in me. "To tell me this, you take me to a back alley, surrounded by rotting vegetables and pigs?"

Bessarion burst out laughing. "You are more humorous than you appear."

I felt myself flush. "No one has found me amusing before."

"No one was listening." Bessarion's expression shifted. "Scholarios is coming to Mystras, ostensibly to attend Plethon's lectures."

"Ostensibly?"

"I suspect he has many motives. You may know that Scholarios is a proponent of the teachings of Aristotle and considers the study of Plato ill-advised."

"You mean heretical."

"That is what Scholarios would say."

"And he is coming to find out?"

"I am afraid he suspects. And when he finds out, Plethon and his students will be in danger."

I thought about what Bessarion was saying. Plethon and Scholarios, taking opposite sides in an argument about the nature of the divine and the cosmos—Plato versus Aristotle, creator versus mover, heretic versus believer. Who was the keeper of the true faith, and who was the blasphemer? "Why are you telling me this?"

Bessarion narrowed his eyes. "If Scholarios gets evidence of Plethon's heresy, we are all at risk. Be careful."

I thought of my parents' uneasy truce. "I know how to be careful," I said. Bessarion, satisfied, led me back into the safety of Mystras's walls.

Ω

The Despot of the Morea, Demetrios Palaiologos, whose governing seat was in Mystras, welcomed Scholarios with a banquet. Charitonymos, more successful at the despot's court than with Plethon, regaled me with details of the menu. "A fat suckling kid stuffed full of garlic, onion, and leeks, and drenched with fish sauce." I had not yet eaten and had to stop him. Charitonymos also mentioned that Scholarios had brought a student with him. I wondered why.

Scholarios soon attended one of Plethon's public lectures. A crowd had gathered to hear the topic of the day: fortune. I watched Scholarios where he sat on a temporary dais. He had a thick beard and long mustache, like most Greek men, and a thin-lipped down-turned mouth. Even when his face was at rest, he seemed to be frowning disapprovingly. Most strikingly, though, he looked like he knew he was always right. That was dangerous.

"Do you study with Plethon?" Bessarion had moved away from my side, and in his place stood a man near my age. He was disturbingly thin, with dark circles beneath his eyes. I had the feeling that if he put a meal into his mouth, he could not be nourished by it.

"I have the good fortune to," I said, cautiously avoiding

mention of our private circle, "by virtue of the lectures we are all privileged to hear."

"An earful of blasphemy is not good fortune." The man spoke Greek like a Westerner. His head jerked forward when he spoke.

"Gemistos Plethon is a man of learning whose belief in God is in keeping with his intellect."

"*My* master, Georgios Scholarios, advises the emperor on matters of theology," the stranger said, and I realized he was Scholarios's student. "*Your* teacher was exiled by the emperor for espousing *the transmigration of souls.*"

The topic made me uneasy but I did not know exactly why. "Does your family reside in Constantinople?" He jerked his head forward again. The movement reminded me of something.

"My family sent me there to study. From Paris," he said smugly. "My ancestors owned yours when La Morée was as dignified as the Frankish court."

I tried to keep my voice level. "We have never been slaves."

"Soon you will be, when the Turks return."

Constantinople was as vulnerable to the Turks as Mystras, but I did not bother to argue that point with a Frank who took what he liked from the scholars and derided the rest. "I don't know your name." I held out my hand in greeting. "I am Elias Sarantopoulos."

His fingers twitched in mine, like a dying fish. "Guarin Lusignan," he said. Then the memories flooded through me, like a river through a broken dam.

chapter twenty-four

HELEN ADLER
July 2015
Mystras

I suppressed my misgivings and scheduled a meeting with Pierre Lusignan about funding. Money for science is hard to come by and worth enduring a fairly large amount of discomfort. Plus, Lusignan was likely to be a source of information that could transform HD genetics, even lead to a cure. I farmed Alexander out to Panos again, who planned a fig-picking trip.

I set the meeting in the most public place I could think of: an outdoor table at the café in Mystras town's main square. We had the company of three middle-aged Greek men chain-smoking and drinking Greek coffee. Lusignan offered me lunch. I ordered sparkling water and asked for a separate check.

We talked through my general interest in neurodegeneration, and my specific focus on Huntington's disease. He knew more about science than I expected and had read my papers. We spent a few minutes reviewing triple repeat disorders, and the accumulation of the abnormal protein in the brain. I made everything accessible and appealing to someone trying to give away money.

Lusignan had made it through his appetizer and main course when we got to the crux. He leaned forward. I could see the sweat beading on his forehead. "Are there therapeutic implications to your research?"

I'd heard this question many times before. Therapeutic implications were a funder's dream. They meant dull bench science could help sick people get better or prevent people from getting sick at all. The holy grail: bench to bedside.

"Of course. Stem cell technology is progressing rapidly, and with evident paths toward treatment."

"Even for Huntington's disease?"

"Brain-derived stem cells are one promising approach, but these cells are hard to obtain. That's a major obstacle, particularly with humans, as you might imagine."

"Indeed," he said.

"A second problem with stem cells is their tendency to cause tumors."

"Is that insurmountable?" Lusignan had left half of his lamb shank uneaten.

"If it were, I wouldn't have a job," I said, almost smiling. But then I remembered who I was talking to. "One solution is using somatic cells—meaning 'of the body'—instead."

"I am familiar with the term," he said drily. "*Soma* is a Greek word."

"Right. Anyway, somatic cells—and when I use that term here, I mean not stem cells—can't give rise to every cell in the body but they can be used for this sort of research. Somatic cells are easier to access and may not pose the same dangers of tumor formation. But there are still risks."

"Somatic cells from where, exactly?"

"Bone marrow, fat. Brain, of course."

"Brain is better because it's closer to the target?"

"That's not what I said. And there are other technologies that don't involve human tissue at all."

I had the sense that he would take whatever I said and turn it to support his own theory. Some people hear only what they want to hear, and once they've justified their preconceived notions, they're done.

He pushed his plate away. "Once you have these pluripotent cells, then what?"

"You induce them to form the kinds of cells you want, in this case neurons without abnormal repeats."

"And then?"

"Then you transplant them into brains of individuals with Huntington's. Ideally, that gives rise to normal neurons in the Huntington brain."

"Clearly this would have occurred already if there were no barriers to success." Lusignan leaned back.

"True. Neural stem cells rather than pluripotent stem cells have lower risk of tumor formation, but there are still safety issues."

"I see. And the source remains a problem. Bone marrow biopsy to obtain stem cells is said to be quite painful, for example."

I didn't like the way he said "painful." "Plus the transplant is risky, since the cells have to form the correct cell types, function properly, and connect to other cells. I am modeling these processes in mice, as a prelude to trials in humans. It's only one of many options."

He ignored my attempt to veer away from stem cells. "Clinical trials, indeed. The source, yes. I see." He did seem to see, if through a distorted lens.

"So, would you like to fill me in on funding?"

He blinked. "Funding, yes." He pulled a sheaf of papers

from his briefcase and spread them out on the table: several European consortia, some private foundations, and individual donors interested in neurodegeneration. "I suggest you provide a letter of intent, a bio, and a preliminary budget. I will initiate contact with organizations that might have interest in your promising work."

This sounded reasonable, though I had a few questions. "How exactly does your work as a professor of Hellenic studies include neurodegeneration?"

He cleared his throat. "My interest is fueled by experience." That smile again. "I had family members with the disease who have unfortunately passed on. I do not recommend growing up with a father with early-onset Huntington's. Nor a sister, whose disease began even earlier. Fortunately, my sister died without having children—I'm sure you agree that is preferable to creating more suffering." He paused to wait for me to concur. I did not agree at all. I moved my head in a noncommittal way. "You may be interested to know that I have tested negative for the gene mutation," Lusignan said. "This leaves me with an intellect unencumbered by the threat of neurodegenerative decline. And I can therefore contribute, as you can, to forwarding the cause of science. With focus and unwavering determination, we may rid the world of genetic defects entirely, so that the human race, free of disease, will recall Eden's brilliant beauty." My unease escalated. Lusignan didn't have the mutation that caused HD, that was clear—it wasn't himself he was trying to save. Maybe we shared the same goal of eradicating a terrible disease, but for sure I didn't agree with his eugenics philosophy.

The waiter arrived, and with a combination of melancholy and disapproval, took the plate of unfinished lamb away. Lusignan was not done with his speech. "I study the evolution of neo-Hellenism—the revival of Hellenic pride that began in the fifteenth century, and how it relates to modern Greece."

"Interesting." I recalled the news bulletin I'd read about Lusignan's views and wondered whether I was about to hear them again.

"The history of ancient Greece reflects a noble past, which modern Greece would be wise to aspire to," Lusignan said, not noticing the dip in my enthusiasm. "Europe has had to work hard to accommodate the Greeks, who have squandered all they have been given." He leaned back in his chair.

"You're not Greek?"

"I am a Greek citizen, but my family is originally French. A civilized culture."

I wanted to throw my seltzer in his face, but we were now on the topic I'd been angling toward. "How long has your family been in Greece?" I waved the waiter over for our checks.

"The Lusignan family dates back to the time when Mystras was first built. Then, it belonged to the French, and the West had better control over Greece." The waiter came back with one bill; I asked again for separate checks. Lusignan went on. "Sometime in the thirteenth century, my ancestors were in Mystras. At least one Lusignan returned to France. Missing home, perhaps." He wiped his lips with a napkin primly. "In the fifteenth century, a Lusignan came to Greece to study with Georgios Scholarios, a master of theology and philosophy in Constantinople. He changed his name from Georgios to Gennadios once he became a monk, and later became the head of the Orthodox church." Lusignan smiled smugly, as if he were personally responsible for Scholarios's erudition and success. "Under Byzantine rule, scholarship flourished. Greek education has since sadly declined."

My hair stood on end. "Your career path suggests Greece is still worth studying."

"Much as the way Huntington's disease is worth studying: disturbing, but necessary. I would go to great lengths to cleanse the human race of disease. As, I am sure, would you. That bodes well for our collaboration."

I smiled stiffly. It was time for the key question. "Do you know of any other families in this region affected with Huntington's from the time of the French occupation?"

Lusignan's expression went from professorial to predatory. "What makes you ask that?"

My plan to discuss Elektra suddenly felt risky. "I've had the good fortune to read a paper by a colleague of yours, Professor Agathangelos."

"How do you know she was my colleague?" The sunlight glinted off Lusignan's round glasses; I wished I could see his expression better.

"She recommended you as an authority on HD in this region. Large families with genetic diseases can be valuable for research." He stayed absolutely still, glasses glittering. It made me nervous.

"We may have even more areas of shared interest than I suspected. Yes, Elektra has done preliminary work on the topic. She promises to develop into a productive scholar." I noticed he avoided answering my question about finding other families while subtly undercutting Elektra's work. It made me more, not less, interested in her theory.

Lusignan's next question took an unexpected direction. "Can you comment on whether forensic evidence from centuries-old remains might provide valuable genetic data?"

"DNA can survive for centuries, if that's what you mean."

"Please continue."

"Well, it depends on the tissue, and the conditions. But in bone, for example—there is DNA in the marrow—the half-life of DNA is estimated to be over five hundred years. So that means under perfect conditions it would take over six hundred million years to break all the bonds in the DNA."

Lusignan looked genuinely pleased. "And that DNA would still be analyzable for, let's say, eight hundred years, for research purposes?"

Eight hundred years got us back to the thirteenth century. "Yes, it might."

"And, for example, one might be able to identify specific mutations—disease-causing or *protective* variants?"

"Variants, yes." He'd said *protective*. I remembered Elektra's excitement.

Lusignan tilted his head to one side. "Are you particularly well acquainted with the tour guide whom I met, once in the museum and again at the House of the Castellan? Or was it just happenstance?"

I did not like the direction in which this conversation was going at all. "He's the tour guide, we're the tourists."

"Given your frequent touristic contact with Mr. Orologas, perhaps you might assist me in making a professional connection with him? He and I have . . . parallel interests. Personal introductions are so helpful in these sorts of situations."

"I don't know him well enough." I hoped that closed the topic.

He allowed himself to be deflected, though I got the feeling he wasn't done. "Well then, Dr. Adler, shall we plan to reconvene after you have constructed a letter of intent? I look forward to sharing our efforts to better the human race."

I wanted to find out more about the other family, whoever

they were, and I was pretty sure he knew more than he was saying. "I've got your card," I said. After he was out of sight, I put the funding material in my bag, getting a nasty paper cut in the process.

Ω

Panos and Alexander weren't back yet, and the hotel staff told me the fig orchard was an hour's drive away. I was child-free and totally at a loss. I wandered back to my room, opened the recalcitrant lock, and sat down on the bed. I could take a nap. I'd napped only four times in my entire adult life, all during pregnancy. I briefly imagined going for a run, then discarded the idea as budding insanity.

I lay flat on the bed and stared up at the ceiling. There was an irregular crack running through the plaster. It looked kind of like a lasso. Then it looked like a constellation. Then a lightning bolt. Why hadn't I noticed it before? I had no one to take care of. What did I *want* to do? I hadn't had a moment to ask myself that question in nine years. The more I lay there allowing myself to do nothing, the more obvious it became. I wanted to see Elias. I spent three more minutes making sure my motives were pure, pushing the question of his ancestral origin out of the way to focus on the unnameable pull. *Be honest: Is this business, or pleasure?* I had a vision of Elias's brown cheek, the curved scar, the way he slowly lifted his head to look at me. *Pleasure.* That was enough to propel me off the bed and out the door.

I stopped at the grocery. The grocery owner confirmed that Elias was at the tourist booth and suggested I bring lunch. I tried not to show my impatience as he cut a slab of cheese and methodically wrapped it in waxed paper. A loaf of bread, two apricots. He glanced up at me. "Perhaps you'll both want lunch," he said, adding two more. He handed the bag to me with an unnecessarily broad smile.

I ended up going for a run after all. The road was steep, and longer than I remembered. I was not at my best when I arrived. Once Elias realized the panting woman bent double outside the kiosk was me, he came out quickly, alarmed.

"Helen. Has something happened? Where is Alexander?"

"He's fine, and I'm fine, sort of." I gasped. "I mean, I would have been fine if I hadn't decided to run for the first time in ten years." As the feeling of being about to throw up receded, I straightened. "But it's nice to have someone share knee-jerk parental panic." He gave me a funny half-smile. "Not that I need another parent. I'm good. Except I just ran a mile and a half up a steep hill and I am brutally out of shape. Plus I'm an overly anxious widowed mom. But that's not your problem. It's my problem. I mean, you don't have to share my problem. I really should stop talking."

Elias's smile grew from half to whole. "I like it when you talk. It masks my silence."

I groaned. "Talking your ear off was not what I had in mind."

Elias put his hand on my arm. I was horribly sweaty but he didn't even flinch. "What *did* you have in mind?"

"Can we go somewhere?" I glanced over at the guard, who seemed to be enjoying our interaction a little too much. "I feel like a zoo exhibit. Or are you busy? If you're busy, never mind. I'll just go." I suddenly felt shy, faced with the bare reality of the reason I'd come. I didn't have any "My kid wants another tour" excuses this time. I would have run off, except Elias's hand was still on my arm. Plus I didn't think I could run anymore.

"We can go anywhere you like." Elias turned to his colleague and said something rapidly in Greek. "I told him you

want a tour." Elias led me up the path through Mystras's Nafplio gate. "That's a good place to start."

As we walked up the hill I remembered my bag from the
grocery. "I brought lunch," I said.

"I'll find us a lovely spot to eat it," Elias said.

We were quiet until we got to the entrance to the ruined
fortress at the hilltop—he called it the *kastron*.

"Sounds like *castle*, but more tough than fancy," I said, repeating the word.

"Precisely."

"I love it when people say that."

"'Precisely'?" Elias stopped and turned to me, raising one
eyebrow quizzically.

"I like being told I'm exactly right. That doesn't happen
very often."

"I suppose it is hard to be exactly right in science."

"Extremely. I think that's what I like, though—trying to find
a solution to a problem, learning the flaws, then trying again."

Elias nodded. "That struggle is not unique to science." I
wondered about his parallel experience.

Elias led us to a flat grassy area surrounded by a low wall.
There were no tourists here, and a stone slab surrounded by
tumbled blocks of marble provided impromptu seating. I unpacked the lunch; the apricots had not benefited from a mile
and a half of bouncing in a bag. Elias gently laid the food out
on a napkin. Watching the way his hands barely brushed the
apricot's soft skin, the slowness with which he put the fruit
down, undid me entirely.

"It is gracious of you to bring food," he said.

"I wish I could take full credit, but it was the grocer's suggestion." I took a deep breath and chose honesty. "I went to
ask where you were. He recommended lunch."

"A wise man, Nano," Elias said. I thought maybe he'd missed my confession, but of course he hadn't. "Why were you looking for me?"

"No reason," I said, failing to sound lighthearted. "I just wanted to see you. Is that enough?"

"More than enough." Elias, putting down the last apricot, reached out to touch my hand with the same breathtaking gentleness. I closed my eyes and opened them again. He was looking at me.

"May I call you Eléni? I keep imagining your name in Greek, and it is strange to hear one sound and say another."

"Eléni's fine. I like it. It's Greek and everything. I mean, we are in Greece." Elias did not let go of my hand, nor did he seem to mind my nervous verbosity. "So . . . can you tell me something about this place?"

"So you *are* here for a tour?" Elias laughed. "Not simply the pleasure of my company?"

"I might as well get all the benefits."

He let go of my hand and pulled a folding knife out of his pocket to cut the cheese. He handed me a slice and took one, too.

"This part of the *kastron* was built after the Turks came," he said. I felt him recede into history and was almost sorry I'd asked him for information. "Seven years after the fall of Constantinople." Elias paused, frowning slightly. He put the knife down. "In fact, seven years to the day. We held on as long as possible, but finally there was no use; the Turks were too many and too strong. By then the Byzantine Empire was just a few small territories in a sea of Ottoman rule. The Turks ruled Greece for almost four hundred years."

"I want to say I'm sorry. But maybe that's kind of odd for

something that happened centuries ago?" I wasn't quite sure about Greece/Turkey conflict etiquette.

"Many Greeks would welcome your solidarity. Or at least your sympathy. There are still older Greeks who insist on calling Istanbul Constantinople." He handed me an apricot. It was the softest thing I'd ever felt.

"You make it sound so personal—like you were there."

Elias picked up another apricot. I stared at the contrast of the pale orange fruit against the brown of his skin. His hands were long-fingered and as graceful as the rest of him. He was brown everywhere, the sort of tan that never quite goes away. His hair was short and dark, but long enough to curl at the top of his head and the base of his neck. I made myself look away.

"History is personal," Elias said. "Some people are bored by facts and dates, but that is because they do not know that history is about *us*. If you feel that way about the past, you can never be bored by it." His cheeks flushed, highlighting the scar. I wanted to ask him about it. I wanted to touch it, too, so intensely my hands ached. Instead I attended to my apricot. It was so ripe, the juice dripped down my chin. Fortunately, Nano had packed napkins. Elias was watching me. "It is remarkable how we can find pleasure and beauty in the world, alongside unimaginable sorrow."

My mouth literally fell open. It was as if he'd reached straight into me. "Yes. Completely." I put my hand out, unable to resist now, to touch his cheek, the one with the scar. He put his hand over mine. "I'm sorry," I said. "Does it bother you?"

"Not at all."

I felt like I could sit there all afternoon with my hand on his cheek, at the top of Mystras hill in the sun, with the taste of apricot in my mouth. "What's that scar from? If you don't mind my asking."

Elias sighed. "It's from living," he said.

I waited, but he did not clarify. "I guess that's what living does."

One second, two, three. And then he leaned forward and kissed me. He tasted like apricots, just like I must have, but also like himself, like mint and thyme, like the Mystras air. I felt like I was falling into him, as if I had known him not only my whole life but for centuries before that, before either of us was born.

When I came up for air, I was dizzy. "Elias, that was the most amazing kiss of my entire life." Then I thought of Oliver, and my heart stopped. Elias must have seen my thoughts reflected on my face.

"Loss does not preclude desire, Eléni."

I started crying. I cried in a way I never had since Oliver's death. I cried for the death of my husband, and for the part of myself that was lost with him. I cried for Alexander's sorrow. But also, for the first time, I cried knowing that there could be joy after despair, and with the relief of being known.

ELIAS OROLOGAS
July 2015
Mystras

It was the apricots that finally broke through my restraint. The apricots, and the honest awkwardness of Eléni's offering, the fruit bruised by her run in the heat, her hand on my scarred cheek, her hilarious bluntness. *I will lose her. As I have lost everyone.* Even if I were to run headlong into the certainty of loss, for the sake of one lifetime's worth of this love, I knew we were on opposite sides of a wall, and always would be. She cannot live in a ruin, and I cannot leave it.

I could not keep myself from touching her hand, and then, with the taste of the fruit in my mouth, I had to kiss her. And then I had to kiss her again. When she began to cry, I held her as if the future could include us.

When she left me with a shy wave, I went back to work, or tried to. The joy stayed with me, joy in the face of sadness. Then, as it often does, the dark end of the day brought memory with it. I had no reason to hope this time would be different. I would outlive Eléni and Alexander, as I did everyone. I had a new set of tasks: a stolen manuscript, a ruined city that remained my charge, even though I did not know from what or whom I was protecting it. I went to bed early and dreamed of being mortal.

Ω

The next morning, there was another note, this time pushed through the letter slot in my door.

> *Dear Mr. Orologas:*
>
> *I regret not having heard back from you. It is such a remarkable coincidence to have met twice by accident, particularly at the castellan's house, when our mutual interests promise fruitful collaboration in historical research. I hope further delay in our meeting to discuss these matters can be avoided.*
>
> *Sincerely,*
> *Professor Pierre Lusignan*

How had he found my address? Had he delivered the letter himself? The proximity chilled me. I crumpled the note and threw it in the kitchen garbage. Then I threw the remnants of my breakfast on top until the letter disappeared under fruit peels and coffee grounds. Compelled by something I could not name, I went back to the castellan's house.

Marceau Lusignan's former home was a place I avoided now. There I had loved, but I had also lost—my love, my future child, and my own life—in one violent moment. There I had rolled with Osanne on the tiled floor, her red hair spreading out around us, and there I had watched her blood fan out in a deadly mimic of her vibrant life.

Now, I stopped in front of number 17 to take in the scene. It looked as if someone had driven an angry bulldozer in front of the house, churning rocks and grass and dirt, leaving gaping holes surrounded by piles of debris. The wall around the house was broken, stones uprooted from where they'd stood since Père Lusignan preached to Frankish soldiers. The stones' unworn sides turned toward the sun, rough and unnaturally fresh. To the side of the house, low bushes were torn from the ground, roots exposed and clumped with dirt. One arch of the facade had collapsed, and its stones were scattered wide, as if thrown by an enraged giant. Worn flagstones of the path to the front door were shattered. The damage was a violation, and I felt it like the memory of the wound in my side.

It was still my duty to defend whatever was left of Mystras; whoever had done this might do more. I would call the police—the modern instrument of defense. They would come with their white Jeeps and their crisp blue shirts. They might rope off the scene of the crime and search for clues. But I knew the police would not find what they were looking for. It *was* the scene of a crime, but a crime so old that there was no evidence to be found. I thought of the missing book at the museum. Theft, and now vandalism, in this place whose last enemies should have died centuries ago. Perhaps someone was looking, as irrational as it might seem, for part of me.

Ω

For though the fortress and the palace were built in the Villehardouin name, still the kastron's walls sang out the name of the Profitis Ilias. And they welcomed his namesake, Elias, the servant of the stones, the guardian of the gates, whose bones would be the marble and whose veins the mortar of the walled city, whose blood would nourish the ground and whose soul would sing from one generation to the next like the nightingales before dawn, as constant as the recurrent sky.

chapter twenty-five

ELIAS SARANTOPOULOS
June 1437
Mystras

After hearing Guarin Lusignan say his name, my mind revealed its hidden secrets, in this, my third life. The memories layered like *koptoplakous*—the sheets of paper-thin dough with sweet cheese and nuts that we made on special occasions. Recent memories—the philosophy I struggled to learn with the *phratría*—dusted the surface like fine sugar. Below that came the riots in Sicily that ended in Anjou's defeat. At the bottom lay Pelagonia and The Six. Each layer was laced with loss. But throughout, like honey, ran the loves that filled my heart: my mother, whom I left twice, my brother, young then old, my father, Demetrios, Osanne. All gone.

Until this moment, I believed I had lost nothing. I had been the content child of a prosperous businessman, with no worries except the mostly distant Turks. I had a vague notion of danger, and none whatsoever of despair. Now my losses multiplied as my past rushed back at me. Terrifying at first, memories appeared like vivid hallucinations, and for days I felt I was in a constant, waking dream. There were no graves to visit, and no one was alive to share my memories.

My father had no inkling of my distress. But my mother noticed. She pulled me to her in a startling show of affection, and I welcomed it—the crush against her chest, the scent of oregano and mint from her cooking.

I shall take your blissful ignorance, the old woman in the Pantanassa had said. She was the seer, my only companion in the endless arc of return. *Whatever is asked of you in the service of this place, do not shrink from the task.* My first mother's words replayed in my head, but I still could not see how my struggling to learn from Plethon would help Mystras.

When I attended the next meeting with the *phratría*, I felt I had aged a hundred years. Plethon coincidentally made me the focus of his attention, like an insect pierced by a pin. He asked me to read one of his writings out loud.

"The Human Soul is immortal; and descended from above to serve the mortal body, to operate there for a certain time. . . . The Soul, if she performs her office well, runs back into the same place; but if not well, she retires into worse, according to the things she has done in life." I stopped, unnerved. Why had he asked me to read this particular piece of writing? I handed the pages back to Plethon.

"What are your thoughts, Elias?"

"Thoughts?" How could I seek the path by which my soul had entered my body, not one but three times? How could the magic of my return be in keeping with the doctrines I had been taught to believe?

"You do have thoughts?"

Everyone in the room was absolutely silent, afraid that if they made a sound, Plethon might turn in their direction. I wished he would.

Suddenly there was a loud knock on the door. Plethon motioned the newest recruit, a profoundly timid fellow whose name I did not know, to open it. Standing outside, one bony hand raised to rap on the door, was Guarin Lusignan.

"To what do we owe the pleasure of this unexpected visit?" Plethon's tone was deceptively mild; I'd heard him use it while brutally dismantling a student's argument.

"Is this a class?" Lusignan asked.

"Not a public one," Plethon said.

"I wish to study."

"You have a teacher."

"I desire another."

After a pause, Plethon opened the door. "Those who seek knowledge are welcome here." He must have seen the danger in allowing Scholarios's disciple to join us. Had he done so to keep an eye on him? Or did he not care?

My thoughts on eternal return were forgotten; I should have been relieved. Instead I felt overwhelming dread.

GUARIN LUSIGNAN
July 1437
Mystras

After his third meeting with the brotherhood, Guarin followed the silk producer's son—Elias Sarantopoulos—down the hill. As the street wound, Guarin almost lost sight of him. Spending so much time watching Plethon fill his disciples' heads with heresy made Guarin restless. He'd gone to Constantinople to learn from a master, not spy on a bunch of boys and their blasphemous teacher with food in his beard. But Scholarios had been quite clear.

"If you are going to study with me, you must accept several precepts," Scholarios said. "First, what I say is law." It was not possible to interrupt Scholarios. Guarin had learned that quickly. He did not wish to be sent home. His mother was dead; his father, who owned enough property to be rich for the rest of his days, was dying of a strange ailment that made him writhe and babble, at one moment furious, the next, laughing. Guarin was his only child.

In his last lucid days, his father had written out his will: Guarin must be educated by a notable theologian and philosopher and make something of the intelligence God had seen fit to grant him, or all his land would revert to the church. Guarin, his father avowed in particular, was not to waste any more time scraping away with a bow on that silly vielle. Guarin was born not to be a traveling troubadour, but a scholar of worth. His father had hired a tutor to teach Guarin Latin and Greek and insisted the vielle be put away where it would not provide an unwelcome distraction from true learning. Guarin had loved the instrument, spent hours coaxing sweetness from its strings—most of those hours carefully hidden from his father, who he knew would not approve of the foolish pastime. He'd packed the vielle secretly when he left for Constantinople; by then, his father was too far gone to notice. Sometimes, late at night after a day full of theology he struggled to master, Guarin would take out the vielle and hold it tenderly, playing muted melodies behind his chamber's closed door.

"Second, you will come with me to the Peloponnese to meet Gemistos Plethon." Guarin had not bargained on another journey—Paris to Constantinople had been enough. But Scholarios's first point prevented his arguing about the second. "Third: Plethon needs watching. I believe he has a secret cell of men he is training to observe the pagan rites. Join it and tell me what you hear and see." Scholarios waved Guarin away with a flick of his ringed hand.

Holing up in a small town under a far-flung despotate of the fading Romaioi empire to ferret out heretics was not why Guarin had come to Constantinople. But he had no choice. He'd done his father's bidding, and his inheritance—much of it already going to pay Scholarios amply for the task of teaching Guarin—held him captive.

Guarin's quarry appeared again, lower down the hill, so he sped up to close the distance. The cobblestones were uneven, and he tripped and caught himself, cursing. Reaching the entrance of the Pantanassa Monastery, Elias disappeared inside. Guarin stopped halfway through the entryway. From that vantage point, he could see his target standing in front of an old woman—a sister of the Pantanassa? She had a voluminous black cloak over a *schema* like all the Romaioi nuns wore. He strained to listen to their conversation.

Give me what you hold dear.

That was a strange thing for a nun to say.

"I have lost my ignorance." Elias bowed his head. "Tell me how I may serve."

So Elias was in service to this strange old crone, who might not be a sister at all. And she was taking payment from him.

I have told you, the woman croaked.

Elias turned to leave. Guarin, fearing discovery, prepared to run. But Elias went the other way, taking the small flight of steps into the monastery church.

Guarin was not sure what he had seen. Had he learned something useful for which Scholarios would provide a rich reward? He edged closer. As Guarin approached, the woman's eyes sprang open, and he was caught in the burning ferocity of that white stare.

You will die of it.

The words unnerved him. "Everyone dies of something," he said.

You will die of it like your father.

How could she know? It had never crossed Guarin's mind that the affliction could be shared, father to son.

As your father's father before him, and his father before that.

Your blood shall give you death, give you death and give your son death and your sons and daughters, and their sons and daughters in turn.

You shall die writhing and raving, it is in your blood.

Guarin saw his hand as if it were disembodied. It flickered with a movement he had tried to ignore, an echo of his father's decline. The old woman spread her cloak wide like a dark angel of death. She reached out one clawed hand for Guarin's wrist, digging her nails into his flesh. She'd drawn blood. His tongue was heavy in his mouth, his limbs frozen. The blood dripped down his arm to the flagstones, splattering red on gray.

Your blood is death.

The blood of the boy is life.

A door slammed, and the spell that held him mute was broken. A cat in front of a nun's cell door yawned and uncurled, a bee buzzed on a flower drooping in the heat. And Elias appeared in the doorway of the church, his eyes wide.

Ask him, he knows.

The crone threw her head back and laughed, her mouth as wide as an abyss, while Guarin's blood congealed on the hot stones.

ELIAS SARANTOPOULOS
1437
Mystras

The seer's words to Guarin—*he knows*—filled me with dread. I waited in the church until Guarin was gone before I made my way back home. Afterward, at the meetings of the *phratría*, which Guarin continued to attend, I often caught him staring at me. I avoided being alone with him.

At the last class before Scholarios and Guarin departed for Constantinople, Plethon's topic took an unsettling turn. Plethon had eaten *krikelloi* for lunch; a ring of the pasta was stuck in his beard. But his words eliminated any errant thoughts of the state of his facial hair. "First," he said, "the gods exist."

When he said "gods," I snuck a look at the other students' faces. Believing in more than one god was heresy of the worst sort. Bessarion's face was calm, as always, but the other monk in the group was scowling. Guarin leaned forward intently as Plethon continued.

"Zeus is chief among them. Poseidon is the second, and the rest are produced by those two with the help of Hera." Plethon stopped in front of me. "The human soul resembles that of the gods, in being immortal." This was too close to home. Guarin was watching me intently. "It is always attached to a mortal body, being sent by the gods from one body to another." Plethon leaned so close that I could see each pore on his nose. Whether I could believe in a pantheon of many gods was questionable, but reincarnation was a heresy I could not renounce; I had lived it. I thought Plethon must suspect that I understood what it meant to have my soul leave my body and enter another. How he knew, I had no idea. But I also felt he was extending reassurance that my peculiar way of being was part of the cohesive harmony of the universe. Unfortunately, Guarin realized he was addressing me, too.

After the lesson, I went to wash my face in Plethon's kitchen, needing a moment to recover. When I emerged, only Guarin remained. "Did you find the topic interesting today?"

"We all did." I edged slowly along the wall. The door seemed far away.

"Reviving Zeus and Poseidon at a gathering of *Christian* scholars," Guarin said, his emphasis barbed, "would have been shocking enough." Scholarios would have ample proof of Plethon's blasphemies soon. "But I was particularly struck by your reaction to the matter of transmigration of souls."

"It is an intriguing topic. Philosophically speaking. Don't you think?" I'd made it halfway to the door, but Guarin blocked my escape.

"I do *think*," Guarin answered. "But you *know*. You know the cure for the curse of movement and madness." He crossed the room in a few steps and grasped my shoulders. "You *must* help me." Sweat beaded along his forehead.

"I am a silk manufacturer, not a physician," I said.

"The crone said *the blood of the boy is life* . . . are you that boy?"

The front door of the house flew open and slammed hard against the wall. Bessarion stood framed in the doorway. "What in God's name are you doing?"

"We were talking." Guarin dropped his hands.

Bessarion's usually peaceful face turned ominous. "You have talked enough. You are no longer welcome here, Lusignan."

Guarin turned and stumbled out the door. I could not tell Bessarion what had transpired; I was not even sure I understood. But Guarin's assault wove the strands together in my mind—the crone's prophecy, my first father's twisting limbs,

Marceau's treachery, Fedryc's violence, and Guarin's desperation.

All the Lusignan men wanted the same thing from me—a cure.

Ω

The following week, Bessarion took me aside in the garden behind Plethon's house. We stood in the patterned shadows under an olive tree and he put his hand on my shoulder. "Do you know the term 'Pater Pneumatikos'?"

"Spiritual father," I said.

"It has a more specific meaning." Bessarion held my gaze. "It also means confessor. We do not need the safety of a church's walls to open our hearts. You may speak your soul's secrets to me, Elias, and I shall not reveal them, except to God."

I wanted to share the burden of my existence, find help to bear the weight of years. Still, I hesitated. I was afraid. It was heresy. It was impossible. But I could not keep my silence any longer; I told Bessarion about the flight of my soul and its return. The branches of the olive tree became the dome of a cathedral over our heads. When I was done, he blessed me in the shifting shadows of the leaves.

Ω

In the spring of 1439, Plethon and Scholarios were both invited to Florence to debate the Union of the Latin and Orthodox churches. Pope and Patriarch had never joined hands to call the faithful to prayer, and papal backing in the resistance of our emperor against the increasingly powerful Turks did not seem likely. The wrong outcome might doom us to Ottoman domination. We had some reason to hope for a good outcome;

Despot Constantine of the Peloponnese had arrived in Mystras in 1443, and began to rebuild the Hexamillion wall, setting his sights on driving back the Turkish forces. For a moment we felt strong again. But it was not long before Sultan Murad returned with his bulldog Turakhan Bey, destroying the Hexamillion for good. Constantine had to submit to paying the sultan a tribute and concede that the wall would not be built again. Despite this defeat, all the citizens of Mystras held Constantine in our hearts, imagining him to be the leader who would recapture our lost land and bring glory to the Peloponnese.

Bessarion was appointed the Metropolitan of Nicaea and left before Plethon. I missed him, but if anyone could argue in support of the Union and win, it was he.

Many of the *phratría* traveled to Florence, but I did not. I had Charitonymos to commiserate with; he moped like an abandoned puppy when Plethon left. His donkey had died, liberating him from its care. He'd been better off with the inconvenient beast to keep him occupied. Now he read and wrote and paced in frustration. I continued factory and family life with my secret to sustain me.

I was, despite Plethon's urging, undecided about whether Plato's or Aristotle's view matched my beliefs. My personal theology did not support the idea of divine intervention in the everyday struggles of human life. But the topic of reincarnation was the most difficult of all. It seemed impossible to believe in reincarnation while maintaining the Orthodox faith, but I had to—because I not only studied reincarnation, but I'd also lived it.

Whatever I believed, that summer I was given, just at my moment of greatest need, exactly what I needed. My mother liked to solve problems, and for a mother of a lonely son, that meant finding me a wife.

Zoe was tiny—she barely came up to my shoulder—and even quieter than I. This posed problems during our betrothal, because neither of us spoke. When I got up the courage to speak to her, she answered in few words, blushing violently. After our fifth meeting, we managed several sentences, and by three months we were able to carry on a nearly normal conversation. Zoe gave me a silver ring at our wedding to symbolize her purity and gentleness, and I gave her an iron ring, as a symbol of my strength and vow to protect her. She seemed so fragile, I wondered whether I was strong enough.

I tried not to allow the memories of my past loves to haunt our time together, but ghosts surrounded me. I remembered the ease of my communication with Demetrios, the way we talked late into the night as if one lifetime was not enough. I missed Osanne's ferocity and will, and the fire she had lit in me. But for now, with my prophesied purpose on hold during Plethon's absence, I found comfort in Zoe's company, and looked forward to our married life together. But I never considered telling her the truth.

chapter twenty-six

ELIAS SARANTOPOULOS
1439
Mystras

In January of 1439, Despot Constantine was chosen as emperor of Constantinople. His coronation was planned in Mystras.

"We are a little Constantinople now," my father crowed, embracing me and my mother so tightly that I could hardly breathe, and my mother's earring got tangled in my hair. The honor was bittersweet, as Constantine's coronation meant he would leave us.

My mother, predictably, took a grim outlook. "Constantine is leaving his loyal subjects in the Peloponnese to command a doomed empire." With the sultan's power growing daily, she was likely right. Despite that threat, I was excited because I had never seen an imperial coronation before, and Zoe was excited because I was.

My father's silk had been used for the coronation robes, so our family had a place inside the church to watch the ceremony. The Church of Saint Demetrios was packed to the walls, and the crowds spilled out into the courtyard, filling the porticos and walkways with cheering spectators. The emperor proclaimed his devotion to Orthodoxy while the garrison raised their shields and shouted their acclaim. Enthroned on a wooden platform built for the occasion, he looked over the crowd: his children, whom he would lay down his life to protect.

I watched Constantine's face at the moment of transformation: despot to emperor, ordinary mortal to the right hand of God. What must he be thinking, as the weight of the empire descended upon him? Was it like parenthood, multiplied a thousand times? Was it joyous or grave? Exhilarating or terrifying? I was not a parent, and I would never be an emperor. But I suspected the roles, one mundane and the other divine, might be similar—joyous, grave, exhilarating, and terrifying all at once.

Ω

Later that year, Plethon returned to Mystras from Florence. Plethon and Scholarios had publicly locked horns over their opposing philosophies. I wished that I could tell Bessarion about the conflict, but I did not dare to commit my thoughts to a letter. Meanwhile, my marriage allowed me to fulfill my desire with someone I was permitted to love. It seemed like an ordinary life. Knowing how extra-ordinary my lives had been, I assumed it wouldn't last.

Within a year of our marriage Zoe was pregnant. She vomited everything she ate, and often when she hadn't eaten. She was constantly ravenous, but food disgusted her. If she ate, she felt sick. If she didn't eat, she felt sicker. She would wake from three hours of sleep in the middle of the day and declare she was desperate for a nap. I took care of her as well as I could, bolstered by my mother's advice.

Over the next few months, Zoe's belly grew, but the rest of her seemed to shrink. Dark circles appeared under her eyes, and her ankles swelled. The midwife visited weekly. She recommended walks and savory foods, neither of which Zoe could manage. By her seventh month Zoe was swollen all over, her slender limbs puffy. I stayed home, giving her sips of warm water. Once I lay in bed next to her the entire day, my head on her belly, feeling our child kick against my ear. Zoe dozed, but I stayed awake, watching the rise and fall of her chest and the light from the window as it moved across her face.

A month later, I awoke in the night to Zoe thrashing in bed with foam collecting at the corner of her mouth. The paroxysm was followed by another, then another. The midwife came running.

Zoe survived the birth, but our little girl was born dead. Zoe and I held each other and our child into the night, touching her pale, almost translucent skin, her delicate closed eyelids, the fine golden down that covered her body. She was ours, and she was gone. We dug a hole and buried her in the earthen kitchen floor by the hearth in the old way, wetting the soil with our tears.

After that, Zoe was even quieter. We half hoped she would become pregnant again, but fear lurked. As time passed, we resigned ourselves to the safety and solitude of two. Zoe turned inward, consumed by her body's failure, and though I tried, I could not find my way into the labyrinth of her suffering to give her comfort.

I kept busy so I would have no time to think, but thoughts are persistent creatures. *Three lives with no children*. Was it life's random cruelty, or was there a message in that failure? Did the fact that I could not lose my life mean I could not make one? Or was I getting closer each time—the first with none, the second with a life barely kindled, and the third with a child stillborn. Would a live child come next, if I had the will to keep trying? And would there be an end to this cycle of return that ensured that I would lose all the people I loved, with no constancy but the blue, recurrent sky? Although I was afraid of what I would find out, I went back to the Pantanassa.

I came bearing a gift: a piece of the fabric that should have been my daughter's swaddling cloth. In the courtyard, a young nun was watering flowers that drooped in the heat.

She looked up. "May I be of assistance?" Her wide-set gray eyes gave her a startled look.

"The old sister . . ."

"Eudoxia?"

I had not known her name until that moment, and then it was abruptly familiar. "Yes."

"She does not see visitors."

"I've brought something for her." The nun raised her eyebrows until they disappeared under her coif.

"I will take it," she said. "Have you come to pray to the prophet? You are welcome." It was the feast day of the Profitis Ilias, the twentieth of July. *There are no coincidences.*

Inside the church, an icon hung on the wall. The prophet rode his flaming chariot, pulled heavenward by red horses. I remembered the amulet I had rubbed smooth over the years and wondered where it was now. I began the formal prayer for the prophet's feast day. My voice sounded strange, echoing into the vault of the church.

Angel in the flesh and the cornerstone of the prophets, you pour forth healing on those who honor you. We call blessed those who showed endurance . . .

Endurance. Was that what the prophet had to teach me? To endure, life after life? The standard prayers seemed out of place. What if I spoke to the prophet with my own words, as my mother had? I remembered what she had told me, two lives ago: *I promised you to the prophet, and I swore you would serve.*

"This is your Elias," I whispered. "Elias who serves Mystras in your name." I knelt, waiting for something to happen, the tiles hard under my knees. How did nuns do it for all those hours? Did practice make it easier, or did discomfort make prayers powerful? There were no open windows in the church, and the door had closed behind me. I tried, later, to explain where the breeze came from, the breeze that grew into a steady wind. The wind lifted my hair from my hot forehead. It cooled the sweat on my neck and caressed my face. And on the wind came a voice that sounded like my own, and I thought: *perhaps the prophets speak to us in our own voices, so we can hear the word of God without shattering from the force of it.* Wherever it came from, it was an answer I already knew.

When you have fulfilled your responsibility, you will be free.

I knelt until my knees burned and my back ached. Then I stayed until the pain was gone. Finally, the young nun came to get me. She helped me up gently and gave me water. I left with the words echoing inside me.

CARDINAL BASILIOS BESSARION
1448
Rome

Bessarion had been a cardinal in Rome for nine years when a messenger came from Scholarios. Scholarios was now a staunch

opponent of the Union between the churches, but Bessarion
tried not to cross his colleague openly. So when Scholarios
asked that he allow Guarin Lusignan to study his book collection on his master's behalf, he said yes, despite misgivings.

"I see you are still a student of Scholarios," Bessarion said,
by way of welcome.

Lusignan's nod was punctuated by a forward jutting of his
head. "I am fortunate. I must congratulate you on your ap-
pointment as a cardinal of the Latin Church. An extraordinary
achievement for an Orthodox priest."

Bessarion did not mention their last meeting, when he'd
found Guarin threatening Elias. "Thank you," Bessarion answered tersely, leading Lusignan into his study, where a servant brought wine and lit a fire in the hearth, fanning the
flames until they glowed.

Guarin Lusignan had aged visibly, and he was not able to
sit still. His arms flicked, a leg jerked. "My master says your
collection of Greek books is notable."

"Are you looking for something in particular?"

Lusignan set his glass down too hard; the wine sloshed
over the rim. "An account of the early days of the Morea,
under Prince Villehardouin."

The request made Bessarion uneasy. "What does your
master want with such a volume?"

"He has requested that I find sources to illuminate the history of Mystras, whose philosophers are renowned."

A singularly poor reason, and unlikely to be the real one.
Scholarios publicly called Plethon "notorious," not "renowned."
Was Lusignan searching for fuel to feed Scholarios's attack on
Plethon, or did he have a personal motive?

"I see. A worthy goal. But it will take me some time to find
volumes that might meet your need. Come back tomorrow at

the same time. I shall expect you." Bessarion rose to make it clear the visit was over. "My servant will see you out."

Bessarion was glad to have Lusignan gone. In the ten years since the conference in Florence, the disagreements between Scholarios and Plethon had turned increasingly acrimonious, and perilous for his friends in the Peloponnese. Bessarion walked to his library. He had built an entire room to keep the volumes in his house; soon a room would not be enough. Rome suited him. Bessarion, still a staunch proponent of the Union, imagined himself the physical embodiment of friendship between the two churches, Orthodox monk become Latin cardinal. But ten years after the council, unity of the Churches had not yet materialized, nor had aid against the Turks. Scholarios, an opponent of the Union, was powerful, vocal, and dangerous. As the agreement languished, the Turks gained power.

Bessarion climbed a ladder to look for the chronicle of the Morea he'd recently acquired. He had to take each book out to examine the cover until he found what he was looking for. He read, standing on the ladder, and then when he tired, sitting hunched at his table. He read page after page, frozen in his chair, until he came to the end.

> For though the fortress and the palace were built in the Villehardouin name, still the kastron's walls sang out the name of the Profitis Ilias. And they welcomed his namesake, Elias, the servant of the stones, the guardian of the gates, whose bones would be the marble and whose veins the mortar of the walled city, whose blood would nourish the ground and whose soul would sing from one generation to the next like the nightingales before dawn, as constant as the recurrent sky.

Bessarion knew this was the text Lusignan wanted. And whether Lusignan had been led by Scholarios or had come for his own reasons, Bessarion knew Lusignan must not find this mention of Elias, whose secret Bessarion must keep. The book felt alive against his body, with a pulse of its own.

Bessarion stared at the pages. No one must know; certainly not an enemy of Platonic ideals, including the heresy of reincarnation. "I am sorry," he said to the volume as if it were a friend. And with a sharp tug, he tore the pages from their binding. Bessarion went to the hearth, where he held the pages over the fire. Slowly the edges browned and began to curl. Before he could change his mind, he threw the sheets into the flames. But he could not let them burn. He scrambled to rescue the pages with a poker, flinging them onto the hearth. Bessarion waited until they were cool enough, then carefully slipped them between the pages of a book Lusignan and his master would—he was certain—never bother to read.

Ω

After his second day in Bessarion's library, Guarin Lusignan left in despair. Bessarion gave him the useless chronicle with a broad, innocent smile, as if he had no idea that the last few pages were gone, their freshly torn edges like a child's budding teeth. Guarin would have to go back to Mystras and wring the answer out of Plethon's student himself.

Guarin's illness was worsening. Soon he'd need a stick to walk; now he stayed close to walls, one hand out for balance. Worst was his clumsiness with the vielle—the bow slid from his grasp and the notes came out wrong, when they came at all. The loss of that music tore at Guarin more than any other facility he'd lost—a missing piece of his heart. He packed the vielle away so the sight would not bring him to tears.

The blood of the boy is life—the seer in the Pantanassa had said. Elias Sarantopoulos *must* be that boy. Guarin had to return to Mystras, and he had the perfect excuse to do so. Scholarios would finance the trip, now that Plethon's writings had grown increasingly blasphemous—he'd find evidence to consign Plethon's writings to the flames. Especially now that Guarin's father was dead, and his inheritance assured. Even monks, for all their professed disregard for worldly things, liked money.

chapter twenty-seven

HELEN ADLER
Late July 2015
Mystras

Neither Alexander nor I wanted to leave Mystras. Each day we woke up in our hotel room and did not say anything about where we were going next. If anyone had told me that we'd be spending our vacation in a one-street town at the base of a ruined Byzantine city, I would have laughed. Now I had more reasons than Alexander's fascination to justify our stay. The first was professional: the existence of two genetically informative families with Huntington's disease, and the possibility of a breakthrough like the discovery of the HD gene in Venezuelan families. But the overlap of that fact with my personal life made me uneasy every time I considered it. Elias was probably a descendant of one of those families. At the same time, he was compelling to me for reasons having nothing to do with genetics. I kept constructing imaginary conversations in my head. *I really like you a lot and hope you like me, too . . . but also, just for the record, I'm wondering whether you want to be a subject in my new research study . . .* ugh. Still, I couldn't let go of the thought that Elias might hold the key to a protective gene, one that would change HD therapy forever. Was I going to let my attraction to him negate the importance of that? Or vice versa? Meanwhile, Alexander had his own preoccupations.

"I wish I could have seen Mystras when it was full of people," Alexander said late one night when neither of us could sleep. We'd curled on the bed—me with a new book that I'd downloaded, and Alexander with a graphic novel about Zeus. It was in Greek, but he didn't seem to care.

"Me too. Having Elias around is a good substitute for that, though, right?"

"Right," he answered, and put his head on my shoulder.

Alexander's breathing grew rhythmic, and when I looked over, he'd fallen asleep. Lulled by his drowsiness, I followed him down.

Ω

The next day at breakfast, Elias was waiting for us.

"I hope you're hungry," he said with one of his slow smiles that I'd liked from the beginning, and now wanted to kiss the edge of.

"Ravenous," I said, feeling it.

"Are you going to order something Greek that I have to try before saying I don't like it?" Alexander went straight to Elias for a hug, which Elias happily provided.

"I've already done so," Elias said. "Very Greek and very likeable. Maybe even to you."

Alexander gave a theatrical sigh. But he stopped pretending to complain when the food showed up. It was an outrageous Peloponnesian feast: peaches, apricots, and piles of delicate green-skinned figs—"I picked those!" Alexander proclaimed—mountain herbal tea steaming in a ceramic pot decorated with blue flowers, *simpoukoukira* cheese (I had to practice saying the word), lamb sausages, fried pastries dipped in honey (Alexander surreptitiously picked the walnuts off before he ate four), *galatopita*, a milk pie that was like firm flan inside a flaky exterior, semolina halva, and lemonade that Alexander drank only when he was convinced that the cloudiness of real lemon wouldn't make it taste weird.

"Where to today?" Elias said as we sat in postprandial stupor.

"I want to see what Mystras looked like when it wasn't just a ruin."

I caught Elias's look. "Not Mystras town," I clarified.

Alexander looked flustered. "I love it. It's just . . . I'm sorry."

Elias smiled. "You are right, it is a ruin. Except for the Pantanassa, but you should save that for another day. I suggest we go back to the museum. Museums are where the past comes alive." Alexander looked doubtful. "Can you trust me?" Elias said. It was, in theory, a simple question. I held my breath, waiting for Alexander's answer.

"Okay," he said. It was just one small word, but with a big meaning.

Ω

As we entered the air-conditioned sanctum, Elias stopped us in front of a glass case. I almost laughed. Inside was a line of metal hooks and eyes, exactly the sort of thing you'd find in a 99-cent store.

Alexander looked up. "These are old? They're on that dress you make me help you put on." *Now that Oliver is gone*, I thought.

"Eight hundred years old," Elias said, "and some Byzantine boy likely helped his mother with her dress, too."

A display of coins got Alexander excited for a while. He

speculated about their value but, having no information to confirm his estimates, lost interest. Elias walked us to the back of the museum, where a closed door read PRIVATE, NO ENTRY on it in English, below a phrase I assumed said the same thing in Greek.

"I'd like to show you a book from the museum's archives," Elias said. "You can't touch it, but I will tell you its story."

Alexander's eyes widened. "Cool. Like a private screening."

Elias smiled. "Working here has benefits." Beyond the door was a windowless modern office. The officious docent sat stolidly at her desk, bent over a museum catalog.

"I require access to the archives," Elias said.

"With *them*?" She looked at us as if we were homeless people who had sneaked into the museum.

"I will handle the documents myself," Elias said reassuringly. She complied, grudgingly.

Elias washed and dried his hands and laid out the trappings of historic manuscript handling. The book he'd brought out was an old Bible. He placed it on the stand and opened it.

"What language is this?" Alexander leaned in.

"*Bible historiale complétée*," Elias said, in gorgeous French. Was there anything this guy didn't know? "It's a medieval French vernacular Bible. That means it was written in the language people spoke at the time, not church Latin, which at that point nobody spoke in daily life."

"We have a Bible," Alexander said. "We call it Torah." I was glad he knew that; I had not spent much time educating Alexander about his Jewish identity. I felt fleetingly guilty.

"Many religions have important books," Elias said. "Now I'm going to tell you the story of this book." Alexander sat back in his chair with what I recognized as his story face.

"This Bible belonged to a French soldier named Jéhan Borghes. He came to Greece with Prince Villehardouin."

Alexander interrupted him. "That same prince who built Mystras? And lost it?"

Elias smiled. "The very same one. Jéhan came from France to Greece."

"How do you know about Jéhan?"

"His wife kept a journal—it is in this museum. We rely on the facts, and we try to fill in what is missing."

Alexander's eyes narrowed suspiciously. "Then you have to tell me what's true and what you're making up."

Elias laughed. "I will try. Let's *imagine* that for Jéhan, at first everything was unfamiliar—the language, the food, the people. He missed France. *Imagine* that he stayed, training and working as a soldier, fighting the Prince of Achaea's battles, and dreaming of home. But one day he saw a woman. She was Greek, a midwife named Chryse. He saw her the day she helped one of the garrison soldier's wives give birth. Jéhan fell in love with her instantly."

"So Chryse was real?"

Elias nodded. "That is one of the facts."

"That's what my mom and dad did," Alexander said, "fell in love instantly." Elias glanced at me quickly. He could not have known what I was thinking: *A French soldier during Ville-hardouin's time who married a Greek midwife.* How many of those could there be? And he knew their story, and their names so well.

"Love at first sight," Elias said to Alexander. "I hope it happens to you someday." Elias told the story as if it had happened yesterday. Did Elias know their stories so well because he was descended from them? The description fit Elektra's perfectly. *Borghes.* I committed the name to memory.

"Did they get married?" Alexander was entranced.

"They did. They had two sons, at first. The older one became a soldier, like his father. But the older brother died from battle wounds, and his mother could not bear to have their younger son become a fighter, too. He became a smith, making weapons rather than using them."

Alexander looked serious. "That's sad."

"Yes, it is. War is terribly sad. But after the war, Chryse adopted a third son and named him after his lost brother."

"That's sad, too," Alexander said, "but nice. What happened to the dad?"

Elias frowned. "He died of illness."

I had to interrupt. "Do you know what kind of illness?"

Elias turned to look at me. I remembered suddenly how my dad used to ask me about his Parkinson's disease, but he did not like the cool, professional voice in which I gave him answers.

Elias cleared his throat. "It is hard to be certain. Then it was called the dancing mania."

"*Chorea* means 'dance' in Greek," Alexander said, making me proud. "Maybe the dad had Huntington's. My mom is a world expert, you know. She's going to find a cure."

Alexander's words echoed through the silence that followed.

"I'm not a world expert," I said. "Have you traced your family back that far?" Elias didn't answer; his quiet made me nervously talkative. "I don't know much beyond my great-grandparents. We have the Jewish Diaspora to deal with, immigration, and name changes. Americans are good at moving forward but not so good at looking back. Unlike you. I mean, unlike you Greeks."

Elias's face went curiously still. I was afraid that my prob-

ing had gone too far. "My family has been here for many centuries, as you know."

I was afraid to ask another question. Alexander broke the
silence. "Can you tell the rest of the story? About the youngest
son?"

Elias went back to his narrative. I listened while trying to
figure out how to get the information I needed.

"The youngest son found his father's French Bible in a
chest. The boy began to learn French from it and would sit in
the shade of the portico of the church right next to this museum, reading and remembering. This way, he kept a piece of
his father in his heart."

Elias turned the page of the book carefully. Two pages
were stuck together, and as he gently separated them, loose
pieces of paper fell out. Clearly not part of the Bible; the writing was in Greek, and the pages were brown and jagged at the
edges, as if they'd been rescued from a fire. Elias slowly lifted
the pages out and laid them on the piece of velvet the book
had been wrapped in. I had an intense desire to pull out my
phone and take a photo, but the sign on the wall (also in two
languages)—ABSOLUTELY NO PHOTOGRAPHS—stopped me.

"What if these are the missing pages of the Chronicle?"
Alexander said in a spellbound whisper. "Wouldn't that be so
cool?"

"Yes," Elias said. His face was flushed. "It certainly would."

"What was the third son's name?" Alexander asked.

"His name," Elias said, clearing his throat, "was Elias."

"Wow," Alexander said. "Just like you."

My heart was pounding. It seemed like the perfect moment to ask my burning unanswered question. "Are they related to you, do you know? The Borghes family? You seem to
know so much about them."

Elias did not look at me. "There is no reason to suspect that two individuals with the same first name, separated by nearly eight centuries, would be related," Elias said, coolly. He touched his face where I knew the scar was, though it wasn't visible in this light. "In this case, though, yes."

Alexander stared at him. "You mean, Jéhan and his wife and their sons are your relatives? Wow, now you really are like a demigod."

Elias closed the book, after carefully putting the pages back where he had found them, and then wrapped the book again. "There were no deities involved," he said, but not un-kindly. Story time was over. As we left, we nearly bumped into the officious docent, who was standing right outside the read-ing room. She'd probably been hovering the whole time.

Ω

Professionally I was intrigued, but personally, I did not like any of my thoughts. One: Elias is descended from a line of people with HD and is at risk. He hadn't shown any signs, but still. Two: Elias wasn't affected, and if so, why not? He might have gotten lucky, and not have inherited the gene at all. Or he might have, but it was too soon to know whether he was headed for disaster. Or . . . he might have a protective gene. The first possibility was hopeful, the second grim, and the third turned him into the subject of my research. I wished I'd never learned any of it. I almost wished we'd never come. *Almost.*

I hated the way Elias's warmth had turned off abruptly, like a faucet. I closed my eyes, remembering my afternoon with him in the courtyard of Agios Demetrios. *It was doomed anyway.* My adaptive strategy kicked in, as it usually does when disappointment looms. *He lives in a minuscule town in Greece that I visited by accident and will never see again. I'm just a recently widowed single mom having a rebound with a dark, handsome stranger. A brilliant, mysterious, erudite, gentle, articulate, compelling, multilingual stranger who kisses outstandingly well and whom my son seems to trust.*

Now that I'd effectively derailed a budding ill-advised romance, I'd be able to divert my energy to finding a cure for HD, which was a much better idea than falling in love. Especially with an as-yet-unaffected Greek man with a centuries-long family history of a devasting genetic disease that I happened to be studying.

MILLICENT BRATHWAITE
July 2015
Mystras

The docent's name was Millicent Brathwaite, and she had never liked it. She should have been named something more romantic—Guinevere, for example. But she had, for better or worse, grown into it: for she was, above all, Respectful of Facts. She had come from Devonshire, inspired by a Love of History, with a broad-brimmed hat to protect her face from the relentless sun.

Millicent disapproved heartily of Mr. Orologas's decision to bring the visitors—*a child! Tourists!*—to the inner sanctum of the museum. The little boy might smear Nutella on an eight-hundred-year-old page, God forbid, and it was her role to prevent such a disaster. And why would Mr. Orologas peruse a French vernacular Bible? He was an odd one. She'd been warned by her parents when she took the job: Greeks, they'd said, were prone to emotional outbursts and might act unpredictably.

Mr. Orologas's find, however, impressed her. Millicent kept her face impassive when she saw the pages, fire-browned and curling, the spidery Greek text still legible. At last, the sort of discovery she'd dreamed of in her lonely youth.

Mr. Orologas left the sheets and book with her, instructing her (unnecessarily!) on cautious handling and reminding her to tell the director. She nodded, pressing her lips together. Once the odd threesome had left the office, Millicent picked up the phone. Given that it had been found inside a Frankish Bible, it seemed reasonable to involve her contact, who had specifically requested that she inform him immediately of the discovery of any pages that might have come from another book. They would, he'd said, be an Invaluable Contribution to Historical Knowledge. And her part in such advancement would certainly be recognized. The conversation she'd overheard regarding Mr. Orologas's relationship to the original Borghes family might be of interest as well to scholars dedicated to these matters. Fingers tingling, Millicent dialed and held the phone a few millimeters away from her ear, as she'd been taught to do. (In case other ears had pressed against it recently. Wise to avoid contagion.)

"University of the Peloponnese," the voice answered on the other end of the line in singsong Greek, "how may I direct your call?"

"Department of Hellenic Studies, please, Dr. Pierre Lusignan," she said, and eagerly awaited the transfer.

HELEN ADLER
July 2015
Mystras

Once I turned Elias from a new love interest to a research subject, we stopped seeing him by accident. The end of our trip was looming, and now I had neither the cure for HD nor the pleasure of Elias's company. I missed him more than I'd anticipated. Mystras felt like a deserted ruin abutting a tiny town, which it was, but it hadn't felt like that before.

Because we were on vacation in Greece and I had to do something other than mope, I planned day trips. The caves of Diros was the most successful outing I came up with, an eerily lit boat ride through caverns studded with stalactites and stalagmites. I could never remember which was which, though Alexander of course did. Outside the caves, Alexander found his ideal playground: massive cement blocks studded with iron poles that seemed to be a remnant of a titan-size abandoned construction project. The blocks were more than twice his height, on the edge of a deep bay lined with sharp rocks, and far enough apart that a death-defying leap was required to get from one to the next. To add to my anxiety, the steel poles protruding from the blocks ten feet above the ground were perfect for a nine-year-old boy to hang from. My main achievement was not gasping when he jumped.

When we got back to the inn, I let Alexander play Minecraft on my phone and headed out to the outdoor café with my laptop to prepare my bio and funding proposal for Professor Lusignan.

When I looked up an hour later, a busboy was clearing the tables. What I'd written seemed clear and convincing. However, I'd left out a key element: how local families with HD might contribute genetic data. I considered the options. Addressing it meant I'd be proposing to study Lusignan's family. That seemed ill-advised, particularly without asking him, which I didn't really want to do. And it meant I might also be proposing to study Elias, or at least get more information from him about the Borghes family, mixing my (now crushed) crush with work.

I took a break from the dilemma by filling in administrative details on the application. In the referral source line, I realized I had to put in Lusignan's contact information. That meant I had to find his business card. I shuffled through the papers Lusignan had given me, unsuccessfully. Then I went through my wallet. Not there either. I started getting that overly warm feeling I get when I think I've lost something. Someone was standing over me, and I got even more hot and flustered when I saw that the someone was Elias. He bent to pick up Lusignan's business card from the ground near the leg of the café table.

"Does this belong to you?" he asked. Not the romantic reconciliation I had imagined.

"Yes, thanks." I felt a little sick. "How are you? I haven't seen you in a while."

"I am well, thank you. I trust you are, too, and Alexander?"

"Yes, we're good." An awkward silence ensued, which Elias seemed to feel no urgency to break, and I felt intense urgency to. "Are you free now?"

"I'm afraid I'm busy," he said. At that moment, a busload of tourists emptied out of their vehicle and stood blinking in the sun. They were wearing matching T-shirts that read NEW JERSEY DOES GREECE: SUMMER 2015 and OPA! *Cringe.*

"Oh," I said stupidly. "Isn't it kind of late in the day?"

"It is cooler at this time," he said with an impersonal smile. "And it is a short tour."

"Shorter than ours?" I said, making one more stab at a personal reference. It failed.

"Certainly," he said. "I hope your work continues to be productive."

He left me gripping Lusignan's business card. I wished I had a tour date instead.

chapter twenty-eight

ELIAS SARANTOPOULOS
March 1452
Mystras

Lusignan came back to Mystras in early March, looking much thinner than I remembered. Though I tried to argue him out of it, Plethon welcomed Lusignan back into the meetings of the *phratría* as if nothing had ever happened. He did agree to meet with me to hear my concerns, though they didn't seem to have any effect.

"Master, you must know that Scholarios gave evidence at Juvenal's trial."

"What of it?" Plethon was working on a new manuscript and barely looked up as I spoke.

"Juvenal is a scholar who was proclaimed to be a heretic. The problem is that Scholarios declared that Juvenal studied in 'Plethon's paganist cell.'" I paused for effect, but Plethon didn't even look up.

"He's wrong about Juvenal. He never studied with me." Plethon crossed out a line and began rewriting.

"But this means Scholarios knows about the *phratría*," I said anxiously. "I think Guarin Lusignan told him."

"And if he knows?" Plethon looked up at me. Today, for a change, there was no food in his beard.

"Master Plethon, after the trial Juvenal had all his limbs broken and was thrown off a cliff into the sea."

"Guarin Lusignan wishes to learn," Plethon said. "That is enough to permit him readmittance." He refused to acknowledge the danger of allowing Scholarios's informant to join our secret society. Scholarios would damn us all as heretics, and then we'd die like Juvenal. After that, I had nightmares about the waters of the Archipelagos closing over my head while my arms and legs flailed helplessly. I added "execution for heresy" to my list of fears.

Follow him, the seer had said—I was already doing that.

His enemies will be yours—this I already knew.

Keep his words safe—if Plethon could not, or would not, take care of himself, then clearly I would have to.

Ω

Plethon introduced us to his new work in progress, the *Nomoi— Book of Laws*—one chilly March morning, after swearing us to secrecy. Plethon, nearing one hundred, sat instead of pacing. His body had given all its energy to his humming mind. At first, the content seemed benign, but within a few minutes we were in perilous territory.

"*It is disputed whether or not gods exist . . .*" My heart sank. Doubting the existence of God was even more dangerous than believing there was more than one, and Guarin Lusignan was taking notes, struggling to hold the pen. *He looks like my first father*, I thought, remembering his abandoned sword leaning against the wall of our house. I feared Lusignan, but I also ached for him. If he had the same ailment, I knew how it would end.

Guarin, listening intently, could transmit the evidence that would consign the *Nomoi* and all the *phratría* to the flames. But what if I burned alongside them?

$$\Omega$$

That night, my parents fought at the dinner table. My mother placed a platter on the table with exaggerated care. "You've been swearing tributes to the sultan, with funds from our business," she said, and began slicing the roast lamb angrily.

"Many prosperous families are." My father smiled.

"The new sultan will not stop at tribute," she said, flinging a slab of meat onto my plate so hard that it slid into my lap. I put it back.

"Mehmed the Second is a surly teenage boy who recites poetry, sleeps with maps, and can't even relieve himself without the aid of an astrologist," my father said, laughing. "Tribute to the Ottomans has kept peace in Mystras and allowed us to conduct our business as we like. So long as Despot Demetrios keeps Sultan Mehmed happy with gold, the Ottomans will leave us alone. The Ottomans know our emperor Constantine is a force to contend with. Mehmed is just a turbaned adolescent. He won't make trouble for us so long as he gets his tribute."

"He's a menace," my mother said, stabbing her meat with a knife. "He had his infant half-brother murdered to keep his dominion safe. He wants Constantinople and will stop at nothing to get it, no matter what agreements he makes with easily fooled Greeks. Like *yourself*." Zoe placed her hands protectively on her belly, in a sad echo of the movement that had marked her doomed pregnancy. "We should be putting our money into defense. Mehmed will come after us once he's rich enough to buy weapons that will reduce Constantinople and Mystras to ruins."

"Our walls have never been breached."

"Walls are useless if you open the door to let the enemy in." My mother pushed her plate away in disgust. "If the defenders of Orthodoxy would agree to the Union of churches, we'd have help from the West. Instead we're standing alone in the face of an oncoming storm."

"You ought to leave diplomacy to those who know enough to advise," my father warned.

"Mehmed will take Constantinople, and Mystras will be next, our citizens left dead or enslaved. You'll be sorry when they come for us with our money in their hands."

"I am the master of this house, and the business I have built provides the luxury you enjoy. Leave business to me, and I'll leave the cooking to you. And"—he paused, considering—"the meat is overdone."

My mother rose from the table, pushing back her chair so hard it hit the ground and broke. "We've got no money to fix the chair," she said over her shoulder as she headed up the stairs. "It's all gone to your friend the sultan."

ELIAS SARANTOPOULOS
June 1452
Mystras

Two months after Guarin Lusignan had rejoined our group, Plethon gave us a lecture so shocking that it left us speechless. He'd covered, in rapid succession, consensual sexual intercourse and its explicit pleasures, prostitution, incest, polygamy, and rape, and then led us in a hymn to Zeus. Afterward, as I was recovering, Plethon put out a hand to stop me from leaving. "I will not live forever, Elias," he said.

"I have learned from you that the soul is immortal," I replied cautiously.

"Today I am speaking of practicality, not theory." He paused. "I must ask you a favor."

"I am at your service."

Plethon finally looked old, as if the effort of fighting to bring his ideas into the world had sapped his strength. "Elias, I need your help." He held two identical manuscripts in his hands. "When the *Laws* are published, I will have said all I needed to say in this lifetime. Many will wish it had never been said." Plethon placed one of the manuscripts into my hands. "I have made this copy of the *Laws* in case my enemies silence me. I shall keep writing, secure in the knowledge that should something befall me, or my work in progress, my words will evade destruction. Protect the *Laws* so that it will be read, Elias. Without readers, writers are lost, our words flightless birds."

"I will." I held the manuscript against my chest. Plethon held his own copy and closed his eyes for so long I thought he had fallen asleep. I was just getting up to leave when he spoke.

"For some, Elias, metempsychosis, the transmigration of souls from one body to another, is only an idea that helps us understand the ends of our lives. But for others metempsychosis is reality." He put one gnarled hand on my arm, and I knew he understood. That understanding was the greatest gift Plethon ever gave me.

Ω

On the morning of June 26, 1452, we came for our usual meeting, but for the first time, Plethon did not answer the door.

We found our teacher dead in his bed. I say we, but even overwhelmed by grief at my teacher's death, I noticed that Guarin Lusignan was absent. I slipped into Plethon's library and searched every piece of writing I could find, from bound books with tooled leather covers to drafts tied with twine. I opened trunks and looked in drawers. I went through Plethon's inkstained writing desk. Plethon had showed me his original version of the *Laws*, the one he hadn't given me. It was nowhere to be found.

And so I knew, two days after our teacher had died on his narrow bed, that his last work had been taken. And I knew who had taken it. My copy was still hidden at the bottom of a chest with the swaddling clothes that should have belonged to my daughter. I shared my worries about the *Nomoi*'s disappearance with the brotherhood, and my fears that Guarin was bringing the manuscript to Scholarios. We continued to study in hiding, with fear as a constant undercurrent.

Ω

The mountains that rose behind Mystras, steep and forbidding, became a second home for the secret community dedicated to Gemistos Plethon's ideals after his death. We called ourselves Plethonists, or Neo-Hellenes, because of Plethon's devotion to the rebirth of Greece's greatness.

"We are Greeks," Plethon had said, deliberately using the word employed by the West to slight us, "and it is time to reclaim our Greekness." Now, in the hidden compound that we built outside the city, the *phratría* became a way of life. New students came to learn history, philosophy, mathematics, and religion. We derived Pythagorean theorems and prayed to ancient gods of the pantheon. We read aloud from Plethon's works and taught his words to others. And we waited for the approaching Turks as they gained control over our rapidly shrinking empire.

I wanted to immerse myself fully in the brotherhood, but I had another life: my father's business, which I was expected to take over, and Zoe, who lay in bed during the day and wandered aimlessly about the house at night. I balanced the double life and waited for something terrible to happen.

In the winter of 1452, it did. Turkish Sultan Mehmed II began to make preparations for the siege of Constantinople. My mother still held out hope for the Union of churches to save us. She had no desire to venerate the pope, but without his support against the Turks there would be nothing left to venerate. She confined her support of the Union to late-night arguments with my father. It was just as well she kept her thoughts secret. Scholarios, now a monk, nailed an anti-Union proclamation on his cell's wooden door and damned Union supporters as heretics: *The Union is an act of Pure Evil, and ruin shall come to those that turn their backs on God.* Any hopes we had for help from the West against the Ottoman assault were doomed.

ELIAS SARANTOPOULOS
1453
Mystras

My father came back from delivering his last shipment of silk brocade to Constantinople late; I went downstairs to meet him. When he embraced me hard, I could feel his ribs through his traveling cloak; he'd lost weight. I got him a drink and sat down with him.

"Constantinople is terribly changed," my father said, as if he were talking about a loved one with a wasting disease.

"Is it worse than you expected?"

"Fields of weeds have replaced half the city, which is pocked with the crumbling ruins of houses. The harbors are nearly empty. One night I met a man writing his will at the inn's table while he ate dinner, he was so certain of the end." Shockingly, my father began to cry.

"Patera, can I help you to bed?"

"Sleep will bring us one night closer to our demise." I did not know how to comfort him. I refilled his glass. "Your mother was right about Mehmed," my father said. "He has garrisoned the Rumeli Hisar." The fortress guarded the straits of the Bosphorus, cutting off access to Constantinople. The completion of Rumeli Hisar was ominous news. "When our ship passed through the Bosphorus at its narrowest point, we saw the three massive towers, bristling with Janissary forces, armed with the largest cannons I've ever seen. Mehmed set up a barrier, requiring that ships lower their sails and pay customs fees to the Ottoman commander. One Venetian trade ship dared to defy Mehmed's orders." My father stopped. "I can't bear to tell you."

I did not want to hear the story. I wanted to sleep unafraid, the way I had before I knew the Turks were coming. But I was not a little boy wandering among the mulberry trees anymore. I put my hand on my father's arm.

"Elias, I've had nightmares since. The Janissaries fired the cannon at the Venetian ship at close range. The ship broke apart and sank. Sailors tried to swim to shore, but as they climbed up the banks they were beheaded; the water of the Bosphorus turned red with Venetian blood. Mehmed's commander impaled the captain alive on a stake at the top of a hill overlooking the strait. I watched him die, writhing as we sailed past." My father began to weep. "Mehmed is a monster. He's taken control of the access to the city from the sea—Constantinople cannot survive his assault. And when the city falls, he will come for us."

I wanted to protect my father, to brush the thinning hair from his brow. I put my arms around him, but we both knew that no degree of comfort could protect us once the Turks arrived.

Ω

Two years later, Constantinople was gone, like a distant family member I had assumed would always be there. I had never been to the city, and now it was lost to me. The day the messenger came to Mystras, I stood listening to the news with my mother on one side and my father on the other. Mystras citizens crowded the plaza outside the governor's palace to hear the story of the end. My parents both wept; the only time I'd seen them have the same reaction to anything. The last emperor Constantine's blood stained the earth where the first Constantine had been crowned more than a thousand years before. I remembered how our new emperor looked out over us at his coronation; we were the children of his empire. The messenger's story made images in my head, like a vivid dream. Constantine stripped his imperial robes so none would know him from a common soldier and died fighting with his men on the ramparts of the city he was sworn to protect. I thought, in my small way, that my life was an echo of Constantine's sacrifice. I, too, was inextricably bound to a city whose end was foretold, sworn to die fighting for its survival. But I fought in secret and, unlike the emperor, had to die more than once.

Word spread through Mystras. Constantinople's Hagia

Sophia church became a mosque. Though I had never seen it, my grief was profound—the way one might grieve for the loss of faith. The Hagia Sophia's bells, altar, and precious relics of the saints were destroyed. Mosaics of Jesus, Mary, saints, and angels were plastered over, and minarets rose around the great dome. In Mystras, we waited for our churches to fall to the Ottoman sword. But two years later, Mystras was still miraculously free and Greek, an island in a sea of conquest.

That year, danger came from another source: Scholarios had a copy of Plethon's *Laws*. We found out through our new and surprisingly useful informant, Charitonymos. He'd finally been allowed to join the *phratría* after Plethon's death; we called him the Posthumous Plethonist, affectionately. He proved his worth by stealing a letter he'd found in the despot's palace, addressed from Scholarios to the governor and his wife, Theodora, who was a close confidante of Scholarios. We crowded around him as he read it.

> *"The Laws took me only four hours to read, and when I finished reading, I threw it aside, unable to bear the touch of the paper sullied by ideas of such depravity. Plethon has been swayed to error by daemons. He is exhorting that his followers make prayers and sacrifice to imaginary gods.*
>
> *"I weep for Plethon's soul, which cannot be saved. The only fitting end to this work of outright blasphemy is to consign it to the flames."*

We pressed Charitonymos for information, but he had no more to give us. The *phratría* despaired that the only copy of the manuscript might be lost; I knew otherwise but kept quiet. After Constantinople's fall, Scholarios was named patriarch by Sultan Mehmed. So by unpleasant coincidence Scholarios was at the height of his power when he read Plethon's shocking manuscript. So far, he'd confined his outrage to a private letter, but if his thoughts became public, the *Laws* and all of Plethon's followers would be in danger.

chapter twenty-nine

GUARIN LUSIGNAN
March 1460
Constantinople

Guarin Lusignan had been handsomely rewarded for the delivery of the *Laws* into Scholarios's hands. By most counts Guarin was fortunate: wealthy through inheritance and well regarded by the patriarch of Constantinople. Those two attributes allowed him to emerge unscathed from the calamity of the city's fall. He was ensconced in a well-appointed house with tapestries on the walls and thick rugs covering the tiled marble floors. He'd been given twenty Greek children as slaves, and they managed his house well. The two-story house on the *Mese* had not been razed by blasts of the Turkish cannons, nor looted in the aftermath of the walls' collapse, and in its garden peacocks strolled. He had no inclination to return to Paris.

He found a wife in Constantinople without much trouble. No father would refuse a man of comfortable means in uneasy times like these. He chose the daughter of a traveling merchant from Carcassonne, and soon they had a golden-haired son, Laurens. When Guarin began to think of traveling to Mystras for the third time, Laurens was two years old and wobbled about the house on his plump feet, babbling in an entertaining mixture of French, Turkish, and Greek.

Money had always been Guarin's answer: it had bought him the posting with Scholarios, safety through the Turkish occupation, and a wife who quickly gave him a son. But when the monster took possession of his body and gnawed away at his soul, gold finally failed him. His limbs twisted with a demonic force, and no doctor, no matter their fee, could do anything. Guarin began to fall—once hard enough to lose two teeth. He carried them home in one bloody hand. Then came the misbehavior of his mind. Memories flitted in and out of his head like moths, and what he read failed to stick. He paid for salves, potions, medallions of the Christian faith, indulgences from the Church, and candles to be lit on his behalf. But the malady's cure could not be bought at any price. Money, for the first time, finally failed him. Guarin, who had never learned another strategy to overcome obstacles, was left helpless. And having a child to protect made Guarin desperate.

Five years had passed since Guarin's last trip to Mystras. Now he had Laurens, whose plump limbs and questioning bright mind might be cursed to wither like his own, and like his father's before him. That Laurens should suffer, and his children and children's children after him, was unbearable. Guarin needed the cure.

Ask him, he knows. The seer's words took residence in his thoughts like a worm in wood. Guarin had tried to find the answer twice, but Cardinal Bessarion had blocked him both times. With Bessarion far away in Rome now, nothing could interfere. *It is too late for me, but not for my son.*

As if Laurens knew he was the subject of Guarin's thoughts, he tottered over to place his curly golden head in his father's lap.

ELIAS SARANTOPOULOS
Early May 1460
Mystras

I'd stayed up late with my father's failing accounts—Turkish domination of the silk trade had hurt business, and we had to let workers go. I slept late and woke up alone. Zoe was gone. I searched the house, garden, and stables. I went to the factories, where our remaining workers had just begun unraveling the delicate silkworm threads, but no one had seen her there. Alarmed, I went to the orchards and began to walk the rows of mulberry trees where we'd strolled before her body betrayed her. The trees were thick with the green of early spring.

I sensed someone following me—twice I turned but saw no one. A twig cracked, but when I turned, I saw only a squirrel cross my path with its tail high. I sat to rest against a spreading tree, trying to imagine where Zoe might have gone. I closed my eyes in the flickering shadows, and when I opened them, Guarin Lusignan was standing over me. I stood up quickly.

"You are a hard man to find," Guarin said.

"If I had known you were looking for me, I would have made it harder." I had not seen him in years, but I had thought of him often, how he had betrayed the teacher whose work he'd pretended to respect. My anger was close to the surface.

"I need to know your secret, Elias Sarantopoulos."

"You are a betrayer of secrets, Guarin Lusignan, and the last person I would tell anything, had I anything to tell."

"You hide behind that innocent face as if you were simply the son of a silk manufacturer."

"I *am* the son of a silk manufacturer." But I thought of my clandestine copy of the *Laws*.

His next words surprised me. "I know you have the cure."

"The cure for what?"

"To the malady that twists my limbs and fogs my brain."

I thought he'd come for the *Nomoi*, but instead, this. Why would he think I had a cure for his illness? I thought of what the seer had said, that day when Guarin stood like a pinned butterfly, transfixed by her stare. Now, in the shifting light of the mulberry trees, I saw the flicker of Guarin's hands, the twist of his neck.

The truth of who the Lusignan family believed me to be began to crystallize. What had saved me, when my first father suffered from the malady that relentlessly pursued the Lusignan heirs through the centuries? I had no amulet of protection, no herbal remedy, and no spell woven by a sorcerer's will. I might have stayed well by chance, or because I had never lived long enough to fall ill like my father, who aged into his infirmity. What if Guarin thought my blood could save him, as it seemed to have saved me? And what if he was right? If I was the cure, did I have to die to provide it for someone else?

Lusignan was armed with a dagger at his hip. I had nothing to protect myself; I'd stumbled from bed wearing only the tunic and leggings I'd thrown on to hunt for my missing wife. I shook my head. "I can't help you." I moved to pass him. "My wife is expecting me."

"I know you have the answer!" His voice rose shrilly, and I saw that he was afraid. His hand shook as he drew his dagger, but not enough to prevent him from killing me.

"I am not a killer," Guarin said. "But I have a son. The seer spoke, and she told me these words: '*Your blood is death, but the blood of the boy is life*.' You are that boy, Elias Sarantopoulos, and for my son's life I would take a life. God, guide my hand to do your will." Now there was no Bessarion to save me; I had only the mulberry trees' shadows and the silent vigilance of the silkworms to bear witness. The seer had led Guarin as she had led me, her tangled words unraveling just enough to allow glimpses forward, like the silkworm's thread. The Lusignan men had spent centuries searching and thought they found what they were looking for in me.

There was a shimmer in the shadows behind Guarin's head, then a soft thud. Guarin folded to the ground, his blade buried in the earth, rather than in me. Behind him, holding a broken mulberry branch, was Zoe.

Ω

In mid-May, Sultan Mehmed encamped with his army at Corinth, five days' march from Mystras. I was delivering a shipment of silk to the palace on the day the sultan's messenger met with Despot Demetrios, accompanied by seven armed guards and seven flag bearers, each carrying a different color banner. The guards, who wore distinctive plumed high cylindrical hats, were Janissaries, the elite infantry of the sultan. Charitonymos slid next to me, and we followed the sultan's party into the main hall of the palace.

The messenger had a disturbingly impassive face; he could have been made of wax. Unfurling a scroll, he laid out the sultan's demands. Despot Demetrios fiddled anxiously with the brooch that held his red cloak pinned at the shoulder. I was afraid he'd stab himself. In contrast to the neatly turbaned representative of the sultan's court, the despot, dwarfed by his large and ostentatious white hat, looked foolish.

"First, the Sultan Mehmed, Allah grant him long life, demands that you pay him your respects in Corinth. Second, the sultan wishes to remind you that tributes in gold are years in arrears."

Demetrios fiddled with his hat. The messenger cleared his throat.

"And finally, the sultan also remarks on how you have not complied with the sultan's request to send your daughter Helena to him to honor his harem." We all knew the despot had sent his daughter to Monemvasia to keep her away from Mehmed. If my daughter had lived, I would have done the same.

Demetrios, eyeing the Janissaries' long-shafted axes, nodded in apparent acquiescence. But in the days that followed, Despot Demetrios did not pay the tribute owed and did not deliver Helena to Mehmed's harem. A few weeks later, Mehmed's massive army began the march south toward Mystras.

For seven years, since the fall of Constantinople, we had feared this moment. Mystras had run out of time.

$$\Omega$$

It is funny, the small things you remember when unimaginably large events occur. On May 29, 1460, my mother picked a sprig from the violets on the terrace and put it in a vase at the table. I remember the spoon sweets we ate for breakfast, made from wild pears and green walnuts that grew on the hill behind our house. I remember the powdery softness of Zoe's cheek when I kissed her, and how she turned to me for the first time in many months to put her arms around my neck. And I remember standing on the terrace with my parents, looking across the valley at the snake of Mehmed's army winding down the slopes of Parnon.

My father did not go to the factory to give the orders to start the looms. We left the dishes on the table until flies came buzzing. We held hands as we had not since my childhood. We watched as the advancing Ottoman army turned the valley's green to black.

The next day, Charitonymos paid me an unexpected visit. He blustered apologetically about the intrusion.

"The despot sent Despoena Theodora to Monemvasia," he said, wringing his hands.

"That seems wise, under the circumstances." I served him a glass of wine, but he did not take it.

"Well, yes, for safety. She'll be with their daughter Helena. No good having his women here when the sultan arrives. Once the Turks come . . ." Charitonymos's anxiety became acute. "What will happen? Elias, I am so afraid." He began to weep.

"We are all afraid."

"Who are we to think we can resist? The Turks will take Monemvasia soon—even the great fortress in the sea cannot hold against them. And the Turks are allied with our old enemy; Mehmed put Scholarios in power in the patriarchal seat."

"And Scholarios is an enemy of Plethon's legacy," I interjected, grimly.

"Exactly. He'll burn the *Laws* to ashes." We looked at each other over the table. "Now what?" Charitonymos said.

"I will take care of it."

"Well, better you than me, certainly." Charitonymos looked slightly relieved. "I'm useless."

"You are far from useless," I said. "Now go back to the palace. Do your job, and don't speak of what we've discussed." I slid his glass toward him. "No wine?"

"Might help. Nothing else seems to." He downed it in three gulps.

That night, I lay in bed, listening to Zoe's rhythmic breathing next to me. *You will serve this city all the days of your life*, my first mother had told me, two centuries ago. I had fought a battle at Pelagonia and fomented rebellion in Sicily in the name of Mystras's survival. What good did my service do now? Hiding a few pages of heretical philosophy on the eve of the destruction of the Romaioi empire's last remnant? My effort was a tiny point of light in the dark of Mystras's imminent demise. Even if I could succeed in bringing the *Laws* to safety, what would it matter if our walls were breached by the Ottoman cannons, our sons taken to protect our conqueror in battle, and our women enslaved to join him in bed?

Plethon was dead, Bessarion was in Rome, and my wife was nearly silent, our child a memory. No prophet spoke in my head, no seer waited in the Pantanassa to deliver cryptic messages meant for me. I had no one to talk to besides myself.

Ω

The Turks' entrance to Mystras was a quiet event; we folded like a pennant in dying wind. There was no cannon fire, no conflagration. Siege engines did not park outside the walls; blood did not run in the streets. We did not resist. I watched as the great gate swung open to let Despot Demetrios pass outside the walls to visit the sultan in his tent. I wondered what it must be like for the despot, sitting face-to-face with his conqueror, a man less than half his age who ruled territories ten times as great. The next time the gates opened, it was to let the Turks in.

It is one thing to be born into an occupied land, as I had been in the days of Prince Villehardouin. It is entirely another to, during the course of your lifetime, have your home become one. Demetrios handed over Mystras's keys. The Palaiologos flag came down, the double-headed eagle folding its wings, and the red banners of the Ottomans rose in their

place. Plaques in Arabic replaced our icons, and the divine lit-
urgy went silent. Within a few days, Theodora was called
back from Monemvasia, their daughter Helena was handed
over to the sultan, and the despot and his wife left Mystras,
stripped of their robes. The town's residents were left to face
the new regime.

Through the wall, I heard my mother weeping all night.
The next morning Mystras's boys lined up in the plaza outside
the palace to submit to the *devşirme*, as the eldest child of each
family was taken to join the sultan's troops. I watched families
sobbing openly or tight-lipped with restrained despair. That
morning was the only time in my lives when I've been relieved
not to have a child. But I knew loss, too. The next day the sultan
chose women for his harem, and one of them was my wife, Zoe.

GUARIN LUSIGNAN
May 1460
Mystras

Guarin woke in the field, where the glare of the light patterns
filtering through the mulberry trees made his head pound. He
put a hand to the throbbing spot on the back of his skull and
it came away streaked with blood. Guarin managed to stand
and stagger out of the field to the edge of town, limping slowly
along the least populated streets, trying to stay out of sight.
He emerged into the market outside the gates, where the stalls
hummed with many languages and he could find a merchant
to provide passage home, but the smell of rotting fish overwhelmed him until he bent over, vomiting into a vendor's
bucket.

The bucket belonged to an arms seller from the Vlora, in Albania. The trader's daughter, who had plump but surprisingly strong arms, helped Guarin up, gave him fresh water and a cloth, and, draping his arm over her broad shoulders, walked him into the shade of her father's tent. There, with his wound cleaned, Guarin found rest, lodging, and a plan for passage home.

The Albanian's daughter, encouraged by his handful of coins and his promise of more, showed him more than therapeutic interest. She did not know he had a wife, and he did not enlighten her. Her father was equally interested in the apparently wealthy stranger who had vomited on their property but otherwise seemed an excellent catch. Guarin also found, in the form of the trader's brooding eldest son, a man who would do anything for money—even kill.

ELIAS SARANTOPOULOS
Late May 1460
Mystras

Zoe's absence gnawed at me like a cancer: a constant, deep pain. She had always been quiet, and after the loss of our child even more so, a ghostlike presence wandering the rooms at night. But her disappearance still opened up a chasm of loss. Every day after she was taken to the sultan's harem, I woke up before dawn, looking into the dark in which the accumulated losses of my three lives wove like hallucinations. I heard nothing of her after she left, and I could not imagine what her life had become.

The only distraction from that despair was misery on a

different front: three weeks after Despot Demetrios left Mystras, Scholarios publicly burned the *Laws*. He preserved only the table of contents and the hymns as a reminder of the depravity of the text, and the wisdom of his consigning it to the flames. Scholarios also issued a patriarchal order to destroy any other existing copies of the manuscript on pain of excommunication.

Now that the Turks ruled us, Plethon's words mattered more than ever. Stripped of the solace of married life, I threw myself into that cause even more fervently. Plethon had called us to grow our Greek beards, to revive our lost gods, and to celebrate a philosophy that illuminated the nature of the divine. Plethon's last work was the final culmination of that Greek paean, and now we bowed our heads to the sultan. Meanwhile, in secret, I kept possibly the only copy of the *Laws* left in the world. I'd failed to save Mystras from the Turks; but I intended to succeed in keeping the manuscript safe. Unfortunately, that meant defying Scholarios, the leader of the Greek Orthodox Church.

I had to get the book out of Mystras, whose walls were surrounded by Turkish troops and whose gates were guarded by sentries. If I could get the manuscript to Bessarion, I knew he would protect it. He continued to support Plethon's teachings, had dedicated his life to preservation of Greek texts, and was the only man alive who could disagree with Scholarios and get away with it. The *Laws* had to get all the way to Rome.

Ω

When the Turks first surrounded the city, the market outside Mystras's gates went quiet, its stalls shuttered. Once it became clear that the Turks' arrival would not lead to bloodshed, it reopened; in fact, business was booming. The narrow walkways between stalls bustled with merchants from all over the world, but now there were new customers: thousands of Turks eager to enjoy the benefits of their new conquest.

At the gate, two Turkish *derbendjis* stopped me. They wore white turbans and ankle-length blue jackets with a row of bronze buttons to the hip. Below the last button, the jackets flared out over pantaloons. One guard lowered his spear to block my exit; the other drew a curved dagger.

"*Orda dur*," the dagger-holder said incomprehensibly. The other *derbendji* shoved the butt of his spear into my stomach.

Once I stopped retching, I managed to say one of the Turkish words I knew. "*Markete?*" I pointed toward the stalls. Another outpouring of Turkish ensued, but at least it wasn't accompanied by violence. I tried again. "*Ipek tüccari.*" I pointed to my own chest, indicating that I was the silk manufacturer.

The guards looked at me suspiciously, but I'd come prepared. I retrieved the bolt of silk I'd strapped across my back. The spear went up, the dagger went down, and I went into the press of the market, heart pounding. Wrapped inside one of the bolts was my copy of Plethon's manuscript. My next task was to find a messenger.

I squeezed past stalls stacked with jars of honey and jugs of wine, bins of aromatic spices that reminded me of my last life in Sicily, and piles of fresh local oregano and thyme. I had a destination in mind: the dyers' tents, where I knew a man I could trust. The dye merchant, a Genoese trader named Alfano, greeted me with enthusiasm and a rapid-fire sales pitch.

"So delighted to see my best customer!" I knew there were many equally good and likely better customers. "Today I have dyes of exceptional excellence. There is Turkey red, for our friends here." He gesticulated with a sideways grin at the soldiers guarding the gate. "I have a new shipment of dyer's rocket, which I assure you will produce yellow of long-lasting brightness. Perhaps you are more inclined to green? I have managed to perfect a *Genista tinctoria* of incomparable purity." When I didn't answer, he tried again. "If blue is what you are after, I have *indikon* today, all the way from India, but that will come quite dear."

I raised my hand to stop him. "Can we go inside?" Realizing this particular visit might be unusual, he raised the flap of his tent. I followed him in.

I told him what I needed. Yes, he could take a package to Rome. Yes, he knew the Via di Porta San Sebastiano. Yes, he knew of Cardinal Bessarion; who did not? And he could keep a secret, especially for money. I gave him the bolt of silk, with instructions not to unwrap it. I left feeling strangely light.

I walked back slowly, taking the path through the armory tents, where polished shields and sharpened swords hung, catching the light. Activity buzzed around me—merchants and shoppers, traders and Turkish soldiers. I'd done what I could, and soon the *Laws* would be on their way to safety. At a sudden movement to my left, I turned as a man appeared from between two stalls, his lower face covered with a cloth. In disjointed sequence, I saw him, then his arm, then the sword held high in his hand. At the same moment, Guarin Lusignan appeared behind him, his head wrapped in a gruesome bandage.

"Stop him!" Guarin's shout made my would-be assassin hesitate—not long, but just long enough. I grabbed a weapon from the closest display—the swing of the blade familiar from my soldier life—and met the masked assassin's neck. Guarin, his face pale under his bandage, caught my eye, then melted into the crowd, leaving me with the bleeding corpse of the man who had intended to kill me.

While I stood stunned, my two Turkish acquaintances from the gates came sprinting in my direction, their blue jackets flying behind them.

"He's killed a man—" That much Turkish I understood before spear and dagger found their mark in me—and then I was lying on the ground in a widening pool of red. *My blood*, I managed to think. I heard the walls of Mystras keening, calling my name, and after that, nothing.

CARDINAL BASILIOS BESSARION
July 1460
Rome

Bessarion almost turned the messenger away. But when the man insisted that he had been given explicit instructions from a silk manufacturer in Mystras, Bessarion led him to a private room.

The sender, the messenger said, had been very specific that the delivery go straight to Cardinal Bessarion himself. Yes, he knew that was irregular, but he was a man to follow instructions to the letter, and no one but Bessarion could be trusted to receive it.

Once the messenger had completed his task, Bessarion shut himself into the library where Guarin Lusignan had once come searching. Every room in the house now overflowed with books that arrived faster than the carpenter could build shelves for them.

Bessarion unwrapped the silk carefully. Dyed a cardinal's red, the message was not lost on him. In the center was a carefully bound manuscript, and when he read the first pages he gasped. He had not known a copy of Plethon's *Nomoi* had survived Scholarios's decree. The writing spidered in the distinctive hand that made him feel Plethon was standing at his side, lecturing as he had in life.

The accompanying letter was brief—

To you I entrust these words, as I could to no other.

Yours in eternal friendship, which I know you understand,
E.S., Mystras

"You knew I would keep it safe," Bessarion said quietly, bringing the pages to his lips.

LAURENS LUSIGNAN
1480
Istanbul

Laurens's father died struggling to breathe. By the end, Guarin Lusignan could no longer eat solid food, not even the soft bread he had come to love after the Turks changed the city's name. Laurens's mother ground Guarin's food into a soft paste so he could swallow, but soon even that became impossible. On Laurens's twenty-second birthday, he lost his father: raving mad, thin as a skeleton, and gasping for breath.

The day after the will was read, the elderly notary handed him a letter and a vielle in a dusty case. Laurens had not known his father played—there was much, it turned out, he did not know about his father.

"Your late father asked that I hold these for you until after his demise," the notary said with ponderous self-importance. Laurens did not open the letter until that night, after his mother slept. The paper was yellowed and fragile, the ink faded. But the power of seeing his father's handwriting made him weep in a way he had not been able to at his father's grave. It had been so long since Guarin could speak lucidly—or even speak at all—that the letter felt more real than his own father had at the end.

June 1460

My dearest Laurens:

Today I almost had a man killed. This is not how I wish to be remembered by my son, whom I love more than anyone in the world. I wish I could forget. But though my memory has begun to fail me, my actions remain preternaturally clear. I recall how much I paid to have it done. I recall the hands of the man I paid to do my bidding—I looked at them because I could not bear to meet his gaze. I remember where the assassin found his target, in the press of the market outside Mystras. Worst—I remember the face of my intended victim.

I knew him, Laurens. I remember that his eyes were dark. I remember the way his brown hair curled over his forehead. I remember that his voice was quiet and measured, and that he was slow to anger.

This is a man I could have called friend, had we not been born in different lands with centuries of animosity between them, had he not been the student of my teacher's enemy, and, most of all, had he not held the key to our family's salvation. Fate makes enemies out of those who

*could be friends. But I did not kill him. Instead, in the end,
I tried to save his life. But others took it from him.*

*I hope your memories of me are not sullied by these
revelations, and that you will understand and forgive. I
am about to tell you what I believe to be the truth, and
it will change you. I sought to help you, Laurens, and
your children, and your children's children. In doing so, I
considered destroying another life, with the belief that one
life spent was worth many lives saved.*

*I beseeched God to provide a sign that my soul at
least might emerge pure in the end, though my body was
possessed by demons. And I prayed to God to give you the
strength to make your own decisions. Either to succeed
where I did not, or to resist the impulse to do ill in the
name of good. Your life and the lives of your descendants
hang in the balance. So do their souls.*

*Laurens, here is what I have learned about a man
called Elias and a city called Mystras, and the secrets they
hold. Keep this letter and show it to your children so that
they may show it to their children in turn. Perhaps this way
we will find an answer to our family's tragedy. I hope the
knowledge serves you better than it did me.*

Laurens continued to read until he reached the end. Understanding was worse than ignorance had been.

chapter thirty

ELIAS OROLOGAS
July 2015
Mystras

The modern Lusignan, despite his academic title and his ve-
neer of cordiality, has begun to pursue me like a hyena who
smells carrion on the wind. I am not carrion, not yet. But hy-
enas are live hunters, too—they kill by tearing off chunks of
flesh as they run alongside their doomed prey, aiming for a
major artery so their quarry will bleed to death.

Lusignan began with pleasant notes left at the museum.
Then came the increasingly frequent calls—even to the museum director's private line—and finally, my own home tele-
phone. I did not answer, nor did I return any messages. I am
not in the habit of chatting with my stalker, particularly not
one descended from a generation of enemies who have wished
me dead. I imagine him now as a mangy predator-cat, becoming hungrier and hungrier, more desperate for a catch. And I
am his prey. I have been pursued for centuries—the feeling is
familiar. So, it is not the pursuit that makes me despair, it is
that I believe he found me through Helen.

Ω

I keep remembering the moment when Helen suddenly saw me as a puzzle, rather than a person. I know that look. I have seen it in the eyes of my enemies for hundreds of years. They believe I am the solution to their problem, and whether they are right or not, they will stop at nothing in pursuit.

She is not my enemy. But to see that calculating look on her face, as she realized how useful I might be . . . was unbearable. Afterward, she was clearly sorry. But it was too late. I will have to forget her: the way she talks too fast when she is nervous, how her freckles stand out, gold against the flush of her cheeks. I will have to forget her breathless run up Mystras hill to find me. I will have to forget the apricots, and the sound of birdsong in the cloister of the Agios Demetrios where she gave me water and I managed to give her comfort. I will have to forget Alexander. But I fear I won't be able to.

Last year, a guest inadvertently left a book of poetry in the Mystras Inn. Panos, knowing my poetic leanings, offered it to me. I kept the book on my bed table long enough that I almost forgot it was there. One night, when the racket of the nightingales outside my window kept me awake, I picked up the book. *Elizabeth Bishop*, the flyleaf said. I opened the book to a page at random and read. "One Art" was the title of the poem.

The art of losing isn't hard to master . . .

I read it seven times. I think of that poem every day.

I have had so much practice, it should not be hard to lose again. But still, it is. Every time.

HELEN ADLER
July 2015
Mystras

I hadn't finished the funding proposal, and it kept nagging at me. Almost three weeks into our trip, the return date to New York was looming. I never like the end of vacation, but this particular end was especially unappealing.

One morning Alexander (unusually) slept later than I did; I took that as a message to get some work done. When I went back to the application forms, I remembered why I'd stopped: the study of the genetic determinants of disease in human populations wasn't what I specialized in, though I knew people who did. I should let them take this on, rather than getting myself wrapped up in finding local HD families in Greece. Particularly one family that included a Eurocentric supremacist and another that included a man I had nearly fallen in love with.

I sat staring at the forms, at the café table where I'd last seen Elias. It felt scientifically unconscionable to ignore information that could transform HD treatment. I got the brilliant idea to call Elektra.

She sounded happy to hear from me. "Professor Adler! How delightful. I was just thinking about you."

"Helen is fine. Why were you thinking about me?"

"I just unpacked the food my mother made for me, and it's the largest *tyropita* I've ever seen. It doesn't even fit in my refrigerator. I need help."

"I wish I were there," I said.

"Actually, I was thinking of you for another reason, besides cheese pie. We've just found a document more than five hundred years old that might shed light on one of the families we're studying. An old woman recently died who'd lived her whole life in Palaiologio, a tiny town between Spárti and Mystras. She'd kept a chest full of old papers, all wrapped in a nightgown. The family discovered it after the woman's death; it's amazing anything survived. Maybe we should replicate the nightgown method for archival protection." She laughed.

"What sort of papers?" I could hear rustling in the background and imagined the cheese pie.

"Mostly letters from the last fifty or sixty years. But also, a document from the middle of the fifteenth century—dated 1460. The family realized it might be valuable and called the university."

"Have you read it?"

"Well, no," Elektra said. "The family gave it directly to Dr. Lusignan."

I felt a stab of irritation, but it wasn't my place to question their professional relationship, even if I *did* question their professional relationship. I tried to frame my next question without sounding disapproving. "Why to him?"

"He is the local expert. But also, the papers belong to his ancestor, a man named Laurens Lusignan. It's not clear how they ended up in this woman's possession."

"Did Dr. Lusignan tell you what it says?"

"Not yet. I know it includes a letter from a man named Guarin Lusignan—a name we already knew, so it confirms the ancestry. The letter is some sort of deathbed parental apology; Professor Lusignan hasn't told me more at the moment." She paused. "He can get preoccupied when he's on the trail of something. Successful people can be like that, very single-minded. I'm a distracted multitasking assistant professor. He's a pit bull—he won't let go until he's done." She laughed again, but it sounded uneasy. "I'm sure I'll hear from him when he resurfaces."

I wasn't so sure. Collaborators would normally share information like that, at least in my universe.

"You must have called for your own reasons," Elektra said, shifting subjects. "Do you mind if I eat while we talk?"

"Of course not. Actually, I have some information *you* might find interesting." *And I, unlike your mentor, am willing to share it with you.*

While she ate, I told Elektra that I might have found the name of the thirteenth-century Mystras-based Frankish soldier who'd married a Greek midwife and then had the misfortune to die of Huntington's: Jéhan Borghes. She got excited—it matched some Frankish names of the period, a family originally based in Paris, with sons who'd traveled to Greece to fight for the prince. I told her there was a Bible belonging to him in the Mystras museum. I didn't tell her where I'd gotten the information, and I didn't tell her I knew a living relative of that doomed soldier—scientific collegiality notwithstanding.

"Professor Lusignan will be excited about the news," she said as we signed off, promising to stay in touch. After we got off the phone, I submitted the proposal, but as I pressed SEND, I pictured Lusignan as a pit bull with his teeth sunk deep in Elias's neck.

ELIAS OROLOGAS
July 2015
Mystras

The next site of vandalism was just outside the city's gate where the market used to be. I found the damage while leading a tour of students. They snapped pictures of themselves and one another with their phones and then posted them, standing around the gaping hole and tumbled stones.

A relentless memory comes with the shape of my lives: I saw the crowded rows of stalls, I heard the merchants hawking fresh-caught fish, brilliant dyes, and gleaming swords. I remembered walking with Bessarion the day he took me into his confidence. I remembered the moment when my life as a silk trader and philosophy student ended, leaving me in a pool of my own blood. The damage went beyond methodical searching; it had an edge of increasingly violent anger. Two sites in Mystras disrupted, and what I suspected was my mother's logbook stolen, with its generations of births and deaths in Mystras. The danger was mounting. I had a name, the usual name, and my suspicions. But suspicions were not evidence. Soon, I supposed, the violence would rise to the surface, as it always had. And I would have to face it.

While the students checked to be sure their posts had loaded, I knelt down and put my hands in the dirt. It was dry from the summer heat, but I shaped it as well as I could into a *kollyva*, in memory of those who were dead and gone.

part four

INDEPENDENCE

chapter thirty-one

ELIAS SEKERIS
February 1821
Mystras

"I'm so tired." I didn't realize I had said it out loud. I had many reasons to be tired. I never slept deeply these days, living in a tent in the mountains above Mystras town, with a rock for a mattress and a pistol ready at my side, but I was more tired than usual.

"We're all tired, up all night because of that infernal rooster. I actually regret stealing it." Fortunately for us, Alexis was particularly good at poaching livestock. He'd escaped a Turkish prison and by some miracle made it to the mountains without being discovered. He usually focused his efforts on larger animals like sheep and goats, but on this occasion had veered to poultry. In theory, it was an excellent idea, as we already had a few hens.

When Alexis joined our band of klephts in the mountains above Mystras, we gained a steady supply of options for dinner. We cooked the meat in a deep sealed pit so the smoke could not give us away. *Klephts* once meant "thieves," which some of us obviously were. We had to eat, after all. But we were more than thieves now. Unlike those who stayed in the settled towns, we resisted Turkish rule. We ruled ourselves, and we plotted our country's liberation.

On a clear day, we could look down on Mystras town and see the brightly colored paint on the houses of the Turks alternating with the drab brown the Greeks were forced to use. The sight made me angry, but it suited the grim situation we Greeks were in.

Alexis was difficult to get along with—he took offense at the slightest insult and picked fights with everyone. He was huge and almost invariably won, so he was rarely challenged. Today I agreed with him—the rooster had been a bad choice. Alexis killed the bird for breakfast.

"Someday, all Greeks will be free," Alexis said as he wrung the rooster's neck. "We will come out of hiding to fight at the front lines. We will be the saviors of our nation, and none will call us thieves." He cut the rooster's comb off with his knife and threw it into the fire. "May the sultan's turban burn like this cock's comb."

"Amen," I said. The rooster, minus crown, made its way into an excellent soup. The next night, we slept through to morning.

No matter how much I slept, the fatigue never eased. My weariness came from relentless living, from an unending duty to a place whose demands I would never escape. And this particular life came with a seamless memory of all the lives I'd lived before. At optimistic moments, I imagined that I had evolved in the wheel of return to a state of greater knowledge, but those moments were rare. Other than wordless babyhood (which no one seems to remember, no matter their mortality), I'd had not one moment of blissful ignorance. Sometimes I imagined myself on a tiny boat sailing apart from the rest of the world. Next to me, visible but out of reach, everyone else clustered together on a crowded, happy vessel, bound by mortality. And though I accepted my strange place in the world, at dark moments, I envied those who lived only once.

There was no one to share my burdens. I could not tell anyone—not Alexis, the livestock thief, though I was happy to eat his meat and share a prayer for liberation. Not Kostis, the crypto-Christian who'd pledged himself to Islam to avoid the non-Muslim's heavy tax, but who, once his devotion to the Church had been discovered, fled to the mountains to escape execution. Not Mitros, the grizzled farmer whose freedom became serfdom overnight as his land was deeded to a Sanjak lord, and who could not bear to watch the fruits of his ploughing feed another man's family. He'd brought his wife and child to our mountain enclave and coaxed vegetables from the rocky mountain soil to feed us. I could not even tell my closest friend, Emmanuel. He'd been an apothecary under the Turks, a stable and profitable profession. But he'd been forced to give up his horse and his dead father's flintlock pistol; the Turkish authorities did not allow Greek non-Muslims to ride or bear arms. Emmanuel pretended to acquiesce, handing over the animal and the weapon meekly. The following night, he knifed the guard, retrieved his pistol, and found us in the mountains. "A knife is quieter than a gun, anyway," Emmanuel said with his lopsided smile. (He'd lost the teeth on one side of his mouth in a boyhood fight.) And he'd stolen his horse back from the Sanjak stables on the way out.

All my klepht brothers had at least one grudge. Most had more than one. What I had suffered and seen was another secret I couldn't share. I'd watched the *devşirme* in person—saw boys ripped from their families to join the sultan's troops—though the *devşirme* had been abandoned two hundred years before. I lost my wife Zoe to a long-dead sultan's harem. I had known a free Mystras, unlike my compatriots born into occupation, and I had seen that freedom lost.

I didn't need a prophetess to tell me what my duty to Mystras would be in this life. We all had the same task: revolution. The success of the French against their government had proven it was possible. Strange, that once the French had been our enemy, while now they were an inspiration. But the knowledge that people could rise up against their king—and win—gave us the confidence that we, too, could fight to reclaim our country.

That shared goal mitigated the loneliness. The singing also made me feel less alone. We klephts had our songs, poetry in music that told stories of harsh lives of resistance and the unshakable belief that our *patridha* could be won back from the Turks. *Patridha* once meant "fatherland"; now we had learned its new meaning: *nation*. But at night when the others slept and I lay awake knowing that I would go on breathing long after those around me had stopped, it returned with aching familiarity.

Ω

I'd been found naked and yelling seventeen years before outside the walls of Mystras's *kastron*. Barbagiannis—whose name suited him because he was both old enough to be uncle to all of us and sported a thick gray beard—was scouting the perimeter of the Turkish garrison for weak spots when he heard my cries. I loved his story.

"I thought you were a dying cat," he said when he retold the events of that night. "A dying cat would have been more useful," he'd always add, but then he'd ruffle my hair (when I was younger) or thump me on the back (once I was too old for ruffling). He found me on the twentieth of July, the name day of the Profitis Ilias, so he named me in the saint's honor. He raised me. Two years after he found me, Barbagiannis's wife and two blood sons were killed in the Turks' attempts to root out the klephts. Only one other fellow brigand survived, and he died of fever the next year, leaving Barbagiannis alone with me. He eventually found other men to join his band and train for the resistance. In addition to being my stand-in for a father, Barbagiannis Sekeris was our de facto leader. Seventeen was young to be a revolutionary, but I had been training for the job all my life.

I saw the humor in my peculiar existence but could not share the joke with others. The last time I'd held a weapon, pistols hadn't been invented yet. Sometimes I'd look down at my clothes and laugh from surprise because I'd forgotten how we dressed now. Mitros would glare at me, incredulous that I found anything funny in this bitter life we led. I could not tell him that the unexpected sight of the foustanella, a white kilt that ended just above my knobby knees, had made me giggle. He probably thought I was a bit mad. If he'd known what I was actually thinking, he would have been certain of it.

We were all on edge. Ottoman generals were strengthening the fortresses throughout the Peloponnese. We stockpiled ammunition, but by the end of January, the Mystras bazaar ran out of shot and powder. When the wind was right, we could hear Turkish soldiers practicing drills all night. War was imminent, but no one knew exactly how or when it would begin. We scouted, trained, and raided villages for supplies and livestock. We sang, and ate, and slept, and prayed to an image of the Virgin Mary nailed to a tree branch, our makeshift chapel. But mostly, we waited.

In February, a messenger from the village of Valtetsi near Tripoli arrived late at night. I was on watch and almost killed him. Despite having my knife pressed against his throat, he managed to squeak out the name of the master who'd sent him. "Kolokotronis," he rasped, just in time.

Theodoros Kolokotronis was the klepht of all klephts. If anyone could unite our ragged, violent, opinionated bunch of mountain rebels, he could. The messenger, whose name was Dionysos, took a few minutes to recover. Once he'd stopped shaking, I brought him into my tent. I questioned him to be sure he wasn't a spy, then gave him some wine and went to wake Barbagiannis, who came back with me to speak to our guest.

"The Elder of the Morea has returned to us," the messenger said. Theodoros Kolokotronis was fifty now and had earned his new title: O Geros tou Morea. I'd never seen Kolokotronis, but Barbagiannis had described him to me: thick white mustache, hawk nose, serious eyes, a red helmet with a high plume he'd worn since his time in the British military. I imagined him riding a forbidden horse, carrying a forbidden weapon, leading us—his rebels—to battle.

The messenger started his second glass of wine. "Tomorrow night, send your best man to the English Inn in Mystras and have him ask for roast beef and port." With that menu, the inn clearly catered to overseas travelers.

The messenger continued his instructions. "The man whom you send will be joining a secret meeting of the Filiki Eteria. Have him sit in the back of the inn and, once his meal comes, ask the red-haired waitress for a glass of retsina. She'll take him where he needs to go." The combination of roast beef, port, and retsina was not likely to happen by accident; a perfect code to enter a clandestine meeting of the Society of Friends whose purpose was to overthrow Ottoman rule.

In the morning, Barbagiannis updated our band with the news and chose me to go to the inn that night. Mitros was not supportive. "I'd just as soon send my ten-year-old daughter as your little foundling here," he said dismissively.

I'm not as young as I look, I thought. I let Barbagiannis defend his choice, though I wasn't sure what made him do it.

Ω

I soon learned that I vastly preferred retsina to port, and that I'd had the wrong image of the redheaded waitress. She was the innkeeper's grandmotherly sister named Sophia, more gray than red. A few remaining strands identified her as my contact, but it was only because of her proximity to a lit wall sconce that I was able to see them. Sophia took a look at my foustanella and gave me a nod of approval. After I made my distinctive order, she led me discreetly to a private back room.

The room was windowless, hot, and dim, lit by flickering candles spaced along a wood table and a fire crackling in a corner fireplace. Three men sat at the table. The first to speak had thick eyebrows like furry creatures perched over his eyes. He also had a dense, unmistakably French accent. It took considerable effort not to speak to him in French. I wasn't supposed to know French.

"Are we so scarce for support that Kolokotronis is recruiting twelve-year-olds?" He laughed. I thought his eyebrows might fly off his face.

The man to his left chimed in. He had hardly any eyebrows at all, and his hair was sparse, like a baby's. "Maybe he's older than he looks, Arnaud. Don't offend him—an aging poet like you is no match for a hot-blooded young klepht; your words won't protect you from a dagger in your chest."

The hairless man turned to me with a nod. "I apologize for my colleague; his humor is not always palatable. Welcome, initiate."

"Thank you," I said. "I'm not armed." Not *visibly* armed, at least. "Also, I'm not twelve. And I'm sure poets can be quite dangerous." The poet Arnaud laughed again, but this time with me.

"Our nation is in peril; this is no time for levity." The third speaker, an elderly man in the dark robes of an Orthodox priest, rose from the table. He was remarkably tall; my eyes were at the level of his shoulders. His cylindrical black hat added more height, and the stillness of his limbs was almost inhuman. It was like being in the presence of a talking black tree. "Welcome," the priest said to me in his gravelly voice. "Introduce yourself. Do you know why you have been sent to us?"

"I am Elias Sekeris," I said. "A friend to the revolution."

"What price are you willing to pay for liberty, Elias Sekeris?"

"Whatever price necessary."

"What words inspire all who fight for our cause?"

"Freedom or death."

The priest nodded gravely. "Are you prepared to learn the aims of our society and take the Megas Orkos?"

"I am."

The priest walked around the table until he was standing over me. The baby-haired man joined him. He held up an image of the Virgin with the Holy Child in her arms.

"Kneel, initiate," the priest said, "and before Theotokos, mother of God, swear fealty to the cause of liberty." I knelt on the stone floor. "Repeat these words and take them into your heart."

I prayed for the revolution as much as anything I had wished for in all my lives. "I swear in the name of truth and justice, before the Supreme Being, to guard, by sacrificing my own life, and suffering the hardest toils, the mystery, which shall be explained to me . . ."

The Great Oath was long, and by the end my throat ached. When I was done, the priest put his hand on my head. "Before the face of the invisible and omnipresent true God, who in his essence is just, by the laws of the Filiki Eteria, and by the authority with which its powerful priests have entrusted me, I receive you, as I was myself received, into the bosom of the Eteria."

I thought of the *devşirme*, thousands of children taken from Greek homes to fight in the sultan's army. I thought of Zoe taken to Mehmed's harem. I thought of the taxes that drove Mitros to poverty, and of Emmanuel forced to give up his profession and his father's legacy. I wanted freedom for my brothers of the mountains, I wanted freedom for my suffering country, and I wanted freedom for myself. I did not know whether this would be my last chance to save Mystras. I also wondered whether it would be my last chance at living. I did not know whether I wanted it to be or not.

CHARLOTTE BOUVIER (NÉE LUSIGNAN)
Late February 1821
Mystras

There were, Charlotte reflected over the roast beef and port she'd taken in the main room of the inn, advantages to having a poet for a husband. One of them was not sexual prowess.

Arnaud had a fumbling appreciation for her body that he translated into rhapsodic poems about mythic beauty, usually relating to Greek goddesses. But in bed she found him lacking. Occasionally the mechanics cooperated sufficiently to allow moderate success, but she was often left awake and restless as Arnaud snored in a postcoital haze next to her. The second, related disappointment was that he had not managed to get her with child. What good was a husband, really, if he failed at those two tasks, giving her pleasure, and, barring that, a baby? She'd heard the whispers among the other wives in the salon where her husband had spent evenings before they'd left for Greece—"Barren, poor thing, and such a shame she can't pass on that lovely red hair. Looking at those hips, you'd never guess."

Charlotte fumed silently but knew it was her husband's failure. She'd been pregnant before her marriage once, and it had ended early. Just as well, as her parents certainly would not have been pleased.

At first, not becoming pregnant with Arnaud was a mild surprise, then an annoyance, then eventually, a constant misery. She stared at other women whose dresses could not hide their expanding bellies, hot with envy. And the women with children were even worse, holding small plump hands and kissing broad, unfurrowed foreheads. The longing began to eat her alive.

When her father fell ill, her desire to have a child became even more intense. At first her father's symptoms seemed a passing malady—he'd not had enough sleep or had drunk too much the night before. But the clumsiness persisted. He stumbled when he came down the stairs of their Paris house and took a stick walking outside. And when she read aloud to the family in the evenings—her father usually chose Duval—

instead of laughing at the humorous turns of phrase, he'd wrinkle his forehead in confusion.

When the doctor finally came, the news was dire. "Connected with rheumatism," he said gravely, "and infections of the heart." Her father took her aside, after a night when she'd had to stop reading altogether. "Charlotte, sit," he said, motioning her to the blue velvet chaise in his study. Arnaud was still downstairs, enjoying brandy before they called a carriage home.

"The doctor says that I had an infection of my nerves," her father said, trying to suppress the twitching of his hand. "But I know something the doctor does not." He pulled a sheaf of yellowed papers from a wooden keepsake box he kept on his desk. Charlotte had to restrain herself from helping him with the lock.

"You married a Bouvier, but by blood you are a Lusignan," her father said sadly, "as am I. That legacy comes at a price." He spread the pages out, letting her read for herself. Once she'd finished, her skin prickling with fear, he told her what he knew, of the generations that had fallen ill through the centuries. She might be spared, or she might not. As might her offspring, should she manage to have any. Some of it made little sense—prophecy, blood, and sacrifice—the rambling of his slipping mind. Modern medicine notwithstanding, there was no cure for this ailment. It should have made her fear to bear a child, but instead it made her even more desperate for motherhood.

When she'd left for Greece with Arnaud on a trip—"to follow Byron's footsteps through the land about which Homer sang," as Arnaud said—her father was confined to his chair, and she was still bleeding every month.

Sitting down to her heavy British meal, she saw a young

Greek soldier, like the dashing klephts in paintings back home. He was dark-eyed and half her husband's age, and she could not help thinking of what was hidden under the white skirt billowing around his bare legs.

ELIAS SEKERIS
February 1821
Mystras

As soon as our meeting was over, Arnaud attached himself to me like a burr. For some reason, he identified me as his ideal Mystras tour guide. I tried to convince him to find someone who lived in the town, but he stayed firm in his choice. "Elias, the Taygetos have shaped your soul. The song of Greek independence sings in your blood, and I see no better man from whom to learn that song." When he finished his impromptu speech, his eyes were actually wet. The more dramatic he was, the more understated I became. By the end of our time together—three days that I stayed at the inn—I found it hard to speak at all. Arnaud, who filled silences effortlessly, didn't seem to notice.

Arnaud, in addition to being fascinated by Mystras, was also profoundly ignorant about it. This led to amusing interchanges during our tours, in which he'd report something he'd heard and I'd gently correct him. He good-naturedly accepted my corrections, but I had the feeling he might not believe I was right, even if he thought the song of Greek independence sang in my blood. He held forth on the first stop of our tour, arms outstretched.

"Is it not miraculous how the walls of ancient Sparta rose

just where we now stand, outside the ivy-choked remnants of the Pandanessi? On this hallowed ground, brave warriors spilled their blood in rituals of passage to adulthood." I'd taken him, at his request, to see the ruins of the Pantanassa. He'd almost gotten the name right. His geography of the city was far off the mark.

"Pan-ta-na-ssa," I said slowly.

"Pandenessi, O Holy Place!" he exclaimed exultantly.

"The city of Sparta was not quite here," I said, trying again, "but farther down in the valley . . ."

Arnaud put one hand to his heart. "And yet it seems so close! The march of sandaled feet, the gleam of burnished shields, O Valiant Sparta, where Leonidas stood against the enemy, three hundred men doomed to die fighting . . ."

I didn't bother to mention that the battle of Thermopylae had been fought not only far from Mystras, but far from Sparta itself. Arnaud took out a notebook and began scribbling verse while I looked at the ruins of the convent. My memories flickered. The Pantanassa was a shell now, the nuns gone. Barbagiannis had told me the story of the convent's destruction the first time he'd taken me to Mystras town. I was just ten, but my head was full of knowledge I shouldn't have possessed.

"What happened to the church?" I stood openmouthed in front of the place I'd once considered a refuge, where nuns walked the quiet paths. I'd asked honestly—my interrupted lives had not included the Pantanassa's destruction.

Barbagiannis scowled. "It was sacked by Albanian troops fighting for the sultan. The Russians tried to help us take back Mystras from the Turks fifty years ago. I was younger than you then. We are hoping for their help again now." He said it quietly, in case the wrong person might hear. "But then the Turks hired Albanians to win it back. They sacked the city, destroyed the convent, and massacred the nuns."

I looked at the ruins, imagining them whole. "Everyone wants a piece of us."

"Yes," Barbagiannis answered grimly. "Franks, Turks, Venetians, Russians, Albanians, Turks again. Our conquerors take what they wish and destroy the rest. Until the next hungry enemy comes along."

"Mystras recovered, though," I said. It was true—the city wasn't what it had been, but we were still here, occupied by an enemy yet again, but alive.

"We always do," Barbagiannis had said fiercely. "We did then, and we will again."

Arnaud snapped his notebook shut with a loud noise that brought me out of my reverie. "What shall we see next? The Metropolitan Cathedral? I'm not fond of domes particularly, but I hear it is dedicated to Saint Demetrios. I imagine you know all about that." He thumped me on the back.

"Certainly," I said. He was right about Saint Demetrios, but I disagreed wholeheartedly about domes.

Ω

I stayed at the English Inn for three days. After my initiation into the Eteria, I learned the names and roles of my fellow members. I was given the first-level title of an initiate: Adelphos, "brother."

The man in the garments of an Orthodox priest, Father Anasthasios Themelis, was a real priest, as well as a secret priest (Iereis)—the third level of initiation—of the Eteria. Under his hands, new initiates multiplied rapidly. In the three days I spent sleeping in a real bed indoors, at least ten new brothers were welcomed. "The moment of truth approaches,"

Father Themelis intoned gravely, "and we shall require the dedication of many men to fuel the furnace of our liberation."

The baby-haired man was Alfred Hartley, a British businessman and philanthropist who remained deliberately vague about the nature of his business back home. He had attained the highest level, Shepherd. No one questioned him. His role was to come up with funds for the society; so long as the till was full, the origin of the funds was not scrutinized. The distribution of those funds, on the other hand, was strictly audited to avoid abuse. Hartley served as the treasurer of our cell. Over the next three days I met several members, always in the dark back room of the inn. The roast beef on china plates was a pleasant change from gnawing stolen meat around a smoky fire.

Arnaud Bouvier was a philhellene poet. I'd been isolated in the mountains and was pleasantly surprised to learn that foreign admiration for Greece was at a fever pitch, inspiring literary and artistic outpourings, as well as military aid in support of Greek liberty. Arnaud had an exhausting tendency to make a joke out of everything, including the way I dressed, which I tolerated. When he wasn't jesting, he incessantly quoted the poet Byron, whose love for Greece was legendary, and rhapsodized about the renaissance of Athenian democracy. I knew Arnaud was indispensable: a major financial contributor and excellent at attracting others to fund the revolution. But I could tolerate only limited doses.

On one occasion, I excused myself from one of Arnaud's read-aloud sessions. He'd gotten through the first stanza of Byron's "Isles of Greece." The verses were slightly embarrassing, perhaps because Arnaud recited them with tears flowing down his plump face.

"The isles of Greece, the isles of Greece!
Where burning Sappho loved and sung . . .
Eternal summer gilds them yet,
But all, except their sun, is set . . ."

I edged my way into the main room of the inn for a drink. Three retsinas and two ports later (I'd developed a taste for port after all), I realized that the woman sitting alone at a table across the room was staring at me. She, unlike the innkeeper's sister, actually had red hair. She wore it in a loose bun, and curling tendrils escaped to brush her cheeks. She reminded me of Osanne, and the directness of her stare made my face hot.

Sophia brought my sixth drink, which I hadn't ordered. "It's from the lady," she said with a sly smile toward the red-head in the corner. After a few more drinks and some innuendo-laden conversation, the redhead joined me in my room. She told me only her first name. When she reached under my foustanella to put her smooth white fingers on my thigh, I stopped thinking about anything. For those few hours, I was exactly what I seemed to be: a lusty adolescent thrilled to find himself in bed with a beautiful older woman, losing my mind in the reckless trajectory of my body.

Afterward, lying in the tangled sheets, I talked too much. Maybe it was the drink, the aftermath of unexpected intimacy, or my years of lonely silence. Whatever the cause, I told her secrets I had scarcely allowed myself to think. I told her my father died of a disease that addled his brain and shook his limbs. I told her I believed I was invulnerable to that malady, because of an accident of my blood, protection from my mother's side—Greek power against French weakness. That made her laugh. And I shared with her the relief and guilt my survival brought with it. She lay on her side, entirely naked with that red hair tumbling over her shoulders, her chin propped on one hand, listening. And when I was done with my story, she climbed on top of me, straddling my hips with her soft thighs, her hands gripping my shoulders for support. She rode me that night until we were both drenched with sweat, and she came back the next night for more.

Not until I left the inn with orders to organize the klephts for imminent revolution did I find out my lover was Arnaud's wife.

chapter thirty-two

HELEN ADLER
Late July 2015
Mystras

I turned on the slow-to-heat shower and sneaked a look at my email. The message from Pierre Lusignan made me drop my phone. The subject of the message read PER YOUR APPLICATION TO THE HELLENIC FOUNDATION TO END HUNTINGTON'S AND OTHER NEURODEGENERATIVE DISEASES. My proposal had been favorably reviewed and was likely to be funded. An in-person interview was the next step.

> *Dear Professor Adler:*
>
> *I spoke with Professor Agathangelos—how fortuitous that your paths intersected—and realized that there is another important line of research of mutual interest you did not mention in your funding application: It seems you might have information about local families harboring potentially protective genetic variants? Perhaps these individuals are even personally known to you. I advise that you consider an expansion of your proposal to include such work (collaboratively, of course) with this additional goal*

in mind. Or, failing foundation funding, perhaps a private
effort with independent sources might be arranged.

Sincerely,
Professor Pierre Lusignan

I suddenly remembered that I was letting the shower run,
and the tiny stall, misdirected showerhead, and flimsy curtain
resulted in a bathroom flood. Lesson: do not read potentially
inflammatory emails while waiting for shower to heat up. A
wave of nausea swept over me, prompting me to sit down on
the soaking-wet toilet seat.

It seemed from this email that though I hadn't told anyone
who Elias was, Lusignan knew. In theory, if Elias's genetics
could inform a treatment or cure for HD, it would be undis-
putably a cause for celebration. But sharing Elias's identity
with Professor Lusignan, the zealous and borderline anti-
Greek eugenicist with a disturbingly excessive passion for the
subject, seemed at best unwise and at worst dangerous. And,
given that Elias was an intensely private person from whom
I'd already estranged myself by stupidly mixing work and pleasure, it also felt like I'd betrayed him. Inadvertently, but still.

How could Pierre Lusignan have learned about Elias? I
hadn't told Lusignan any specifics. Elektra communicated
with Lusignan; he was her mentor. I'd told Elektra about
Borghes, but not about his living descendants. I remembered
the hovering docent listening in the Mystras Museum, where
Elias told us the story of the French Bible. Then I felt acutely
sick. At that exact moment, there was a knock on the bathroom door, which turned out to be Alexander, absolutely unable to wait.

I came out of the bathroom and hung my wet pajamas on the radiator to dry. In doing so, I moved Alexander's backpack off said radiator, discovering he'd been secretly stockpiling hotel keys. His collection fell out of the front pocket, proving that my lecture about the stolen wheat penny hadn't worked. Yet another parenting fail.

I confronted Alexander as he emerged from the bathroom, wiping his feet on a towel.

"Where did you get these?"

Like a good witness, he said the minimum. "Front desk."

"Did someone say you could have them?" Silence. "Did you ask?" More silence. "You didn't ask?"

Alexander shook his head.

"Did you think it was okay to take them?"

"I wanted them," he said in a small voice.

I took a deep breath. "This is stealing," I said. "Do you understand?" He nodded. "We're going to the front desk." We dressed in uneasy silence and headed to reception. "Kleptomaniac," I said, under my breath, then immediately regretted saying it.

Panos was there when we arrived. He beamed and came around the counter to put his arm around Alexander's shoulders. When he didn't get the expected reciprocal warmth, he stepped back. "All is okay?"

I pushed Alexander forward. He stood wordlessly with his hand in his pocket, jingling the stolen keys. I tried the verbal method. "Hello, Panos. Alexander has something to tell you." More key jingling.

Panos put his hand under Alexander's chin and tipped his face up. "You talk, I listen. Then we have *galaktoboureko.*"

It sounded like a good deal to me. Alexander shuffled his

feet, and then brought out the handful of keys. "These are yours," he said, mumbling.

"Ah." Panos took the keys gently. "Thank you." He didn't say anything else about it. No reprimand, no elaboration. He turned to the front desk, where a tray of sweet cheese pastry sat with its fractured golden-brown top. He cut Alexander a slice and handed it to him on a napkin.

"I'm sorry," Alexander said, almost inaudibly. He held the pastry in his hand like a fragile treasure.

"You eat," Panos said with a smile, and graciously disappeared into the kitchen, leaving us alone to process.

"What does *kleptomaniac* mean?" Alexander said, not looking at me.

I sighed. "It means someone who can't stop stealing things."

Alexander's face flushed. "I'm not a kleptomaniac," he said. "I can stop."

"I'm glad to hear that," I said, feeling bad. The silence was long and painful. "It's a Greek word," I said, hoping that would extract us from the vortex.

Alexander looked up. "Cool." And then over my shoulder something caught his eye. "Look, there's Elias! I'm going to give him some pie." Alexander nearly knocked me over in his eagerness.

I turned, slowly, my heart thumping. Elias stood in the doorway, looking more beautiful than I remembered. He smiled at Alexander with genuine warmth, then at me, with distant politeness. Probably the two smiles were not as different as I imagined, but I couldn't help my interpretation.

"I learned a Greek word," Alexander said, handing Elias the pie. "It's *kleptomaniac*. Do you want a bite?"

Elias broke a piece off and gave the rest back. "*Klepto*," he said thoughtfully. "It means *thief*. Thieves were called *klephts*, a few hundred years ago. But they weren't just thieves. They were outlaws who lived in the mountains and fought against the Turks, for Greek independence. They turned into heroes."

"Like Robin Hood?" Alexander said hopefully.

"Yes, very like Robin Hood." Elias smiled. "I hope you haven't encountered any thieves, here in Mystras."

"No," Alexander said. "Definitely not." He looked back over his shoulder at me with a warning glance.

"Nope," I said, "no thieves."

"Can you have breakfast with us?" Alexander turned back to Elias.

"That would be lovely." My voice sounded squeaky. I waited the longest three seconds of my life.

"No, I'm sorry, I'm giving a tour today," Elias said. "I do hope your research is going well."

"It's okay," I said miserably. "I'm on vacation. Not doing much work."

"Yes," he said. "It is better not to work excessively on vacation."

Alexander handed Elias the rest of the pie. "Do you want this? Since you are too busy for breakfast?"

"Thank you very much. I will certainly enjoy it."

Alexander licked honey off his fingers. "Maybe we can have another tour later?"

"Later, certainly," Elias said graciously. But it sounded like never. I watched him leave.

"I miss Elias, Mama," Alexander said as we sat down in the café.

"So do I," I said.

I did not enjoy breakfast, not even the *galaktoboureko*.

ELIAS SEKERIS
Early Spring 1821
Mystras

After my alcohol-soaked, unexpectedly sexually active days plotting revolution at the English Inn, I came back to camp with news. The start of the revolution was set: time, mid-March, and place, here in the Peloponnese. General Kolokotronis was mustering the klephts for military action against the Turks, building a revolutionary force of mountain outlaws. I did not meet Kolokotronis myself, being a lowly initiate, but Shepherd Alfred Hartley had.

"O Geros tou Morea has called the klephts 'the yeast of liberty,'" Alfred said before I left, and put his heavy hand on my shoulder. "With your men of the mountains, we shall overcome oppression." Alfred had a flat and monotonous voice, but somehow the effect was more intense for its restraint. I imagined him as a modern oracle of Delphi, a vessel for the messages of the gods.

The Peloponnese, however, is a big place, and Mystras was not the center of the struggle. Alexis, whose constant state of belligerence was heightened by the distant plan, drew his pistol. "I've waited my whole life to castrate those bastards down the hill. Who's in?" He glared at us. After a few tense minutes, Alexis put away his weapon.

Mitros, predictably, was grimly suspicious of me. "Three days, and he comes back reeking of drink, spoiled by a soft bed. Why should we trust a child to tell us how to fight for what we have lost?" Mitros brought his face so close to mine I could see every pore on his nose. He grabbed the neck of my shirt.

Barbagiannis put his hand on Mitros's wrist. The grip looked casual, but Mitros grimaced and let go. "You will trust him because I do," Barbagiannis said. "Or we will manage without you." Mitros did not touch me again, but I had no illusions that he'd changed his mind.

We stockpiled weapons and ammunition, and other bands came to join us. Soon our numbers grew so large that there was no more room to pitch tents, and we either were sleeping crowded inside them or on bare rock outside. Latrines overflowed, food was scarce. Alexis was in a constant state of barely restrained fury, taking his frustration out on the carcasses of the animals he stole to feed us. At least he'd torn a dead sheep apart rather than a living person, but it was frightening to watch. Kostis prayed for hours every day, fingering an icon he wore around his neck.

Every few weeks, I went down to Mystras town for a meeting of the Eteria. The English Inn was still serving roast beef, though portions were smaller. Alfred told me Arnaud had gone on to Tripolitza with his lovely wife—had I met her? A woman of taste. "Tripolitza is a good place for Madame Bouvier; better than little Mystras." Alfred made a gesture with his hands to illustrate how little Mystras was. "It's a bit stifling here when you are longing for Paris. Madame was not as enamored of village life as her husband, I'm afraid."

Mystras was not always little, I thought. *And in any case, Madame amused herself just fine with me.* Instead, I said only, "That is understandable."

Ω

"I don't know whether to be relieved or disappointed," I said one night to Emmanuel, whose tent I now shared. He was large and radiated warmth; good company, even asleep. "I'm not eager to die with a Turkish sword in my belly, but I can't take much more waiting."

"They say 'we shall go to sleep in Turkey and wake up in Greece,'" Emmanuel answered in the dark, "but no revolution happens in a day. This war will be a marathon, not a sprint. There is no point rushing to start." I could not foretell the future, but what I knew of the past told me he was likely right.

The fighting began at Tsímova, a Maniot town a day's march away from us. We were not called to join the battle. I heard afterward that armed Greeks assembled in the streets, carrying sacred icons, cheering, and singing, as priests chanted thanks to God. Kolokotronis wept openly, heading a force of the Mani's leading families and more than two thousand men to meet the Turks of Kalamata and defeat them. The next day, Tsímova changed its name to Aereopoli, city of Ares, god of war. We wished we had been first.

On March 25, the Metropolitan Archbishop Germanus raised the flag of revolt at the Monastery of Agia Lavra. Barbagiannis and Emmanuel raised our revolutionary flag, too, driving the staff into the hard spring earth. We knew that all over the Peloponnese the same flag was flying: the horizontal stripes of yellow, blue, and white, the central white cross of our true faith, flanked by green branches, the olive tree of our suffering *patridha*.

"*Eleftheria í Thanatós!* Freedom or Death!" we shouted in unison.

Our turn finally came at the beginning of May. We were sixty men now, plus our families, pressed close together on the small patch of level ground where we'd set up camp.

"Omer Vrioni, the commander of the Ottoman army, is heading into the Peloponnese," Barbagiannis announced.

"I'll bleed them white and dance on their corpses!" Alexis's savage enthusiasm was welcome now.

"Quiet," Barbagiannis said. "Vrioni divided fifteen hundred Greek fighters at Alamana, leaving Commander Diakos on the bridge with only forty-eight men. Diakos's sword broke; the Turks killed him along with his soldiers. We must learn from our failures."

"How many men does Vrioni have?" Emmanuel said.

"Ten thousand." Barbagiannis's answer fell like a stone into a lake. Silence rippled around it. *Ten thousand.* "We have been called to join Commander Odysseas Androutsos. He is a klepht like us, and it will be an honor to serve him. Tonight we march to Gravia to meet Androutsos—he has sixty men, as we do; he needs more. Vrioni is coming to put an end to the rebellion. Our job is to stop him."

I calculated in my head: 120 of us, 10,000 of them. Seventy-five Turks for each Greek. Next to me, Emmanuel called out into the nervous silence: "We shall go to sleep in Turkey and wake up in Greece!" Soon, we were all chanting. I remembered what Emmanuel had said to me in the tent. Even if we won at Gravia against those impossible odds, war is a marathon, not a sprint.

Ω

Gravia, where we had to stop Vrioni's progress, was north of the Peloponnese. Alexis grumbled as we packed up camp. "Thousands of Turks to fight right here and we're going four days' journey to get massacred?"

"Think of it like Thermopylae," I said. "Or don't you want to be compared to a Spartan warrior who died to keep the entire Persian army from invading Greece?" That silenced him effectively. I was not afraid of dying, since I'd had the unique experience of having done it before. I was afraid of starting over.

When we arrived on the seventh of May, scouts told us Vrioni's troops were only a day's march away. At the low-slung redbrick inn at Gravia, we met our commander, Odysseas Androutsos. He had the most impressive mustache I had ever seen, facing stiff competition in nineteenth-century Greece, particularly among the klephts, whose facial hair was the stuff of legends. What made his mustache particularly remarkable was its shape—miraculously horizontal, defying gravity. He was dressed to kill, with three pistols stuffed into his ornamented belt and a sword at his hip.

Our band stood in the back of the crowd of klephts assembled outside the inn's walls to meet our new commander. Emmanuel whispered in my ear, "He's prepared to kill each enemy four times, just in case."

"Or four enemies at once," I whispered back, "which would greatly improve the ratio."

We were a rowdy, unruly bunch, exchanging stories and showing off our weapons. While we waited, a group of men began to sing, tunelessly and raucously. Alexis started a fight on a patch of grass. But as Androutsos began to speak, we all went quiet. His voice carried easily to the last row of soldiers. "Men of Greece, I salute you." Androutsos held out his hand. I could not take my eyes off him.

"You have come from different villages and cities. Some of you worked land you lost. Some risked death to kiss the icons of our beloved saints, to prostrate ourselves before the divine."

"*O Theós na se evlogeí!*" Barbagiannis exclaimed, and the chant went up around him, blessing our leader.

Androutsos gestured for quiet. "You may have traveled many days' journey here, to defend land you've never set foot on. Or you may have spent your childhood in the shadow of Mount Parnassus, which looks down on us today." He scanned the crowd seriously. "We have one shared purpose: to defeat ten thousand Turks tomorrow." A few cheers erupted from the group, which he acknowledged with a hand to his heart. The gold decorations on his red vest gleamed in the sun. "The Turks have killed our priests, stolen our sons, and claimed our country as their own. We are the only barrier keeping Vrioni from the Peloponnese. Remember King Leonidas at Thermopylae, when he faced Xerxes' millions with just three hundred warriors. 'Surrender your weapons,' the Persian commander said. And what did Leonidas respond?" Androutsos looked to us for the answer.

"Come and get them!" I shouted, repeating words the King of Sparta had shouted at his enemies more than two thousand years before.

"*Molon labe*," Androutsos repeated. "To defeat our enemies tomorrow we need five things: faith in God, trust in one another, strategy, luck . . ." He paused for emphasis. We all waited, holding our collective breath, for the fifth.

"And plenty of ammunition!" Androutsos shouted. Our cheers echoed to the slopes of Parnassus. We had all five. God willing, it would be enough.

Ω

The inn at Gravia was not meant to hold a hundred and twenty guests. We would have to sleep on the floor of every room, with two exceptions: the kitchen, where stew bubbled in a huge pot on the woodstove, and the cellar, which had become an arsenal. Rifles, pistols, and crates of shot were stacked along the walls; I tasted gunpowder in the air. Androutsos outlined our strategy. We would barricade ourselves in the inn and kill off Turks as they came near.

In the walled courtyard, soldiers assigned to the night watch stationed themselves beneath the windows, and two stood inside the massive wooden entry doors. It was time to sleep, or at least to try. Emmanuel lay down next to me.

Six hundred years ago, the last time I was a soldier, I slept beside Demetrios. Then I'd been a *gasmoule* follower of a wordy Frankish prince. Now I was a mountain bandit, led by a Greek revolutionary fighting to win back freedom from the Turks. It was, as many moments in my layered lives were, a strange juxtaposition.

Emmanuel, who had more flesh than I, was perfectly comfortable on the bumpy flagstones. I struggled to find a position that did not grind my bones against rock. Emmanuel put his hand on my arm. "You are thrashing like a fish on a line."

"I'm sorry I'm keeping you awake," I whispered, trying to lie still while a stone dug into my left hip.

"Are you thinking about tomorrow?"

"How could I not?"

He gestured at the soldier on his other side, who was lying flat on his back, snoring fiercely. "You're not like that. You think instead of sleep."

"Sadly," I said, "you're right."

"It's one of the many things I love about you, my friend."

I imagined kissing his cheek, where the bristly stubble of half-grown beard ended and his smooth skin began. "I love many things about you, too, Emmanuel," I said. Words instead of caresses. It was just as well. Then Emmanuel surprised me, kissing me once on each cheek. For him it was an easy act of affection, not the longing of a lover. But for me, it was no less sweet. *At least I will know love before I risk death*, I thought, not for the first time.

"Sleep well, Elias," he said. And, lulled by his affection and his heavy arm draped over my shoulder, I did.

Ω

At dawn we lined up in the grassy courtyard, guns loaded. The inn's walls were like the *kastron* of Mystras, stone with slits to fire weapons. We had no priest to bless us, but Kostis led us in a soldier's prayer.

> *"The Lord is my refuge and my fortress. He shall cover you with his feathers, and under his wings you shall take refuge. God forgive us as we defend our beloved patridha and watch over those we love."*

It was the most I'd ever heard him say.

I offered to serve as lookout. Barbagiannis did not challenge my offer, even though it was safer behind the walls than on top of them. "It is the right task for me," I said. I didn't think he'd understand if I told him I needed to see more than to survive.

The sun rose on Vrioni's enormous army: thousands of soldiers spread through the valley, surrounding the inn on all sides. Ten thousand is a number so large it is hard to grasp. Standing on the wall, I saw the army two ways. First, a single mass, stripped of humanity, a symbol of imminent violence. That is how we must see our enemy for war to be possible. I also saw the other side: thousands of men. A man is harder to kill than an enemy. But I would have to—we all would—to survive. A turbaned emissary broke from the group. I watched him approach on the stone-flagged path. "Now is your chance to surrender," the emissary said, in Greek.

Androutsos, below me, shook his head. "Shoot," he said without a trace of uncertainty. And I, though uncertainty was my constant companion, did. Killing a man with a rifle is not like using a sword. The emissary fell slowly, his blood pooling under him. It was too easy. I climbed down to congratulations, but my hands were shaking.

The Ottoman attack came from all sides. First the Albanian mercenaries—"Vrioni sends his irregulars first, the coward!" Alexis snarled. When they were close, we began to fire a barrage through the narrow windows. The courtyard filled with flashes of powder igniting and the deafening noise of pistols and rifles. Within minutes, enemy corpses covered the path, but they kept coming, stepping over bodies. One soldier managed to climb to the top of the wall; his head appeared disembodied, topped by its red cap. Alexis shot him in the face and left the bleeding corpse draped there as a warning. Soon the air was filled with clouds of acrid gray smoke. Half the Albanians were dead, the rest fleeing. Alexis crowed with delight.

Mitros brought crates of shot and barrels of powder from the cellar. We reloaded as the next assault came, then the next. Soon hundreds of bodies littered the grass, and we were slipping in blood. My ears rang from the noise, my throat burned from smoke, my limbs felt detached from my body. Finally the gunshots subsided, and turbaned fighters stopped coming over the walls.

"Have we won, or are we dead?" Emmanuel looked nightmarish, his face dusted with black powder.

"Neither? Both?" Honestly, I wasn't sure.

Barbagiannis looked through an opening in the wall, then quickly pulled his head back. "Vrioni is bringing the cannons," he said to Emmanuel. "Tell Androutsos." Emmanuel pivoted on one foot with the incongruous grace some big men have. I remember he looked back over his shoulder at me with a smile.

That's what a friend looks like, I thought. Why do I remember all this so well? Because as he turned, a bullet from a Turkish soldier who'd climbed the wall struck Emmanuel in the temple, tearing through his head. There was no time to stop and grieve. I delivered the message about the cannons to Androutsos myself. There was nothing else I could do for Emmanuel.

We counted; Emmanuel was one of only six Greeks dead. Androutsos shouted out his orders. We left our dead and slipped out the back entrance of the inn. Six of us dead to their three hundred—I later found out—and another eight hundred of them wounded. Vrioni retreated in frustration, and Greece declared a victory. It sounds like a triumph, and by all historical accounts it was. But numbers tell only part of the story.

chapter thirty-three

CHARLOTTE BOUVIER (LUSIGNAN)
September 1824
Tripolitza, Peloponnese

Three years before, when Charlotte began to suspect she was pregnant, she'd laughed out loud. She had not bled since she'd had the klepht Elias in the inn's rickety bed. Her husband, Arnaud, looked up at the sound of her laughter; she'd barely smiled since they'd come to Greece.

Charlotte had taken to doing needlepoint, sewing tiny stitches to pass the hours. Even Tripolitza, the self-important capital of the Peloponnese, was a bore. Tripolitza was better than Mystras, where Arnaud took them on his periodic and overdramatically secretive business voyages, but still pitiful compared to Paris. No concerts, no theater, and the food hopelessly rustic. But when she felt stirrings of nausea, and then her dress tightened across her tender breasts—she began to giggle with delight. She no longer cared where she was because of the miracle inside her. The Greek boy had done his part, in more ways than one. She lay in bed repeating his words like an incantation: he'd said he was invulnerable to the malady that had shaken her father's limbs and gnawed at his soul. Because of an accident of blood, the klepht had said, he'd been granted protection—*Greek power against French weakness*. He helped her make a child, and the power, whatever it was, would keep her son safe. She recalled the nights with a languorous stretch: Greek power indeed.

Arnaud began to call her beautiful again and lifted his head from his writing more often. He even invited her shyly to bed and managed to stay hard until she was done. And she'd pretended to enjoy his brief success. It mattered less, now that she had what she wanted.

Arnaud was delighted when she'd told him the news. He fluttered about her with his plump hands, reminding her of the puffed-up pigeons that trotted after crumbs outside Notre Dame.

"Should we return to France?" Arnaud's forehead wrinkled with concern. "I worry physicians in Greece may not be suffi-cient to keep you and our precious new life safe on the peril-ous path of your womanly labors." She'd jumped at the chance, but when Arnaud still hadn't made arrangements weeks later, she resigned herself to more years away from home. At least she'd have a baby to keep her busy until her husband's part in the war was over. The French government had become pas-sionate about the Greek Cause. Her Greek passion had served her purpose; she could afford to be sympathetic.

The birth was uneventful, and soon little Remy curled against her side, keeping her company when her husband stayed up late emulating Byron or fanning the flames of the revolution.

"I don't care about the world," she whispered in Remy's ear while he slept, "I have you."

Then the trouble with Remy's sleep began.

"All babes struggle," Marie said reassuringly. Her husband was a French army doctor who, like Arnaud, was passionately loyal to the cause of Greek independence. Of the French wives-in-exile, Marie was her preferred companion. Marie had a two-year-old with dimpled knuckles and a mop of gold curls and was a source of useful advice. "Don't fret, *ma chère*, he will settle soon."

But Remy did not settle. Many nights he lay awake restless and whimpering, and within an hour of drifting off woke again. Charlotte frayed as her own sleep followed Remy's erratic pattern, and she snapped at Arnaud at the least provocation.

Then Charlotte began to drop things. At first, she thought it was lack of sleep that made objects—the full dinner plate, a cup of tea—slip from her hands. Arnaud tried to clean up the mess but often made things worse. Their sullen maid, Myrtile, tailed Charlotte like a bloodhound, waiting for the next accident.

By the time Remy was a year old, Charlotte began to lose her footing on uneven ground. She ordered Myrtile to take up the rugs so she would not trip on their raised edges. When the twitches began in her hands, Charlotte knew her father's ailment had come to haunt her. Remy was her consolation. Other than his sleep, he was a perfect cherub of a child. Charlotte remarked often how like Arnaud Remy was, to offset suspicion that this dark-skinned, dark-eyed baby was not the son of a blond father and a redheaded mother.

I may be doomed to hell on earth, but at least I made an angel. It gave her strength to know that as she descended into darkness, her son would remain in the light. *His mixed blood will protect him*, Charlotte told herself when she lay alone in the bath, watching her limbs move without her volition. The more she said it, the more she believed it to be true. *His father's blood will protect him*.

But it didn't. In Remy's third year, his endearing child's sentences began to recede, first to short phrases, then a few words. By summer, as the Turks prepared to send their Egyptian sword-for-hire Ibrahim Pasha into the Peloponnese, Remy had only two words left: *mama* and his own name. Charlotte imagined he said them sadly—but her misery colored her hearing. Soon, Remy's headlong toddler gait stiffened, and he, like his mother, began to lose his balance. He cried when he fell—which to Charlotte was heartbreaking.

Soon, it was impossible to hide her own ailment or her son's. The emigrée wives began to shun Charlotte's company, whispering behind their fans and shaking their heads with distaste. When the doctors had no answer, Arnaud retreated into his work, leaving Myrtile to attend to Charlotte's needs. As summer faded, Remy stopped eating solid food and went back to his bottle. Soon, Charlotte had to hold it for him. Myrtile would only touch them both with gloves, as if she thought their miasma could infect her. Charlotte's fear turned to despair, and despair to fury. *I will die an outcast with my dying son.* She had only one person to blame, other than herself. The despair and anger gnawed at her. She had been wronged—by God, by Fate, and most of all by the Greek soldier who had promised her heaven and given her hell instead.

On the first day of September, Charlotte stayed awake until Arnaud was snoring. She crept into his study, where she took money from his collection for the Eteria. After a moment's hesitation, Charlotte took his pistol, too. The next morning, she bundled Remy in a blanket, packed an unobtrusive bag, and hired a cart and driver to take her to Mystras. "The English Inn," she told him. It was the only address she knew.

ELIAS SEKERIS
Early September 1824
Mystras

A marathon is measured in miles. That challenge is physical distance; it is not over until the last mile is done, but at least you know when it will end. A war is a different sort of endeavor. We had no idea when our revolution would be over, and the longer it went on, the less clear it became. Three and a half years after Archbishop Germanus raised the flag on mount Chelmos, we were still not free, and we were still dying. The Peloponnese was mostly in Greek hands, thanks to the klephts, and sometimes we managed to reclaim Turkish territories in other parts of Greece. But every win was followed by a loss. We were also miserably divided. As if our Ottoman enemy were not bad enough, we fought one another: two civil wars in three years. By the autumn of 1824, there were two governments claiming to rule Greece.

"The best remedy for a divided nation is a common enemy," Barbagiannis said as we gathered around a fire for the evening meal. The temperature had dropped abruptly, heralding fall. Barbagiannis was still our leader, but we'd shrunk below our prerevolution numbers. Kostis died during the battle of Tripolitza, just after Gravia. A few men from Gravia came back to join us in the mountains above Mystras, but most stayed where we'd found them. Mitros's wife and daughter died of a fever that swept through the crowded camp.

I did not find another friend after Emmanuel's death. I could not even try, not while I was remembering the way his face came apart as the bullet entered his skull. Each love lost was like a piece torn out of me, and it seemed easier to manage alone than risk another wound. Barbagiannis was as close as I could get to anyone.

Alexis was still stealing, so we were still eating, though barely. Meat was at best a once-a-week event. The last week I'd had a hard biscuit and a handful of olives each day, with a slice of raw onion at the end of the week for a special treat. Tonight's meal was goat, but as I chewed on the gristle of Alexis's latest, I realized that the goat probably hadn't had much to eat either.

"We have a new enemy." Barbagiannis gave up on the piece he was chewing and spat it out into the fire.

"Someone else to kill?" Alexis looked up, hopefully. He had not changed at all, which I found reassuring.

"The Turks have hired an Egyptian general, Ibrahim Pasha, to take back the Peloponnese."

"*Molon labe*," I said, and Alexis laughed out loud. He didn't seem to be having the same difficulty with dinner as we were; maybe he swallowed without chewing.

"They're offering him the Pashlik of the Morea," Barbagiannis said grimly, "if he can take it from us. And his army, unlike ours, is trained by the French and armed with real weapons, not rusty farm tools." Mitros grimaced. "I'm not denigrating your former livelihood, Mitros," Barbagiannis said, "but I'd rather face an Egyptian soldier with a pistol than a pitchfork."

We had informants who brought news about Pasha's approach. Alfred continued collecting funds from international donors (whose names he did not reveal) to back the revolution. With the money that he doled out carefully, I had to find sources for the dwindling powder and shot and weapons to hand out to local bands. I looked at the clumsily repaired pistols and rifles I'd scrounged up and thought of Pasha's army sailing from Crete. Seventeen thousand men, professionally trained by the late General Napoleon's commanders, and led by a general whose payment would be the Peloponnese. Alexis's bravado, inspiring when we were sitting around our mountainside fire, seemed absurd.

Sophia, the now entirely gray-haired innkeeper's sister, gave me the same room where Charlotte took pleasure with me three years before. Every time I slept in the narrow bed now, I remembered how the frame shook, the joints creaking. I remembered the pounding of the headboard against the wall. I remembered wondering who we were keeping up and deciding not to care.

Ω

Ibrahim Pasha did not need stealth to win. Pasha's forces sailed from Egypt to Crete, and from there to Methone on the coast. Efficient and relentless, he took the harbor at Navarino, then went on to Corinth. In September, Pasha and his soldiers entered the Vale of Sparta. At an emergency meeting of the Eteria, Alfred Hartley told me the news, which he declared to be "almost all bad."

"Pasha is burning every town and village he passes through, leaving smoking ruins behind. He's destroying fields and slaughtering every living Greek he sees, whether they are fighting against him or not."

"*Almost* all bad? I haven't heard any good yet."

Alfred cleared his throat in a fashion I imagined to be distinctively British, though I had few examples to compare it to. "Here is the good: the British government has become so alarmed they mean to intervene."

"Finally," I said bitterly. "And how exactly will this intervention proceed? Do you plan to have a cup of tea and a biscuit with the Egyptian killer and suggest perhaps he'd like to come to a peaceful agreement?"

"More or less." He looked at me pointedly. "I am arranging a diplomatic mission with Pasha. Perhaps he'll agree to an exchange of prisoners, rather than full-scale massacre and conflagration throughout the Morea. In fact, I think you'd be an ideal representative."

"I don't drink tea," I said discouragingly. But my beverage preferences had no bearing. The following day, I was on the way north to join a British Army captain named Hamilton, stationed at Nafplio. From there we'd travel to meet with Ibrahim Pasha himself.

I strongly believe that a man's soul should not be judged from his appearance alone. Ugliness is so subjective and inextricably bound to prejudice. I knew that a British captain was unlikely to find an Egyptian general appealing to look at under any circumstances, and Hamilton certainly did not.

"He's a squat, stout, pox-faced, crude, and vulgar oriental savage," Hamilton said to me. "There is no reasoning with a born killer who is evil to the core."

I knew Hamilton, who imagined himself as a paradigm of grace, thought he was preparing me for the meeting in the best way possible. Still, I decided to draw my own conclusions about Ibrahim Pasha.

The Egyptian commander received us cordially. He had a thick white beard and mustache that partially covered his pockmarked cheeks, and pale cold blue eyes. He served us tea, and I drank it, in the spirit of diplomacy. At the end of our visit he smiled indulgently, as if we were small children asking for a sweet, rather than diplomats trying to avoid the death of thousands. Pasha finished his tea daintily, the delicate china cup incongruous in his thick fingers, and rose from his chair.

"I will not cease till the Morea be a ruin," he said. His

smile deepened. "And once I've killed all the Greeks, I'll replace you with Egyptians." He nodded toward Hamilton, whose jaw was unpleasantly slack. "Find someone else to protect with your British might. This particular fight won't go well for you." Pasha's words, not his appearance, told me the sort of man he was.

If I'd been brought back again to save Mystras through the art of diplomacy, I'd just failed spectacularly in my mission. Pasha was coming for us, and the only way I could protect Mystras now was by force.

Ω

On the morning of the fourteenth of September, 1824, I stood with an army of klephts and every Greek citizen who could hold a weapon. We were unshaven and disheveled, armed with hastily repaired pistols and rusting farm tools. We were hungry and thin and tired. We had slept on the ground for months. Most of us did not know how to read or write, but we knew we must escape Turkish occupation. We marched beneath the standard of revolution: Freedom or Death.

Pasha succeeded where others had failed because he did not seek to take Mystras; he sought to destroy it. He set fire to the city as his army swept in. Every building burned: the markets, the houses, and the palaces, the government offices, inns, and apothecaries. Our lush hillsides, fertile fields, and fall-blooming gardens turned black with ash. Horses, donkeys, sheep, and goats roasted in the flames. Pasha's soldiers shot every Greek in range and finished off the rest with their curved swords until limbs and heads littered the streets. Greek blood ran down the hill in grim imitation of mountain rivers in the spring. Barbagiannis died with a *kilij* in his belly, and I could not even stop fighting long enough to close his eyes.

Alexis took a bullet in the forehead, and his body burned where it fell. The grand houses went up in flames and their timber roofs caved in, showering orange sparks. The Church of Agios Demetrios—the church where I had once brought *kollyva* to remember my dead father—swarmed with Pasha's men. They hacked through soldiers, slaughtered grandmothers huddling in the doorways of their homes, massacred women holding children against their chests, then killed the children, too.

In one day, Mystras was transformed from a living city to a smoldering ruin full of corpses. Some fled through the gates, but troops posted outside shot them down until piles of bodies blocked the exit. The few left alive ran toward the mountains, where I had taken refuge with the Plethonists, then the klephts. I directed those who could run and carried those who could not. By the end of the day, Pasha was done; he moved on with his troops to the next town on his list. Mystras was left empty except for a single singed cat and a terrified dog.

Of all my comrades, only Mitros survived. It felt like a perverse jest from the universe that we were left together. We stumbled back to our mountain camp without speaking. Mitros limped away under the trees where we'd once eaten soup made from a noisy rooster.

I lay on the bare hillside, not bothering to find shelter.

Whatever is asked of you in the service of this place, do not shrink from the task.

I had served, but Mystras was still dead. *I should have died, too.* Everything was gray and black: the sky, the hills, the trees, the stone. I looked at my own palm. It was too dark to see the lines that crisscrossed it. *This is the hand of a soldier who did not defeat the enemy.* I pulled my knife out from my belt and held the point against my palm. I could not bear that I was whole while all my friends and family were broken and bleeding, that I was alive when the city had been crushed out of existence. I drew the tip of the knife slowly across my hand. Blood welled up dark from the wound. Once I had crossed the line it was easy. I did it again, a second cut, then a third, then a fourth. The stellate pattern of lines throbbed. I turned my hand over, smearing my blood on the rock.

Am I done? The first time was just a thought. The second time, I said it out loud. "AM I DONE?" And once I was speaking, even though there was no one to hear, I couldn't stop. "I failed!" I shouted as loud as I could.

Maybe Pasha's troops would hear and put a sword in my chest. Maybe a wild animal would smell the blood and have me for dinner. I sat up on the slab of stone I'd chosen for a bed and shouted into the sky. "I failed my brothers of the Eteria and my brothers of the mountains. I failed the city I'm pledged to guard. I failed my first mother. Now, *AM I DONE?*"

The only answer was the chirping of crickets in the grass.

EUDOXIA

This time, she came to the boy in sleep. He shouted his question into the night and the words came to her, carried on the smoke of Mystras's destruction. *Am I done?* he cried, and she knew he longed to be.

In the dream, she found him in the ruins of the Pantanassa. There, dreams wove themselves around broken stones like stealthy cats, and the fractured convent walls and roofless cells let in the night sky, dusted with stars and mourning. The ghosts of murdered nuns drifted where once birds sang. She called him in his sleep, and he came.

You are not done.

Guardian of the gates, watcher in the shadows.

You carry the blood of death and the blood of life. Half-blood, half-breed.

You are not done.

In his dream, the guardian of the gates wept, weighted with the endless task of living.

MITROS GIANOPOULOS
September 15, 1824
Mountains above Mystras

He'd lost his land, then his wife and child, then a battle, and then the city he'd called home. There was only bitterness left, and the company of that boy Elias. Barbagiannis should have put his trust elsewhere. The secret meetings down the mountain, and the trip to Nafplio had done nothing. Now, the Peloponnese was burning.

There was no hope of sleep while he was thinking of Barbagiannis's guts pouring into the street, and Alexis with a bloody third eye where the bullet had entered his skull. The survivors of Pasha's massacre were scattered now, hidden in the Taygetos foothills. What use is there in hiding if you don't care whether you live? After dark, Mitros loaded his gun and walked down to what was left of the city, while the smoke of burning homes and fields filled his lungs. As the moon lit the plumes of smoke filling the Evrotas valley, he thought—*Why not?* He would walk to the house that had once been his, and to the fields he had farmed. Rubble and ashes, like the rest of his life.

He saw a stray dog sniffing at a corpse. He saw rats having a meal of charred goats and sheep. Mitros walked down the street that wound past the English Inn. The door was open, and the doorframe intact, though the building's roof was gone. Maybe there would be food. Better than the rotting onions they'd been eating for months. He drew his pistol and peered in the window.

He saw a woman, her back turned, feeding a baby. Not a baby, a child, too big to be fed. He thought of his dead wife and daughter. This was some Phillhelene, by the looks of her fancy dress. A lot of good they'd done with their foreign money. And who knows whether they were as Greek-loving as they professed themselves to be? Barbagiannis said the Egyptian soldiers were French-trained. How did they get that way if the French were allies of the Greeks? Maybe this was one of them, ally in name, traitor in her heart. *Greece was better off before you came.*

Mitros backed away from the window, where shards of broken glass clung to the blackened frame. Soon the woman came out carrying the child awkwardly against her chest. What was this woman doing here, alone, with a child in the shell of a ruined inn? Nothing good, he was sure of it. The child could be used as a decoy, or a shield. He saw the glint of metal in her free hand—a gun. The woman headed up the street that wound into the hillside, where the ruins of the Pantanassa looked out over the smoking city. She struggled with the weight of the child balanced on her hip. Mitros, suspicions rising, followed her.

ELIAS SEKERIS
September 15, 1824
Mystras

I thought I might have died, and that the gray sky was the arching roof of purgatory. It must have rained in the night; my clothes were damp, my hair heavy with moisture. Does it rain in the afterlife? Everything hurt. My hand burned. I looked at the crusted scabs of the star I'd cut into my palm. It had healed despite me.

I sat up, which hurt more. Then I remembered: the feeling of my pistol recoiling in my hand, the bleeding bodies, the blank dead eyes, the burning houses, Pasha's army swarming through the city like a plague, the long climb up the dark mountain path. I looked for Mitros but could not find him. Even though my only acquaintance left in the world was a miserable man who disliked me for no obvious reason, he was better than no one.

My dream echoed in my head:

You are not done.

I could still hear the guttural voice and see the figure in tattered robes, standing in the burning ruins of the Pantanassa.

I stood up slowly, drank cold water from the stream that ran through the deserted camp. Below, smoke hovered over what was left of the town. The jagged walls of the Pantanassa clung to the steep hillside, gray-white against the skeletons of burned trees. I thought of the hours I'd spent in the peace of the cloister, the hum of the bees, the bright scent of flowers, the kind nuns, the old crone with her overflowing pail. *You are not done.* I started down the path that led to the ruined monastery.

The Pantanassa's gate hung open on a broken hinge. I

walked into the empty courtyard. The earthenware pots along the wall were shattered, the soil spilled out onto the stones, rivulets of cloudy water spreading after the night's rain. It was eerily still. No birds sang, no nuns walked through the slanting light. I heard the distant whinny of a donkey and thought of Charitonymos, dead for four hundred years. A cloud moved out of the sun's path, flooding the courtyard with light. It should not be so beautiful, not in the wake of this devastation. Beauty disregards tragedy. I closed my eyes, wanting the world to reflect the ugliness in my heart.

A peculiar cry made me open my eyes again. The cry sounded like that of an animal, but strangled, like a baby trying to scream and failing. I turned, and the doorway of the Pantanassa darkened. A misshapen figure walked through, silhouetted by the sun. Then the figure spoke, and I knew the voice.

"Charlotte?"

"You are hard to find." She stepped out into the sunny courtyard. She held two things I could not reconcile: a child and a gun. Her hair was down and in disarray. Her gown was torn at the hem and streaked with mud.

"You are looking for *me*?" It was the only thing that came into my head.

She raised the pistol. Her hand shook violently, but not enough to ensure that I'd survive if she pulled the trigger. "You said your Greek blood kept you safe." She began to weep, tears spilling down her cheeks. "This is the child you made with that Greek blood of yours."

I stared at the bundle in her arms. A head of dark curls, large eyes fringed with heavy lashes in a round face. He looked startlingly like me, except for his eerily immobile features. The child raised one hand slowly; it was twisted in an unnatural shape. He tried to grasp a tendril of his mother's hair and failed.

"We are both doomed." Charlotte stepped toward me clumsily, tripping on the raised edge of a flagstone. She was not close enough for me to take the gun, not far enough for me to run. "I am an outcast, while my son withers in my arms. Look what you have done!" She was sobbing now, her face distorted. The child—my son—began to cry, too, with that choked sound. One more life I had failed to protect.

I remembered what I had told her. I remembered the confidences I'd whispered in her ear. I'd believed, and I had led her to believe, that I *was* the cure. She saw me as the antidote for her family's future. She had used me, but her plan had turned against her.

"Look what you have done!" Her scream was frantic as she stumbled toward me, the gun flailing in her free hand. The child started screaming, too. I was so stunned I could not move.

There was a shot, earsplitting in the closed courtyard. I waited for the pain of her bullet hitting my flesh. Shock widened her eyes, and she folded slowly to the ground. Mitros appeared behind her, holding a pistol, silhouetted in the entrance she'd come through.

Mitros waited until he was sure Charlotte had stopped moving before he lowered his weapon. "Just because I don't like you doesn't mean I'd let you die," he said to me. The child cried desperately, grabbing his mother's dress in his feeble hands.

$$\Omega$$

Mitros left and I did not see him again. I took care of my son as well as I could, with help from a midwife who'd sought shelter in the mountains while Mystras burned. I learned my son's name from a note Charlotte had tucked into his clothes. I wondered whether all along she had meant to leave him with me. There was no way to know whether Charlotte's intent in her final trip to Mystras was revenge or a desperate plea for help. Remy lived six months, enough that I believe he knew me, though he could never say so in words. I remember the feeling of his soft cheek, and his sweet, powdery smell.

War is a marathon, not a sprint. In 1829, five years after Mitros shot the mother of my only child, Commander Demetrios Ypsilantis defeated the Turkish general Aslan Bey at Petra in the last battle of the war. It was three more years before we flew our Greek flag over an independent nation.

Mystras remained a shell of its former self. I found a barely habitable house in the lower town, as did a few other stubborn folk who would not leave. We claimed the remnants of what had been first a Frankish prize, then the capital of the Romaioi world, then the Turks' plaything. A few of us stayed on, even after King Otto built the new center of Laconia, renaming Sparta as a modern town. The streets echoed with loss.

This time, I lived long enough to learn I would not fall ill from the disease that destroyed both my first father and my only son. Was it an accident that the curse did not find me, or was I truly immune? Perversely, my longest life was the one in which I had no one left to love.

part five

A LIFE IN RUINS

chapter thirty-four

ELIAS OROLOGAS
January 1981
Mystras

The next time I returned, I was found by a nun on the doorstep of the Pantanassa, the only inhabited structure left in old Mystras. I grew up with six nuns, four cats, one donkey, and a city of crumbling buildings clinging to the sun-baked hill. Once I was old enough to ask, I learned that the last few residents—other than the nuns—had been forced to leave in 1953. It was, Sister Iosiphia told me, to make way for Mystras's restoration—not as a living city, but as a memory.

The day I was found became my birthday, New Year's Day 1981. That day, Greece became the tenth nation to join the European Union. It was a triumphant moment for Greek democracy, but also marked our entry into Europe's tight grasp. The irony did not escape me.

MILLICENT BRATHWAITE
July 2015
Mystras

Millicent Brathwaite had at last found someone who recognized her potential. Professor Pierre Lusignan had plans for a new exhibit in Mystras, and he had placed the logistical aspects in her hands, with the understanding that she would work with him to obtain the documents of interest. He also impressed upon her the need for discretion, until all was ready to be revealed. She did not need reminders, being, by nature, exceptional at keeping confidences. Once assembled, the exhibit could be presented in its entirety. It would be groundbreaking.

Millicent knew Professor Lusignan's approach to Greek culture mirrored her own. There was much to appreciate in this country, whose history and resources were valuable. However, the struggling nation must take direction from those with a stronger work ethic. Professor Lusignan, much like Millicent herself, gleaned the wheat from the chaff. The best would be celebrated, the worst put aside.

Now, because she had identified important information, and wisely communicated it only to Dr. Lusignan himself, he trusted her even more. She had stayed close when the Americans—that grubby boy and his unappealing mother—were given access to archival material by Mr. Orologas. She thereby learned that Mr. Orologas himself was actually descended from Jéhan Borghes, the original owner of the French Bible dating back to Mystras in the thirteenth century. She shared this information with Dr. Lusignan, along with the loose pages Mr. Orologas had found in said Bible. The pages had cemented the trust of their burgeoning collegial relationship. Professor Lusignan had asked many questions about the tour guide, which she answered with great seriousness and accuracy. Yes, Mr. Orologas lived in Mystras town. Yes, he spent a great deal of his time at the site—his job, after all, required it. Yes, he demonstrated long-standing dedication to Mystras. In point of fact, Mr. Orologas's attachment to the place was, to her taste, a bit outsize. Yes, Mr. Orologas would likely go to great lengths to protect what was left of the ruined city. Professor Lusignan had been quite satisfied by her answers.

The professor was deeply appreciative of her late hours, her reliability, and her avoidance of gossip. *She had not told anyone else of the documents they were assembling, had she?* He sounded grave on the phone. Of course she had not. And after she'd hung up, she smiled. *I am appreciated and sought after for my subtle gifts, by a man of stature.*

She carefully assembled the documents he'd requested. One was the handwritten log kept by the thirteenth-century midwife Chryse Borghes, wife of Jéhan Borghes. She'd removed it from the archive's collection, at Dr. Lusignan's request. She'd spent some time perusing the deaths in the log. The author seemed to have had an unusually heavy burden to bear; she'd lost two sons and a husband in a short time. Both sons with the same name. Millicent would not have used such an ill-fated name twice. But all mourners mourn differently. And then there was Mr. Orologas here in the museum, yet another Elias. The Greeks were not especially imaginative with their choices of names.

The second item he'd asked her to assemble for the new collection was a first edition of Sir Steven Runciman's treatise on the history of Mystras, *The Lost Capital of Byzantium*. She read several chapters and found it overly emotional, but thorough. One section, marked for review, detailed the origins of the name Mystras. She supposed this would be useful for the

project, given the focus on origins. She took a moment to read
the marked passage:

> *The hill was known as Myzithra, probably because it was*
> *thought to resemble a local cheese made in the form of*
> *a cone . . . later shortened to Mistras or Mistra. It was*
> *uninhabited, but there was a little chapel on the summit,*
> *dedicated no doubt to the prophet Elijah, the patron saint of*
> *the mountains.*

Millicent stopped to consider. There was no chapel now,
nor evidence of worship of any prophet. She checked again.
Dr. Lusignan had clearly marked it, and on an appended sheet
of paper, written several words: *Mystras/Mistras/Mistra/Elijah/*
Elias/Ilias. It seemed to be a bit of a word puzzle. Elijah again.

Millicent herself was an atheist, but the biblical stories
were appealing from the perspective of literary analysis at least.
It was interesting, though, that the prophet and the tour guide
had the same name. Coincidence, of course, but interesting
nevertheless.

HELEN ADLER
July 2015
Mystras

The night after Elias refused to join us for breakfast, I woke up
with a headache. Since there was nowhere to go at midnight
in Mystras, I decided to drown my misery in work and try to
figure out the Byzantine Mystras ancestry puzzle, which was
preferable to leaving it to the dubiously trustworthy Lusignan

and the tight-lipped English museum docent, his probable informant.

Byzantine history was about as far from my area of expertise as is possible, but within a few minutes of internet surfing, it became obvious even to me that the Dumbarton Oaks Library Collection in Washington, D.C., was an oasis for Byzantine history and surprisingly had a stupendous website. I started searching through their perfectly indexed online primary sources for tax records, and a sort of medieval version of a local census with genealogy swirled in.

I checked the time—12:30 a.m. in Greece meant 5:30 p.m. in D.C. I might be able to get someone on the phone. I grabbed the pen and paper from the wobbly hotel room desk, stepped outside (being careful not to lock myself out), and crouched against the wall under the all-night light. My first call got someone at the Oaks, and, remarkably, she was able to help.

I asked about the history of local families of French and Greek descent, dating back to the thirteenth century. When the voice on the other end of the line asked who I was working with, I panicked and said Pierre Lusignan. Luckily, my false affiliation made the librarian extra-helpful. On the French side, four individuals with the name Lusignan (!) had been identified in tax records from the several hundred years of Mystras's illustrious history: Marceau, Fedryc, Guarin, and Charlotte, who had changed her name after marriage to Bouvier. The last lived in Mystras long enough for her husband to contribute financially to the Greek cause of independence. The librarian guilelessly mentioned that Professor Pierre Lusignan himself descended from that original Lusignan line. Yes, it was remarkable, I agreed, that a family could be traced for so many hundreds of years. Meanwhile, my mind was racing—Elektra had told me he'd traced his ancestors to that original French family . . . and now the librarian confirmed it—the French line from which the HD gene originated was Pierre Lusignan's. That's why he was so interested.

The librarian gently mentioned that it was getting a bit late, but perhaps she could send PDF images of the pages so I could review them with the professor at my leisure? Assiduous graduate students had already converted the documents to digital format. I made a silent vow to include the Dumbarton Oaks in my will.

Within three minutes, my email alerts started firing. The first document was a list of deaths from the thirteenth century in Mystras, written, said the document header, by a local midwife, Chryse Borghes. It was a warm night, but I felt a chill. The document was in Greek, but I knew the alphabet well enough to spell out the names one by one. Fortunately, the name I was looking for was the fifth one down, and it made my hair stand on end: Elias, *Ηλία* in Greek, and the last name—Borghes—in French. In the margin was a handwritten note, legible on the PDF: *Naos*. I had to look it up: shrine. I went back to the marginal scrawl: *Naos Profitis Ilias*. Shrine of the prophet Elijah. Why had Chryse Borghes scribbled that next to the death date of her eldest son? *She lost her son*, I thought. *How could she survive that? I would die.*

Below the entry I made out the next words: *Anapáfsou en eiríni*, which with Google Translate I managed to figure out meant *Rest in peace*. I felt the tears starting. My Elias's (if I deserved to call him my Elias, which I didn't) ancestor eight hundred years ago, maybe his namesake, died young enough to be mourned by his mother. I couldn't bear to read any more, and my headache was definitely worse. Back inside, I lay down next to Alexander and tried to fall asleep.

Ω

The next morning at breakfast, someone turned on the TV attached to the café wall. Alexander pointed to the screen. "Mama, that's Mystras," he said, alarmed. Hotel staff started to gather around the TV. They, unlike us, understood what the reporters were saying.

On the screen, a police officer in a pale blue shirt was being interviewed, serious behind his dark glasses. In the background, two other officers roped off an area with yellow tape.

"It's like a *murder* scene," Alexander said under his breath. The police activity focused outside the *kastron*'s walls, where a grove of trees grew in a circle. As the camera panned in, I could see multiple freshly dug holes, each big enough to be a grave.

Alexander whispered in my ear, "Maybe the police are digging up bodies." I couldn't tell whether he was horrified or hopeful. A waiter flipped channels to a station showing a baby-faced reporter standing next to the *kastron*'s outer gate. Lucky for us, it was broadcast with English subtitles. The reporter had earnest blue eyes and a carefully trimmed goatee, which he smoothed self-consciously.

"Dusty Byzantine Mystras hasn't seen this much action since the sack of the city by Ibrahim Pasha in 1824. We're here with breaking news from the UNESCO World Heritage Site of Mystras in the Southern Peloponnese." The reporter's Adam's apple bobbed in his skinny neck. "Two locations in this remarkable city have been vandalized. The most recent damage is right here outside the impressive walls of the fortress. Police have identified another site of damage, a structure called the House of the Castellan." Alexander gripped my arm hard. "Reasons are not yet known for these devastating acts of vandalism. Local police are working on leads."

"We have to tell Elias," Alexander said.

"He already knows." I turned to see Panos standing outside the double doors of the inn's kitchen, Elias behind him. Alexander ran up to Elias and hugged him tightly. I wished I could, too. "I'm sorry about Mystras," Alexander said.

Elias had a smear of dirt on his face. He put his arms around Alexander. "I, too," he said. He sounded like he might be about to cry.

"Mr. Elias takes this very personally," Panos said. "It is like old Mystras is his home."

"That's because Mystras *is* his home," Alexander said gravely. Even though it wasn't technically true, it sounded absolutely right.

ELIAS OROLOGAS
That Same Evening
Historical Site of Mystras

I went home and locked the door, which I never used to do, and sat down at my kitchen table to think. The danger felt nearby now, closing in. Officers had been assigned to patrol the crime scenes: the walls of the *kastron* and the castellan's house. Neither was necessary. Whatever the perpetrator had been trying to do, it was done. New dangers would arrive elsewhere.

When I saw the holes in the ground where the shrine of Profitis Ilias once stood, where my mother and Demetrios had buried me under the arching branches of the then-young trees, I felt fear, then anger. Fear because my enemies, whoever they were, were looking for me—whatever part of me they thought they could find in the earth and the stones of the city, in the places where my blood had spilled and my body had been laid to rest. Fear also because I suspected they had not found what they were looking for. But I was also angry: angry that as a result Mystras—what was left of it—had to suffer, yet again. I picked up an empty vase and put it down again.

I had no proof. I could not make officers of the law hunt down an esteemed professor of Hellenic studies and accuse him of a crime he'd committed or planned. The certainty of my lives and a prophecy unfulfilled were not the sort of evidence the law demands.

I would have to either find hard evidence or stop him myself, before he did more damage. And whatever I did, inside or outside the confines of the law, had to be soon.

chapter thirty-five

HELEN ADLER
End of July, 2015
Mystras

The next day, Alexander—without asking me—invited Elias to go on a picnic. Elias, perhaps because he didn't want to hurt Alexander's feelings, agreed.

"We're meeting outside the grocery," Alexander said, leaving me in our room to finish getting ready. Flustered by the imminent prospect of seeing Elias, I forgot and flushed the toilet paper, again.

Elias directed most of his attention to Alexander. This was a relief in a way because I felt like I couldn't help staring at Elias, and it was just as well if he didn't notice. He didn't seem to have any difficulty not looking at me, unfortunately. I missed the way he used to, that steady gaze and slow smile that turned me inside out. I tried not to think about it. He had a large bag on his arm, printed with the name of the grocery. I hoped there were apricots inside.

"I know you asked for a picnic, not a lecture," Elias said as we walked through Mystras's plaza, "but we have to spend a moment with this statue."

"I like your lectures." Alexander took Elias's hand with a careless ease that I envied. "Especially since they're usually short."

Elias smiled. "I've spent many years saying very little." It was nice to see him smile again.

We stopped in front of a statue I hadn't paid much attention to. It fell into the category of Military Bronze Guys with Explanatory Plaques that usually made my eyes glaze over.

Elias made it interesting, of course. "Do you know who this is?"

Alexander bent down to read the sign. "Constantine Ex-One?"

"Sounds like a superhero," I said, leaning in to read it, too. "Oh, *XI*. Those are Roman numerals—it's eleven."

Alexander traced the numbers. "Was Constantine Eleven a soldier? He looks super tough."

"He was," Elias said. "He was the last emperor of Byzantium, and his coronation was here in Mystras."

"What happened to him?" Alexander said.

"He died the day Constantinople fell, on the twenty-ninth of May, 1453, fighting on the ramparts to save his city from the Turks. The last words he said were, 'The city is fallen and I am still alive.' He took off his imperial garments and he led his troops into a final charge."

"He looks like someone who would die for his country," Alexander said. Alexander turned from the bronze superhero to Elias, who had the sad faraway look I'd seen him get when telling stories about the past. "Why was he the last?"

Elias sighed deeply. "Because there was no empire left to lead."

Elias and Constantine Ex-One. I suddenly had an image of

them as a pair of tragic selfless superheroes devoted to their two cities, fighting in their defense. "What do you mean? Did all the Greeks die?" Alexander asked.

"We didn't have to," Elias said. "Constantinople was lost. Only three cities were left in Greek hands: Monemvasia, Trebizond on the Black Sea, and Mystras, which became the capital of what was left of Byzantium after the fall of Constantinople. But everyone knew the end was coming. Eleven hundred years of continuous rule—the longest living empire in the history of the world. And it ended here."

Alexander looked up the hill toward the ruins. "It must have been awful, waiting for the end."

Elias took Alexander's hand and brought it to his heart. I wished I could be in that circle of affection again. "You understand the past as if you have lived it," Elias said to Alexander. "That is a great gift."

Alexander blushed. His freckles stood out against the vivid pink of his cheeks. "Thanks." He sighed the way Elias just had, in unconscious imitation. "But it's so sad. Now Mystras is all gone."

"Not quite gone," Elias said, lowering Alexander's hand. The three of us walked in silence to the car.

Ω

As we started driving, the mood lifted, and Alexander piped up from the back seat. "Where are we going?"

Elias kept his eyes on the road. "To the Evrotas river."

"Isn't that where the Spartan boys went to train?"

"They did. Boys enrolled in the *Agoge*—the Spartan soldiers' training—had to pull the tough reeds from the Evrotas river with their hands, then make their own beds from the reeds."

Alexander was quiet for a while, imagining. We passed through the modern town of Spárti, where we'd had our first run-in with Pierre Lusignan. We crossed a river that I assumed was the Evrotas, and after a short bumpy ride on a dirt road, stopped in a sunny spot by the riverbank. Here the river was edged with a stone wall, but farther along, the wall ended and greenery began.

Elias pulled a blanket and the bag out of the trunk. Alexander walked down the path along the river's edge, looking for reeds. I lost sight of him in the tall grasses. Elias and I walked behind. It was the first time I'd been alone with him since my work eclipsed our pleasure. I wished I could hold his hand. Suddenly, a dark bird flying overhead took a dive toward the water—a breathtaking torpedo of folded wing, sleek body, and pointed beak. As it neared the river's edge, it extended its legs, talons outstretched.

"A falcon," Elias whispered next to me, the awe in his voice echoing the way I felt. And then there was a yell of alarm and a rustling of the grasses where Alexander had disappeared. Then a splash, and Alexander's voice screaming for me. Elias took off running for the water's edge, with me after him.

ELIAS OROLOGAS
July 2015
Evrotas River

I have never loved the water. Twice it nearly took me—*a friend to some, but not all*, my mother had said. Now it was Alexander's enemy. His plight left no room for my own fear, and it drove me straight into the cold rush of the Evrotas. I hit the water hard, aiming toward Alexander's bobbing head as he was carried along by the current.

The water was still cold, despite the July heat, and strong enough to sweep me downstream. Alexander was moving fast but resisting the current, so I, using it, moved faster. His head went under, then up again. "Mama," he yelled, his voice shrill with fear. Helen was running along the bank to intercept Alexander where the river narrowed. Alexander came up briefly, just long enough for a breath, then went under again.

I put my face down and swam hard. When I lifted my head again, Alexander was close enough that I could see his terror, and then I caught sight of something around his neck, glinting in the sun. Two more strokes and I caught his wrist, then I was pulling him to the shore, where Helen dragged us both, gasping and streaming river water, onto the muddy bank.

HELEN ADLER
July 2015
Evrotas River

I don't know where my speed came from, or the strength that let me pull two people from a river that wanted to keep them for itself. I know science would call it adrenaline, but "maternal love" was my sister's answer, later, when I could not tell the story without crying. Panos, who heard it first, proclaimed: "Profitis Ilias," with a knowing look at Elias. At the river's edge, though, it didn't matter what had fueled me, because Alexander was wet and sobbing and alive, with Elias wet and sobbing and alive next to him, gripping Alexander's wrist so hard I couldn't pry his fingers off, and I was also sobbing and alive, and soon

I was almost as wet as they were, hugging them both as hard as I could.

I remember the rest of the morning in kaleidoscopic fragments: Elias touching the *enkolpion* around Alexander's neck and whispering a prayer in Greek, the three of us sitting together drying in the sun on our blanket, sharing a bag of warm apricots, the sticky juice running down our chins. The way the back of Elias's head looked, the dark curls drying at the base of his neck while he drove us to Mystras—I sat in the back seat with Alexander, who leaned into me and fell asleep, as if I were the safety of the land.

ELIAS OROLOGAS
July 2015
Mystras

I took them back to their hotel. Panos, outside directing newcomers to parking, intercepted us. He saw we were damp from the river, but he also saw what was inscribed on our faces. He brought three cups of hot mountain tea and one hot chocolate.

Once the chocolate was down, "I need help with the spanakopita," Panos said, and Alexander's face lit up. How do kids move into the hopeful present with such ease? Panos looked at Helen. I saw the war in her: what she wanted for herself, and what she wanted for him.

"Sure," she said, and Alexander disappeared happily into the kitchen to learn to make phyllo for what I knew would be many hours.

Helen and I finished our tea with days of unspoken hurt, regret, and resentment humming under our silence. I watched

Helen as she drank, the way her freckles appeared and disappeared in the flickering sunlight under the trees that shaded the outdoor tables. I watched her small hands curving around the cup. She looked at me over the rim, knowing I was watching.

"Eléni, will you come with me?" I said. She knew what I meant, and she came.

HELEN ADLER
Late July 2015
Mystras

We walked wordlessly. I followed Elias, thinking how I always seemed to follow him. Because he was a tour guide, obviously, but also because he knew where he was going, and I did not.

At the door of his house, I had to say something. "Should we talk?" He turned to look at me, slowly.

"Yes, we should. But later, please."

Silence was not my strong suit. "Can I say just one thing? A really short thing?"

He smiled. I hadn't seen that smile in too long. I took a deep breath. "You aren't just my science project," I said.

Elias took my hand and kissed the back of it. "Good." He turned my hand over to kiss my palm, then unlocked the door.

Ω

I woke up uncertain where I was. By the bed, a blue curtain shifted in the breeze of an open window. A note lay under a smooth river rock, next to a vase of geraniums. My favorite.

On the terrace, the note said. Elias's handwriting was careful, sweetly irregular. The letters reminded me of him, that deliberate measured grace, the slight awkwardness. Then came the memory, flooding back. His hands, slow and relentless, his mouth, and finally his weight on me, the feeling I might break apart, the smell of sweat and thyme, his voice gruff and urgent in my ear. I remembered making sounds I did not know I could make. I thought fleetingly about being embarrassed, but I felt too spectacular.

"Do you always cry like this?" he'd asked afterward, brushing the tears from my face as he slowly withdrew. He had not been gentle a moment before; I'd begged him not to be. I touched carefully where I'd scratched his arm. He put his hand over mine.

"Never," I said, and it was true. Never that searing abandon, never that pleasure on the verge of pain, never that blind, wild hunger. I wanted him again. I thought of the words I'd cried into his ear, and my face went hot. "I was a little out of control," I said, sort of apologizing.

"I am honored," Elias said. "Lose control as often as you like." He kissed my wet cheek.

"You are *honored*," I said, smiling at the old-fashioned elegance of his words. "I am blown away." I started to giggle, and then soon I was laughing uncontrollably, then crying, then laughing and crying at the same time. I laughed at the unbelievable delicious reality of where we were and what we'd done. And then I laughed and cried even harder because I was laughing, which had seemed impossible a few months ago. At first Elias looked startled, but soon he was crying and laughing with me.

Now, after a blissful nap, I was lying in bed wrapped in rumpled sheets, the blue-and-white-striped blanket on the floor. There was a cat watching me, a calico with green eyes. *I didn't know Elias had a cat.* There was a lot I didn't know. I wondered how much the cat had seen. That thought made me suddenly hot all over. I looked at my watch on the bedside table; I had no memory of having taken it off. *Glad phyllo takes so long*, I thought, and did not feel guilty for thinking it.

ELIAS OROLOGAS
July 2015
Mystras

How long had it been since I'd allowed myself to want someone? *Centuries* was a word I thought meant forever, before I knew how I'd inhabit time. Almost eight centuries since I'd taken my first breath, six since I'd last loved. I learned to keep love in check, ready to lose it. I thought of the book of poetry I'd found at the Mystras Inn—*so many things seem filled with the intent to be lost that their loss is no disaster.* For me, everything was like that: filled with the intent to be lost.

So how had she slipped through, this curious Helen with her sharp mind and agile hands, her startling forthright speech and her green-gold eyes, her vivid emotions so close to the surface? I did not manage to keep her at a distance because I did not want to. I wanted to hold her hand, know her thoughts, share her grief. I wanted to experience, at close range, her outrageous abandon in the heat of desire. She was more beautiful in that moment than I could have imagined—radiant, weeping, and overflowing with laughter. And I'd outlive her. Her and Alexander, whose trust I had managed to win.

I sat on the terrace of the house I'd always been alone in, which now had Helen in it. I'd reluctantly left her asleep in the bed I'd never before shared, her legs tangled in the sheets, her long back bare. She did not wake when I cut a geranium from my garden and put it by her bed, or when I pulled the curtains to keep the sun from her face. I had vowed not to need anyone again, but now I was longing for her to wake up, so I could see the green of her eyes and listen to the rhythm of her voice. And I was not the least bit sorry.

chapter thirty-six

HELEN ADLER
Late July 2015
Mystras

That evening, Panos joined us for dinner in the hotel restaurant. The combination of Alexander's near-drowning, my afternoon with Elias, and looming worry about vandals tearing Mystras apart made the meal a little strange. We ate the spanakopita Alexander had helped make. I proclaimed it delicious, which it was. Panos taught us how to say delicious—*nostimo*—in Greek. I wanted to sneak my hand under the table to touch Elias's leg, but I restrained myself.

"It was even better fresh," Alexander said, now the spanakopita expert. It was a Tuesday night and the restaurant was nearly empty. "Did they find out anything about the holes?"

Panos finished his fourth piece of spanakopita. "Police will find out."

Alexander picked up a fry, then put it down again. "How do you know?"

"Maybe we should go to bed." I ate his fry, though I wasn't hungry. "It's been a long day." It felt like a lifetime packed into fourteen hours.

Alexander leaned against my side. "I am pretty tired."

"I'll walk you," Elias said, following us into the quiet street.

"It's a thirty-second walk, we're fine."

He touched my hand, and I stopped arguing. He waited until we were in the room with the door closed behind us, and even tried the knob to make sure it was locked.

"We're fine," I yelled from inside, "thanks." I heard his steps receding on the gravel path. I'm a reasonably independent person, but it was nice to have someone taking care of me for a change.

Alexander was out in minutes. Now that I didn't have to keep up a parental facade of calm, the sight of him undid me completely. I was afraid to leave him, but I felt like I couldn't breathe. After a brief breakdown in the bathroom, I changed out of my pajamas, wrote a note telling Alexander I was taking a walk, and headed out, closing the door softly behind me.

I went outside to the triangular plaza where we'd first looked at the *thessaloniki* outside the cheese shop. It was closed now, the windows dark. It was the same plaza where the old woman in black had talked to Alexander, where the cold spring water poured from a spout at the base of the tree. We'd pulled up to it in the bus we'd shared with Catena and an Orthodox priest, and sat at a café with Elias at breakfast, eating the Peloponnesian feast he'd ordered for us.

I felt like we'd been here a thousand years instead of three weeks. Once I didn't know how to reach Alexander in the darkness of his loss. Once I could not imagine love and desire coming back into my life without guilt. And now Alexander and I were starting to share grief rather than struggle in separate corners. I'd admitted my marriage's faults, and the world hadn't fallen apart. And Elias, of course.

I sat on a bench in front of the cheese shop. The breeze brought a faint smell from the bakery across the street, despite the late hour. I walked over to the bakery, which was, as one might expect, closed. The door and window were covered by a metal pull-down shutter. It started to smell more like something burning.

Imagining every terrible possibility at once, I ran back to the hotel and threw open the door of our room. Alexander was still sleeping peacefully, now in the exact center of the bed, which was not engulfed in flames. I checked the garbage pails for smoldering embers and examined all the electrical appliances. When I went back outside, the odor was gone. I searched around the hotel grounds, feeling a little ridiculous, then went back out into the plaza.

At the far end, Elias was walking quickly on the street that led from his house. I had an overwhelming urge to follow him, but I couldn't leave Alexander alone. I made a quick stop in the restaurant, which I noticed also wasn't the source of the burning smell. Panos was decanting olive oil into bottles again. "Panos, I'm going to go talk to Elias—he's outside. Can you check on Alexander while I'm gone?"

Panos smiled at me. "Of course. We are *oikogéneia*." When I emerged from the restaurant, Elias was just rounding the bend of the street that led up to the Mystras site. Accelerating, I caught up with him on the path that led up to the wall of the lower town. The towers of the Pantanassa loomed above us on the hill, the moon behind them. Elias turned quickly when I called him.

"Helen, what are you doing here?"

"You don't sound very happy to see me."

"This is not a good time to be out wandering in the ruins."

"*You're* out wandering in the ruins."

He took a moment to let my logic soak in. "I'm not you."

"Obviously," I said.

"You remind me of someone."

"A good memory?"

"Quite. She was a fiercely independent person who did not let me get away with any nonsense."

"Sounds about right." I felt slightly jealous but didn't want to pry. I figured whoever she was, he wouldn't have told me anything if I had something to be jealous about. I hadn't told him much about Oliver either. "I'm coming with you."

Elias sighed. "I'm not sure it is a good idea. Where is Alexander?"

"He's in the room. Panos is checking on him. What kind of not-good idea? Maybe neither of us should go."

"I must," Elias said.

"You can't explain?" Clearly, there was something I didn't understand.

Elias shook his head. "What if there was something I couldn't tell you? Would you be able to live with that?"

"Do I have to?"

"It's likely that you do."

My mind started racing through unpleasant reasons. "You don't have cancer, do you? Or some other fatal disease?"

He did not laugh, which I appreciated. "No. I'm exceptionally well."

My next fear surfaced quickly, as it often does. "Don't tell me—you're already married? Please give me the details so I can decompensate properly."

This time he laughed. "Not married in the least. And although I am not in the habit of thanking God for that, at this particular moment I am grateful, having met you, that I am not."

I blushed in the dark. Just at that moment, the scent of smoke got stronger. "Do you smell that?"

He frowned. "Helen, please don't come with me."

It was definitely smoky; maybe campfires? There were hiking trails on the other side of the gorge. I hoped that was the explanation, rather than the next trick from the vandals. I didn't back down.

Finally, Elias shook his head in resignation. "I can't stop you."

"No, you can't. And if you won't tell me your secret, then . . ."

Elias looked at me, waiting for the end of the sentence. I let him wait, but not very long. "Then I guess I'll have to live with that. But I won't like it."

He leaned in and kissed me. There was so much warmth in that kiss—not just desire, but something slow and patient.

"Then come with me," Elias said, beckoning, and I followed him up the hill.

ELIAS OROLOGAS
Late July 2015
Site of Mystras

We stopped outside the gate on the slope where the market used to be. I remembered walking with Bessarion the day he took me into his confidence. And I remembered the moment where my life as a silk trader and pupil of a heretical philosopher ended, leaving me in a pool of blood that soaked into the ground. That is why I was almost certain that this was where Pierre Lusignan would come next. Now, though, the ruined walls were lit by electric floodlights, and the market was only a memory.

I'd ventured outside at the smell of smoke. Ever since Ibrahim Pasha burned Mystras to the ground, I still think I smell the burning, unsure where memory ends and reality begins. I hoped it was the wood-burning stoves where local bakers fire their loaves, or hikers camping on the mountain, though even campfires can bring danger in the heat of summer. I followed the smell up the hill.

Now, standing where I'd died for the third time, I was afraid. I wished I had not let Helen follow me, because now I was afraid for her, too. Seen through a twenty-first-century lens, the threat seemed silly. Professors do not hire assassins, they do not wield daggers and swords, they do not cut their enemies to ribbons. This particular Lusignan had done nothing but harass me with messages and vandalize a World Heritage site, as far as I knew. If he wanted to hurt me, he would have done so already. Vandalism is a long way from violence.

Helen was quiet while my thoughts ranged, but as we looked up at the outside of the gate, she cleared her throat. "You know that amulet Alexander has? We got it from an old woman from Monemvasia who I met on the plane. She told us it would protect him. You saved him from drowning, of course. But maybe the amulet gave Alexander the extra bit of courage that made him swim just hard enough . . ." She stopped, collecting herself. "It's amazing sometimes how the past comes so close that you can hold it in your hand. Being here is like that."

She did not realize the effect her words had on me. I took her hand and leaned in to kiss her again.

Then, abruptly, we were no longer alone. Out of the shadow of the gate's arch, Pierre Lusignan appeared, his face lit by the white floodlights at his feet. He was holding something by a handle in one hand: something large, cylindrical, and heavy.

"I knew you'd come, Mr. Orologas, but I did not expect Dr. Adler as well. You've made my job so much easier." Lusignan smiled and gestured slightly with his empty hand. "Shall we talk together? It appears you two are well acquainted."

As he moved, light glinted off the object he was holding: a red safety can of kerosene. Lusignan caught my gaze. "I burned a bit of grass, just here outside the gate. It's so dry this time of year, isn't it? Just a small spark and the whole hillside would go up in flame. Is that what brought you here tonight? The smell does carry remarkably well."

In place of Pierre Lusignan's face, I saw Marceau's: pale angular cheeks and cold blue eyes. The eyes were eerily the same, as if he were looking out from the past at me. But out of his mouth I heard Ibrahim Pasha's words: *I will not cease till the Morea be a ruin . . .*

"I smelled smoke," I said.

"I knew you'd come to save your precious Mystras. Your devotion to the ruins is so . . . predictable. You didn't answer any of my messages, until this one." He almost snarled.

"Now I've answered. After Dr. Adler leaves, we can talk further."

But Helen didn't move. I saw the patch of ground Lusignan had burned, the blackened grass and ash. Left unattended, a fire would sweep the hillside, tear through the Monemvasia gate and what was left of ruined Mystras, carried on the light breeze that made this the first bearable summer evening we'd had in weeks. Everything would burn: the seven churches, the frescoes, the palace, the geraniums blooming in the Pantanassa courtyard.

"How gallant. But we must include the doctor in our discussion. Perhaps you don't realize that our goals are synergistic." Helen bristled at my side but kept silent.

I changed the subject. "I assume the castellan's house and the spot outside the walls were your doing as well?" If we managed to emerge from this encounter, at least we'd know the truth.

"I'd hoped to obtain blood or a bone, perhaps. Even a bit of DNA, extracted from human remains . . . from a massacre, let us say, or a grave. But alas, the yield at these sites has been disappointingly paltry." *Remains.* The word made the hair stand up on the back of my neck.

"Burning won't get you any useful remains," Helen said suddenly.

Pierre Lusignan tilted his head. "Dr. Adler, you are an extremely valuable resource. I count myself fortunate that our purposes are aligned. But the burning wasn't intended for archaeological investigation. It was designed to attract you, Mr. Orologas. Since you were so obstinate in refusing to respond to my reasonable overtures, I had no choice but to use more extreme measures to initiate contact." Lusignan laughed, a short bark. "Now I have you, instead of the fragments of your ancestors. Much better. I'm a modern scholar, not a relic-worshipping idiot." He turned to Helen, and I wished again that I had not brought her with me.

"Dr. Adler, my kindred spirit. We are both dedicated to eliminating the scourge of disease, bettering the human condition. We stand at a crucial juncture; together we could save lives. I know, because I've read your work, that you don't hesitate to sacrifice thousands of animals for your cause."

I was surprised when Helen answered him. "You're wrong. I *do* hesitate. I think about *every* life."

Lusignan shrugged. "We must make difficult decisions in order to change the world, Dr. Adler. If you knew the Huntington's disease gene ran in your family, knew it could take

your son, is there anything you would not do to protect him?"
This time, Helen said nothing. "We both know the utility of
studying cells of individuals with unusual resistance to disease.
So much can be harnessed from genetic clues, hidden in those
with desirable traits—characteristics that if propagated could
improve the human condition. I am fortunate to understand a
bit of the genetics you have dedicated your career to pursuing." Lusignan reached into his pocket and pulled out something small. A cigarette lighter. My chest hurt.

Lusignan put the can of kerosene down and unscrewed the
cap. "So much is at stake. Small things, like Mystras, as well as
larger matters, the eradication of disease, for example. Dr. Adler,
what if I told you that your new friend, your excellent tour
guide, held the hope of a cure in his very own body? But I suspect you know that Mr. Orologas's cells are particularly well
equipped to alter the course of disease." The floodlight glinted
off Lusignan's round glasses.

Helen was not in a position to disagree. "Professor, this is
not an optimal time for a scientific meeting. Let's talk tomorrow? I'm eager to collaborate, but not in the middle of the
night."

Lusignan shook his head. "I'm afraid we have to start now.
Delay might lead to your distraction from the true path."

"I suggest you leave Dr. Adler out of this conversation.
This matter is between us," I said.

"Only part of it is," Lusignan said. A strange look lit his
eyes, the look of a zealot. A frustrated zealot, whose efforts had
failed too many times.

"Dr. Adler: I invite you to help me harvest the cells from
Mr. Orologas's body. We'll start with superficial cells that can
be taken without sacrificing the well-being of the individual.
Skin—or blood, for example—an easily renewable source. I

will assure that you have adequate funding to keep your laboratory running, with every piece of equipment you require to forward your research. And if those tissues fail to produce acceptable results . . . then we can move closer to the source, shall we say. You did say *brain* tissue conferred particular advantage in the study of this disease, Dr. Adler, did you not? Brain cells would be a last resort, certainly." Lusignan's monologue was increasingly alarming. "I feel fortunate that we met at the moment when I am at last approaching a solution I've pursued for decades, and when I am in the best position to advance your work. I count myself fortunate that I have not inherited the Huntington's gene myself, despite my membership in a tainted family. We must, you and I, as avid gardeners caring for our mother earth, weed out those who diminish its beauty and strength." Spit gathered at the corners of his mouth. He looked like a rabid dog—but with glasses and a cigarette lighter. "I'm sure you agree, Dr. Adler. And you can convince Mr. Orologas of the importance of the sacrifice he must make. If not, I will use other methods."

Lusignan picked up the opened kerosene can and poured the contents onto the ground. The smell wafted toward us, acrid, dangerous. "The welfare and purity of the human race is in our hands. We can remove the scourge of disease, bring the world back to the state of perfection that God intended. Imagine if there were no individual on this earth with any deforming illness: Eden as it was before the serpent. The keys to paradise, to unblemished humanity, are within reach! Dr. Adler, will you join me in this divine mission?"

Helen kept her voice remarkably steady. "We differ in our perspectives, Professor Lusignan. I want to get rid of *disease*. You want to get rid of the *people* who suffer from it."

Lusignan's veins stood out on his temples. "Here's a threat

you can't solve with your perspective," he said savagely. He lit the lighter and bent toward the kerosene-soaked patch at his feet. A few dry patches of grass caught fire, then a few more. I saw the kerosene splash onto the leg of his pants, the droplets briefly highlighted by the glare of the floodlights. "Mystras is so vulnerable. Mr. Orologas, you can make a small personal sacrifice for the greater good. Submit to the research plan I propose. Alternatively, I will burn your precious little ruined city to the ground. Humans, such as your thus-far uncooperative paramour, are not immune to burning either." He smiled viciously.

The Meltemi, Greece's late-summer wind, began to blow, and the fire ignited another patch of dry grass.

Whatever is asked of you in the service of this place, do not shrink from the task.

"Helen, run!" I yelled, but I, with my first mother's words in my head, ran hard up the hill, toward the fire, toward my grinning enemy. I tore off my shirt as I ran and threw myself on the ground, rolling over Mystras's earth and stones and grass, trying to extinguish the flames with my own body. I heard the wailing of the stones, a sound I had not heard in centuries, filling my ears. And then Lusignan was on top of me, like the savage dog he resembled. "You will not escape me, Elias Orologas," he screamed, "nor will your precious ruins."

And then, with a flash, Lusignan's kerosene-splashed pants burst into flame. His screams grew shrill with horror, and his grip on me loosened. He rose, backing up and stumbling, trying to escape the fire, but he was the fire; there was no escape. That's when I saw Helen, who had, not surprisingly, not done what I'd said. Instead she sprinted to close the distance and threw herself hard at Lusignan, knocking him to the ground. It took me a few seconds to realize, as I saw her roll him away from the fire, then roll again, that she was saving his life.

HELEN ADLER
July 2015
Site of Mystras

Lusignan passed out, likely from shock. He was burned to the knee, but not higher. Elias somehow managed to emerge with only superficial injuries—nothing a bit of ice and antiseptic wouldn't handle. We got the guards to come from the site they'd been unnecessarily guarding. Paramedics arrived to deal with Lusignan, and firefighters to manage what was fortunately just a small fire. Lusignan woke up as he was being lifted onto a stretcher for transport to an ambulance waiting down the hill. He tried to catch my eye—I think he genuinely believed we had collaboration in our future. I wouldn't look at him.

$$\Omega$$

We walked down the hill behind the paramedics, far enough behind to have a reasonably private conversation. "We need to talk," I said quietly. "I mean, we *really* need to talk."

"Yes, I know." Elias nodded.

"I wouldn't have agreed to kill you to end Huntington's disease, in case you were wondering."

"Good."

"Or even harvest your skin cells."

"Excellent. I am fond of my skin. I am glad I did not lose any tonight."

I touched his bare arm. "So am I." That would have been a perfect time for me to stop talking, but silence is not my strong suit. "We should revisit the whole protective gene issue, in a nondeadly context, at some point."

"Agreed," Elias said. We went silent for a while, walking down the steep path.

There was so much I didn't know. I chose one of my many questions, one I thought would be easy to answer. "So . . . how old are you?" Elias didn't say anything. "I don't mind older men, if that's what you're worried about."

He laughed gently. "That's good to know," he said.

He hadn't answered me. "You seem to have an awful lot of secrets."

There was an unbearably long pause. Finally, he sighed. "I was born, for the first time, in 1237."

This was not the sort of conversation that comes with a script. *Born in 1237. FOR THE FIRST TIME.* I could hear my heart beating. How was I supposed to deal with the fact that I and my nearly eight-hundred-year-old reincarnated boyfriend with a protective gene against HD were walking down a hill in the dark in the middle of a ruined Byzantine city, after nearly being kidnapped by an unhinged pseudoscientist?

It made sense, in an irrational way. Everything I'd learned about Elias fell into place, like the glittering fragments of a kaleidoscope.

"You're saying I'm in love with a seven-hundred-and-seventy-eight-year-old man?" I guessed love hadn't changed so much since Byzantium. Why would it? And Elias was, at least now, a twenty-first-century man.

Elias made a sound, almost a laugh. "Are you saying you're

in love with me?" Then he kissed me. That probably hadn't changed much in the last eight centuries either.

We got to the bottom of the hill as the ambulance doors were closing on Lusignan's prostrate form. The old woman was sitting under her tree. The cat wrapped around her ankles, its tail flicking slowly back and forth. Elias crossed the plaza, and I followed him. The woman's eyes were open, the corneas hazy white.

"*Échete ekplirósei tin efthýni sas,*" she said, her voice rasping. She shaped the words with her hands as if they were made of clay.

Elias leaned against the tree; I thought he might fall.

"What does it mean?" I put my hand out to steady him.

He took a deep breath. "She said, 'You have fulfilled your responsibility.'" He added, whispering, in Greek: "*Efcharistó ton profíti.*"

That I understood. "Thanks to the Prophet?"

Elias began to cry. He wept with his whole body, his shoulders shaking. It made me want to cry, too. I put my arms around him. "Elias, what is it? Why are you sad?"

"I am not sad," he said. He was crying while smiling. "This, *agápi mou*—my love—this is relief."

ELIAS OROLOGAS
Late July 2015
Mystras

I felt the weight of years fall from me. I was fully in the sweet, evanescent present, in a life that would begin and end only once. The smell of smoke receded, and the scent of fresh bread baking rose in its place; the bakery's lights gleamed. I was standing in the quiet center of Mystras town with Helen, who, along with Alexander, had managed to break through my solitude and join me.

And there was no other place—or time—I preferred to be.

HELEN ADLER
End of July 2015
Mystras

Our flight back to New York was two days away. Alexander and I sat in the café on Mystras's tiny square. Alexander knew how to order in Greek now—Elias had taught him. "*Vissinada kai tzatziki, parakalo,*" Alexander said, his voice lilting easily over the syllables. In addition to the soda, he'd ordered yogurt and cucumber dip. He said "please," too.

I asked for a cup of the milky sweet Nescafé I'd gotten used to. We watched the village cats circle the tree full of birds in the center of the square. The old lady was gone. Alexander got through a few bites of tzatziki and then his words spilled out, full of longing. "Mama, my heart is here, in Greece."

A million thoughts flooded my head, none of which I wanted to say. *We have plane tickets. I can't really take more vacation. We have to get back to New York. I have a big job.* And then two more: *Mine too.* I put my hand out, and Alexander wrapped his fingers around mine. Elias was walking toward us. He had a way of appearing and disappearing as if he moved through different air than the rest of us.

Alexander finished his thought. "But I *wish* I knew Greek."

Elias greeted us. "*To paidí mou*," Elias said, "I can teach you."

The thought of our plane tickets faded. My head filled with the chorus of birds in the big tree, and the murmur of voices from the old men who spent the afternoon drinking coffee at the tables set along the narrow sidewalk.

Alexander wiped tzatziki on his shirt. "Here? Or you could come to New York. We have a spare bed."

"I would teach you anywhere," Elias answered gently. "If your mother wishes it." Elias looked at me.

I surprised myself by answering fast, as if I didn't need to think about the answer. "Yes," I said. "Yes."

And Elias pulled up a chair and joined us at the little table.

author's note

A novel's copyright page generally includes something like: "This is a work of fiction. Names, characters, places, and events are a product of the author's imagination. Any resemblance to actual events, places, or people, living or dead, is entirely coincidental." You have probably read those sentences before, or some version of them.

In fact, this book has a paragraph such as this on the copyright page. But for historical fiction, at least some of the names, characters, places, and events are, by definition, taken from history. Some, however, are not. And that is where the author's note comes in: to explain where history ends and fiction begins.

Unlike *The Scribe of Siena*, my first novel, *Anticipation* has many characters who were historical people. I hesitated before taking on that task, since for me it's more frightening to fictionalize a real person (what if I get it wrong?) than to make up a character from nothing. There are a lot of "real" people in *Anticipation*: Guillaume Villehardouin (who, incidentally, did have unusually prominent teeth); his third wife, Anna Komnene Doukaina, and his eldest child, Isabelle; Anna's father,

Despot Michael of Arta (ruler of Epirus); his son John "the Bastard" of Thessaly; Emperor Michael Palaiologos the Eighth; Emperor Constantine the Eleventh; the Ottoman sultans Murad and Mehmed; Georgios/Gennadios Scholarios (his name changed when he became a monk); the philosopher Gemistos Plethon; the scholar and cardinal Basilios Bessarion; Despot Demetrios of the Peloponnese and his wife, Theodora; Hieronymous Chrystonimos Charitonymos (that really was his name, believe it or not); and later, during the War of Independence, Greek generals Theodoros Kolokotronis, Odysseas Androutsos, and the savagely destructive Egyptian general Ibrahim Pasha. I tried to do them justice.

Elias, Helen, and Alexander, the three characters at the heart of this story, come entirely from my imagination, and so do the generations of the Lusignan family. They are all imagined, but they feel the most real to me. I didn't read about them, but I know them inside and out.

I had to make some decisions about what to simplify to prevent readers from losing their minds. Insanity is a serious risk with the study of Byzantine history. While I was researching this book, it seemed to me that at least half of the important people in Byzantium were named either Michael or John, and I spent a lot of time tearing my hair out trying to tell similarly named people apart. Meanwhile, other historical figures each had multiple names and titles used interchangeably for no clear reason. I tried to spare readers from experiencing similar suffering by choosing one distinct name for each person whenever I could, and when I couldn't, giving each one just one title, rather than the three or four different titles I'd sweated over.

I also had to make decisions about when to use Greek versus English words. I chose to use the English word for the

Peloponnese region, for example, rather than the Greek "Peloponnesus"—which I much prefer the sound of—to make things easier. Sometimes I had to break my own rules. One particularly difficult decision I faced was the name to use for the city of Mystras, the heart and soul of this story. Steven Runciman, the scholar best known for writing about this ruined former capital of the late Byzantine Empire in his wonderful book *The Lost Capital of Byzantium*, calls the city "Mistra." If I kept to my decision to use the English word, I would have called it Mistra, too. But I couldn't. Because my first glimpse of the city's name was in Greek, on the roadside sign we passed as I drove with my family through the Evrotas valley on the way to this mysterious place I'd heard about, the place I thought might be the subject of my next book. I was right, which meant my three kids, who were then eight, eight, and ten years old, had to trudge up and down the steep hills of Mystras for six hours while I got my fill. It wasn't my fill, of course; it was just the beginning. As a reward, they (eventually) got a nice long story (a novel) to read later. The sign said, in Greek (which I could, thanks to my high school ancient Greek teacher, actually read), Μυστρᾶς, which in English is pronounced "Mystras." After seeing that sign, with my heart beating as we wound up the hill toward the magical place that would fill my imagination for the next five years, I could never think of the city by any other name.

This would be a great place to end my author's note (and I almost did), but there's something missing. I haven't told you why I wrote this book. I haven't said anything about what compelled me to spend years re-creating life in a now-ruined city on a conical hill in the Peloponnesus. I didn't explain what led me to intertwine neurogenetics and Byzantium. And I also haven't told you what made me tell the story of a mother and

her young son—a story about how parenting can be both profoundly sweet and terrifying at the same time, how the unimaginable huge love pairs with an equally vast fear of loss and
the desire to protect that child above all else.

I can't possibly answer all those questions in a page or
even two. But I will say this: I strongly believe the past is still
with us—it's not a dusty faraway thing, but a living, breathing
force. History is not obsolete; it teaches us who we are now. If
we ignore it, we're lost. And Greece's current joy and tragedy
are wrapped up in the history of the Byzantine Empire. That's
why I wrote about Mystras. I am a historical novelist, a neurol-
ogist, and a neuroscientist. I can't help thinking from all three
of those parts of myself at once: this novel is the result. And
the parent part? I'm also a mom of three kids. Mothering is
one of the greatest joys of my life, but it has also produced
some of the most intense fear I've ever felt. All the pieces of
me are here in this novel: doctor, scientist, lover of history, and
mom. It seems like an impossible task to fit them all into one
story, but the truth is, I couldn't help it.

acknowledgments

This book could not have been possible without my incredible team at Gallery Books, who welcomed me and *Anticipation* with open arms: Aimée Bell, Molly Gregory, Shelly Perron, Jen Bergstrom, Jen Long, Nancy Tonik, Caroline Pallotta, Lisa Litwack, Michelle Podberezniak, and Abby Zidle. I am also incredibly grateful to Kate Dresser, whose early round of edits were the perfect combination of ruthless and kind. I owe my sincere thanks also to Professor Anne McClanan at Portland State University, who helped me navigate the complexities of Byzantine history.

I deeply appreciate the input of the Columbia Health Sciences Huntington's Disease Society of America, whose physicians, genetic counselors, and social workers helped me understand the challenges and struggles families with Huntington's disease face. I owe special thanks to Dr. Karen Marder, director of the Huntington's Disease Center, and Jill Goldman, genetic counselor, both of whom spent extra time helping me understand. I also have profound gratitude for the patients with neurological and neurogenetic conditions whom I have been privileged to care for and learn from for more than twenty-five years.

My family deserves special mention for this particular book, which I wrote on deadline (don't ask them what it was like!): Chiara, who helped me figure out tough character problems on a very long and unpleasantly muggy hike without enough water; Ariana, who told me I was great when I wasn't feeling great; Susanna, who managed to tolerate my alternating irritability, exhilaration, and sheer panic for far too long; my mother, Bonnie Josephs, who read and commented on the manuscript with too little time and extraordinary good will; and Leo, who read and loved every word and gave me the courage to keep the story going.

I am constantly in awe of Michael Radulescu, wizard of international sales, who patiently guides me through incomprehensible paperwork. And last, but certainly not least, thanks to my wonderful agent, Marly Rusoff, whose ferocious dedication to writers and the written word, unflagging support and enthusiasm, and extraordinarily warm and generous heart, have made it possible for me not only to bring my books to readers but to feel I deserve to call myself a writer at all.